To Linzi , best wishes

To all ye who ⸺

The Good Housewife's From⸺ ⸺hite Matters…
By Jane ⸺
Published by Jane Durston, Pound Farm, ⸺ ⸺ch Lane, Rudford, Gloucestershire
GL2 8DT

Illustrations by William Charles Durston
Printed and Bound by: BookPrintingUK, Peterborough
ISBN: 978-0-9932827-0-6

<u>Acknowledgements:</u>

Permission for textile for background cover design was kindly granted in person at
"Nature in Art" by artist in residence Liz Brooke-Ward of Stroud, Gloucestershire.
Website: www.lizbrookeward.com

Permission to reproduce parts of historical research in his excellent book *Gloucester's
Asylums 1794-2002 Parchment:Oxford* was kindly granted in person by Ian M.C.
Hollingsbee of Gloucester.

Reader's comments:

"When you write about such personal experiences…it has to be rich with humanity and have pace. It can't just rely on science and stats but must also have something that elevates it from a journal article. If you want to make a difference with such stories, you have to show it's worthy of a whole book that people will pay for. So I was pleased to see some beautiful imagery in there."
Becky Thomas, Fox Mason Literary Agency

"One of the best things about the work is the huge empathy that the author so clearly has for the much put-upon central character whilst at the same time not shying away from the more problematic aspects of her personality. "
Martin Randall, Author

"There was a great deal I admired about your novel, not least the fact that the book has such a clear, strong message and theme, and one with which I could wholly sympathise, from both a scientific and feminist point of view."
Vicky Blunden, Senior Fiction Editor, Myriad Editions

"The structure has been astutely chosen, with the key events – the crux of the narrative – inserted proleptically at the start. The Good Houswife's Frontal Lobotomy tells an exceptional story of human courage with empathy and vivid detail. It's a tale that resonates through the decades."
DD Johnstone, Author

"It is brilliant…you are so descriptive about everything which makes both people and situations seem so real. I have found it difficult in places especially when you spoke about Coney Hill and the way the time is spent as a day patient, and obviously the ECT treatments. Close to home for me and memories I would rather I didn't have, but I have persevered through and I am pleased I did. It's a great read and I honestly think it could do very well although because of its graphic descriptions it is not for the faint hearted!"
S.C.; Former patient and latterly Counsellor, and Reader.

"I think your book is stunning. not many peoples words move me but yours do. I was spellbound, didn't expect it, tearful too, where for the future? The next cuckoo's nest perhaps? Don't rush, I can't believe how much you have achieved."
D. Oliver, Reader.

Prologue:

The black stitches crimped a roll of soft skin upright into a crude sausage. It stretched horizontally across Rebecca Denby's scalp. Her hair, half-shaven and jagged, was caked in black blood. They'd promised to wash it before her husband visited, but never quite got round to it. Medusa-like strands fused together and protruded stiffly. She didn't know. She couldn't see the mirror from her bed.

In June 1967, at the Maudsley Hospital in London, Rebecca Rose Denby underwent a brain operation. It lasted just under two hours. In England the psychiatrists and neurosurgeons called their modified version of a pre-frontal lobotomy a "bimedial leucotomy". This was psychosurgery, a surgical operation that destroys brain tissue in order to alleviate the symptoms of mental disorder. This permanent destruction was known as ablation. Under general anaesthetic, two four centimetre holes were drilled into Rebecca's skull using a trephine. This was a circular implement with serrated teeth, rather like a saw. It allowed Mr Svante, the neurosurgeon, to gain access to the soft brain tissue beneath. He angled a brain needle into the centre of the hole. Applying downwards pressure until he reached an area of the anterior cingulated gyrus, he removed out two spherical centimetres of the white matter in the medial area with a metal sucker.

Whether these held childhood memories, personality or humanity, he didn't know. He believed it was that troublesome "emotional" part of the brain. If he cut some of that out, she wouldn't *feel* so much anxiety and depression. She'd been in and out of asylums for years. Mr Svante was determined to put an end to that.

These parts of Rebecca would be discarded and incinerated alongside other people's diseased body parts – like the leavings from a butcher's block. Yet they were not diseased. Some may consider the experience of emotions as an encumbrance to rational thought. Others would argue that even the most basic decisions are influenced by emotions and without them, people could not live well.

Chapter One:

Look. The nurses on the ward are striding, prodding, turning, patients. But in Rebecca's room, an antiseptic smell lingers from the bed, waiting for her presence in starched white expectation, of changing those that lie down. The drawers are bare, the wardrobe empty, but for the wood hangers and peeled paint, and a single marble, stationary, at the base. A sink sits on the wall. Her suitcase is on the leather chair, the clasps shut, the clothes undisturbed. Through the window, one lady returns from surgery, drooling inside her nest of cellular blue, hair carelessly strewn out. An intravenous bag hangs bloated on a frame nearby, and only that marks time, drips measured, needle punctured to refill tired, flat veins. Rebecca's room is removed from others on the ward, beside wide corridors, on the third floor of the block. This denotes a barrier between well and ill, where crepe soles squelch, controlling slippered feet. A centre of excellence. One mustn't dwell upon the people here, gone as they will be with the change of shifts, nurses, patients, porters, consultants, flying through with their coat tails and stethoscopes, files and smiles.

Still, she's here, while others are swinging, in summer, in the 1960's. The shiny floor slides to the bathroom – communal. In the store cupboard, lint and liniment, iodine, swabs and syringes, sharps and blunts, crinkle in sterile packets under hard fingertips. A monitoring machine beeps out of time with the swish-splat of a waterlogged mop, squeezing waterfalls into a bucket. The nurses watch. The patients watch. Rebecca, perched on the side of the bed, waits, as though the theatre is full and she's in the wings. So the curtain rises; as her door opens. Sharp female voice, instructions and rules read, the latches on the suitcase snapping open.

"Unpack your things, dear, and get into your nightie!" someone says, as they turn the tap on hard, squirting pink soap on their hands.

She's thirty three, though only just. She is taking off her wedding and engagement rings and handing them over for safekeeping. She wears a floral dress from Liberty; the flowers are small and yellow, buttercups perhaps. She's unpacking her suitcase and the knitting bag, with the black cardigan in moss stitch, just started, for her son, Charlie. She hopes to finish this, when she's better. Her toothbrush stands lonely in the cup. She doesn't see the pigeon that has landed on her window sill. She slides off, and folds her petticoat, putting on the flannelette nightie, and smoothing the crease from the sheet. Opening up the prayer book, at the frayed ribbon bookmark, she starts to murmur:

Be not afraid of sudden fear, neither of the desolation of the wicked when it comes, for the Lord shall be thy confidence, and shall keep thy foot from being taken.

She believes in God. She holds the book closer, as her eyes swim and the letters seem to rearrange themselves. Now, without knocking, the Vicar strides in. His spectacles are round and his nose thin, his hair is wild, long at the back and half shorn at the front and his eyes, bloodshot. She stands, not gently as she normally would, with measured movements, she bolts upright, bare feet stamped cold on the floor, dropping the prayer book into a kidney dish, which upturns with a clang.

"Where is it?" he growls.

She stares at him, unknowing, waiting. He takes the three steps between them to clutch at her nightie, bunching under her throat with his fist. His mouth is so close to hers; hot breath, panting. Her mouth begins to move.

"Father, what are you looking for?"

"You know what I want, you fucking bitch."

He flings her away from him to the bed and begins to scour the room. He turns out the empty suitcase and shakes, hard. A penny, forgotten after some long-ago holiday, falls to the floor and rolls in an ever-decreasing circle.

"Nurse! NURSE!" she shouts. He ignores her, pulling open drawers and throwing out her clothes. As the steps approach the door, the nurse shouts.

"Jackson. JACKSON! Over here! Now!"

The nurse attempts to restrain the Vicar, pulling firmly at his sleeve.

"Father John! What's the meaning of this? You simply cannot burst into other people's rooms!"

"Away from me, you fucking whore of Babylon! Where the fuck's my world gone? You've fucking hidden it, haven't you? That's what you've done! Because of the bed! Was that the reason?"

He pulls open the wardrobe and climbs inside, throwing aside the two pairs of high heeled shoes, scrabbling around at the base. Flakes of paint rub off, on his arm.

"AHA!" he shrieks, holding the marble in the air, jubilant.

Jackson, the shiny Negro orderly, wide as a tree trunk with arms like branches, lifts the Vicar from under his arms as though he's a doll and pulls him, from the cupboard, backwards. He doesn't resist, but clutches the marble in the air.

"Behold, Sister! Oh, ye of little faith! I have the whole world in my hands! Praise the Lord!"

Moments later, the corridor returns to ordinary sounds. The nurse returns to bring two pink tablets and check her over. Rebecca takes the cup and swallows the pills, allowing the sheet to be pulled back; her legs moved and tucked in tight, bars erected at the sides, like a cot.

The nurse rights the kidney dish and hands the prayer book into trembling hands and, closing the cupboard doors, she begins to pick up the clothes and pop them back in the drawers.

"I'm sorry you had to witness that. Father John is sick. He'll be right as rain tomorrow, you'll find."

The room begins to whirl and as Rebecca's eyes roll up to the ceiling, she fancies she can make out a face in the craggy polystyrene tiles. Someone begins to sing to her, but she can't make out the words. As her eyes close, the blood-red blackness envelops her until morning.

Rebecca squints, confused with her half-view, through the bars of her cot to the window, where sunlight streams in. Cot-cage, she says. Cot-cage, cot-cage. A sign above her head reads *nil by mouth*. Aware of the figure in the room, she looks harder at the shape, which forms into Sister; who's holding a chart.

"Good morning Mrs Denby!" Her own response sounds muttered.

"Good news! You're first on the list. Dr Svante has ordered more X-rays this morning, before we take you down to theatre."

She's hungry and thirsty. Sister allows her to rinse her mouth, but she mustn't swallow. Then Sister brings a bowl, towel, scissors, a soap dish, a horsehair brush and a disposable razor. Not like Arthur's cut-throat Sweeny Todd one, with the strop. He's abandoned her here. He has to get to work. And see to the children. The home help can't be expected to do everything.

"You're aware, Mrs Denby, that I need to shave your head?"

"Yes Sister," she replies.

"We'll save what we can. Ready?"

Rebecca nods, so she arranges the towel around her shoulders. The scissor blades gleam in the sunlight. They make dancing shapes on the wall. Her fringe is held for the first snip of nine. Nine is divisible by three. Clumps of her auburn curls float silently into the enamel bowl. Her head seems colder, lighter, except the top towards the back. The brush is swirled in the soap dish. The soft lather, though cold on her head, is soothed by the swirling of the brush. Not the razor, which scrapes rather, in fifteen firm strokes. Nine and fifteen make twenty four and that is divisible by three, eight times. Sister pats the towel around Rebecca's scalp to dry it and stands back.

"There!" she says. She doesn't fetch a mirror to show her the back and sides.

"I expect I look like a convict."

"I've seen worse. Your head's a nice shape."

"Thank you. Is it time?"

"You need to put the gown on. It's a little draughty at the back, I'm afraid."

She's never undressed in front of anyone, not even Arthur, but tries to remember that they are medical. She changes quickly, looking away from Sister.

That porter's a jolly young man. He tells her she's pretty as a picture and she laughs, as she's expected to. He squeezes around the side of the bed, at the lift doors and pulls her bed in backwards. The doors close behind them. Rebecca's stomach lurches with something she last experienced on the waltzers, but instead of music and candyfloss; an uncomfortable silence. This lift opens at the back, to another corridor and into the X-ray room. A big room, bereft of all but the black bed and a little window, but nothing behind. Strong arms remove the bars and lift her, sheet and all, onto the bed. Three staff with six arms, which is divisible by three. Then they all leave her. Close the door behind them, leaving her in the darkness. A hum, a flash of light and then a thud. Nausea threatens. Eleven flashes and thuds. This is not divisible by three. The lights go on and she senses her pupils contract, blinking. Mr Svante enters the room.

"All done, Rebecca!" he says.

"Could you take one more?" she asks, reaching out to touch his arm. He moves.

"I think we've plenty now."

This is a bad omen. She's moved back onto the bed. Wheeled out, quickly now, into an ante-room. This is the pre-op room, so they say. This room is green. The Sister puts in the pre-med and sharp, cold fluid enters the back of her hand before they tape down the hard plastic tube. Nine men in masks wait outside the theatre. This seems a lot.

"You're not all going to have a go at me, are you?" she quips.

"They're here for observation, Rebecca. Remember we talked about that?" Mr Svante says.

"Yes. Where's Rupert?"

A tall young man lifts up his mask, to show marshmallow pink lips and straight teeth.

"I'm here, Rebecca."

"There you are, Rupert."

Rupert is Rebecca's student. He's a lovely young man. He's going to learn all about the operation today, from her – lovely manners. They wheel her into the white theatre, under a big lamp with nine bulbs. A metal frame puts her in mind of a sextant in the museum. At the SS Great Britain. They had fish and chips that day.

"This is the anaesthetist, Rebecca. He'll be popping you to sleep in a moment. First, I need to make some marks on your head. This'll feel a bit odd."

"Right you are, Mr Svante."

8

He's drawing a treasure map on her head; a thick nib makes two X's. She remembers making one of these with Robert, for his homework. They stained the paper with the teapot leavings and left it out to dry in the sunshine, until crisped up. Took the edges and burnt round them with a match. Robert drew a palm tree, a blue ocean and a treasure chest with his colouring pencils. They rolled it up and tied it with a red ribbon. Then she sharpened them all again, to make sure they were all the same size.

"Now, if you can count backwards from ten for me please,"

"Ten, nine, eight, seven...." She must get to six, but her lips won't move. "Iths" comes from her throat.

Away with the fairies, they say.

Chapter Two:

Arthur sips his tea, which is very strong today, with three sugars, just as he likes. Mrs P is a Godsend. Arthur doesn't believe in God. His sons, Robert and Charlie are washed, dressed, hair combed and sitting nicely at the breakfast table. They've had Frosties and are now having toast. She's washing up the other things, with the fag hanging out of the corner of her mouth, the ash precariously low. Almost as soon as this one's out, she'll put another in. She's forty eight years old and the front of her fringe is stained yellow-brown, as is the space between her right and middle forefinger. Her fat arse wobbles as she brushes the inside of a glass. He glances at the clock, noting he must leave for work in ten minutes.

"You alright here, Mrs P? I'll need to pop upstairs and get going,"

"You go ahead, Mr Denby. I'll sort them out."

He scrapes the chair on the lino. He brushes his teeth and glances in the mirror. The foam makes him appear rabid, he thinks. His eyes are bloodshot. As he rinses the brush and replaces it in the holder, he fingers the hole where his wife's should be. He wonders if she's had her breakfast and decides she hasn't.

Downstairs, Robert has finished his toast. He sneaks behind Mrs P, taps her on the left shoulder and as she turns, he slides his plate into the bowl under her right arm.

"Stop that, Robert," she says, firm.

"You can wash my plate up now," he says.

"Don't speak to me like that!" she raises the brush in a threatening manner.

"You work for me, remember? You'll do as you're told."

"I work for your father, you cheeky beggar."

He turns to his younger brother, who is sniggering, guilty. "That," he pauses, pointing the finger of authority at Charlie, "is how to treat staff."

"Get yourself off to school! Who d'you think you are?"

"Your boss!" Robert snatches the last piece of toast from Charlie's hand and runs out the back door, which slams behind him. Mrs P mutters. Charlie stands, placing his plate and cup neatly to her right and murmurs. "Thank you."

"You're a good boy," she says, patting his hand with her wet one. He stares at her and his eyes fill up. She puts a plump arm around him. He shrugs her off and, grabbing his satchel, runs out the door. Mrs P gazes out to the garden, shaking her head and wiping away a tear on the back of her sleeve. The lawn could do with a cut. She'll speak to Mr P.

Arthur treads heavily down the stairs, pulling on his jacket.

"Now just what time d'you think you'll get back?" she asks, brisk.

11

"I'm going straight from work. Visiting ends eight. Not until about half ten."

"That's fine. I'll make their dinner."

"Thank you. Best be off."

"Right you are."

She wants to kiss his cheek and pat his back, but she doesn't. "Your sandwiches," she says, sliding the Tupperware box into his hand. He nods.

Charlie, eight years old, is running through the alley and his knees are scratched from the brambles. A nettle sting has lumped into three little white blotches, on his shin, just above the knee-length socks, which he's pushed down to his ankles. He stops to scratch and then searches for a dock leaf. Rub the juice on, Grampy says, when they go fishing. They always grow together, nettles and docks. *The cure for everything will be found beside the cause.* Grampy has lots of sayings Charlie doesn't understand. When he has long trousers, at big school, he won't get stung. He's forgotten about Mrs P's quick hug, just as he has forgotten about his mum's lingering one yesterday, until he had to wriggle away from her. She doesn't usually say goodbye to him. Normally he gets in from school and she's already gone in for *a rest.* He can't wait to get home, to the four bird's eggs waiting to be blown, labelled, and lain out carefully on cotton wool, in the wooden box with segments. His mouse, Delilah, has given birth to six babies, candy-floss pink and hairless with claws like hands and wrinkles. Their eyes are shut. Their father, Samson, needs to be separated from Delilah tonight, in case it happens again and Dad says they've no room for any bloody more. Charlie thinks he will sell four babies and keep two. He's going to save up the money he makes for a dog.

He hopes they won't visit his mother in the *nuthatch* later. It's boring, apart from the salamanders and frogs in the garden pond. If he's good, he'll get a packet of spangles and a bottle of coke from the canteen. Sometimes, after school, he and his mates climb the big wall and laugh at the loonies in the allotment. Occasionally, they throw stones at them and run away. As he squeezes through the hole in the hedge and runs across the playing field, dodging the dog mess, he swings his satchel round in big circles.

Eighty-three miles from Gloucester, in an operating theatre in central London, Mr Svante, consultant neurosurgeon, trained under the expert tuition of Hugh Cairns at the Radcliffe Infirmary, is about to perform the first of the four surgeries scheduled to take place today. He lifts the patient's head, in order to fit the Horsley-Clarke stereotaxic apparatus, which ensures the accuracy of the position of the incisions and lesions. He demonstrates to the student observers how the screws are fastened and encourages Rupert to try. Rupert keeps a steady hand, and Mr Svante is satisfied. They depart the theatre to scrub up and return, ready to begin. He makes two incisions into the skin on the scalp, about four centimetres wide each, and folds these open either side, neatly. The suction machine drains blood and fluid down a transparent tube, like a child sucking up the last drops from a plastic beaker, through a straw. The skull is exposed. He motions to the nurse assistant for the drill, which she passes, gazing at him through long lashes. Mr Svante ignores her. He drills two four centimetre holes into Rebecca's skull, using a trephine. He narrates each step to the student observers. The trephine is a circular implement with serrated teeth, similar to a saw. Rupert will describe the smell of burning bone to his lady friend later. He will compare this to a variety of things, sulphur from a match, rotten eggs, but most of all he repulses her with the grisly details of the grinding sound which makes his teeth ache. Rupert remembers the smoke rising from the trephine.

Arthur pulls out the choke and pumps the accelerator three times before turning the key. He'll need petrol. He's held up in a queue at the level crossing. A goods train – he counts seventeen carriages of coal. He enters Alphonse Reyer, Dry Cleaners *by Royal Appointment*, greeting the receptionist and making his way to the workshop. Shelves of cardboard boxes hold wires, screws, parts. He's labelled them all, so it's a good system now. Checking the worksheets, he notes the ventilation system in the office needs maintenance. The boiler in the ladies' toilet has an intermittent fault and the fan belt has gone in one of the driers. The raffle's on tonight at the Sports & Social club – he must remember to give the stubs to the Treasurer. He writes this down.

Wait. The teacher will not allow Charlie's class out into the playground until they're all perfectly still. Charlie's feet fidget. Capper has brought his football today and they're going to skip lunch to play. The games master has said Charlie's in the running to be picked for the junior team. Charlotte Dundry, aged ten, has other ideas for Charlie at lunchtime. She swings him around by his hair until, enraged with pain, he punches her in the face to make her stop and he receives six of the best for hitting a girl and no-one listens or cares.

Arthur passes a director, who ignores him. When he winks at the secretary, tagging along behind, she smiles back. Everyone knows him here. He loves this workplace, always something different to do and everyone's grateful when you fix things for them. Mightn't be the best job in the world, but he's not chasing money any more. Not after the bankruptcy. Here, they understand, sometimes he must go home at short notice. He always makes the time up. His wife can sit outside in their car, staring into space all day, if necessary. If they wonder how he stands her, they don't say so. One secretary even offers a little comfort – good old Enid, practically putting it on a plate. Can't take things too far, so he doesn't drink. Wouldn't like to get himself out of control, however other people live. That's up to them.

He checks the clock, often. He wonders at how quickly the time goes today. He experiences a chill, when he passes the well. The low level waste pit with concrete sides contains the discarded perchoroethyline, which has a sharp, sweet odour. A few months back, he'd brought his family in, to show them round the factory. Charlie went missing. They searched for hours, calling his name. He was last seen running around by the pit. Eventually, Arthur took a long wooden pole used for opening the top windows and started swirling round in the chemicals. He met with something solid. He began to swear and sweat, poking frantically at the object. His wife howled, held tightly by his colleague. And then the shout from above "found him!" came. He almost sank to his knees and cried with relief, but he didn't. Charlie, bored with his parents and with the hide-and-seek, had settled down on some old sacking inside the store cupboard and fallen fast asleep. Arthur will never forget this. He makes his way to the drier, unscrewing methodically, replacing the fan belt and screwing everything back together.

In London, Mr Svante angles a long metal instrument above the exposed tissue. This is Rupert's first sight of a live brain. He remembers the folklore at University College about a student like himself, Danny Abse, watching a neurosurgical procedure. When the incision was made, the patient began chanting..."leave my soul alone." Rupert wonders whether this was true, and decides not. These are merely axons and neurons in Brodmann's Area 24.

"Can anybody tell me where the word leucotome originates?" Mr Svante asks his observers. They gaze at one another, wide-eyed, with minor shakes of the head and one shrug. Mr Svante tuts. "It's Greek," he says. "Originating from *leukos*, which means white, and tome, meaning cut". They nod and murmur, but he knows they will not remember this. "This is a brain needle. Though others favour Ytrium rods, or freezing, I find one should not underestimate the precision of the suction method. Attend." They watch the narrow shaft as he angles the instrument into the centre of the hole in the skull and pushes down. It disappears like a knitting needle puncturing blancmange, going in very deep.

"I am applying downwards pressure until I reach the anterior cingulated gyrus. Our target, is to remove approximately two spherical centimetres of the white matter in the medial area, subjacent to the grey matter medially and inferiorly. I shall divide the thalamo-frontal bundle. This will isolate the cortex of the frontal pole and disrupt the fibres lying in the midcentral segment." He withdraws the plunger to suck out a spherical centimetre of the white matter. Whether these contain childhood memories, personality, or humanity, Mr Svante is unaware. He believes it is the troublesome "emotional" centre; the encumbrance to the rational. If he removes some of this, the patient won't *feel* so much anxiety and depression.

She will dispense with her obsessive routines and counting. He has reviewed twelve years case-notes and around half of her time has been spent in asylums. He's determined to put a stop to that, once and for all. The operating room is quiet, tense now, save for the sucking and the breathing and the beeping of the heart monitor. As Mr Svante withdraws the first centimetre of white matter, he places this to one side. It reminds Rupert of the herring roe his mother cooks up on Fridays. It's quite wet and the gauze spreads with pale pink brain juice. Mr Svante repeats the process. Finally, the skull bone flaps are replaced, using small metal plates – each about an inch square, destined to stay in her head forever. The operation lasts for two hours, including sewing up. Painkillers are administered intravenously and Rebecca is returned to her room. Over lunch, Rupert and his colleagues marvel at the skill of their mentor. The canteen serves steak in ale pie for lunch.

Arthur works through his break and eats his sandwiches in the car at the end of the day. At half past five, he sets off. He drives for an hour before the countryside begins to give way to concrete. The engine smells hot, with a strong undertone of petrol. He hopes the head gasket won't go – he'll take a gander at that tomorrow. Perhaps stop to fill up with water, just to be on the safe side. He keeps a plastic bottle in the boot for this. After a time, the smell is a little nauseating. Winding the window down, the warm air blows in a floating dandelion clock. Once into London he'll close the windows to stop the traffic fumes choking in. Over halfway now, he fiddles with the radio button, through the crackling, upbeat music, searching for another sound. Perhaps a story, to override the one in his mind. He stops at the black-treacled tones of Richard Burton reciting *Under Milk Wood*. For the next hour, he does not hear the engine's drone, or the light beat of the wind. The traffic becomes more congested and his eyes water from concentration. Other drivers push and shove the noses of their vehicles ahead of and around him, vying for position. Everyone's in a rush here.

He's almost grateful to pull up in the car park of the hospital, but not quite. He turns off the ignition, stretching out his cramped legs and stares at the blue and white sign. Maudsley, Guys & Saint Thomas's, it says. Saint Thomas. He's the doubting Thomas. The one who can't quite believe in the resurrection. Arthur doesn't blame him. Seven pips on the radio indicate the start of the news, so Arthur switches it off. The respite of the play is over.

Charlie decides not to tell his father about getting caned today. He bursts in through the door, to find Mrs P outside, hanging up the sheets. Starving, he can smell the stew in the oven. She won't make him wait, though. She knows boys. On the table are two doorstep white bread thick buttered sandwiches filled with yellow cheese and a glass of milk for him. She's got the radio on, loud. Charlie eats them quickly and drains the drink in four gulps. He calculates the distance between them. Mrs P is walking towards the door, but he reckons it will take her five more seconds. He belches. He swills his plate and leaves it to drain, leaving the greasy white glass on the table. He jumps up the first four stairs, landing crouched and holding on to the bannisters, then puts his right hand up higher to jump the next two, until he reaches the landing and then his bedroom.

First, he checks the eggs are still whole and Robert hasn't smashed them, as he'd threatened to, if he was home before Charlie. Next, he walks over to the desk in the corner, to check on Samson and Delilah and the babies. The sawdust has been kicked up out of the corners and the base of the cage is littered with sunflower seeds and empty wheat husks. Delilah's head seems to be buried in the sawdust. As Charlie pulls her up by the base of her tail, her head is gone and he's holding half a body, little pink and white guts and entrails and intestines hanging out. There are no babies. Delilah has an oblong mouse turd on her back, perfectly smooth at both ends. Samson stands on his hind legs, sniffing Charlie and the air, white whiskers, twitching. Charlie scoops him up and holds him close to his face, searching the eyes to find out what's happened. He squeezes Samson a little and this makes his eyes pop out a bit. Samson pees and Charlie drops him onto the plastic floor of the cage, wiping his hand on his shorts. He closes the door, twanging the metal bars, running his finger along their full length. Samson runs around in fast circles – over Delilah's body, kicking up the sawdust with pink paws and white hairs on top of them.

Charlie walks downstairs, one at a time, slowly. Mrs P is scrubbing the dried poo off the toilet bowl and singing a song about the day she went to Bangor. She doesn't sing lovely right, she sings loverly and Charlie finds this makes him feel something evil and powerful and knowing inside. He scratches hard at the stinging nettle place again and thinks grown-ups lie, really and dock leaves don't *do the trick*.

He searches the kitchen drawers. Cutlery, string, elastic bands, foil, tea towels, cloth, scissors, a biro, cocktail sticks in a hexagonal plastic pot. He opens this and they all fall out. He pricks one to his fingertip and it hurts a bit. He stabs, hard, into a maggoty apple from his Grampy's orchard, lying in the fruit basket on the worktop. The fruit oozes white spit. He stabs it harder until the stick snaps in half.

He slots all the cocktail sticks back into the plastic tub and fits the lid on, rotating the clear top, until it clicks into the red base. After shutting the drawer, he walks into the sitting room. He goes to Mum's sewing basket. Her knitting bag and wool are gone. He finds the embroidery needles and tapestry and little skeins of coloured wool she separates and squints to thread, one eye closed, and sits for hours to make pictures, so other people say aren't they wonderful and aren't you clever and how artistic, but are not. They don't resemble anything and people talk to her as if she's a child. Sometimes she sews words which are supposed to mean something, like Grampy's sayings. *Samplers* - she calls them. The needles are small. He puts them back. Robert'll be home soon, he'd better hurry up. His bus gets in at four o-clock and the walk only takes fifteen minutes.

He tries another drawer, in the dresser this time, next to the crystal glasses he must keep away from and not touch because they are heirlooms. Here, he finds something different. A half-finished cloth, fine squiggles of thin cream, intricately woven and a long needle with a hook at the end, not sharp and still stuck in the material, like a spider's web on a frosty morning. He unhooks it carefully from the work. Too blunt, perhaps, but he returns to the kitchen. Mrs P is scrubbing the cloakroom floor and her big bottom is wobbling, the patterns on her smock swirl into purple eyes, staring at him. She's singing something else now, about weighing pies over the rainbow. Why is she so happy? He stabs the apple again, which fizzes. He tastes the bubble-spit, the sharp tang and then cold metal. He takes a huge bite right over the maggot hole and spits out the peel and flesh into his palm to look. The inside is dotted with dark brown spots. He looks at the gap left in the rest of the apple in his palm, right down to the core. That, too, is spotted. He remembers another of Grampy's sayings; *the apple doesn't fall far from the tree* and wonders why an apple would. He has helped collect those apples up, sometimes they're mushy-brown, with a wasp's arse hanging out, munching juicy flesh up like a cancer. He doesn't know what a cancer is, and we don't use that word, we say the big C. The Big C eats people. Perhaps him, too.

He takes the stairs back up, one at a time. Reaching his bedroom, he closes the door behind him, quietly and rolls the bed across, to block entry. The carpet underneath is a paler, cleaner brown and the wheels leave four dents. Samson is running in the red wheel, round and round. Sometimes his feet are overtaking him and he spins three hundred and sixty degrees, scrabbling and then continuing. He unclips the sides this time, where the wheel is attached, and tips Samson out on the cage floor. Samson rests his paws onto the edge of the ridge, which reaches his chest, ready to investigate the world outside his cage, and hikes himself up to balance, wobbling. The whiskers move with the sniffing nose. Charlie grabs him round the middle and squeezes him up to his face once more. He looks into Samson's eyes. "Are you sorry?" he says. Samson struggles, flailing in the air. He turns his head to one side and bites the webbed skin between Charlie's thumb and forefinger. Charlie throws him down onto the cage floor, hard. Samson's legs splay out with the force. He scrabbles to right himself, but before he can, Charlie stabs him with the crochet hook, aiming for his middle. Samson squeals and his legs flail. Charlie lifts up the impaled Samson, and holds him up to his face once more. He looks into the brown eyes without whites and says:

"You don't hurt girls, no matter what they do. Is that clear?" He watches to see if Samson understands. Samson's blood pours down over Charlie's hand. Now, Samson's limp, and his eyes are open, shining, like beads. Charlie pulls out the needle, putting Samson gently onto the cage floor, with his dead wife. He replaces the lid.

When it's finished, he feels the tears coming, hot and plentiful and the two clear streams of snot from both his nostrils, running down to his lips. They plop onto grubby knees. He whispers *why did you to do it Samson, why've you make me do this. This is going to hurt me more than it hurts you. I had to do it, Samson; it's for your own good. You can't go round eating your wife and children.* He wipes his hands over his face and rubs them to the sides of his knees. Moving the bed back in place, he hears the door slam downstairs and Robert begin speaking to Mrs P in his bossy, teasing voice. He puts the cage in the bottom of the wardrobe and throws a blanket over it. Running to the bathroom, he turns the cold tap, splashes his face with water, turning it sideways to drink, just beneath the stuttering spout with its dotted grey-white scale on the rim. The pipes groan and judder. He switches off, drying his hands, leaving smudgy marks on the white hand towel.

"Tea time!" Mrs P shouts.

Later that night, he will cry in rage again, as Robert lies full length on him and he is trapped under the sheets and blankets Robert has pulled over his head and is now suffocating him with, knowing that he's not big or strong enough to fight him off yet, understanding he must wait until Robert tires of torturing him, certain that Mrs P doesn't hear over the radio and positive, too, that his Dad won't be back in time to catch Robert, realising he's nobody and everyone else is more powerful. This will continue, once a week for the next three months, until his mum returns. In a few days, his Dad's going to ask how the mice are getting along and Charlie will tell him they died and he doesn't understand what's happened. His Dad will say, that's a shame, sunshine. These things happen. His father, uneasy, wants to ask more, but he won't.

Arthur measures his steps from reception to her room on the polished floor, so shiny, sometimes it reflects the wheeled bed legs. She'll not be staying in here, they tell him. She's to be moved onto the ward tomorrow. He must not expect too much because it's too early to tell. Probably best that he visits weekly after today, so as not to disrupt her routine and occupational therapy. He is afraid to ask his questions about whether she will still be his wife, or will she be blind, a vegetable, or paralysed. Just as approaches her room, he hesitates and looks up the ward. A vicar sits in a chair, next to a bed, staring at him, clenching and unclenching his left hand.

"Evening," Arthur says, to put himself at ease.

"Fuck off," the vicar replies, quietly. Arthur takes one step back and almost laughs. His mother's words come to him; *you ought to leave her, Arthur. She's been nothing but trouble to you. No-one would blame you.* Turning away, he sees her first. This gives him just long enough to fix his face to one of greeting, from one of horror, where his mouth has opened involuntarily, as he inhales the syrupy scent of iodine. His wife looks like a badly stitched rag doll. Her hair, matted with Medusa-like strands of black blood, is half shorn. She doesn't know, because she can't see the mirror from her bed. She sees him, then, and begins to sob, holding out her arms to him. He feels compelled to turn and run, but he doesn't.

"Help me die, please, I want to die now!" she cries.

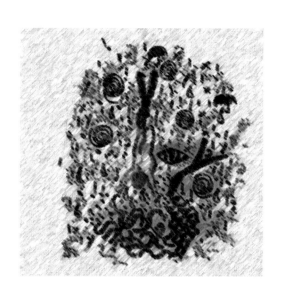

Chapter Three:

The twenty second day of April, 1934, is a Sunday. At 2.00am, three hours after Faith Lindsay's waters break, she watches the midwife turn the clock forward an hour.

At 11.30pm, Faith Lindsay has been in labour for 23 hours. "You're doing well, Mrs Lindsay." Dr Turnbull's tone conveys nothing but competence. He'll need to act quickly. It's stuck. He can't afford to consider the half protruding lump a baby - yet. The patient's exhausted. He's seen plenty of screamers. Faith Lindsay is quiet. He thinks her dignified – even as her resignation disturbs him. He hopes this isn't indifference. Most women submit to the pain, eventually. When he asks if they want his help now, they accept, gratefully. Mrs Lindsay has persevered for twenty three hours, only grunting involuntarily with each contraction. Her legs tremble, elevated in the stirrups, sagging like sailors in a hammock. He's already performed an episiotomy and the nurse has stemmed the bloody flow with cotton wool and gauze. He tries an upbeat tone.

"I think we're going to give baby a helping hand. I don't want you to push any more. Just lie still."

Mrs Lindsay says nothing, bud nods compliance. The midwife squeezes her wrist and looks away from her eyes. Dr Turnbull concentrates on positioning the padded bars of the forceps. He pulls. The lump shifts an inch. It's too big for this slight woman. He begins to sweat as he pulls, stops, pulls and stops. His arms ache. At the last pull, the baby slops out. One side of the forceps slips and leaves a deep red scratch on the left frontal lobe. Bugger, he thinks. They'll be bruising of course, and this is damned regrettable. He dips a cotton wool ball in the iodine and wipes, gently, across the scratch. The skin stains, but this is only a graze. The baby's quiet, but has good colour – no bluish tinge on the lips. He can tell it's alive. Noting the sex, he cuts the cord. Clamping the baby's belly with gauze and a clip, he hands her to the second midwife and speaks to his patient. "She's a girl, Mrs Lindsay. Well done." It is ten minutes to midnight.

She nods. He asks her for one last push to expel the afterbirth, which slops out like liver and then begins to stitch the incision. He takes more time than usual to make the stitches neat and of equal size.

The second midwife is only just visible to Faith Lindsay, above her raised knees. The midwife holds up the baby and smacks her bottom. The baby begins to cry – a coowah, coowah, coowah sound. At this, Faith looks. A look, should anyone see, of remembrance, realisation, and resignation.

"Congratulations, Mrs Lindsay. We'll just clean little one up for you and pop her off to the nursery so you can get some rest. She's a big girl alright! D'you know, I think she might be nine pounds! I'll weigh her in a jiffy," the midwife says, with all the buxom enthusiasm of the barren despot.

"Thank you," Faith breaths.

Dr Turnbull hears them tell her the weight, ten pounds in impressed tones, as though it is a matter of pride. She seems unmoved by this news. He tries to engage her. "Do we have a name for a baby girl?"

She shakes her head and closes her eyes.

"Isn't it Princess Margaret's birthday today? What about Margaret?" he realises he sounds uncharacteristically desperate. But he senses she needs direction. The midwife at the bedside smiles, because this is a matter on which she believes in her superior knowledge and can prove so, now asked.

"No, Doctor. Yesterday was Princess Elizabeth's birthday. Is that what you meant?"

"No, that won't do at all. I'm sure it's Princess Margaret's birthday."

Faith is silent. The second midwife swaddles the baby, and tries to show her, very briefly, to Mrs Lindsay, whose eyes are closed.

"Quite sure. Margaret seems perfect – don't you agree, Mrs Lindsay, she looks like a Margaret?"

Faith Lindsay opens her eyes and stares at the baby. "Don't know," she whispers and shuts them again. Tired, they say. They take the baby away to the nursery.

Dr Turnbull tries to rest, sweating in the dormitory, damning alternately the forceps and his own hands. He closes his eyes and thinks of his father and a cricket match during the long summer hols, far from the grind of Harrow. He smiles, a sad, lonely smile that no-one can see. His thoughts are often clinical now, but when they aren't, he finds some comfort in prayer. Not aloud, of course. Not often. It's a habit. Dear God, please bless that little girl and let her be someone's princess.

He sleeps before he reaches Amen.

Dr Turnbull is wrong about the princesses. The midwife tells him so, the next morning. It was Princess Elizabeth's 8th birthday on Saturday – the shift changes confused him and he's lost a day. In any case; he learns the father came in and named the baby "Rebecca Rose" – his favourite names. Seems Mrs Lindsay didn't argue. She won't breastfeed, so they've bottle fed Rebecca to the ward routine, four hours. Mrs Lindsay's episiotomy scar is healing nicely, but she says she's too weak to hold the baby. The midwives did this for her. Her face is turned to the window, where the rain trickles down the pane in silver strips, one drop joining the next, like glass eels. It rains all day.

Chapter Four:

Rebecca drops the needle and stares at the oily red blob on her fingertip. She wonders if Mother'll notice. The sting stops quickly and doesn't hurt so much, so she decides not to cry. There will be a fuss and everything will be put away. It was all going so well. As Mother rests the cotton reel on her smock, Rebecca watches closely. She licks the thread's end, closes one eye and pokes this through the needle's hole, drawing the white cotton through, deftly pulling together the ends equally, snipping them with the scissors and looping them around to a tiny knot.

"I've knotted the end. Don't poke yourself. Be sure not to leave the bits when you're done. Put them in the hearth."

"Yes Mother. Thank you."

"You're not to use my sewing scissors for that cardboard. You'll blunt them. Use the paper scissors."

"I will."

"I must get on." Mother walks away and begins scrubbing floors, wiping worktops in the kitchen.

Rebecca doesn't want to spoil the lacy folds with stains. Putting her finger in her mouth, she sucks blood so hard it stings again. Mother's emptying one of the kitchen drawers, filled with pencils, on the table. Rebecca wants the pencils, but she's not allowed them yet. They're not *right*.

Mother counts, quietly - five piles of different colours, red, blue, green, yellow and black. She sharpens them with a knife, sweeping each one's shards into a uniformed pile. She measures each one against the next of the same colour, sometimes making a clicky noise with her tongue and shaving more off the end, sometimes launching them, exasperated, into the bin.

Rebecca is allowed the scissors and the blue and brown sugar boxes. When mother's not looking, she sticks her finger into the grains in the corner of the box and licks. She cuts out the cots. Carefully collecting the trimmings from the floor, she places them into the fireplace, already arranged with rolled newspapers, small sticks and coal. Just before tea, Mother will light the fire in readiness for Daddy's return.

Rebecca pokes the needle through the card and the lace and cotton strips, covering the big capital letters TATE & LYLE. Sometimes the cotton tangles into a funny loop, just one knot in a strand. When she gets stuck, Mother puts the needle's end into the loop and pulls one side. The knot goes tiny, and she removes the needle and pulls hard and the knot disappears. Rebecca tries this, but the cotton breaks and Mother does the clicky noise. Rebecca knows how to do this for herself now, so she doesn't *interrupt* Mother any more. That makes Mother cross and Mother will say *you're so cack-handed.* If only she'd use the other hand instead of being *awkward*, it would be so much easier. Rebecca tries, but fails. She sews the cot blankets, all ready for the babies to sleep. They'll be very content in here. She'd love to have some babies to put in.

The clock on the mantelpiece bongs dolefully; marking o-clocks. The little hand is on the two. Mother will light the fire soon. Clive, her big brother and Doris, her big sister, will be home from school at four o'clock. Rebecca wishes she could go with them. She should have started a week ago, but the doctor says not until January now. Daddy will be home at six o'clock.

Mother sweeps the pencil shavings into her hand, walking to the fireplace to throw them in, rubbing her hands together. Next, she fetches a cloth and a round yellow tin. She dips the cloth in and begins polishing the wooden mantelpiece round and round. Rebecca's nose runs as she smells the beeswax. She reaches up her sleeve for the hanky and blows her nose, folding again, so that the pink curly letters RRL are on the outside. She stitches the last corners of the cots, finishing with two little stitches, and cut off the ends close to the base. After picking up all the bits of cotton and putting them in the grate, she walks to the kitchen and replaces the scissors in the top drawer.

"Please may I have the pencils now?"

"Tomorrow. They're all sorted out now. I'll light the fire and start the dinner. Why don't you play outside for a while?"

"Yes."

"Shoes off when you come in. I've washed the floor."

"Yes."

"Put your hat and scarf on. We don't want any more septic throats."

"Yes."

Rebecca pushes the tortoiseshell toggles through her coat straps and puts on her woollen hat, tying the scarf around her neck. She runs up the garden path. Past Daddy's vegetable plot, where the lines of string are pegged so straight, next to the feathered-green carrot tops. The sheets billow to and fro and she runs in and out between them. They smell fresh as they float, against her cheeks. At the far end of the washing line is the hearthrug, woven from tiny pieces of cotton, all different oranges and white. The beater has been left out, like a wooden flower with a white metal cap on the handle. Rebecca peeps at the window. Mother isn't looking. She picks up the beater and whacks the rug hard. The washing line shudders. She whacks, harder and harder until her arms ache, and specks of dust fly into the cold sunlight.

Tired of this, she finds the box of clothes pegs and pinches each one open. As one goes on the end of her fingertip, her skin goes white, then red. She puts one on her lip, which hurts. She pinches a peg on her nose, which makes it squelch and itch. After rubbing it with the back of her hand, she begins picking up sodden leaves and pegging them on the washing line. Mother raps on the window, shaking her head and beckoning. Daddy's face appears at the window next to Mother, smiling and waving. He's home early. Rebecca drops the pegs and runs to the kitchen.

"What has my Miss Rebecca been doing today?" he says, leaning down towards her for his kiss. She kisses his scratchy cheek.

"I've made babies cots. Shall I show you?"

"Presently. I must get washed up for supper."

Rebecca wriggles from foot to foot, as the draught from the open door whooshes around her bare knees. Daddy's in the bathroom. She can hear him coughing and hacking up again, spitting into the sink. Daddy can't help that – he's been gassed with mustard in the Great War and it gets down him on damp days. Rebecca often wonders why he still eats mustard with his roast beef. Clive bursts through the front door, wiping his feet and dropping his satchel. Rebecca stretches out her hands as Clive lifts her over his head, swings her round and pulls her ponytail.

"Friday Freeday Becky! I met a bear on the way home. He was so fierce Becky – I had to fight him off with my bare hands, look at these scratches!"

Rebecca looks at his hands. He has two scratches. "Did you get him? Where is he?"

"I tied him up down the road. Look out the window, you're sure to see him."

As she runs to the window, Clive sprints upstairs. Rebecca pulls the net curtains aside, and stares at the road. A man rides by on a black bicycle with a basket. No bear. Clive is telling stories again. Just above the shop on the corner is the biscuit tin lady on the sign. At the other end of the street, she spots Doris, walking arm in arm with another girl, laughing. Her curls bounce underneath her blueberry-coloured beret. When these friends leave each other at the corner, Doris puts her head high, looking right down the road. Rebecca waves but Doris doesn't see, so she runs to greet her at the back door. Doris bites the middle finger of each glove to remove them and pulls each tip off, popping them on the side. Mother smiles a big smile. After saying hello to Rebecca, Doris goes upstairs to change for dinner.

The family eats their fill of shepherd's pie and spotted dick. After mother washes up the plates, they gather in the lounge. A little dribble of spit hovers around Daddy's pipe, drooping from his lips. The pipe's gone out, as he concentrates on tuning in the wireless, turning buttons and squinting as he listens. Clive sits next to him, watching and listening but not moving, nor smiling. The box crackles loudly, then softly. Rebecca peeps over the armchair, listening – as the man's voice comes crisply from the wireless. Doris and Mother squeeze hands and laugh.

"Shhhhhh." Daddy says.

Clapping and cheering. "Orf come the hats", the man says. "People are crowding around the machine". Another man thanks the British people for their letters in these anxious times. A paper from Herr Hitler. Peace for our time. Someone in the crowd shouts three cheers for Neville and they start singing: for he's a jolly good fellow. This seems to please Daddy and Mother. When the voices stop, Daddy switches off the wireless. He goes straight to the cabinet and pours himself a brandy and a small sherry for Mother. They tap their glasses together. Rebecca takes the cots up to her bedroom to play. She'll show Daddy tomorrow.

Chapter Five:

The box sits on the wooden desktop, the long string trailing in a loop and two thin white strips at either end. Miss Cranleigh claps her hands.

"Pay attention children. Listen carefully to my instructions. From now on you must carry this box with you everywhere. It may save your life."

Rebecca fiddles with the string, loops and pokes the end in the inkwell. This promises to be more exciting than chanting the times tables.

"Now, open the box."

Thirty five children stare at the contents. Rebecca sees two huge round glass eyes, framed by metal, on a dark red face, with a long nose and underneath, a blue ring and a black strip with holes; like the inside of Mother's mincer.

Frankie holds his up, turning to Tommy, beside him.

"Woooooooooooo!"

Rebecca giggles. He's a giant bluebottle.

"Francis, don't touch until I tell you."

Rebecca stares at the blue writing under the lid. *Packing of Respirator.* Underlined.

"This, children, is a gas mask. If Hitler decides to use chemical weapons, these will filter the air you breathe. Take them out."

They obey, feeling the smooth red rubber and tracing circles around the eyes; poke fingers into the holes, and try, in vain, to unscrew each section.

"Familiarise yourself with the parts and then we'll practice. The straps go round the back. They may require adjustment. Put your hand up if you need assistance."

"Now hold them thus, your chin goes inside, like so, drawing the straps over."

When she removes her horn-rimmed spectacles to demonstrate, her eyes look small, but somehow she appears kinder. The mask is too small for her and her skin is scrunched up at the sides. Some children giggle.

"Breathe slowly and normally and above all, don't panic. You must remember that the air outside will be poisonous and could kill you. Under no circumstances should you remove the mask," she says, removing hers. Her sturdy heels clump on the parquet floor, as she walks down each of the three rows of desks. The petticoat under her skirt swishes with every brisk step.

Rebecca's straps pull her hair and become tangled. Inside, the overpowering scent of disinfectant and rubber is nasty. She thinks she might be sick, but wills herself to swallow and carry on. Her face is hot and red - rogue strands of hair over her eyes are damp and cling to her skin. Her hissing breath muffles the other sounds, rather like when she slips her head under the bathwater. As she breathes out, the whole mask moves outwards with a farting noise. Turning her fly eyes to look at her classmates, Rebecca notices Frankie's shoulders shake, with muffled laughter. Miss Cranleigh boxes his ear. She's checking the position of everyone's gas mask, eventually striding to the front and clapping.

"Remove! Well done. Place them carefully back in the box and shut the lid. I'm going to show you when you should put them on."

She takes a wooden object from underneath her desk, with a handle, a cog and a paddle.

"This will be the signal. Listen carefully. It's different from the air raid sirens."

She twirls the object round – Rebecca covers her ears. The paddle makes a brash clacking sound. Tommy retches, cupping his palms over his mouth. By the second gag, orange vomit seeps through his fingers. He stands, releasing his hands. His sick hits the floor with a blunt slop, like the dropping of a sodden dishcloth, as he runs to the front. Delighted shrieks of ueagh and *Tommy's spewed up* begin as Miss Cranleigh opens the door to release him.

"Thomas! Get to the cloakroom."

She decides to evacuate the room, before the class descends into pandemonium.

"Form an orderly queue to the right hand side of the classroom. Silence! We shall move to the playground for early break while this is cleared up."

Chairs scrape; little feet scuttle to the line. The children poke, prod and shove one another. Pony tails are pulled, arms pinched. Some hold their noses as the stale sweetness begins to rise. Miss Cranleigh fetches a long pole with a hooked end and opens the top windows. They file past the pool, gawping. Rebecca thinks it smells like rotten milk. She holds her breath as she passes, trotting down the corridor and out to the concrete playground, where her classmates whoop at the prospect of extended playtime.

Outside, the high-meshed fences hang with frozen water droplets; which glisten in the sunlight, slowly melting and dripping. Several larger puddles are iced over and the boys are sliding across them, their hot breath steaming the air. They shoot at one another with imaginary guns, clutching their sides and falling down. Others are trying on their gas masks, waving their arms with their eyes shut, as if blinded. One clutches at his chest, collapsing and pulling at the mask, gasping: "I'm dying....help me.....argh!" Some use the boxes as weapons, twirling them and trying to aim at one another's heads, or bashing them into the others, as though playing conkers. The boys whirl like human aeroplanes, arms outstretched and running.

Several of the girls stand in pairs, clapping their hands together and chanting. Another crowd has gathered around a long skipping rope, one at each end twirling round in a large arc, which smacks the ground. One at a time, they run to the centre and jump three times, then duck out to join the back of the queue. Rebecca hovers at the edge, wondering what to do. A girl called Peggy approaches her.

"Want to do *under the bramble bushes?*"

"I don't know how."

"C'mon, I'll show you."

Peggy angles Rebecca's arms – right palm up, left one down.

"Clap up with me, then hands facing. Again."

They finally get a rhythm, Peggy chants:

"Under the bramble bushes, down by the sea, boom boom boom
One kiss for you my darling, one kiss for me
And when we're married, we'll raise a fa—mi—lee
One boy for you my darling, one girl for me."

At each boom boom boom, Rebecca has to clap her open palms three times with Peggy. She begins to enjoy herself.

The classroom has an odour of disinfectant. Rebecca pores over her handwriting. Her hot hand covers her writing as she toils; griping the pencil, as grey smudges dirty the page. She glances up at the teacher, who peers directly back at her from the front desk, over her spectacles. The expression on her face is familiar, sort of cross and puzzled. Rather like Mother's does, when Rebecca's in trouble. Rebecca tries to cover up her work with her right hand.

"Rebecca Rose Lindsay!" The teacher calls, in the sharp voice she uses for Frankie.

"Yes Miss Cranleigh?"

"You are writing with the wrong hand. That won't *do.*"

Rebecca looks down at the smudgy page. Mother's right, she is cack-handed. The class turn to stare. Frankie laughs and points.

"Rebecca Lindsay's wee-ird!" he sings.

"Be quiet Francis. The word is pronounced weird, and *someone* in this classroom would be well-placed to mind their business. Let *him* who is without sin among you be the first to throw a stone at *her.* Eyes front." The children turn, trying to peep at the entertainment under one arm.

"Sit on your left hand Rebecca. Pick up the pencil with the right one and start again."

No-one understands but Daddy. He's cack-handed too. He's told Mother to leave her be, never did him any harm. She's stopped telling her off, in front of him. Rebecca wishes he was here. She wants to cry, but remembers what he'd say, *making a silly fuss over nothing.* The lines and curves wobble as she struggles. You're allowed a grown-up fountain pen if your writing's neat enough, which might be a long time away. Tommy has returned to his desk, pale-faced. He wears a knitted jersey, the wrong colour and size. Rebecca is relieved, when Miss Cranleigh moves on to story time. Now and again, Miss Cranleigh's voice over-rides Rebecca's wandering thoughts. Rebecca concentrates on the inkwell, imagining it leads her down a rabbit hole with Alice to a bottle that says drink me and a cake that says eat me. Too soon the book is snapped shut and the bell rings. Rebecca is quite sorry the day is over and if she can just use the other hand, she might enjoy school.

Rebecca arrives home to find the house unusually dark and smelling of paint. She closes the door quietly and peers through the kitchen. The lounge lights are on. Mother appears not to notice her. She's standing on a chair, fixing black material underneath the curtains, over the windows.

"I'm back!" Rebecca calls, walking in. "What're you doing?"

"Fitting blinds for the blackout. Did you have a nice day?"

"Yes! I've got a gas mask. Tommy was sick on the floor, so we had extra playtime. I made a friend called Peggy and we played clapping. Have you been painting?"

"Yes, over the smaller windows. No point making blinds for those."

"What's a blackout?"

"Blacking out any light, as a precaution. If German planes fly over at night, their pilots can't see the ground."

"Will they crash?"

"What a curious child you are. So many questions. Perhaps they'll turn around and go back to Germany."

"Won't we be in the dark?"

"We don't use them during the day, you silly girl. Run along and wash your face."

Rebecca runs up the gloomy stairs to her bedroom. The house is a den, like the Andrestrun shelter, where there were packets and tins of food, *just in case*. Everyone had huddled inside. Clive had even brought Nigger, his black Labrador puppy, who'd snuffled round, sniffing everybody, wagging his tail, licking bare knees or hands. One lady said a bad word to Clive about *bloody* dogs in here. The inside was cramped and stale with all those people, squashed like sardines in a tin. If only she had some tins and packets, her room could be an Andrestrun shelter too. Peggy says Frankie got the cane for pinching a packet of biscuits. He never even shared them out. You weren't allowed to eat anything, food was for *emergencies*. Rebecca wouldn't stop people eating - she'd put on a tea party.

When Daddy's home from work, she rushes downstairs to show him her gas mask, whirling it around by the string. He's not excited. His eyes are watering, but men don't cry, everyone knows that. Perhaps he has a sneeze coming, because he puts the box to one side and excuses himself, pulling out his handkerchief and striding to the bathroom. He's taking a long time. Mother's laying up the table now. Rebecca hopes he wouldn't much longer; she wants to tell him about the writing. Perhaps after tea.

Chapter Six:

Rebecca stares at the flowers on the wallpaper so long, they travel in diagonal lines. Her feet are propped on the lower spindle of the little wooden stool; her woollen skirt is raised, exposing her knees. The grey socks pinch her shins. She squeezes her hands into fists and pushes hard again. Her bottom stings, raw, and the poo won't budge. Her gas-bloated tummy gurgles, mocking, as a compressed fart escapes, squeaking, into the bowl, with an obnoxious stale stench. She's been in the bathroom for ages and they'll notice soon. Someone else is bound to need the lavatory and will knock on the door. What would she do if the sirens go and the house is bombed, exposed to the world, with her drawers around her knees? Eyes closed, she strains once more, to no avail. She should've come home and gone to the toilet earlier, instead of holding on.

The middle stair creaks, under someone's feet. Perhaps they'll go past, to their bedroom. Rebecca prays for them to walk on, but the steps pause at the bathroom door. She holds her breath.

"Are you alright, Rebecca?" Mother. Rebecca doesn't answer.

"Rebecca?"

"Mother....my job is stuck...and won't come out."

"Oh." A long pause. "When did you last go?"

"Thursday."

"That's three days ago. Why on earth didn't you say something sooner?"

"It's embarrassing."

"Just a moment. CHARLIE!"

"No don't, please!"

Rebecca stands and wipes, flushing away the toilet roll and scrambling to pull the big drawers up. Their elastic leaves a purple-red line round her thighs. She replaces the lid, grabs the green square from the basin and lathers her hands, running them under the tap and drying them on the hard towel. Too late, Mother's calling him from the banister.

"Charlie, can you come up here directly please."

She listens, pulling the sleeves of her cardigan over her fingers. He thuds upstairs. Her voice, reproachful and pleading, his own deeper and calmer. Knock knock. Rebecca stifles a frightened giggle as she thinks of the man on the wireless and toys with replying "who's there?" but Dad won't laugh.

"Yes?"

"Open up, Rebecca. Let me in." She slips the bolt and turns the doorknob, opening slowly. He walks in, tailed by mother, who closes the door behind her.

"Mother says you're having a problem."

"I'll just try later. I'm alright now."

"I understand you haven't done a job for three days."

"No....won't seem to come out."

Dad turns to Mother, who has backed up to the basin with her arms folded. "Did you try the soap?" he asks her.

"I don't like to, Charlie. Perhaps we should call the doctor."

"For heaven's sake, Faith, we don't want all this fuss. That's what my mother did when I was constipated."

"Can't you? I never had this trouble with Doris or Clive."

"Very well." He says. He unbuttons his shirt sleeves, rolls them up and moves his wife aside with one arm. She perches on the edge of the towel box, crossing her legs.

"What are you doing?" said Rebecca, alarmed. Her mouth waters. Dad avoids her eye as he takes out his pocket knife, cutting two long slivers of soap from the green bar.

"Now, Rebecca, we'll get this sorted out. You'll be better in a moment. I want you to take off your drawers and skirt, and bend over the bathtub please." His tone indicates she mustn't fuss, or refuse. Rebecca stares into her mother's eyes for something that isn't there. She won't stop him. Mother catches her look for a second and her right eye twitches, as she turns to the window.

He reeks of stale Digger Plug tobacco. His warm calloused hand pulls open the soft cheeks of her bottom. His sharp thumbnail digs into her skin. Rebecca begins to weep. Please God make this over and I'll never tell them again. I'll come home from the farm earlier. I won't stay to feed the cows salt block if I need the toilet, or eat the chips with spring onions. No, I'll get straight back. Her eyes travel from the bath taps, from the engraved *Standard*, down the chain to the plug, which lies upturned. She stares hard down the void of the plughole and imagines diving down it, like Alice down the rabbit hole, travelling through the pipes, out to the river, down to the sea.

Dad pushes the slivers of soap up into her bottom, wriggling them up and down, either side of the compacted poo. This hurts less than her thoughts.

"That should do the trick" he says eventually. "Stand up now."

Rebecca cups her palms over her privates, still facing the bathtub, as he briskly washes his hands and dries them. Her Mother stands up and floats towards the door. Dad opens it for her, turning to Rebecca. He avoids directly witnessing his daughter's nakedness any longer, and says: "We'll leave you to try again now. Then come down for a cup of tea."

He closes the bathroom door behind them and Rebecca's shoulders begin to shake. She can cry properly, at last. She slips the bolt over and sits down on the toilet for a long time. She thinks of Peggy and Edith. She'd been sitting opposite them on the scratchy hay bale. How wonderful, to be invited to go and play with them, on the farm. She pulls on the drawers and skirt and decides to tell her first lie. She flushes and washes her hands, looking into her red eyes in the little round mirror; splashes cold water on her face. With a forced smile, she rehearses the words, in case she should be asked. Yes, I have gone now thank you. She pads down the stairs softly, gripping the handrail.

She can't bear to meet his eyes, though she's aware of him in his armchair from the fresh-lit pipe. Mother sets down a cup filled with tea, with a small biscuit in the saucer; resting her hand lightly over Rebecca's, before Rebecca pulls away and Mother turns her back. Rebecca glares at her and pictures her sliding from the room. She sits gingerly on the chair and sips the tea - she wishes she was bigger than her, towering above. In Wonderland, when Alice ate the cake, she grew tall. She nibbles the biscuit's edge – which is soft, stale. Stupid Alice; her adventure was all a dream. Stupid Rebecca, full to the brim with dirty smelly poo.

"Tickety-boo, now!" Dad says, not looking up from his newspaper.

Chapter Seven:

The splayed triangle of the birthday cake oozes dark home-made raspberry jam on the crocheted doily, exposing the yellowy-cream sponge. Mother says she made it with powdered egg, which won't be the same, hasn't risen properly and all the coupons were saved up to make *a cake*, she hopes Rebecca appreciates the sacrifices. Rebecca watches Doris, whose hair is swept underneath a headband. She's tipping white powder into a bowl, adding water and stirring, with a paintbrush. Rebecca's eleventh birthday tea is a minor distraction, before her own night out. She's used Doris's bathwater, six inches deep, lukewarm now and smelling of rosewater. Left the water for Clive, he's next, followed by Dad.

"What's that Doris?" she asks.

"A face pack."

"What for?"

"You put it on and leave it to dry. Makes your skin beautiful."

"Ugh. Don't forget you promised to finish the jigsaw."

"In a minute."

"Where are you off to?"

"Morelands. To a dance."

"Is Mark going?"

"I should think so. Plenty of yanks, if not. The war's almost over and they'll all be gone."

"Can I come?"

"No. You're not fourteen yet."

"Why must I always be older to do anything?"

"You'll grow up soon enough."

Doris daubs the mixture all over her face. Rebecca giggles.

"You're like Coco the Clown!"

Doris dabs the brush onto Rebecca's nose, which she rubs. The jigsaw is of a steam-train, painstakingly completed between them each night. The sisters sit together for half an hour and finish the puzzle, Rebecca putting in the last piece.

"Shall we carry it up to the lounge?"

"Alright, hurry up, I need to get ready." Doris hisses through her teeth, her cheek muscles frozen under the set mask. They manoeuvre the board down the dark corridor. Halfway, Rebecca glances up at Doris's face, which appears ghostly. She screams. The volume startles Doris, who drops her end. The pieces scatter into jagged clumps all over the floor.

"For heaven's sake, you silly girl! See what you've done now? My face pack's cracked too."

Rebecca runs away to the door at the other end, into the light, roaring with laugher. Doris's cheeks are covered with cracks, like a monster. She pokes her head round the corner.

"Won't be beautiful tonight, will you?"

Doris picks up all the jigsaw pieces, cursing.

They play rummy after Doris leaves, and Dad pours her *a real one*. Mother doesn't approve. *That's far too big. I don't hold with you giving her strong drink.* The delicate thin-stemmed glass from the cabinet is filled. *Lift it by the stem* Dad said. The sweet brandy burns her throat, warm and thrilling. Rebecca tries to sip but drains the drink, too quickly. She smiles, but mother removes the glass from her hand, strides to the kitchen and washes it up. She glares at Rebecca. Rebecca stares back.

"Go upstairs now. Time you were in bed."

"She's a big girl, let her stay up for another," Dad says. His face is ruddy.

"Don't encourage her. She's already been up an hour later."

"She'll be getting a job in a couple of years."

"Ladies shouldn't go out to work. I'll thank you not to put silly ideas in her head. Upstairs, Rebecca. I'll be up in a moment to speak to you."

Rebecca kisses Dad goodnight and he smiles, as though they share a secret. She climbs the stairs, wondering why Mother's coming to talk to her. She undresses, slips the nightie on, wrestles with the tightly packed blankets, fidgeting her feet together to warm them against the cold sheets. Everyone else is out enjoying themselves, she's not the slightest bit tired and life is all so...boring. She can hear children, younger than her, shouting and playing in the distance. The door opens and Mother appears, carrying a box. Another present? As she perches on the end of the bed, Mother doesn't look at her. She speaks, quietly.

"Now Rebecca, soon you might find some bleeding from your private parts. This happens to all girls – perhaps in a few months, or in a couple of years, but when you start, these go inside our knickers to prevent a mess. Once they're dirty, you must tear them up and flush them down the toilet and put a fresh one in. You'll bleed for four days every month."

"What's the blood for?"

"When you're married, it means you'll be able to make babies."

"Does it hurt?"

"You might get a small tummy ache. You can take aspirin."

"Why don't men bleed?"

"That's the women's curse. Now, go to sleep, please. Goodnight."

Rebecca can't ask any more questions, because Mother tucks the packet marked *Dr Whites* into her underwear drawer. Not until she leaves the room and is safely downstairs, does Rebecca open the box. Long thick white pads – looped at either end, with some tiny safety pins. To become a lady seems a sticky sort of business, what with face masks and bleeding.

She begins to check, three times a day, whether she is cursed yet. A month later, while the street party is in full swing and the traffic is stopped, when everyone's out with their flags and their tables of food, laughing and celebrating Adolph Hitler's suicide and Mr Churchill announced the war's over, Rebecca is slipping away to check the curse hasn't started. In the three years to come, she won't remember the bombing, the greasy margarine, the powdered egg, the first time she ate a banana, the twisted packets of sweets from the corner shop that she can buy with her pennies now, not coupons any more, or the arguments. She will remember all the things she needs to check.

Chapter Eight:

Enforced rest and the resultant fuss from mother proves inextricably boring, but the only time Rebecca knows Mother really loves her, is when she's *poorly*. From the plumping of the pillows, checking that the light in the room is *just so*, to the pulped grapefruit, sugared mashed banana or fluffy scrambled eggs, brought to her bedside on a tray. Mother's concern and the soft touch of her hand, as she feels Rebecca's forehead. Another septic throat is a small price to pay for the ministrations of the doctor, pills, potions and instructions to Mother. Rebecca is ambivalent about recovering. She's missed so many months of school over the last three years; they all agree exams are a waste of time. She can get a little job until she meets someone and gets married. Anyway, term finishes, in a few weeks.

After she's been confined to bed for three weeks, school officially ends – so there's no other obstacle to getting up and about. Before long, she's taking a walk into town each day – avoiding stepping on the cracks between the paving slabs. She notices an advertisement in the window of Clarendon's. They require a sales assistant for immediate start. On impulse, she goes in to enquire and after half an hour's discussion, she's offered the position.

For the third week running, Rebecca places the brown envelope containing her wages on the mantelpiece, as she's seen Dad and Clive do. Mother reminds her every Friday that *ladies shouldn't work*. The job at Clarendon's is simple. This isn't a busy boutique due to the nature of the clothing - expensive and exquisitely made. The Assistant Manageress, a dour woman; well-groomed and efficient, wears lily-of-the-valley talcum powder. Mrs Curtis approves of Rebecca, who does her best to be polite to the customers and is diligent.

Mother proceeds to spend all Rebecca's wages on items to perfect Rebecca's appearance. Make up, matching gloves and handbags, stockings and underwear arrive on Rebecca's bed each week, wrapped in tissue paper. After tea, Rebecca washes and changes into the new dress of deep pink, the full skirt lined with scratchy netting. Her friend Peggy knocks at the door to accompany her, on their night out to Morelands. They attended regularly for months, until Rebecca's recent illness.

The Morelands Youth Club hums with the usual noises. At the snooker tables, the brightly coloured balls snap into Bakelite pockets and are greeted with cheers and groans. Clouds of cigarette smoke hang in the warm air, as Rebecca and Peggy tap in, on high heels. In one corner, a record player blares out *"Open the Door Robert."* The singer "talks" in a deep Southern American accent and the lyrics are broken by five "knocks". The people near the speakers rap their knuckles on the table each time, laughing and tapping their feet. One couple are in a clinch, trying out their dance steps. The girl's dress twirls out as she turns under his arm, almost showing her stocking tops.

Collecting two bottles of coke with straws from the kitchen hatch, Rebecca and Peggy scan the clubhouse.

"Shall we go up?" Peggy says.

"Alright."

It's quieter upstairs. They pass a side room, containing three ping-pong tables. The players concentrate hard, one with a Woodbine hanging from his lips as he serves. The noise forms a rhythmic pattern, when they play well, ker tap tap for a service, tap tap tap and back again in a volley. They almost resemble dancers, prancing sideways.

The older lads gravitate up to the lounge, to the licensed bar. Peggy nudges Rebecca and points to two of them in the corner – one familiar, one not. They recognise Neville.

"He's here," Peggy hisses.

"What should I do?"

"Nothing. Act normal. We'll chat in a breezy way. Maybe drop another man's name into the conversation –that'll show him."

"I don't want him to think I've found someone else."

"He's a cheeky bugger. Bit of the green-eyed monster will do him good!"

Peggy gives little quarter to the Neville's of this world. Rebecca wishes she was more like Peggy. Last month, she'd been on a date with Neville. After the cinema, he'd diverted Rebecca to the alleyway near her house for a kiss. That was pleasant – until he had begun pawing her breasts. He became angry when she pushed him away, saying she'd led him up the garden path. Between pleading and persuasion, Neville said he wouldn't get her in the family way because he had a French letter. He'd only stopped after she started crying. He gave up and walked her home. Not right to the door. She'd not heard from him since – and it wasn't until Peggy had explained a French letter was a *johnny*, that Rebecca realised what he was *after* – as Peggy said.

Peggy evens out her lipstick by rubbing her lips together and pouts, smoothing the rigid pin curls with her free hand and flouncing across the room like a movie star. Several lads eye her – one half-stands, thumbing his bracers and letting them snap against his chest, as though to ask her something, but is felled back to a seated position by one contemptuously-raised eyebrow. Peggy sits down at the table close to Neville and his companion, patting scarlet nails on the seat beside, to indicate where Rebecca should sit and smoothing out her skirt. Rebecca follows tamely, trying to emulate Peggy's walk. The red linoleum is sticky underfoot and Rebecca inhales the smell of stale beer and Woodbines. Glancing at Neville, whose dark hair is brylcreem slick, she sits down. He eyes Rebecca and Peggy, smirking and elbowing his accomplice.

"Good evening girls," he begins. "Won't you join us?"

"If you want," Peggy responds.

Neville pulls out two chairs for them. "Can I fetch you both another drink?"

"We're fine thanks."

"Yes please," says Rebecca.

"What would you like? More coke, or something stronger?"

"Champagne and brandy," Rebecca replies. She's tried this Thursday night; after Dad secured his biggest contract yet, to supply gravel to the Highways department. Neville laughs.

"Not sure they stretch to champers here. They might have brandy. What would you like with it?"

"I'll have it neat." Neville seems surprised and amused.

"Righto. This is Arthur, my cousin, by the way," he says, gesturing towards the other man, who's quietly sipping a pint. "Arthur, this is *Rebecca* and this is Peggy." Rebecca doesn't miss the emphasis on her name and wonders whether he's been talking to Arthur about her, but there's no clue from his expression.

"Hello Arthur," Peggy says, smiling, perhaps too brightly.

"Ladies!" He smiles, revealing a set of crooked teeth. Rebecca is quite fascinated with uneven teeth— she considers they give a man character. He has large brown eyes and wide shoulders, thick, curled black hair which is slightly too long at the neck.

"Refill Arthur?" Neville points at his glass.

"No thanks, Nev. Early start."

Peggy stares at Neville's back as he walks to the bar.

"D'you work on Saturdays then?" Rebecca asks Arthur.

"No. I'll be shivering on a riverbank tonight!"

"You're going fishing?"

"Elvering. You like elvers?"

"I do. Mother cooks them with bacon and egg."

"If you're coming in tomorrow night I could bring you some?"

"That'd be lovely, thank you."

"About 8.00?"

"Alright."

Peggy's a little put out, at this exclusive conversation. She bestows her attention on Neville for the remainder of the evening, by which time they've arranged a date for the following Saturday at the town hall dance in Cheltenham. Rebecca spends her time trying to sip the burning brandy and talk with Arthur.   He walks her home. He wants to kiss her, but he doesn't. She wanted him to.

Chapter Nine:

Two weeks later, the fears begin. Rebecca senses someone's listening to the family through the telephone. Dad sometimes takes orders over the phone, late at night. She begins to lift the receiver to check. The first time; Dad is still talking to some man, so she replaces it quick – going back twice more. On the second and third occasion, only the dialling tone. Reassured; she goes to bed. This becomes a nightly ritual. Always three times – once, Dad catches her, as he's plodding up the stairs. He doesn't comment, so he can't mind. He seems sad, coming to bed alone. Mother never comes with him – she stays downstairs, until late. Sometimes Rebecca listens to him, tossing and turning. He takes at least an hour to settle down before his snoring starts; loud at first, then softer as he settles, more constant. Mother creeps up, always stops halfway to listen. If the room's quiet, she goes back down. Rebecca's taking much longer to fall asleep, while she replays the thoughts of the previous day's journey.

The fears start coming when Rebecca's pedalling her bike to Clarendon's. She becomes a bit disorientated, as the other traffic races towards her. A bus, quite a long way ahead, looms up, as though giant-sized, cutting out the light. She's tempted to ride straight for the bus and embrace being run over. She squeezes her brakes, closing her eyes; sure of the impending impact, embracing the whoosh of the slipstream, the rumbling growl of the engine and the choking diesel clouds leave her trembling. The bike wobbles. She's compelled to stop, slipping her fingers into the glove of her left hand and touching her finger rings, three times. She believes this will keep her and her family safe. This annoying, but essential habit becomes increasingly frequent.

Fairly certain everyone is asleep, she tiptoes onto the landing, picking up the phone and listening, replacing the receiver. On the third replacement, she retires and thinks about Arthur. After a fitful few hours sleep; Rebecca wakes up, shivering. Her bed and nightie are soaked. She leaps up, wondering what has happened, touching the sodden under sheet. She sniffs her hands and the faint, familiar whiff of urine makes her wipe them quickly, on her sides. The house is silent. She wonders what to do and decides to strip the bed and wash the sheets before anyone can find out, she gropes for a fresh nightdress in the bedside drawer, slipping off the wet one and throwing this down. The top sheet is wet, but not the blanket. Lifting the mattress, she pulls hard to loosen the tightly tucked under sheet. As this comes away, she crumples and throws the bedding on the floor.

The mattress is wet. Still in darkness, she turns the door handle and gropes her way to the bathroom. She runs her face flannel under the tap, lathering with carbolic, slinks back to the bedroom and rubs over the wet patch. Now to turn the mattress, which is so heavy, the misshapen feather bulk makes her stagger back a few steps. She begins to sweat – periodically stopping to listen. The downstairs clock bongs four times.

To manoeuvre the dead weight over into place takes ages. The iron springs squeak in protest, so she has to do this in stages – slide and hold. Rebecca's eyes have adjusted to the dark and she can make out the accusing white sheet and nightdress, glowing by the door. She'll have to take them with her in the morning and throw them away somewhere. The clean sheets must be in the airing cupboard downstairs. She'll get two plain white ones – Mother need never know. Rebecca bundles the wet linen in a ball, and creeps out to the landing. Dad snores, their door remains open, the customary three inches, the gap akin to an inescapable eye, watching her every move. Rebecca knows which stairs will creak, so she skips these, stepping at the edges.

Nigger the dog snoozes in his basket; his greying whiskers and bushy eyebrows resembling that of an old man. He's pretty deaf now; though his sense of smell remains acute. Rebecca passes him in the lounge and he grunts a grumpy growl-snort and makes her start. She stoops to stroke his head – which, mercifully, he lays back down on his paws, with an almost human sigh. She stuffs the dirty linen into a straw shopping basket, hidden behind the longer coats.

She opens the airing cupboard door in the scullery. Piled high are pressed and folded sheets, so she pulls two out. A lavender bag plops to the floor and she bends to retrieve this, pausing to finger and squeeze the little seeds through the muslin for a few moments, closing the door, with one hand laid flat against the wood – she knows the click is quite loud.

After tiptoeing back up the stairs, Rebecca pauses. Dad is still snoring. The telephone's round face stares at her, taunting. She balances the sheets on her right arm, she picks up the receiver. No-one, this time. Again. And once more, before she goes to her bedroom. Her arms ache as she makes the bed, folding under and smoothing straight. In the end, she decides she's safer to spend the last two hours on the floor, just in case. The draught under the door chills her, so she pulls the bedspread off the bed and round herself. Her neck begins to ache, and she retrieves the pillow.

No one should wet the bed at her age. Something's wrong with her. She'll make sure she does three wee's before bed, from now on. If she goes three times, she'll be safe.

"Out! Bad Dog!" she hears her Mother shouting in the morning. She's complaining to her Dad about Nigger.

"He's had the sheets out from the ironing basket and peed on them! And one of Rebecca's nighties! The dirty bugger..."

"Calm down now Faithy, he's getting old. He can't help himself."

46

Nigger had torn the bedding all to shreds and was caught asleep on top.

Chapter Ten:

Rebecca and Arthur have been walking out together for four months, and now, Doris and her fiancé Mark's wedding invitations are ready to post. They're to be married on Boxing Day and last week announced they'll immigrate to America, as soon as they can. Doris teases Rebecca, whether she should address the invitation to her and Arthur *as a couple*. Yes, now Rebecca's got a fancy man to accompany her to Doris's wedding. Well, she'll be next.

She taps up the Morelands staircase to their usual meeting place, pausing to check her make up in the mirror of the powder compact. She dabs at the little shine on her nose, slips her right finger into the lace gloves and touches the rings of her left hand, three times. She smiles as she spots Arthur, sitting at their table with half a pint in front of him, and a brandy and coke for her. As she bends to kiss his lips, he turns slightly, to offer his cheek instead. Undeterred, she takes the invitation from the clutch bag and slides it across the table to him.

"What's this?" he asks, looking at their names, elaborately written in calligraphy.

"Open it!"

He opens the envelope and pulls out the card, reading the words. He seems to take a long time studying them, before he speaks – avoiding meeting her eye.

"I'm sorry, Rebecca. I won't be able to come."

"Why?"

"I've been posted to Yatesbury in Wiltshire, for my National Service, so...I don't think we'll be seeing each other, from now on."

"Perhaps you could get leave? I can write to you, too?"

"I can't make any promises. D'you mind if we call it a night after this one – I need an early start at the farm tomorrow?"

"Alright."

He doesn't arrange to see her, when he drops her off at the corner, just kisses her on the cheek. Despite checking the post every day for the next three weeks, she hears nothing from Arthur. Doris says he's *messing her about*. She won't believe that, though sometimes she imagines how she'd manage, if she never saw him again. She pictures herself on her deathbed after some dreadful illness, not a painful one mind, only a life-threatening one. Someone, a mutual friend perhaps, sending him a telegram and his return to her bedside, (in his uniform) crying and begging forgiveness and asking her to marry him, her, weakly agreeing and then making a dramatic recovery. The wedding, all the elderly ladies, commending her bravery, taking their vows and their guests, throwing rice and confetti, Doris, looking dowdy in the background, Mother, eaten up with jealousy at their happiness, listening to the stories about how much Arthur loves her.

The fears and the rituals increase. She checks the telephone three times a night, getting progressively later, and interspersed with going to the bathroom. It's easy enough at Clarendon's to touch the finger rings without being noticed and for much of the time she's distracted with her tasks. The fear becomes heightened during the bike ride to and from work, with the volume of all the traffic rising to a crescendo, pulsing in her ears, which means stopping every two hundred yards or so.

Rebecca arrives breathless and shaking, ten minutes before opening time. She spends the morning checking the sizes are all in the right order. The monotonous counting calms her. At lunchtime, she wipes the till over and prepares to re-open in the afternoon. Shortly after she turns the sign around to open, the gold bell tings. The door opens to an extremely tall woman. She wears an ostentatious fox fur, its head and tail clasped as though hugging her neck between eternally paralysed paws. But what strikes Rebecca most, are her eyes. One of them is brightly fixed, unmoving, rather like the beaded ones of the fox. Imperious, the woman strides in, surveys the room. Mrs Curtis, assuming an obsequious expression, scurries to greet her. They speak in hushed tones and Rebecca tries not to stare.

"This is Miss Rebecca Lindsay," Mrs Curtis says, warmly extending her hand.

The woman holds out a gloved hand to shake Rebecca's, scanning her from head to toe, with pursed lips.

"Pleased to make your acquaintance at last, Miss Lindsay. I understand you have been *walking out* with *my son* for several months now," she said. Her voice sounds like those people on the BBC.

"I'm glad to meet you – I'm sorry, but are you Arthur's mother?" Rebecca replies.

"I am indeed. My name is Kate, Lillian, Shelagh Denby. You may call me Shelagh."

"Thank you, Mrs Denby."

"Shelagh."

"I'm sorry...Shelagh." It feels unnatural, to be so over-familiar. She'd no idea Arthur was from a rich background.

"Rebecca, you may use my room to talk with Mrs Denby. She needs to speak with you on a matter of grave importance," says Mrs Curtis, who has adopted a more upper-class accent than usual. Rebecca leads Shelagh into the office and closes the door behind them - Shelagh takes the higher chair, brushing imaginary crumbs from the seat, before sitting down and removing her gloves.

"I'll not take too much of your time. I expect you might be wondering why Arthur has not been in touch."

"A little. I was expecting a letter – but Arthur did explain he'd been called up for his National Service, so he'd be away, for a time."

Shelagh appears puzzled. "I see. Well, *Arthur* is in hospital, I'm afraid."

"What's happened?"

"He's been involved in an accident with a shotgun."

"Is he badly injured?" Rebecca begins to picture herself at his bedside – his weak hand gripping hers *("I'm dying Rebecca, before I go, swear you'll marry me" – I will Arthur!)*

"The doctors say he's likely to recover. They are concerned about lead poisoning, but they managed to remove most of the shot."

"Is there anything I can do?"

"He has been asking for you."

"Has he?"

"Yes, he was insistent that I contact you and request that you visit. I've written the visiting times and ward number on this card for you."

"Thank you. I'll come tonight, as soon as I finish."

"Arthur will be pleased, I'm sure."

Shelagh stands, to indicate the meeting is finished and promptly leaves the shop. For the remainder of the afternoon, Mrs Curtis treats Rebecca with the utmost respect – even asking if she would like to leave, a little earlier. Rebecca pedals furiously home – only stopping once to touch the rings. She changes her clothes and rides the two miles to Gloucester Royal Hospital, flinging the bike against the wall of the alleyway.

Henry Denby, Arthur's father, sits at the edge of Arthur's bed with Shelagh, puffing on a woodbine. He stands to greet Rebecca, smiling kindly. Shorter than his wife, he has the beginnings of a pot belly and a small neat pencil moustache, rather like Hitler's. His skin is softer than Dad's as he kisses her cheek and peers at her, over little round glasses. Shelagh wears a frostier expression and constantly fusses over Arthur, smoothing his bedclothes and putting her hand to his forehead.

Arthur lies in the bed, looking pale in his striped pyjamas, the dark chest hair curling over the button top, covered from his torso to toes in pristine white sheets. She's never seen this much of him and wishes it wasn't in front of his parents. It is difficult to know where to look, instead of his body, as she wants to. The top of his arm is bandaged, but the shot is, apparently, widespread. Lower down are little black dotted marks that she imagines would make a picture; if only she could join them. Rebecca longs to kiss him, and touch him, but instead sits in the spare chair, further away from him than his mother and father, making small talk with them. Shelagh's accent seems to be less upper-class; she sometimes slips into a broader Gloucestershire one. Arthur recounts how his friend accidentally discharged the shotgun. His life was only saved by the wad of electronics textbooks he'd been carrying, but the blast had knocked him to the ground. She listens, enthralled. After half an hour or so, his parents step out to fetch tea for them all.

"C'mere and give us a kiss," he said, as soon as they leave the room. Rebecca leans over him and from under his arms came a familiar, comforting smell – just like her father. It isn't really pleasant, more...earthy.

"I thought I might never see you again. We'll be together now, won't we? I know you've going to Yatesbury. I'll wait for you, if you like."

"I do. I'm not a big writer, but I'll do my best and apply for leave to attend the wedding, too."

"Is there shot on your chest?" she asks.

"Want a look?"

"What about your mother?"

"She's seen it all before. Check outside."

Rebecca stands up and checks the corridor. It's clear. She closes the door and turns, just as Arthur rips the sheet away to the side. He's naked from the waist down and Rebecca's expression changes from curiosity to horror, as she's confronted by his poker-stiff Johnson – all purple. He looks her in the eye for a moment, then flips the bedclothes back and clutches his stomach, breaking into raucous laughter.

"Your face!" He slaps at his Johnson over the sheet. "DOWN BOY!"

"Arthur...How could you? You...dirty bugger!"

He's still laughing when his father opens the door, carrying two cups and saucers.

Chapter Eleven:

Rebecca slips her hand into Arthur's, as she shimmies down Innsworth Lane. He lengthens his step, pulling her along, laughing. She has to trot quicker to keep up, heels tapping. As he squeezes round the kissing gate, he smacks a loud kiss on her lips, and runs backwards, laughing and beckoning. She can't keep up, her heels are sinking in the grass and she doesn't want to stumble and ruin everything.

"Come on!" he shouts. Rebecca slips off her shoes, taking them in her hand, and runs after him, the skirt of her dress billowing out. Dandelion clocks and grass seeds rise up and yellow baubles of buttercups and celandines peep through the green, with wild garlic scenting the air. Doris's borrowed stockings pucker underfoot, as a thistle stabs Rebecca's heel. This wouldn't happen in the movies. Doris'll be cross. On Monday, Arthur's leaving for Yatesbury and Rebecca might not see much of him for two years. Bugger Doris. She's going to give him something to remember.

At the edge of the meadow, Arthur reaches the willow tree which stands dancing, by the brook. He scoops up the curtain of branches into a bunch, inviting her underneath. As Rebecca follows, he whips and spreads his jacket over the mossy patch, lying down with his arms outstretched to her.

"C'mere."

She lies down next to him and their teeth bump as he kisses her hard, fiddling with her thick bra strap, through the dress. She slides her arm under his bracers at the back and twangs them.

"You little Madam..."

"Someone might see us!"

He stands up and parts the branches, surveying the meadow. "We've got the place to ourselves. Come on."

As they kiss, he reaches up her dress and tugs at the side of her underwear. She lifts her bottom, but they stick at the suspender belt. She realises she's clipped them over the knickers.

"Wait a minute," she says, reaching into her handbag and retrieving a tanner, fumbling with the wire clasp. The clips ping free at the front, and she wriggles them off. The stocking tops sag, helplessly. Rebecca gazes up at him, searching, but he wears a serious expression and a brown curl has fallen over one eye, as he fiddles with his trouser button. He seems to take ages.

"Bugger" he mutters, stopping to undo it.

Rebecca glances down at his Johnson. Purple – aggressive - exactly as she remembered. Afraid and thrilled, she shuts her eyes. She feels she might pee with excitement, as he lies on top of her. Her privates burn when he pushes in – no-one said sex would hurt. He moves up and down three or four times slowly - twice quickly and he pulls out.

"Whoops." He fumbles about a bit and exhales loudly, lying on his back. His elbow brushes past her face as he puts his arms behind his head. She drags her dress down. This makes her a woman now, like Doris. Sex is quicker than she thought. She opens her eyes and smiles at Arthur, who grins back.

"Alright, my darling?"

"Yes." she replies. "I love you Arthur."

"And I love you. Did you like that?"

"I did." She reaches for her knickers. "Could you turn away please?"

"Nothing I haven't seen," he says, laughing and rolling over.

She stands, fumbling with the stockings, as the ladder creeps, silent, to the back of her knee.

"Arthur, I'm bleeding!" A single line of blood runs slowly down her thighs.

He pulls a hanky out of his jacket pocket.

"That can happen, your first time. Here."

She wipes herself three times, folding the cloth. "What shall I do with it?"

"You give that to me. I'll keep it for a souvenir!" He kisses the handkerchief, punching the air in glee, before stuffing it in his trouser pocket.

"You won't tell anyone, will you?"

"Nooo."

He lights two Players, handing one to her. She puffs, without inhaling and lies down, turning her back to him. He presses in behind her and lifting her head with his right arm, weighting his left across her, he squeezes her breast. She smiles. Now and again, the harsh cak cak cak call of a magpie disturbs the peace, but they are the only lovers in this world, and nothing and no-one can disturb them, so they doze, both content in body and the other, for the first time, content in the mind, too.

Rebecca's eyes fix on the black silver ones above her head. The creature is motionless, with a musky-stale scent. Upright on hind legs, white front paws dangling – poised, edged with stale yellow claws, slightly upturned at the end. A pointed face, with whiskers sprung out either side. The perfectly curled ears are wide yet neat, like folded velvet.

She leans hard into Arthur's arm.

"Arthur..." she whispers, though her teeth. He doesn't stir.

"Arthur!"

He murmurs: "Whas' the trouble?"

"Look!"

"Christ. Don't move." His voice is grim, suddenly alert. He slides his arm down to his ankle, slipping off his shoe.

Rebecca shrieks as his shoe smashes down on the creature's head with a crunching blow. They stare at the body, which the force appears to have reduced to half-size, like a peg in a hole.

"He's a goner." Arthur says.

"What was it? My God Arthur, I thought I'd die of fright!" Her hands shake.

"Stoat. Big bugger, too. He 'ad you in 'is sights."

"What would he do?"

"Bite off your beautiful nose, like this" he pinches her nose, between his thumb and forefinger, sharp. They break into relieved giggles. She can't stop staring at the stoat.

"I'll buy you a coat from his fur one day. Know what they call them?"

"No?"

"Ermine."

"Mother says Mink's the finest."

"I'll rob a bank". He checks his watch. "We'd better go. You'll be late for tea. Knock the grass off that dress, or your Dad'll have my guts for garters."

They kiss a lingering goodbye twice, at the end of her road.

Rebecca eyes Mother, inhaling her scent, of rosewater and disinfectant with distaste, as she leans over Rebecca to reach her plate. Mother picks the bone away from the chop, cutting the meat into little pieces, before withdrawing, to begin her own meal. Tomorrow, Rebecca thinks. Tomorrow, I'll tell her to stop cutting up my dinner, but she doesn't.

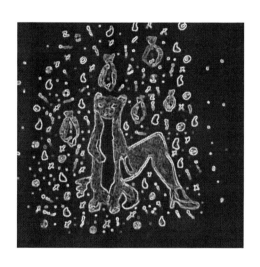

Chapter Twelve:

She's written to him every day for eighteen months; and he's written to her twice a week; returning for furlough when allowed. They became engaged on her sixteenth birthday, just as he promised; two months ago. Now, they lie under their willow tree once again.

"We've got no money. My mother and your father will kill us. You trust me, don't you? It's the only way. I'll still marry you, of course I will. The time is wrong. You do see? D'you love me?"

"I do love you. I'm frightened. Will it hurt?"

"Yes, but it's for the best. Just lie still."

She lies back on the grass. He aims the first punch just below her belly button with his fist sideways. She gasps with the pain, but nods and looks away. He punches her stomach again, twice. Then he cuddles her and tells her how much he loves her.

That night; Rebecca's parents are sound asleep. The cramps in her stomach become unmanageable. The sounds of the stop-start drone of the milk float and the milkman clinking bottles on his round, in the dark, filter through the open window. She can't take the pain any longer and must move, so she goes to the toilet. As she sits, her insides are dropping out from her. Frightened, she checks between her legs into the bowl. The blood clots turn the water scarlet. She clings onto the basin as waves of pain radiate from the left to right of her stomach. She cries out for her parents and they come – as a larger lump torpedoes into the water.

Mother stands, stunned. "Ring the doctor Faith. Get the doctor!" Dad shouts, and at this, Mother jumps and scuttles to the phone.

Dad kneels down beside her and puts his arms around her, rocking, soothing.

"Alright, my pet, alright. Doctor will be here soon."

Rebecca holds him, sobbing in gulps. Now Mother and Dad know everything. All over - her perfect secret exposed. Dad reaches over, placing the hand towel on his knees and he slides Rebecca off the seat and into his lap, cradling her and stroking her hair. She shivers with cold as he hugs her close, quietly reaching behind her to shut the toilet lid.

They are still in this position when Dr Lewis arrives. He issues brisk instructions. She succumbs as they clean her up, and put her to bed, with a huge pad wedged between her legs. Her Mother is silent as she tucks a towel underneath her, but Dr Lewis glares at her, sternly.

"You're an extremely silly girl. You might have died. This is why people wait until they're married before they start a family. I hope you've learned a lesson and you must never do anything like this again. What a good job this happened, or you'd be bringing down a great deal of shame on your parents and yourself."

"I'm so sorry," she replies, crying and turning to her Dad.

"I know you are – but heed what Dr Lewis says now. I'll be having words with Arthur."

"Yes. It wasn't all Arthur's fault."

"I think we've said enough. This is nature's way. We'll put the unfortunate business behind us."

He doesn't kiss her goodnight. Arthur will be happy, of course – he's been so worried about what his mother would say, and the pair of them without much money. In fact she hates him just now, grinding her teeth to try and stop the tears until her jaw aches - she cannot bring herself to be pleased, about losing their first baby. She's sure God will punish her for this in some way. The toilet is flushed four times.

Rebecca is left in bed long after everyone else is up and about.

Chapter Thirteen:

"You'd better come in, young man," Charlie says, opening the door to Arthur. His expression looks grim.

"Thank you," Arthur replies, removing his cap.

He follows Charlie into the kitchen. Charlie shuts both doors.

"Rebecca's in the bathroom. She'll be down presently."

"Is she...alright?"

"She'll recover. Now then; I think you'd better explain your intentions to me."

"Of course. I'm so sorry. I'd like to ask you for her hand in marriage – please. I know I shouldn't have taken advantage of her; but we got carried away. It's not her fault."

"I'm aware of that. I hold you entirely responsible – she's naïve. Now I'm a man of the world, Arthur. I've seen plenty of young women land themselves in a situation and have to carry the can for it. Especially during the war."

"I just want you to know I love her."

"It's probably for the best she miscarried. She still has her reputation, at least. But we can't have a repeat of this. You're not to touch her until after the wedding – and that should be sooner rather than later."

"I promise, I won't. Does...does this mean you will give us your blessing?"

"I'll give you my permission. That's it. I expect you to do right by her and you'll have to earn my trust again."

"I will. Thank you Charlie."

"She needs looking after, that one. You got off lightly – this time. If you let her down again, you'll have me to answer to. Is that understood?"

Arthur nods.

"What do you parents say about it?"

"They don't know..."

"Don't you think they ought to know?"

"I'd rather not. It'd break my mother's heart. I'm her only son, you see – she'd be so ashamed."

"Pity you didn't think about that before you decided to knock up my daughter!"

"I'm sorry."

"It's too late for that now. We'll put it behind us. Probably best they don't know – no point upsetting another set of parents. Now you just go in there and make it up to her."

"I will."

Rebecca finds little respite from the secret fears and the rituals. She's hopeful they'll go, after her wedding. She's sure she'll be safe with Arthur, he'll protect her. Busying herself with the arrangements; she becomes distracted from the bad thoughts. Doris's heavily involved with setting the date. She's keen to be Rebecca's Matron of Honour, before she sets sail for America to join Mark.

The week before Rebecca and Arthur's wedding, their plans to rent a flat from a friend of her father's, fall through unexpectedly. They'll need to live with her parents until something else turns up. They are married in the Spring of 1953 at the Holy Trinity Church in Longlevens. Every pew is adorned with yellow tea roses. After the reception, everyone throws rice and confetti, as they set off for their honeymoon in Bournemouth, with tins on strings rattling at the rear of the car.

Arthur unlocks the door to the light and airy hotel room at The Connaught. A vase of fresh lilies with a heavy sweet scent sits next to the double bed, which has a continental quilt. This ought to be idyllic; but she's got up to use the toilet four times tonight; frightened she might wet the bed.

After their first full night together, Rebecca sips tea on the balcony, watching the sea, remembering the times she's stayed in this hotel. She's visited Bournemouth on many occasions for family holidays, and only ever played on the sand once. Of course, the last time she came was shortly after she met Arthur. Such a lot has happened. He tried to finish with her, just before he went to Yatesbury. Only last night, he confessed, laughing under the sheets. When he'd been shot, he considered whether he might die. He'd contemplated his death in the hospital bed and concluded he didn't want to die a virgin. Rebecca was the best woman he could think of. She was affronted – though as always, he'd made her laugh again within half an hour. Like their first date, when they left Morelands, him, whistling, her, carrying a smelly plastic bag filled with elvers. They walked past the undertakers, and Arthur said it's where he lived. The next five minutes of the walk home were silent, as she'd worried herself silly how she would tell him she couldn't possibly marry an undertaker. She asked some polite questions about undertaking – which he answered, until he failed to keep up the pretence any longer and owned up to pulling her leg.

Rebecca lights a cigarette and blows out the smoke into the sunshine. She can see all the holiday visitors passing by from this balcony. One is pushing a Silver Cross perambulator. She'll buy one of those, when their next baby arrives – hopes it'll be soon. He's forgotten about their first one already. She puts her hand to her stomach and rubs.

Arthur comes out to the balcony and kisses her forehead.

"So what d'you want to do today, Mrs Denby? Back to bed?"

"I'd like to play on the sand, Arthur," she replies.

On Tuesday morning, they set off for Southampton to meet Rebecca's parents; Doris, and baby Greg. The family stand at the quayside, exchanging goodbyes and crying, retrieving their handkerchiefs, to wave. The brass band plays a variety of tunes; one of which even makes Charlie Lindsay take out his hanky. *We'll meet again.* Faith is devastated to witness her daughter and grandson leave. This is compounded by her terror of crowds. At five feet tall, she stands even shorter than Rebecca; immaculately dressed in a mid-brown twinset, with matching shoes and handbag as she scans her surroundings, visibly discomfited. As Doris waves from the gangplank with Greg in her arms, Faith grips Charlie's arm for support. Rebecca reaches out her hand to squeeze her mother's. Faith shakes it off and dabs her eyes.

The Queen Elizabeth departs from the Solent, with people shouting over the hooters which blow periodically, deafening the watchers and passengers alike. When they lose sight of Doris and Greg, the family turn, fighting their way back through the crowds to their cars. No one attempts conversation on the way home. Charlie glares at the road ahead, as though his will can devour the distance faster. Faith snuffles and dabs her eyes with the handkerchief. The newlyweds in the back seat squeeze hands and gaze out of opposite windows at the hedges rushing by.

Chapter Fourteen:

Four months later, Rebecca and Arthur are delighted to discover she's expecting a baby. Arthur's working as an electrician – installing wiring systems at the Government Communications Headquarters. Rebecca's healthy – proud of her pregnancy, her skin white-smooth and flushed rosy cheeks from frequent walking, her nails, smooth, strong and white and her hair glossy. Faith, morose since Doris's departure, perks up with a new focus and begins knitting bootees. Shelagh Denby's delighted at the prospect of her first grandchild and she knits cardigans and bonnets with little ribbons, to tie under the baby's chin. When Rebecca's around three months pregnant, she hands in her notice at work, which is customary as soon as one begins to show.

One evening, Charlie Lindsay calls his daughter and son-in- law over, looking pleased with himself.

"I've bought Cherry Cottage. We think the time has come for a place of your own, what with the babby coming along soon!" He slides a set of keys over the table to Arthur.

"Dad, this is wonderful!" Rebecca says, jumping up to hug him and kiss his cheek.

Arthur stands to shake his hand. "Thank you so much Charlie. I'll take care of the place, don't you worry."

"The house in my name, of course, but you needn't pay any rent. You just concentrate on looking after my daughter and the little one to come."

"I will," Arthur smiles.

"Can we see it now?" Rebecca jumps up, stopping to hold her stomach, she must be careful.

"We'll all go, shall we?" Charlie replies.

Cherry Cottage has three bedrooms, two doubles and a little box room for the baby, only a few hundred yards from Charlie & Faith Lindsay's house. "Blossom Orchard" lies behind, where the long grass ripples, beneath the trees full of flowers. Sometimes when the wind blows, petals fly into the air like pink snow – yes, Rebecca's sure she'll make this beautiful place their home. They move in, next day.

Rebecca finds herself ill-prepared for becoming a housewife - Faith hasn't taught her to cook or clean and this a steep learning curve. For much of the time she's distracted from the bad thoughts. With no telephone, she can't check the receiver at night. Different routines take over - a never-ending round of tasks making her back ache and her ankles swell, but she continues trying her hardest, borrowing recipe books from her mother and taking hints and tips from Shelagh. Seems Rebecca isn't aware of all the rules - a proper way and a day to do each large chore and you try to fit the others around.

Monday is wash day, Tuesday for ironing, Wednesday for sewing and mending. Thursday for shopping, Friday for a big house clean, Saturday for cooking and baking. Sunday's supposed to be a day of rest, but after the effort of making up and putting on her best clothes to go to church, she's still to cook the roast dinner and clear up. She's no-one to talk to and Arthur's not much company – he's always tired. Even if he does spend time at home, he seems to want to be tinkering with something that needs fixing for some other bugger, or he's anxious to go fishing. Sometimes she talks to herself, just to break the silence.

One Monday, when Rebecca is about seven months pregnant, she's working up a sweat in the kitchen and her ribs ache – the baby's turning cartwheels. She didn't light the fire this morning after cleaning out the grate. The weather's unusually warm for April, so she's determined to hang the washing outside, rather than hanging it on the clothes maiden in the sitting room. This always seems common and scruffy, somehow – all that underwear on display and the steam that rises, when're drying, makes the whole cottage seem smaller, cloying and stuffy.

She puts on her apron and lugs the whites into the Belfast sink, soaking them for an hour in this new Super Oxydol Shelagh's recommended. Her hands sting, as she scrubs them with a hard brush, the bristles clogged with soap. As she rubs the stains out of her husband's underwear, she reflects - you just don't know people until you live together. Especially men and their habits – they pee round the toilet and leave drips on the rim, sometimes on the floor. How nasty it is to scrub another person's shit from the bowl – a wife was no better than a charlady really. It wasn't long ago her Mother used to do this for her - some people out there were rich and had someone to "do" for them. Her hands are still soft, but she knows if she doesn't put cold cream on later, they'll be itching and dry. Her fingernails aren't what they were a few weeks ago –she never finds the time to paint them these days.

As a sweaty lock of hair dangles limp across her eyes, she brushes her forehead with back of her arm and stares out of the window. The gate clangs. Mother's traversing the path, casting a glance either way, as though she expects someone to pounce on her. She's always so bloody...jumpy. Rebecca dries her hands on her apron and walks to the door, just as Faith knocks. She's brandishing an envelope, like a weapon and looking excited.

"They're coming home, Rebecca! Isn't that wonderful?" she asks, handing Rebecca the letter.

Rebecca scans her sister's scrawled handwriting, skim-reading the first few paragraphs:

Hope you are all well and that Rebecca is enjoying pregnancy. Onto our news – Mark's job hasn't worked out as we planned and now I find I'm expecting again! Baby's due about seven months after Rebecca's. With this in mind, we have decided to come home.

Greg is growing tall and misses his grandparents so much. We'll be with you in around one month and hope you can put us up, you until we find our own place? I'll write further when we've got the itinerary. Give everyone our best.

Much love, Doris, Mark & Greg.

No wonder Mother's happy. Rebecca wonders whether Doris's return will overshadow the arrival of baby Denby. What an awful thing to think. Such fun; they can be new mothers together and help each other out. She makes her mother a pot of tea and listens to her twaddle for an hour – watching the clock, conscious of getting behind.

"Doris's got all the latest fashions. I expect she'll bring presents, she keeps talking about the amazing chocolate in America – Hershey bars."

"How *marvellous.*"

"Mark's carpeted their house right the way through. Can you imagine?"

"I wonder why they're coming back."

"Well, they miss us, obviously. She wants to be near me when she's having a baby – only natural."

Rebecca shifts in the chair. "I must get up – sorry. My ribs hurt. Did yours hurt, when you were expecting?"

"The others weren't too bad. *You* put me through hell to bear you!"

"Did   I?"

"Oh yes. I'd only wanted two children. No one understands what I've been through." Faith pauses to consider for a moment. "I expect Doris'll feel the cold when she comes back. And poor little Greg. I've missed him. Perhaps I'll knit him a cardigan. "

"He probably won't recognise anyone, will he?" Rebecca says, sly.

"I'm sure he'll know his grandmother."

"He was so young when they left."

"Children always know their grandparents." This is said with enough conviction for Rebecca to retreat.

"How long are they staying?"

"I wish they wouldn't go back. Too far away. You'll understand when the baby comes – it's hard to be separated from your child, no matter what age they are."

"Mmmm."

"Well, I must let you get on – it's obvious you've a lot to do. What are you cooking for Arthur's tea?"

"A chicken pie."

"I presume the pastry's prepared?"

"Not yet."

"Better look sharp then – that needs a rest before you roll. Being organised is the thing."

"Actually Shelagh's given me a new recipe."

"Hmm. I'll see you at church on Sunday?"

"I don't think Arthur will be able to come – he's busy at work."

"I hope you're looking after him, Rebecca."

"Yes. I'll ask him."

"Good. Toodleoo!"

"Bye."

Rebecca closes the door behind her mother and leans back against it, heavily. Returning to the kitchen, she turns the sheets over and over again in a roll, squeezing the soap out in stages and slapping them hard on the draining board. Their heavy limp weight oozes dirty suds into the sink, as she refills it with plain water. The tap judders and sprays. She turns it harder than necessary – on, off - on, off - on, off, drenching her face and apron. She stares out of the window with water dripping down her cheeks and allows her eyes to cloud enough to make the scenery slightly blur and the lane becomes slug-like, cherry blossom fading into pink clouds and the grass merges into a tempestuous sea, swirling and rising.

Throwing in the muslin bag to rinse the washing, she gazes at the blue circles expand in the water and disperse, poking the garments viciously with the wooden tongs. Fuck off Doris. Fuck off Mother. Fuck off washing. What a dreadful word – only bad people have those thoughts. I am sorry God. I didn't mean it. Turning the handle of the wringer makes her arm ache, so she tries alternating them. The drips make a mournful twang in the aluminium bowl underneath. She imagines squeezing the life out of the sheets and when she's put them all through three times, Rebecca drops them into the wicker basket and lugs it out to the back garden, hanging them up with dolly pegs. The scent of sweet blossom from the orchard is soon overpowered by the sterile washing, but she's freer out here and her mood begins to lift a little. Time to start the fucking shitty bastard pastry. She allows herself a giggle – what a good job people can't read your mind.

Chapter Fifteen:

Doris and Mark move in with Rebecca's parents and become frequent visitors at Cherry Cottage - Faith appears to be driving Doris "nuts", fussing over her – another of those Yank expressions she's picked up. Her accent's tinged with a slight drawl, that everyone (except Rebecca) finds charming. Her sister has reinvented herself as someone even more interesting.

Mark secures a job as an Office Manager and becomes so friendly with Arthur; they begin discussing the possibility of building a couple of houses together. Rebecca is expected to be thrilled and so she acts, but she isn't. Charlie Lindsay gives them each a plot of land to build on. Doris suggests she and Mark move into Cherry Cottage with Rebecca and Arthur, on the premise of "keeping Rebecca company", which is not discussed; rather, sort of...settled. Rebecca tries so hard to keep the place tidy and Doris slips into being looked after, in the manner she was with Mother – she doesn't do much to help. Alongside all the housework, Rebecca helps out with Doris's toddler, Greg, thinking it'll be good practice for her. Doris lets her.

On 12 June 1954, Rebecca goes into labour. She tries hard to wait until the last moment before calling the midwife. Although she's in a lot of discomfort, Arthur takes her out to visit friends and drop in on her parents – but she won't tell Mother the labour has started; realising she'll only get into a panic and make Rebecca frightened. She plods around the orchard until she can't bear the pain any longer and Arthur calls the midwife. Two very young midwives attend, in shifts. The first arrives alone – and when the second comes to relieve her, she advises that the doctor should be summoned immediately. Both are rather nervous and inexperienced.

The doctor examines Rebecca, puts sweet-smelling chloroform on a cloth over her mouth and nose and tells her to breathe deeply and slowly. On the fourth breath she passes out. She doesn't know how long for, but when she wakes up, the pain is coming in waves. Then it's constant. A curious mixture, as though she's constipated and needs an enormous poo, mixed with intense period pains. She's frightened she'll be destroyed by the outcome – this won't be a baby that comes out, but her whole insides and she'll die in this room. First she's afraid of this prospect, the world will carry on without her and she can only observe from a distance, her mother, her sister, taking her baby away and bringing him up, together with her husband, he now loves them more than her and she'll be forgotten. Then she thinks dying could be a blessed sleep and wishes for the end, if only someone can make the pain stop for longer than a few seconds, she would drift away. She has no pain relief.

People are getting busy. The burning of the episiotomy scalpel on her perineum, reminds her she's alive, earthy, and animalistic. Incessant voices instruct her to stop pushing for a minute, but she can't – her body appears to be working independently, out of control. Alien hands on her most private parts stabbing, shifting, like she's a machine with something stuck and then a cry, of someone new, overwhelmed with rage and need. She will never separate who it belongs to...as though this voice was once owned by two people, wrenched apart by the greater force of others.

Baby Robert Denby is born thirty six hours after Rebecca's labour starts, on the 14th of June, 1954. She receives fourteen internal stitches and sixteen external. She's bedridden for a fortnight, staring at the wall, woken every few hours to Robert's sucking mouth clamped furiously on her fiery, aching breasts. He's so angry. On the fifteenth day, left alone, she drags herself up to continue with her routine. Doris's out visiting. Arthur's at work and Robert keeps crying, like a rabbit with a paw caught in a snare. She tries again to breastfeed him, but he's never satisfied – as though he can't get enough. Eventually, she changes his nappy, tucks him into the perambulator and walks away to the garden. He doesn't want her. She's no good to him. When Doris returns home, she finds Robert, red-faced, squalling uncontrollably in the pram, legs kicking, tangled in the blanket. Rebecca has collapsed, while hanging out the washing and lies prostrate, unconscious on the lawn – still clutching a terry nappy. Low blood pressure, the doctors conclude.

Chapter Sixteen:

Shelagh Denby often invites Arthur, Rebecca and Robert round for meals. The atmosphere in their home is much more convivial than at Charlie & Faith Lindsay's. Rebecca even visits without Arthur and is made welcome. She confides in Shelagh.

"I love being over here. I miss Arthur when he's at work. Doris doesn't understand – it's all about her pregnancy now. She's always out with Mother."

"Rebecca, if it ever gets too much, we've always the attic room. We'd love you all to stay with us, while Arthur finishes the house. It must be lonely for you."

"D'you mean that?"

"Of course. Grampy suggested the idea, more than once. He adores you and Robert."

Rebecca determines to speak to Arthur this evening, about her idea. They talk at length, into the early hours, whispering so that Doris and Mark don't overhear and they won't wake Robert. Arthur seems content to go along with the plan, anything to keep her happy. In any case, it'll only be temporary – just until the house is finished; maybe four months or so. For the first time, Robert sleeps through.

Doris makes no attempt to dissuade them from moving out of Cherry Cottage. She thinks this a sensible suggestion – the cottage is obviously over-crowded. The day after Rebecca, Arthur and Robert move out, Doris begins re-decorating the master bedroom and moves in.

\#

The Denby's home, "Sandbanks", is an Edwardian three-bedroomed end-terraced house, with a garage at the side. The other permanent resident is Eddie Mustoe, Shelagh's father - always dapper in a three piece suit and Panama hat, setting high standards and frequently complaining about other's lack of them. Eddie's bedroom is on the second floor of Sandbanks, beside Henry and Shelagh's, alongside what appears to be a cupboard door, but behind this are the dark, narrow steps leading up to the attic room. With only one little window, the attic room is rather gloomy. The double bed has a lumpy feather mattress, which smells damp and musty. There's only just enough space to fit the cot alongside, with a small gap between. Rebecca and baby Robert spend most of their time in here. Arthur goes straight from work to the site where he's building their house, and when he comes home he's exhausted. All he wants to do is eat a meal and go to bed.

Breast-feeding Robert isn't working. He seems discontented. Rebecca's conscious about his crying disturbing her in-laws, particularly at night, although they say they don't mind and they're kind to her. Despite a sense of failure, she agrees with Shelagh's suggestion to start giving him a few solids as well, a little rusk softened with boiled water. Sometimes she digs her fingernails into the palm of her hand, to try and take her mind off the bad thoughts. This only creates a temporary distraction and one which brings tears to her eyes. All she can imagine is lying on a bed and crying herself to sleep, but her duties won't allow time. Trapped and desperate, her growing sense of being overwhelmed is unbearable. She's unable to complain to Arthur again. She tells no-one.

One afternoon, Rebecca eventually manages to settle Robert for a nap. She sits on the edge of the bedside watching him; strangely detached. If she leaves the room he's bound to cry, alerting the world to her abandonment. Still, she might risk slipping downstairs to re-do her face and start preparing the dinner. Getting up, she pads away from the cot, her finger over her lips. Best to leave the door ajar, in case the click disturbs him. As Rebecca creeps down the stairs, she's startled by Eddie Mustoe and a woman – leaving his bedroom. She's much younger than him, perhaps forty or so and dishevelled, her red lipstick's smudged. Her skirt's far too short to be decent. Eddie, self-assured, squeezes his arm around his companion's waist. Rebecca has overheard the lascivious comments about Eddie. A ladies' man; the way he appraises women.

"Well, young Rebecca. Asleep at last, is he?" he asks.

"Yes. I thought I might start the dinner for Shelagh."

"Good girl. Have you met Cynthia?"

"Hello Cynthia."

"Cynthia's an old friend."

"Less of the old! Charmed to meet you, Rebecca," Cynthia smirks, extending a taloned hand.

Rebecca shakes it. "Glad to meet you, too."

She follows the couple downstairs. Eddie disappears to the toilet and Cynthia sits down in the kitchen, as though she owns the place. Rebecca fetches the potatoes from the larder and fills the bowl with water. She senses Cynthia watching her.

"You're pretty, aren't you Rebecca?" Cynthia says, grinning.

"I couldn't say, but thank you."

"How old's your baby now?"

"Robert's four months."

"Eddie says he's handsome."

"He's very fond of him."

"Fine pair of lungs on him!"

"I'm sorry if we disturbed you." Rebecca's tone is sharp.

"Breast feeding, are we?"

"Yes."

"Come here, Rebecca."

Rebecca obeys. Cynthia seems a bit excited, yet furtive, watching the door for Eddie.

"Don't you bother with that malarkey," she says. "Put him on the bottle. Look what it did to me..."

She hikes up her blouse. She's not wearing a brassiere and reveals an inverted hole where her left breast should be. A hollow, purple and lined with white scars next to a puckered, sagging right breast, the brown nipple erect. Rebecca recoils and steps back.

"What...what happened to you?"

"Cancer. Four of the little bleeders. Never you mind any nonsense about doing it nature's way. That's never natural. They'll be the death of you, if you let them. I 'eard your babby grizzling. Ee's hungry. Put him on the bottle, quick smart."

Cynthia pulls down her top, cackling.

"Shocked are you Rebecca? Get used to it. You're a woman now. Think you're a cut above, don't you? I can tell. "

"I don't understand what you mean..." Rebecca falters, horrified.

"They're all the same." Cynthia draws hard and extinguishes her cigarette in the ashtray, the greasy lipstick smearing her fingertips. "Mark my words."

Eddie Mustoe returns to the kitchen and Cynthia greets him with a smudgy swollen-lipped grin. He holds the back door open for Cynthia and follows her out. Rebecca sees him grasp one of Cynthia's ample buttocks. She shudders at their sleazy display. The door bangs shut carelessly behind them - never mind about the waking the baby then. She listens...silence, for now.

Rebecca peels the potatoes, her hands shaking. The knife nicks the webbing between her thumb and forefinger. She watches the blood disperse in the water. Robert cries out and her stomach contracts. This time she carries on peeling, until they're all done. His crying has escalated to braying. Grinding her teeth and squirming; she succumbs to the instinct to attend to him. She lies on her side and tries to draw him to her breast, but he alternates between writhing away, his little limbs taught and outstretched in protest and hard gums biting, struggling, fists kneading, clutching and hurting her breasts, punishing her for his hunger.

By the time he latches on, slurping, her nipple is so sore, she could slap him off, but she tolerates his mouth and he settles for a moment. Then his head pulls away, red face contorted with frustration. As Rebecca prays up to the ceiling for God to help, he isn't up in the rafters...the dusty line of a spider's web sways in the draught, mocking. She'll get that down tomorrow, filthy dirty things. Cynthia's hollow of a breast stays in her imagination, like a crater of insatiable need.

Chapter Seventeen:

Two months later, by February 1955, Rebecca is desperate enough to book an appointment with the Doctor. She leaves Robert with Shelagh, and walks the half mile to the surgery with her head down, counting the paving slabs - they don't quite add up to be divisible by three, so she doubles back several times until they do. Despite feeling lonely for months, this is the first time she's been alone. She's daunted by the combination of freedom and anxiety at the prospect of change. The waiting room is peaceful, and she skims an article about the *real* Prince Philip in *Woman's Own*. Here's a knitting pattern Shelagh would like, a jersey in moss stitch. Rebecca doesn't find time to knit any more. She reaches the problem page when Dr Lewis calls for her, too soon. She closes the magazine and follows him. He greets her with warmth.

"Motherhood suiting you, Rebecca?"

"Quite well, thank you, Doctor."

"How old is baby now – he must be coming up for eight months, mustn't he?"

"Robert will be six months next week."

"They grow up so fast. Now - what seems to be the trouble?"

Rebecca starts to cry. Dr Lewis is taken aback and opens his desk drawers to hunt for the box of tissues. He can't find them and he pulls a handkerchief from his breast pocket.

"There, there now. Dry your tears, that's a good girl. I'm sure things can't be as bad as all that."

She dabs at her eyes, ashamed – what would Dad say about her making this fuss?

"I'm sorry. I can't seem to stop blubbing."

"I see. Quite natural, things take a little while to...settle down after one's had a baby. Are you eating properly?"

"I think so."

"The trick is to have plenty of fresh air and exercise. A brisk walk, every day. Good for Robert, too."

"I'm frightened to leave the house."

"What on earth for?"

"I keep thinking bad things will happen to me, or my family."

"Because you're going out? Come now, that's hardly sensible, hmm?"

"I can't bear it any longer. I'm like this all the time. I'm an awful mother, Doctor."

"I'm sure you're not, dear."

"Robert's always crying. I don't think he loves me."

"Of course he does. You're his mother."

She begins to sob. Dr Lewis is silent, thoughtful. He takes out a sheet of headed notepaper and writes. When he's finished, he folds and inserts the paper in an envelope, addressing the outside.

"Rebecca, I want a colleague of mine to take a look at you."

"Alright."

"He's a psychiatrist. He's based at Horton Road – now, do you know where that is?"

"You mean the asylum? Is there something wrong with my brain?"

"I think you're very troubled – and I'd like him to assess you, for mental illness. He'll just ask you some questions and you can talk to him about your problems. Go directly from here, give the receptionist this letter and she'll book an appointment for you."

"Thank you."

"Good luck," he says, standing to usher her to the door. "I'm sure you'll be fine."

Chapter Eighteen:

The first appointment with Dr Hitchman takes place in his office at Horton Road. Younger than Dr Lewis, he's sympathetic and rather handsome. Rebecca tells him everything, all the bad thoughts, the fears – even the rituals she uses to try and take her mind off things. The relief is almost like going to confession. He appears concerned at the length of time she's been struggling with this alone. When she's finished talking, he speaks:

"You poor thing. What a terrible time you've been having. I don't want you to worry - we're going to sort you out. Now, here at Horton Road, we have the latest equipment to treat mental illness."

"Am I mentally ill, Dr Hitchman?"

"I believe you are. I'd say on the basis of my notes from our discussion, you're suffering from hysteria, compulsions and depression – possibly neurosis, too."

"Then it's not my fault? I'm not just an awful wife and mother?"

"Certainly not. The brain can become diseased, rather like a wound that doesn't seem to heal. Without treatment, it'll get worse. You've done the right thing."

"Can I be cured?"

"I've achieved marvellous results from the latest treatments. You might have heard of ECT?"

"No."

"Well, what happens with mental illness, the mind becomes so muddled; the worries people experience don't make sense."

"You're so right. You do understand."

"Well with ECT, we almost give the brain a little jolt, a kick start; if you will, back to normal. Life gets into kilter again."

"Does it…hurt?"

"ECT produces a natural anaesthesia. After we've started, you'll not be aware of any pain."

"Must I stay overnight? I have a baby, you see and my husband doesn't know."

"Well, you must certainly tell him. The treatment only takes about an hour, but you mustn't be left alone for several hours after – someone needs to look after you. Can you make the necessary arrangements?"

"I think so."

"I'll prescribe a course of treatment. You'll come here, once a week. I'm going to prescribe eight sessions to begin with, and we'll monitor how you get along. We can always top up with a few more if necessary. But you should start to feel a difference within the month."

"I'm willing to try anything, to be better."

"We'll book you in Friday. Ten o'clock."

#

Horton Road, Gloucestershire's first county lunatic asylum, opened July 21st 1823 at Wotton. Built on rising ground, about half a mile from the City of Gloucester, with grounds spanning 45 acres that afforded extensive views of the surrounding country, the semicircular centre of the building (with the wings) originally extended 250 feet. In 1873, additional buildings were erected, including a chapel, providing accommodation for 640 patients. The Asylum became known as Horton Road Hospital. At the introduction of the National Health Service in 1948, the two county asylums became known as Horton Road Hospital and Coney Hill Hospital respectively. From 1948, the hospital, left under the control of the governors, suffered financial problems.

This year, the Gloucester Citizen edition of 7 May 1955 reported a record increase in voluntary admissions to Horton Road & Coney Hill Mental Asylums; 70% of the total 652. There was a severe shortage of nursing staff; in particular, student nurses. The records also indicated some presence of wartime evacuees. The management committee reported "the increase was not an increase in the prevalence of mental illness, but more a willingness by the public to enter the hospital for early treatment."

The annual report makes no mention of a scathing attack in the London Morning Newspaper on the conditions alleged to be prevailing at Horton Road Hospital, by an unnamed author, after visiting 27 mental hospitals throughout the UK, stating that they were "a disgrace to a nation that calls itself civilized." In particular, of Horton Road, it says:

"It should have been condemned 50 years ago. Behind its grimy windows are 748 men and women. The entertainment hall is packed with beds. 83 women sleep in a corridor nine feet wide and long enough, according to the Health Ministry, for only 64 beds. I saw rooms no bigger than a prison cell, with peeling plaster and damp-streaked walls that were big enough for two beds and contained four." A doctor is quoted as having informed the paper twelve old people had died, from the cold conditions. The Citizen prints all the allegations and the article is highly condemned by the hospital authorities.

Since 1940, enthusiastic reports concerning a new treatment for mental illness began being published in the United States. A far cry from the earlier, more violent treatments such as the whole-scale removal of teeth and tonsils, or enforced tight packing in wet cold bandages; they were called shock treatments or convulsive therapies. Somehow the new treatments gained a scientific credibility formerly lacking. Electro-Convulsive Therapy (ECT) was considered a major breakthrough in treating a growing hospital population of seemingly intractable cases. ECT Equipment was first installed in the Horton Road Asylum in 1942. In the basement.

Chapter Nineteen:

With so many steps down; she's walking into the bowels of some huge living creature. The walls are painted green, but tiled white from waist-height to the floor. Matron leads and Rebecca follows the starched cap bob down in front of her, perched on top of her chignon like a small boat. Matron's shins are thick in their tights and her crepe soled shoes squeak on the linoleum. The keys hanging from her belt jangle with each step. Rebecca has the urge to turn and run back up, saying this is all a huge mistake; she's better now. But she trails behind, the echo of her own heels tapping, her floral dress swishing. Her fingers, swollen with the heat, make the finger rings too tight to turn. She tries to rotate them with her thumb, but they won't budge and the lines across her palms ooze sweat. Acid rises in her throat.

The room emits a scent of cloves. Despite the multitude of people inside – the bed is the focal point. Flat, with the straps and buckles – open and waiting to be filled - like a belt without a belly. Her eyes seem foggy as she complies with the instructions, delivered in an indifferent tone.

"You'll need to remove all your jewellery, please."

"Even my wedding ring?"

"Everything."

"My fingers are swollen,"

"Come to the sink – we'll get them off with lubrication."

She smears pink soap all over Rebecca's fingers, sliding and turning the rings until they slip over white knuckles. They're put in a brown envelope with her earrings, necklace and watch.

"Take off your shoes." Matron holds out her hand for them. Navy blue high heels – her favourites. She wants to say, look after them, please.

"Put these on."

She's handed ugly, shapeless, flat pumps. She recognises the stale rubber stench. Her head sweats and her breath shortens. She takes herself on a journey – disengaged from her body, as they move her around. Alice, after leaving the mad hatters' tea party, arrives in another burrow. The white rabbit straps her into the buckles and they are tight - this is for Alice's safety, because people can jump around and might hurt themselves. Alice knows her hair'll be ruined by the grease smeared onto her temples and when she returns to her family – they'll know where she's been. The mad hatter is putting something both sides of her forehead, which clamps tight and makes her panic – her nose is running, but since she can't move her buckled-down arms, the snot slides down on her lips, in an itchy trail. They don't wipe. The Queen of Hearts orders: open your mouth and bite down and pushes something hard in - tasting the wooden spoon from the cake mix her mother lets her lick, this time without sweetness, only salty wood. She runs her tongue over the smooth surface, nips, bites down, wanting to gag – someone else pushes up her bottom jaw – not sure who; they're behind her.

The people step back – away from the bed. The humming starts like a swarm of bees, softy first, louder now and she's being stung – mostly in the head, next, all over. Now, she's stabbed by red hot pokers. She writhes and twists to get away – her screams won't come out, so she gnaws at the wood. She's not afraid to die any more – can't wait. Her eyeballs roll up as it comes – black and red.

#

Matron witnesses the patient's body jerk up, initially – straining against the straps, as though she will throw herself from the bed. She's used to it now - the way their limbs go poker-stiff while the electricity is administered – heads forced back, neck muscles taut. Mrs Denby's eyes are bulging open and for a few seconds, the horror and pain registers and sticks like a mask, before she passes out. Thank God she won't remember this. They never do.

These patients don't make a noise. When the electrodes are removed, she's witnessed an intense, pregnant pause...before they all step forward to hold them down through the convulsions. This is necessary; otherwise they bruise as they flail against the straps. Matron moves first, remembering some broken bones, ten years ago, when they'd started doing this. Always at the joints, patients seemed instinctually to draw them up and into a foetal position. The convulsions were so strong, it often took five staff. Some salivate, foaming at the mouth as they gnaw down on the paddle.

Matron counts. This patient is going on longer than usual – she seems uncommonly strong. Normally they're settling by forty seconds. She glances at the clock as the red second hand judders for a further nine, before the exhalation and the limpness takes over –like a wall collapsing beneath you. Matron's hands are sweating now – she wipes them on her apron. She takes the pulse. It's returning to normal, as they administer the oxygen. Matron stares at that ring finger on the patient's left hand, never'd seen that happen before. It keeps right on twitching.

#

The tea, Rebecca imagines like nectar and the biscuits, honeycomb. Then they start asking questions. She can't answer any of them and wishes they'd leave her alone.

"What's your name?"

"I don't know."

"Where are you?"

"I'm here."

"What day of the week are we on?"

"Today."

"Which year is this?"

"Year?"

"Rest for now. We'll come back in an hour. Try and see if you can remember."

Not for three more hours, will Rebecca realize who she is and why she's here. She only wants to sleep; but they're making arrangements for the taxi driver to take her home. What a lovely man, talking away. He's got such a soothing voice – sort of a drawling singing – she doesn't register the words, as they drive through the streets. Those biscuits were sweet – she could have eaten a packet. She imagines eating them all over again, like some mashed banana with the sugar on top and being tucked up in bed and cared for, long ago. She tries to reply to him, but she can hear her words slurring. The taxi driver doesn't seem to mind. He squeezes her hand as he leads her to the front door. Once she finds her keys, he leaves her.

Sandbanks is deserted. Shelagh Denby has taken Robert out to her friend's house today. Rebecca's dizzy as she reaches the second floor, so she crawls up the steps to the attic bedroom on her hands and knees. She sleeps until the pounding headache wakes her, accompanied by the realisation that she should start the dinner – how selfish to lie here when Shelagh's looked after Robert all day. She can hear movement downstairs. Henry must be home already – surely that can't be the time? She glances at her wrist, puzzled and fishes in her handbag, finding the brown envelope, earrings, necklace, wristwatch and her wedding rings. Of course, they took them off her – something about conducting. She slips her jewellery back on and straps on her watch – gone six o'clock. She'll splash water on her face and take aspirin. Tell them she'd taken to her bed with a migraine. All night, Rebecca's sleep is troubled with nightmares, as well as Robert waking up. Her head pounds continually and she sweats. Next Friday she repeats the whole process. It does not improve.

#

The following Saturday, Arthur leaves home to work on their house. Robert's eaten his porridge and Rebecca's holding him in her arms. She wipes the grey lumps from his dribbling lips with a muslin cloth. Shelagh left early for a gathering at the Women's Institute. Henry – still in his slippers, relaxes in the living room with his newspaper and lights a woodbine. Suddenly, Rebecca becomes disorientated and faint; steadying herself against the drinks cabinet – which wobbles slightly and the crystal glasses tinkle inside. Henry looks up.

"Rebecca love...are you alright?"

"No..." she says. She starts crying.

Henry gets up quickly, tossing the newspaper aside and takes Robert from her arms, placing him face down on the rug. Robert, in intense concentration, begins to grasp handfuls of the wool and hold them to his mouth.

"I thought something was wrong. Why don't you tell me everything?"

"I've been having bad thoughts."

"What d'you mean?"

"I think of hurting myself. I can't manage. It's all too much. I'm not a proper wife or mother. I don't even feed him properly. I'm a failure."

"You poor dear."

"I went to Horton Road and Dr Hitchman prescribed some electric shocks - the latest treatment. I'm mentally ill, you see. I've only had two so far. It was awful – but he says I'll be better in a month."

"Dear me. You should have said something, Rebecca. You've done this all on your own?"

"I'm sorry – I don't want Arthur to worry, he's working so hard, you know and I'm ashamed."

"No reason for you to feel shame. Now listen, Nanny's going to be out most of the day and I think we need to get this sorted out. You fetch your hat and coat and I'll ring the doctor."

"Doctor Lewis won't be very happy – the treatment isn't finished."

"Never mind him. I'm taking you to my doctor."

While Rebecca is in the Doctor's office, Henry entertains Robert in the waiting room, showing him the pictures in the magazine. Robert's only interested in the noise they make as he crumples the pages between sausage fingers. After half an hour the Doctor sends Rebecca out to wait and calls Henry in. His manner is conspiratorial.

"She's completely overwrought," he says, tapping his forefinger on his temple. "She was crying hysterically for quite a while. She seems to be hearing voices. The trouble is; they're specialists at Horton Road with this sort of thing. I strongly advise you to take her back – since she's already their patient. Tell them what's happened and they'll admit her for a rest. Probably what she needs."

"How long d'you think she'll need to stay? I've got Shelagh out all day and no way of contacting Arthur. And Robert, too."

"Can you manage Robert until Shelagh comes home? I'd rather you took her straight in."

"I should imagine so."

"Right you are. That's the best place for her." He lowers his voice. "Between you and me, ladies can go off the rails – hormonal. They often suffer these peculiarities, during menses, after childbirth and of course later on, *the change*."

Henry nods, thoughtful.

When they arrive, Henry is quite certain his beautiful daughter-in-law doesn't belong in Horton Road, with all those disturbed people. But the nurses seem to take over and admit Rebecca onto a ward, with 7-8 other patients. Rebecca cuddles Robert close, giving him a long kiss on his forehead, wiping off the lipstick mark. She passes him to Henry, who is led away by the nurse.

They hand her two pills – big as horse pills; and a plastic cup of tepid water. They're hard to swallow, but she gets them down. These are supposed to calm her and make her sleep. Curtains on wheels are pulled around the bed for her to change into one of those nighties. They're all in the same nightdresses – like uniforms. Long and white, with tiny blue flowers, maybe cornflowers – she isn't sure, but as she stares at them, they start spinning.

One or two other patients turn to stare at Rebecca, when they take the curtains away. The fading evening light dapples through the bars on the window, on a small drop-leaf table standing at one side of the room – mahogany perhaps; such a pretty doily on the top, maybe hand-crocheted. A vase contains two white roses in stagnant water. An elderly lady rocks backwards and forwards. Yet another moves her lips in animated, silent conversation. Someone appears to be holding their breath repeatedly until her face is bright red, before blowing out. Is she, Rebecca, ill like that woman tracing figure of eights on top of the bedspread with a finger? Or the other one, who plays an invisible piano, turning the pages of an imaginary piece of sheet music. Her companion in the next bed appears to be conducting, though the pianist ignores her.

One lady holds her arms around no partner, dancing what a waltz, in perpetual circles. When the nurse passes her, she manoeuvres her back into bed, but as soon as she walks away, the patient gets out and begins her barefoot dance again, thick yellow toenails scratching the floor. Rebecca's eyelids droop. She remembers the subscription rooms in Stroud – the candles lighting all the tables and Arthur, sitting with mother and Dad. Not sure if Arthur couldn't dance or whether he just wouldn't – such a shame, she loves dancing. The white Coney fur stole, her pride and joy, too warm on her shoulders. Here comes the neighbour, Mr Brown, in his dark, tailored suit – holding out his hand to invite her to the floor. They are together for four, five dances in a row, her whirling under his arm, the dress floating out – returning to the table with a shiny nose and then Arthur. He's turning into a black bear – with claws extended. Mr Brown's suit is covered in the fluff – like a white rabbit. Arthur's making a scene now, angry faces, mustn't think what came next. Arthur frightened her that night, as he took her so passionately – "you're mine," he'd said into her ear. She was excited by his rough display; which meant he loved her. Her last memory was that she shouldn't flirt. She sleeps.

#

Henry leaves Rebecca reluctantly, wheeling Robert home. He can't escape his remorse for abandoning her. When he passes the cinema; he notices the blaring advertisements "Smoke Signal" and "The Looters" coming soon. Who wants films about some bloody redskins sending a message no-one else understands, or people thieving – taking advantage. He wonders what the world's coming to.

Robert nods off in the perambulator. By the time they arrive home, Henry has chosen the words he will use, to break the news to his wife and son.

Chapter Twenty:

Charlie Lindsay is beginning to realise everyone around him is weak. They can't identify what's needed and get things done. This would be sorted out, if he'd been told at the outset. The trouble is, people come to you too bloody late – keeping their secrets until they can't manage them and then expecting him to pick up the pieces during a crisis.

He turns away in contempt from his son-in-law, masticating Arthur's words that permeate the plans he's already making. A good job Arthur doesn't work for *him*. Charlie's rage is silent; contained, as Faith weeps at the kitchen table. For the first time, he experiences an intense wave of dislike for his wife. These displays of emotion are undignified. He loves her, is responsible for her, but she is pathetic. Those quivering lips never looked thinner. When did her hair get so gray?

"If I wasn't hard at work on the house, I might've noticed. She didn't say anything to me about being upset. I'm as shocked as you are."

Charlie realised at the time, Faith didn't want any more children – Lord knows she was clear enough and he'd been careful. In the seven years after Doris's birth, she hardly let him near her. One night, she started enjoying herself for a change, knocked back a few sherries at the Connaught and told him he could anyway – though he'd no French letters. Why would he carry them, with no expectations any more – not even for a cuddle.

He listens to Faith's snuffles. Arthur's forehead is propped up by his elbows on the table, his face obscured. The clock's incessant ticking is like a nagging reminder – each second his daughter is in the nuthouse is one too long. He'll need to act by eight o-clock, no longer – ten minutes to.

"She needs more company. Of course she's got Robert, but she needs some women friends. Mum's asked her out to the WI a few times, but she wouldn't go. Mum's always out organising somebody or other. She might be lonely."

Faith's fiddling with her ear lobe. Charlie notes the plain gold earrings – another peace offering to make up for the beastly night of Rebecca's conception. Faith lay on the quilt; stony and immoveable as the sacks of gravel he'd lugged away for years; until his promotion to Foreman. He wonders whether Faith ever enjoyed sex. Always dutiful though; no-one can criticise this immaculate house and their impeccable children, all grown up now. Faith's greater cruelty lay in her oblivious indifference. She's punished him and the daughter she didn't want, ever since. He's lost count of the times Faith complains to Rebecca "you put me through hell to birth you."

She's contributed to their daughter's problems, with her silly panicking over nothing, fussing through the minutiae of every action, constantly checking. Kept her childish too, picking over her bloody dinners and cutting everything up. Molly-coddled her for a simple cold – keeping her off school all that time – small wonder she'd only worked in a shop, without exams behind her. Almost as though Faith wanted Rebecca dependent, to control her.

"She had a dreadful headache last week and then vivid nightmares, she said."

Lots of women give birth to unplanned children and learn to love them. Faith's been as cold to Rebecca as she is to him. Well, not Rebecca's fault, any more than her being born a Southpaw – all from his side of the family. He'd got pissed off enough with Faith one day to tell her straight – it'd never done him any harm. All those bloody teachers at his school and their cane marks on his left hand – not for his Rebecca. Faith shouldn't have withheld her love. It wasn't natural, not towards her own daughter. God knew Charlie did his best to compensate, to make life better for Rebecca. He knew this wouldn't be enough, but he hoped when she got married, with Arthur to love her and a baby, she'd come right.

Rebecca might do better, looking the way she did. A man who'd take care of her and provide for her. She loved him, but Charlie never thought Arthur was up to the job. Clearly not. Why couldn't the man understand her? She wanted spoiling, just like he'd done. All women needed attention and Rebecca's a loving girl, headstrong and passionate. Charlie'd even provided the cottage near him and she was happy there, surely. Arthur took her off to live with *them*. Shut inside a silly room you couldn't swing a cat round in. Left her with those people for company and ignored her and his lovely grandson. This is all *his* fault.

The sheepish, sorrowful monotone of Arthur's voice begins to grate on Charlie as he scans the rhetoric for details.

"I've only just found out, Charlie. When I got home from work, Dad said she had a funny turn this morning. Course, I'm on site, so they couldn't get hold of me at the office. Seems she went giddy – she's been having treatment for two weeks and didn't say a word – electric shocks. I put it down to baby blues; even Mum thought so...."

"Go on."

"She started crying and he couldn't comfort her, so he took her to his doctor. The doctor didn't want to interfere with her treatment. He told Dad to take her straight to Horton Road. They admitted her right away and put her to bed. Dad's taken care of Robert all afternoon while Mum's been out. He's so upset – he thought this was for the best. I went straight down, but they made me wait an hour until visiting time, before they let me see her."

"How did she look?"

"Not too good. She's slurring her words and crying. She asked me to fetch you. I promised I would. I came straight here to tell you. I think she wants to come home – but they said discharging her wasn't possible until she's been seen by the consultant. I didn't want to leave her, but they gave me no choice."

The clock bongs eight. Charlie stands and scrapes the chair across the tiles, in the way Faith hates. She flinches. No-one's going to leave his daughter with those fucking loonies and halfwits. Now he's a foreman, he won't let all them bloody navvies have a field day, nudging and sniggering, talking about her behind his back. It'll totally undermine his authority. All Rebecca needs is a break from this lot. A rest. He'll make this happen. They're not calling *his* girl a nutter.

"Leave this to me. She's not staying *in that place*. She'll be taken care of properly. You go on home and I'll bring her back directly."

"Alright." Arthur replies. He can't muster the energy to argue.

Chapter Twenty-One:

Horton Road lunatic asylum is one of the best Georgian structures in the city of Gloucester. The cast iron roof, with the intricate patterns, stands over the terracotta terraced houses in the surrounding streets, commanding respect. Charlie Lindsay appreciates the architecture. Nonetheless, this is a palace containing idiots – as he supposes most palaces do.

Striding past the spiked railings, he pushes open the left side of the double doors. He notes the impassive expression of the nurse at the reception desk with some distaste; and deduces she is a cold fish. Her face is covered with downy hair and his eyes are drawn to the brown mole, underneath her ear, which sprouts two wiry grey strands.

"Good evening," she says. "I'm afraid you've missed visiting time."

"I'm not here to visit. I'm after Frank Lorimer."

"I'm sorry, but Dr Lorimer is doing his ward rounds. May I ask the nature of your business?"

"My name is Charlie Lindsay. My daughter was admitted today in error and I'm here to collect her."

"Is she a voluntary admission?"

"Yes."

"And she is?"

"Rebecca Rose *Denby*." He spits the surname.

"Take a seat please, Mr Lindsay. I'll fetch Matron."

Her mouth twitches at the edge. Charlie logs her discomfort with some satisfaction. She's not used to being challenged.

\#

Dr Frank Carter Lorimer works seven days a week. He's done so for 25 years now. He doesn't believe in holidays – though he takes the wife and children to Bridport for a week's duty each year. He's consumed by his work and the improvements, he hopes will be achieved, in the pioneering treatments for mental patients. These fascinate him. The ECT equipment was installed under his charge nine years ago. The insulin treatment works in conjunction – but now there are the leucotomies.

He's signed authority for ninety-eight cases so far, to be performed on his recommendation for referral. The violent patients became much easier to deal with – placid. One or two had even been able to return to their grateful families – manageable if not bright, but in his experience, intellect often precedes rebellious behaviour.

As an active member of the parish council; the Lindsay name is familiar to him. Something of a star in ascendance – nouveau riche. How the man had gained entry to the freemasons was a mystery, but Dr Lorimer suspected bribery. New money often belies vulgarity. A different lodge, of course – or he'd have applied the black ball. Not that Lindsay didn't know how to conduct himself; simply that he was rather outspoken and too flash.

Dr Lorimer is discomfited to learn of Lindsay's presence in reception. Still, something of a coup. The daughter, quite a popsy, had been admitted today. He'd not made the connection; of course, the married name struck no chord. Not the usual type – he concluded hers was little more than a temporary condition; baby blues – but she had this disturbing sexuality. Compliant with it, too – and secretive. Lindsay had obviously indulged her. He'd wondered about the husband; who was very distressed when he'd visited this evening. Seemed he had no idea his wife was having trouble coping.

Matron hovers at the door. Dr Lorimer keeps her waiting as he contemplates his notepad, while doodling a cartoon-style bomb, with a fuse. He leaves a rectangle of light. Matron's a dab hand on the rounds. She runs the wards efficiently, with a relentless routine - walks them round in the fresh air, whether they want to, or not. Dismisses any discussion of cases, very sure of herself – reassuring that she never questions diagnoses. He looks up.

"Would you show him up please Matron?"

"Yes, Doctor," she replies. Though her expression reveals little, he senses her surprise. He waits.

Charlie Lindsay removes his Trilby hat and extends his hand.

"Dr Lorimer?" His handshake is firm and he applies thumb pressure in the relevant places to indicate the Masonic connection. The doctor is intimidated by Lindsay's height and the roughness of his hard-grafting hands; he's conscious of standing a good six inches shorter. Lindsay's charismatic – he seems to take charge of Dr Lorimer's domain. His thick black hair is streaked with striking white lines, gruff yet dignified, like the Badger in *The Wind in the Willows*. Dr Lorimer involuntarily imagines himself as Toad of Toad Hall, determined to assert his imperative.

"Mr Lindsay. Please, take a seat. How may I be of assistance?"

"I'm here to collect my daughter." Lindsay sits on the edge of the chair, knees apart and feeding the hat around by the brim, between his forefingers and thumbs.

"I see. Rebecca Rose Denby?"

"Yes. My son-in-law informs me his father brought her in earlier. I wasn't aware and should have been notified."

"I've reviewed Rebecca's case notes from Dr Hitchman. He prescribed eight ECT treatments – Rebecca's only received two, so far."

"As I'm told. I'm afraid that's not good enough. I want a second opinion. This is not a suitable environment for my daughter. Rest is what she needs."

"It's a delicate matter. Rebecca believes she hasn't been coping for some time."

"I'd be grateful for you to arrange her immediate discharge. I'm taking her out of here."

"Might be better to leave that, until tomorrow. She's under sedation and slept well this afternoon."

"She's not spending the night. She can sleep at home."

"Of course, Rebecca is here as a voluntary patient...but my advice would be to wait until morning. Mull things over – you might change your mind."

"That won't be necessary."

"I can assure you she'll be cared for."

"That's all settled. Rebecca's attending an appointment with a private psychiatrist tomorrow. Should anything require treating – I'll decide where and how."

"Right. Well, since you're determined – I won't stop you, of course."

"Thank you. I'll wait in reception."

"I'll arrange for some refreshments, while you wait."

"Thank you, Dr Lorimer."

Charlie stands and marches back downstairs. He drums on the armchair until the tea arrives...hot and sweet, in a flowered porcelain cup and saucer. He can't fit his fingers through the handle, so grips the whole thing like his mug at work. A brandy would be better – he'll pour a large one, once he gets home. He checks the pocket watch on the chain from his waistcoat four or five times until half an hour passes. A side door opens and he catches sight of his daughter, a yellow cellular blanket edged with frayed ribbon around her shoulders, on top of her short jacket and floral dress. Rebecca clings onto the nurse's arm, as though she will topple if she lets go. Her auburn hair's wild and unkempt, she looks – well, pissed as a Lord. Her eyes are glazed and vacant and she can barely support herself on her heels. He notices the ladder in her stockings.

"Rebecca love!" He stands and rushes to her side.

"Dad...oh Dad, I want to go home!"

"Alright my darling. I'm here. You just come along with me. Take my arm." Charlie replaces the nurse, glaring at her. Rebecca feels heavier than usual, she leans her full weight on him and he needs to support her with his other arm around her back. He wonders what the hell she's taken.

"That's the ticket, through the door love, you hold onto me. We'll get you home in no time."

The cold air bites, as he helps her down the steps. She's relieved – he can tell. It's not the first occasion he's taken his daughter back drunk and tonight is no exception. Pale and disorientated, she holds him and wobbles to the car; shivering. Charlie props her up with his leg, as he opens the passenger door and manoeuvres her into a seated position, tucking her head in to avoid hitting the roof. When he lets go, her chin drops, as though she'll fall asleep. Charlie ferrets in the boot, retrieving the tartan blanket, unfolds and tucks this over her knees. He closes her door, strides around to the driver's side, feeling for his keys. He turns the ignition and fiddles with the heater.

He drives her back to his house. She falls asleep, although the journey only takes ten minutes. After turning off the engine, he looks at Rebecca and wipes the tears from his eyes. The kitchen light is still on. He fingers a curl of her soft hair, which bounces back into position.

"Daddy's little girl," he whispers, but she doesn't stir.

Charlie gets out and lifts his somnambulant daughter, shutting the car door with his foot. Faith's already gone to bed – so he sits Rebecca, slumped, in his chair in the lounge, and stokes up the fire – poking the dying coals viciously until they glow and spark, throwing on another log.

Faith pads down the stairs, in winceyette, hair already in rollers.

"How is she?" she asks, stifling her yawn.

"Not good, Faith. I'm going to give her a brandy, and then I want you to put her straight up to bed."

"Yes, Charlie." Faith potters to the drinks cabinet and retrieves a round crystal glass.

"Pour me one, too," he says, gruff, willing her for a challenge. Faith obeys, decanting two generous measures.

Charlie taps Rebecca's cheek, until she stirs. "Rebecca. Wake up, darling!"

Her pupils expand as she opens her eyes, wildly scanning the room.

"Dad – where am I?"

"You're home now. Listen, I want you to drink this, and go up to bed."

Charlie tips the thin glass edge to her lips. They're slack, and half the brandy dribbles out. He pulls out his handkerchief and mops her mouth and chin.

Rebecca revives a little. Charlie helps Faith tuck Rebecca in bed and returns downstairs, refills his glass, four more times, before stepping heavily upstairs. He notices the telephone receiver is askew from the cradle and replaces it. Faith is already asleep, with her back to him. He turns to the wall and shuts his eyes.

Chapter Twenty-Two:

The familiar curtains come into focus; the warmth of the bed and the fresh smelling sheets transport Rebecca to a safer time. The comfort taunts and dissipates; as the vague recollections of the last few days return, piecemeal. Underlying each; is a palpable sensation of anxiety. Reaching for Arthur; she realises she's in the wrong bed. She sits up, trying to understand what's happened. Vague phrases: depression, obsessions, panic attacks, agoraphobia make vulture circles around her mind - but they are disconnected from any source. She wonders if she is mad.

Rebecca makes her way to the bathroom. She passes the telephone and stops to pick up the receiver. Her father is talking to another man, so she replaces it quietly. Having washed, she puts on her dressing gown. Padding down the stairs, her father's voice sounds clipped and quiet, as he ends his telephone call.

"Good morning love. How are you feeling?"

"A bit tired. Dad, where's Robert?"

"He's with Shelagh. Don't trouble yourself."

"What about Arthur?"

"He's going into work and Shelagh's looking after Robert today. Now, Rebecca, I don't know how much you remember..."

"I was in Horton Road."

"Yes. That's not the right place for you. You're probably just over-doing things. To be on the safe side, I've made an appointment for you with a private psychiatrist at lunchtime."

"Where?"

"The Burden Institute, near Bristol. I'm assured he's the best in his field. We'll find out exactly what's wrong, if anything. You'll get the proper treatment. You're not to worry."

"Arthur's not angry, is he?"

"Of course not. He's worried about you – we all are."

"Dad, am I going mad?"

"I think you're just tired. Now run along and have your breakfast. We'll need to set off in an hour."

"Alright."

In the kitchen, Faith prepares tea and toasts pikelets. Her movements are methodical, but she seems quieter than usual. Her eyes are red and swollen.

"I'm sorry Mother. I was so frightened. Are you upset with me for going to the doctor?"

"No, Rebecca, I'm not. Life's often difficult with a new baby. I do wish you'd told Dad and me earlier."

"I thought I might be able to manage on my own,"

"Yes, well everyone needs help sometimes. Now eat up, and Dad will take you to Bristol. I can't believe they put you in with *those* people."

"They were strange."

"Don't upset yourself any longer."

This is their longest conversation in months. Rebecca eats ravenously and begins to brighten up. Hopefully Dad's psychiatrist will sort her out and she can go home. She goes back upstairs and brushes her teeth, returning to her bedroom. Mother's placed her clothes on the bed, a pressed dress, clean underwear, stockings and hat, scarf and gloves. The shoes she'd worn into hospital are freshly-polished on the floor.

The journey to Purdown passes pleasantly. The A38 is fairly clear of traffic. The road is lined with trees and fields, containing benign-eyed Friesians or sheep with twitching ears and dopey, slitting yellow eyes, munching at the grass and startling occasionally for no good reason – a bit like her, Rebecca thinks. Everything seems vibrantly green – so many shades – she's never noticed them before. Dad talked about various landmarks along the route; Travers & Scudamore's – pointing out the gravel pits where he sometimes works, lined with the poplars bent by the wind, like ballerinas doing bar work, all synchronised and elegant. Until he broaches the more *delicate* topic.

"You tell the psychiatrist everything, Rebecca."

"Yes."

"He's going to help you. Whatever you're unhappy about, we can fix."

"I want to be better."

"Of course you do. Listen to me, Rebecca. I realise things weren't always easy for you. Your mother does her best, but she had a terrible time when she was having you. She wasn't very well at all. She suffers with her nerves, but she worries because she loves you a great deal."

"Yes. Dad, I do think badly of people sometimes. Everybody's trying to do their best for me and I just feel so, selfish for feeling sad. I'm wrong to think bad thoughts."

"Well, you're married now, Rebecca. You need to learn to be a good wife to Arthur and take care of Robert. I know the situation isn't ideal, but you really must be brave, and make the best of things. Do you understand?"

"Yes, Dad, I'm so sorry."

"Not to worry. We'll get you sorted out."

The Dower House, part of the Burden Neurological Institute in Stoke Park, stands like a small yellow castle on top of a mossy tump, yet devoid of a moat. Five arched windows come into view, covered by shutters, as the car cruises up the long driveway. Behind the counter is a middle-aged lady with a mouthful of big straight teeth. She wears a tweed suit and cream blouse and her benign expression is welcoming to Charlie, a smile conveying empathy, for the patient. You get what you pay for, in this world. The waiting room contains four dark red Chesterfield chairs - low, with an inviting width. Rebecca focuses on a painting on the wall. A street scene, in shades of brown, red and white; filled with people. They have no facial expressions or features, but she can tell what each one is doing. Her father leans over. "You like that?"

"Yes, all the people are busy."

"What else d'you like?"

"You don't see their faces, do you? So you can't tell what they're thinking."

"That's a Lowry. Good taste! You take after your father."

She smiles and he winks, patting her knee. After five minutes, the receptionist approaches.

"Mrs Denby? Dr Townsend is ready for you now."

Rebecca stands, turning to her father. "Aren't you coming in?"

"I think you'll see him on your own first. Don't forget what I said."

"No."

"Off you go."

The psychiatrist's office is housed on the second floor. Dr Townsend is approaching middle-age. His hair is thick and dark, with a slight curl and his eyebrows are going a little grey, She stares at them, noticing that they join together and remembers her mother's warning: "Never trust a man whose eyebrows meet in the middle." Still, he's clean-shaven and his eyes are kindly.

He wears a white jacket and is seated behind a large mahogany desk with his feet stretched out in the gap. His shoes are good, brown brogues, the little paisley dotted patterns, well-polished and laces slightly askew. To the right is a chaise longue, with a curved rolled back and a striped cushion like a Swiss roll. The ornate legs with upturned feet are highly polished. He stands, to welcome Rebecca.

"Mrs Denby? Dr Townsend, I'm pleased to meet you."

"Hello, Doctor."

"Now, your father's told me all about you Rebecca, but I want to hear your story. Would you like to lie down on the sofa?"

"Should I take off my shoes?"

"Whatever makes you comfortable? Most patients feel more relaxed that way."

"Right." She slips off her heels and reclines. From this position, she can't see him. The rolled cushion presses into the back of her neck, supportive.

"You may close your eyes if you wish. I want you to tell me everything. I shall take notes and I might stop to ask you questions. Are you ready?"

"Yes." She closes her eyes.

Dr Townsend holds a fountain pen, which scratches across the page as he takes notes.

"Perhaps you could tell me what's been troubling you?"

"At Horton Road, the consultant diagnosed me with obsessions and anxiety hysteria – I think they said I was neurotic, too. And depression."

"I understand you had two sessions of electro-convulsive therapy?"

"Yes. I couldn't bear it. I lost my memory afterwards, I couldn't remember what day it was, or my name, for hours."

"A temporary side-effect, quite normal. Has your memory returned now?"

"Oh yes. Most if it. I got a frightful headache afterwards. During the night, I woke in a cold sweat. There were nightmares, too."

"I think if you could tell me exactly what you said to them to begin with, I'd get a better idea."

Rebecca tries to ignore her stomach, which is beginning to rumble and squeak. The breakfast is working its way down and she's frightened she might break wind. She was constipated again this morning. Clenching her buttocks, Rebecca opens her eyes and searches for something to focus on. She stares at the tree outside the window, a silver birch. The white bark, scarred with black. Some of the leaves and catkins cling on, relentless – not ready to die. Some are shrivelled where they sway in the wind, not wanting to let go.

"Rebecca? Can you hear me?" She smells the musty scent of damp – just like the attic room – but here, overpowered by beeswax polish.

"Doctor, I think wicked things. I've become frightened to leave the house. It's as though I'm going to be punished for these thoughts – something will happen to me or my family."

"I see. When did this start?"

"I think this first happened when I went out to work. I was about fourteen. But it wasn't too serious. I just had to turn my finger rings three times. Then there's the telephone."

"The telephone?"

"I'm sure someone's listening to me on the other end. So I'd pick the receiver up and check. But I needed to do that three times, too."

"Any particular significance with the number 3? Are you religious, perhaps?"

"I believe in God. I do go to church, when I can. I wouldn't say religion has anything to do with the counting."

94

"Catholic?"

"Church of England."

"Hmmm. These rituals were continuous, for the whole five years?"

"Well, no. It was alright, to start with. They went away a bit when I first got married. I was safe, with Arthur, you see. In any case, we had no telephone at the cottage. Now we live with Arthur's family, so I couldn't possibly. They don't have one upstairs, only in the lounge."

"Your relationship with your husband – feels different since your wedding? Unsafe?"

"I'm so lonely, Doctor. Arthur's always out at work, the poor man. I know he's doing the best for us, working all day and off building our house in the evenings. Robert (he's my baby) cries a lot, too. Sometimes the two of us are stuck in our bedroom for hours on end."

"Does Arthur know you feel this way?"

"Only now. I've let him down."

"You're worried these bad thoughts make you a bad person?"

"I must be evil, to think this way. I try so hard to be a good wife and mother."

"I'm sensing conflict here. As though your life is an act and only the good part of you can be acceptable to others?"

"You're right."

"You believe your thoughts belong to someone else?"

"Yes... they're too bad, nasty and unkind. I just want them out of my head. Can you help me get them out?"

"What is the nature of them? Can you tell me? I promise not to be shocked."

"I sometimes feel that other people are better than me, happier than me."

"Anyone in particular?"

"They all are."

"Everyone can't possibly be happier than you. Who is happiest?"

"My sister. She's so wonderful, I'd like to be her, not me. Mother seems to love her more."

"Well, I'm sure she doesn't."

"You see, what an awful thing to think – you understand what I mean?"

"Not so terrible. But is there anything else?"

"When it gets really bad, I picture things."

"Picture things – can you say a little more about those images?"

"Last week, for example. Robert wouldn't stop crying. I couldn't go to him straight away, I was so...tired and I can't do anything for him at times, so I did something for my mother-in-law instead. I was chopping up the

95

potatoes and I found myself looking at the knife and imagining what would happen if I had...an accident...like the knife slips and I cut off my finger, or something..."

"I see. And what did you imagine next?"

"There would be a huge fuss, of course. But they'd notice me and I'd be taken to hospital, maybe sleep in a clean bed and be looked after."

"A *clean* bed you say...your bed isn't clean?"

"Of course it's clean...sometimes it doesn't feel, clean..."

"What would make it feel clean, do you think?"

"I don't know."

"Do things often feel dirty, to you?"

"Not if I clean them myself – the right way. The trouble is, when you're in someone else's house, you have to do things their way. Sometimes they take over, too."

"Do *you* feel dirty?"

She cries then, because she does. She doesn't answer him. He waits until she stops.

"Has it ever got so bad that you think about hurting yourself?"

"Once or twice. But sometimes I just think about doing it to take my mind off the thoughts...to stop them, because I'd be feeling some pain then."

"A different sort of pain?"

"Yes. A real one."

"You've been have some very distressing experiences. Are other people around when you feel like this?"

"No, I'm always alone, with Robert."

"What about alcohol? Do you ever drink?"

"I used to, quite a lot. Not so much now I have Robert – there's too much to do. Anyway I don't see Dad so much, and we used to have a little brandy together in the evenings."

"I see no real need for you to be alarmed about these episodes. They're what we call a fugue. In your case, your desire to flee, from the outside world means your personality has dissociated with reality. This is characterised by these bad thoughts, or messages that you hear about hurting yourself."

"So can anything be done?"

"I feel sure that you can be helped. Your mind is rather disordered and you need to achieve reorientation and adjustment to the outside world. Although keeping busy at housework is often the best therapy – life sometimes becomes too much for people, particularly women. After having babies, some show a complete loss of contact with reality."

"That's how I feel!"

"Quite so. Now, if we were to consider taking you away from your environment, for a complete course of treatment, say over six months or so, you could be proud to face the world as a proper woman again. Return to your tasks with goodwill, and good humour."

"That's all I want…but I don't know about leaving my family."

"Well, it would be entirely voluntary for you to submit yourself to treatment, of course. You clearly pose no threat to others, only yourself. In the place I have in mind, behavioural improvements are rewarded with added privileges, light working tasks, occupational therapy and so forth."

"I do want to be a better wife and mother."

"I'm certain that you will emerge from this, rather like a butterfly from a cocoon. Where you will be encouraged to take care of yourself and look after your appearance, too. Though I might add, it looks as though you have managed that very well."

"Thank you, doctor."

"But you'd be surprised, Rebecca. Why, I've seen occasions where wives become slovenly, and simply a visit to the hairdressers in one of our care homes, for a permanent wave, serves as an epiphany in terms of their self-respect. After all, we can't expect others to care for us, if we don't take care of our appearance."

"You're right Doctor. Though it's so difficult to find the time. I try ever so hard, make-up every morning and freshen up before Arthur's return."

"I see that you do. I cite it merely as an example. But you must realise that you are ill. It's as though you have become someone else – though I might add your case isn't a textbook one, but rather more complex."

"Really?"

"Yes."

"I feel sick sometimes. There's so much work piling up, it's overwhelming. I'm exhausted, some days. Poor Arthur, he doesn't deserve a wife like me. You see, I can see his mother is such a good wife and mother and she thinks I don't look after him properly. I heard her say it to my father-in-law. Even though I cooked Arthur's tea when we lived at the cottage, she kept cooking extra treats and things for him. Now she adds to his lunchbox after I've packed it. Sometimes she even re-does the flask I've made up."

"She sounds like a good woman concerned for her son. That can only be a good thing. Perhaps she's trying to support you, because she can see that you're not coping."

"I know. You see, I am even saying bad things about her, and she's been so kind to me – welcoming me into her home. She's proud of Robert, too – she can settle him. She takes him out for walks, you see, which I'm finding difficult."

"Yes, your problem's clear to me now. Finally, tell me how you are sleeping?"

Rebecca's feet are beginning to sweat. She hopes he can't smell them, – if only he leaves her alone for a minute, she can check. She wiggles her toes and feels the stocking toe snag on her toenails. They need trimming.

"Rebecca?" He repeats. "How are you sleeping?"

"Badly. I find I toss and turn a lot and of course it's hard to settle down after feeding Robert in the middle of the night. He wakes often – he wasn't getting enough on my milk, I'm sorry to say. They've put him on the bottle by now, I suppose."

"Very sensible. I suggest you bandage round your breasts tightly to dry up the milk. Well, now Rebecca, thank you for being so frank. It's clear to me that you need a complete rest and proper treatment. Shall we call in your father and discuss what happens next?"

"Yes, thank you Doctor. "

"If you'd like to sit up and pop your shoes back on, I'll fetch him in."

As Doctor Townsend leaves the room, Rebecca lifts her foot to her nose and sniffs. Sweaty, but not awful, hopefully he didn't smell them. She pulls out the nylon from between her toes, which are stuck together and slips her feet into the shoes, smelling her fingers to be sure. A bit ripe; not too bad.

The receptionist shows Charlie Lindsay in, behind Dr Townsend.

"Rebecca's is a very interesting case," he begins.

Her Dad seems nervous, but this pleases Rebecca.

"I think she may be suffering from schizophrenia. I'd like her to see a colleague for a second opinion, since she's not a text-book case. I know an excellent facility in Northampton called St Andrews."

"Will she need to stay?"

"Oh yes, for formal assessment. If she's suitable, I'd like her to take a six month combination course of insulin treatment and electro-shock therapy, as an inpatient. In the meantime, complete rest. I don't want her to return home to her usual duties – Barnwood House is the closest private facility to you. We'll need to discuss the delicate matter of fees."

"I'll pay for whatever she needs."

"Marvellous. In any case, I think we may be able to get some assistance with those. With your approval, I'd like to apply to the Banbury and Oxford Hospital Board for funding. Although St Andrew's is private, they also have a number of charitable places.

If we're successful, it's my opinion Rebecca will be a suitable candidate to participate in their research of the latest treatments, if she's willing to be observed and share her experiences? All in complete confidence, obviously."

"I don't mind," said Rebecca.

"How much are the fees?" Charlie Lindsay asks.

"Ordinarily they're £24.00 a week. We'll apply to get £20.00 covered, if you can cover the other £4.00?"

"I will. You'll make the necessary referral?"

"While you wait in reception, I'll draft the letter immediately."

"Thank you Doctor Townsend." Her father stands.

Rebecca and her father leave Bristol with the letter. Having found her voice, Rebecca chatters about the understanding Dr Townsend and how much better she feels. Her father doesn't interrupt, at all. After a cup of tea at home and a lunch of corned beef sandwiches and pickled onions, while Charlie Lindsay makes various telephone calls to the Denby's and other parties, the arrangements are made. Faith packs Rebecca's case, ready for her departure. Robert will stay with her parents for six months, leaving Arthur free to finish the house while she's away. She'll return to her new home after a good break and with her treatment completed. Charlie drives Rebecca the three miles to Barnwood House, where she'll stay for the next three weeks, until her place at St Andrews becomes available. He kisses her goodbye, after she's admitted to her single private room. She unpacks, slowly and carefully – smoothing out each item three times.

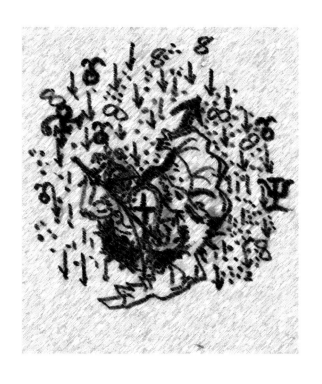

100

Chapter Twenty-Three:

Barnwood House has a reputation for being at the cutting edge of treatment for mental disorders. This was the first place in England to install and use ECT treatment. This is a private registered hospital for the care and treatment of ladies and gentleman who suffer from nervous and mental disorders. The wide building with multiple rectangular chimney stacks has two water turrets; which were used during the Second World War by wardens, to watch for German bombers. This building escaped any bombing, standing in three hundred acres of landscaped grounds at the foot of the Cotswold Hills, affording patients a tranquil environment detached from the bustling city centre, just three miles away. Three accommodation villas are entirely separate from the main hospital and the male and female patients are segregated. Inside, there are grand marbled halls; a laboratory, a theatre showing films (there's only one projector, so the patients must wait for the reel to be changed every 20 minutes). During the annual staff dance; this stage is decked with fresh flowers. In the ladies drawing room, the tables are laid with linen and silver and a huge aspidistra makes the centrepiece. There are two sets of padded cells, some with manacles on the walls. Outside; the two greenhouses contain eight different varieties of grapes. There is a farm, a laundry and provision for many occupational therapies; croquet lawns and a cricket pitch. Spiritual wellbeing is addressed by two services being held in the chapel each day.

Rebecca follows her new friend Clarissa Needham-Wright past the rock garden and the swans floating gracefully on the pond. They proceed down the walk known as the "Ladies Mile" and into the leafy glade; before crouching together inside the laurel bush, watching the other patients being wheeled out for their constitutional, or shuffling along, arm-in-arm with the nurses. One male patient wears leather slippers and a dressing gown, but only one foot lies on the foot-rest of the wheelchair. One pyjama leg is folded underneath his torso, as though he's kneeling on it. He reaches down now and again with some agitation, as though scratching the lost limb. Clarissa passes Rebecca the hip-flask and she sips at the brandy.

A white-coated gentleman walks past them towards the main house, carrying a worn briefcase. He has a small, unsmiling mouth and large brown eyes, which Rebecca fancies are a little sad and tired – as though he is misunderstood and deep in thought. His dark hair is slicked back. From Clarissa and Rebecca's vantage point, they can observe people without being witnessed. Clarissa is giving Rebecca a potted history of those she recognises. Some are from titled families and Rebecca listens in awe to their family stories, diagnoses and peculiarities. Now, Clarissa points out the Doctor.

"They say he built a human brain, made entirely of magnets, in his laboratory."

"Who is he?" Rebecca asks.

"Dr Ashby," replied Clarissa. "I don't think he sees patients much. He's only here on Thursdays at present."

"Is he part-time?"

"Gracious, no. He works down at the Burden at lot of the time, in the Institute."

"That's where I was assessed," Rebecca says.

"Really? But you're moving on from us soon, aren't you?"

"Yes, to St Andrew's. They think I'm schizophrenic. I'm a special case, so I'll be taking part in research."

"Do you have different characters?"

"What d'you mean?"

"You know. Talking to you in your head."

"I don't think so. I, sort of, speak bad thoughts to myself."

"Well we all do, at times. I wonder about clairvoyants. Some people who hear voices end make a fortune with the tales they tell. The rest of us end up being condemned as nutters, in places like this."

"You mean gypsies?"

"Quite. Still, you seem pretty normal."

"Thank you. So do you,"

"I'm better since the shocks."

"Clarissa, d'you mind my asking, what's wrong with you?"

"Hysteria - according to them. I'm angry a lot. Father's a Major, you see and he won't tolerate my being out of control. He threw a dinner party and I suppose I drank a bit too much booze – still no more than him. Two courses later, we're on the dessert and the *men* started this discussion about politics - they were so bloody opinionated. P'raps they should have waited until they went for billiards, but things got quite heated. I listened for a bit to this absolute oaf next to me. I joined in the conversation and he squeezed my knee under the table and asked whether I'd soon be finding a husband. Couldn't help myself and ended up pouring my Chablis into his lap. Hilarious – just as though he'd wet himself! I was laughing so hard at his outraged look, even when Father marched me out by the arm. I caused a terrific storm, I can tell you."

Rebecca laughed. "Why did you want to talk about politics?"

"Don't you know? Why should you, I suppose? Not many women seem to take an interest in politics. But I read the newspapers."

"No, I don't understand politics. You must be terribly clever."

"I think they're rather ashamed of women liking anything other than knitting or needlework. *Frigid* I heard them say, about me."

"Don't you like men?"

"I enjoy sex with them, if you want to know. Don't fancy being trapped in a marriage though. They think all we're good for is housework or charity work - they even admire some of these missionary types, well, you try voicing an opinion about anything important and you might find yourself carted off to one of these places."

"My Arthur's not like that."

"No, but here you are. Funny."

"I'm leaving soon."

"I wish you luck. Don't tell them everything Rebecca – take my advice. Shall we go in? We'll miss afternoon tea and I don't mind about you, I'm famished!"

"Alright."

Three days after Rebecca leaves Barnwood House for Northampton, the bill for £12.00 arrives at Sandbanks, addressed to Mr .A. Denby. The remaining £60.00 has been covered by the hospital board. Since his father-in-law will be funding the £4.00 weekly shortfall for Rebecca's next six months at St Andrews; Arthur feels obliged to pay it. He goes to the post office and withdraws all their savings. He delivers the cash in person. The receptionist writes him a receipt and as he leaves, she could have sworn she heard him mutter *robbing bastards*.

Since he earns £6.00 a week in order to provide for his family; he knows it will be long time before he can save this amount again.

Chapter Twenty-Four:

St Andrew's Hospital for Nervous and Mental Disorders is situated in one hundred and thirty acres of park and pleasure grounds. The land was purchased at auction from the Cluiac Prior of St Andrew's in Northampton and the building purpose designed by Mr. George Wallet of the Bethlem Hospital, with the works being funded by charitable donations from the Northamptonshire Yeomanry. The second Earl Spencer was elected a Vice President of the proposed institution in 1834. St Andrew's opened in 1838; founded on the principle of "Moral Treatment". Inside the building, the walls are lined with fine oak panels and ornate high ceilings. The doors off the wide corridors lead to light and airy lounges with sash windows. Accommodation for patients is in private rooms. The latest technology has been installed; with an operating theatre, a Dental surgery, an X-Ray room, Ultra-violet apparatus and a department for Diathermy and High-frequency treatment. In addition, two laboratories are available for biochemical, bacteriological and pathological research.

St Andrew's gained exemption from the National Health Service in 1948 and remained a charitable organisation. The building was bombed by the Luftwaffe during the Second World War and was re-constructed to include libraries, a gym and further recreational facilities in 1954. In its long history, St Andrew's patients consisted of many influential members of the aristocracy; as well as notable artists and poets. The hospital board of Governors included knights, nobles, captains of industry, Generals, Admirals and even a Duke.

The patients are given every opportunity to engage in occupational therapy. The grounds include a 650-acre farm, supplying milk, meat, fruit and vegetables for the residents and staff. There are cricket grounds, football and hockey pitches, lawn tennis – both grass and hard court, golf courses and bowling greens. Facilities are also provided for handicrafts, such as carpentry. The patients in St Andrews are actively recruited from the middle and upper classes. Rebecca finds herself surrounded and befriended by rich and glamorous people – eccentric perhaps, but clearly moneyed.

There are observation rooms with two way mirrors. Rebecca is well aware of the faces behind the mirrors, during those interviews. She imagines Alice through the looking-glass, where she can almost step through to another world behind. She conducts herself with an air of modest and compliant dignity, answering their incessant questions with the facade of a femme fatale whom no-one could understand. Determined to defy any simple explanation, she ensures each time they appear close to discharging her, she thwarts them with a small tidbit to retain their interest.

Well rested by now, she finds being looked after such a relief - she's feeling a lot better. Sometimes, she feels pretty fake, and wonders whether the bad feelings are always strong, or real. They were so intense at home, terrifying. In St Andrews, they seem paltry compared to the palsy of those veterans, crying, shaking and muttering…a genuine loss of life and limbs. She's guilty. What, truly, can she complain about? If they find out, she'll be sent home. The house isn't finished yet and she's not rested enough – besides which, she's making friendships and getting invitations from people she wants to cultivate. She's been prescribed the whole six months. Some of the others don't seem too ill either; who seem to be indulged. She reminds herself, she's a special research case.

The Medical Superintendent summons her to attend an interview panel, with three of his colleagues.

"Well, Rebecca. You've been with us a month. How are you settling in?"

"Well, thank you Doctor. Everyone's been kind."

"You seem to be integrating with the other patients. Any problems?"

"No, they've taken me under their wing."

"Sleeping alright?"

"Yes."

"What about those bad thoughts?"

She warmed to her topic. "Always with me. But I try my best."

"We think you're trying very hard."

"Thank you, Doctor."

"Would you like to hear your diagnosis?"

"Yes, please."

"When you were admitted, we believed you had schizophrenia."

"Yes, Doctor Townsend said so too."

"But after our first week's observations, we've revised our diagnosis."

"Oh…so what is wrong with me?"

"You've got some negative thoughts, anxiety, obsessions and deep depression. After consultation with my colleagues, we're all agreed that six months of insulin therapy would cure you, for sure."

"I'll try whatever you suggest."

"You'll have to take some tests before we start. Fairly routine, just to ensure you're fit and healthy."

"I'm willing to do whatever you say. I just want to be normal, so I can get back to my family."

"That's the spirit. Now, do you want to ask any questions?"

"Does it hurt?"

"Not at all. The procedure is straightforward and you'll be with other patients having the same treatment. We administer a dose of insulin every morning through a little tube in your hand. Your limbs feel paralysed, temporarily. You'll be very relaxed and your body becomes anaesthetised from your toes upwards."

"How long will I be asleep?"

"A few hours. We'll put a small tube up your nostril and feed in some glucose to wake you back up. You'll take a bath, then it's off for a hearty lunch; we always find patients have a good appetite afterwards! How does that sound?"

"It sounds fine. So when do we start?"

"I'm pleased you're embracing things this way. Often our best results are achieved with a positive frame of mind. We'll do the physical tests over the weekend and begin first thing Monday. Agreed?"

"Yes."

"Attagirl."

There are blood tests, blood pressure taken, weight, height and measurements – even of her head. Certainly they are thorough, urine samples and questionnaires, until answering questions becomes tiresome. Rebecca is proud when they announce to her on Sunday she's passed. Not only is she fit and healthy, she qualifies. With a proper treatment (particularly one that doesn't hurt) she can demonstrate to the world how ill she is.

At 6.00am, there's some sense of camaraderie between the three patients sitting in the preparation room. The two men make conversation with her, too.

"What brings you here?" The man to her left asks.

"Deep depression and obsessions. I need to be cured you see, to return to my husband and my lovely baby."

"How old's the baby?"

"Robert. He's eight months now. Do you have any children?"

"Not yet."

"Anyone special?"

"Yes, but my situation is…complicated." He lowers his voice. "We had to keep things secret. This trouble I have. I'm not conventional. Should we introduce ourselves, since we're talking about such things? I'm Jack." He extends a hand.

"Rebecca," she replies. "What were your troubles, if you don't mind my asking?"

"I fell in love with the wrong person. Made a bit of a fool of myself, truth be told."

"No need to explain. Where do you work?"

"Navy."

"How interesting! On a ship?"

"Yes, I was an Officer. But I've been medically discharged – because they found out about the relationship."

"I'm sorry. How harsh, all for love. I expect it was the rank, they're rather stuffy. Though I confess, I didn't know women could serve aboard."

"Women? Ah, I understand what you mean – foolish of me. Still, here we are and let's hope they sort us all out eh?"

"Oh yes."

The other man listens to the conversation with a slight smirk and interjects into the pause.

"What regiment were you, *Jack*?" he asks. Rebecca thinks him impertinent.

"Why d'you ask, old chap?" Jack replies, slightly defensive.

"Sorry, all amongst equals here, obviously. Force of habit."

"Are you nervous?" Rebecca says, trying to change the subject.

"Of course. Who knows what might happen? One writes best, with personal experience. Should make a good article."

"You're a writer?" she asks, in awe.

"Journalist. Or former, at any rate. May be some material in this little lark." He laughs; a harsh, fake laugh, Rebecca fancies.

"How romantic. May I ask your name? Mine's Rebecca."

"Edwin Cottle," he replied. "Silly surname! Can't chose your parents."

"I think Cottle's a dignified name. Which newspaper do you write for?"

"Whoever's paying! I'm freelance. A literary prostitute, if you will. The Northamptonshire Chronicle and Echo you might've heard of, round here."

"Yes. We take the Gloucestershire Echo, at home."

"Cotswolds eh? Lovely part of the world – superb hunting, I'm given to believe? Are you a hunter, Rebecca?"

The pleasant interlude is interrupted by the entry of Sister. She indicates Rebecca should accompany her. Rebecca smiles at her two companions and wishes them luck, following her to an ante-room containing three beds. The nurse passes Rebecca a plain white cotton hospital gown and as she changes; she turns to allow the nurse tie the bows behind, before getting into the bed. The needle stings the bony back of her left hand, just above her knuckle, as the intravenous drip is inserted.

Her toes become warm and tingle, almost as though she's about to get pins and needles or cramp. This sensation creeps slowly upwards. She finds she can't wriggle her toes any more. When her legs become paralysed; she's alarmed and reaches down to touch them. They're like heavy lumps of white meat, as though they belong to someone else – she can't feel the pressure of her own hand on her flesh. A few minutes later, she passes out.

When Rebecca wakes up, she's soaking wet. Her throat and nose are dry and sore. The gown clings to her skin in patches and in dismay, she realises she's wet herself. The nurse seems unconcerned and helps her to the bathroom next door. The cloying steam rises from the white tub.

"You take a nice wash, Rebecca, and then we'll get your lunch. I expect you're hungry?"

"Oh yes, ravenous. I'm sorry…about the bed."

"Perfectly normal – sometimes the treatment makes one lose control of bodily functions. We always give you a bath straight after. I've put some carbolic and a fresh flannel out for you. I'll fetch you in fifteen minutes, but here's a little bell here for you to ring if you feel faint. You've got quite low blood pressure, I see from your notes?"

"Yes, I fainted before."

"We don't want fainting in water! If you feel at all dizzy, you must ring. Alright?"

"I will, thank you."

After a hearty lunch of solid rounds of ham and cheese sandwiches, Rebecca is led out to a sunny verandah and handed some magazines to read. A nurse perches on a chair with a notebook, but she doesn't speak. A little under an hour later, Edwin Cottle is brought out in a wheelchair. His hair is matted and his eyes bloodshot.

"Edwin; are you alright?" she asks.

"I'm not sure yet. Had to be strapped down – seems I had convulsions. Messy business. How did you get along?"

"I was rather clammy, too. I'm alright now I've had a bath. Did you eat anything?"

"Got through half a sandwich – but it came back up."

"Where's Jack?"

"Back to his room. He had a worse time – a bit of trouble with the old bowels. He seemed to be hallucinating, poor chap, kept ranting about "bloody queers". I think they'll take his lunch into him. We'll see him at dinner, I expect."

"Right." Sensing Edwin could do with some peace, Rebecca returns to the Woman's Own. But she's wrong, Edwin needs to talk. He leans forward, and grasps her arm, hard.

"They're all still around us, Rebecca," he hisses, so the nurse can't hear.

"Who, Edwin?"

"Factions. You're not safe anywhere. Even in here."

"What sort of fractions?"

"Halves, quarters and whole! Fascists. Buffs. Hitler's minions. He might be dead - his ideas aren't. One of the bugger's in here! I recognised his father. They think I'm nutty, - well, I'm the only one who knows the truth!"

"Edwin, you're hurting me. Will you please let go of my arm?"

"I wrote about her, Rebecca. Norah Elam. She was at the rally, too. She's from Northampton. I bet he's in here to infiltrate!"

"Where?"

"Are you being deliberately obtuse? The Albert Hall!"

"Edwin, you're in St Andrew's. You're confused."

"He's in here! I've seen him, I tell you! Bringing his son in! They'll infiltrate everywhere in the end!"

"Edwin, you're scaring me…stop now! STOP IT! I won't listen to you anymore. Nurse, NURSE!"

Edwin is taken away. He's shouting all the way, but then he breaks into song, in a foreign language: "Die Fahne hoch, die Rihen fest geschlossen!" and his left hand makes a Hitler moustache with his forefinger and the German salute from his right. She wonders what possesses him.

Robert has gone to live with Rebecca's parents; so that Arthur can work. On weekends, Arthur, Rebecca's parents and baby Robert visit Rebecca. Her sister Doris never visits, but her brother Clive comes once or twice; he doesn't approve of these places and can't understand why Rebecca has been admitted. Grampy Denby comes regularly; but Shelagh's afraid of mental institutions and can't bring herself to visit. Instead, she parcels up all the local newspapers and magazines in brown paper and string, once a week and sends them on to Rebecca.

Arthur completes the home he's building for them; furnishes it and moves in, with a work colleague staying to share the costs, but Arthur finds this a lonely arrangement. He misses his wife, so he decides to move up to Northampton and secure work and lodgings near St Andrews. He works nights in an engineering factory and his employers let him a flat close to the hospital, although he explains he can't stay longer than six months. Occasionally he shares a fishing trip with a friend from work, but the rest of his time is spent between working and visiting Rebecca, where he'll occasionally enjoy a game of billiards with one of the male patients.

Rebecca's regime continues each morning for the next three months. The patients receiving insulin are confined to walking around the hospital or accompanied around the grounds, in case they lapse into a coma. Their diet is strictly monitored, to control their sugar intake, but Rebecca is bored and fancies she'll take a day off. She eats a whole box of Cadbury's chocolates one evening; as an act of sabotage.

"I'm sorry nurse, I couldn't rresist!" she says. She's rolling her r's and training herself to enunciate all her words; like the other ladies. She's never rebelled in her life; this seems fun. She wonders what they'll do if she provokes them. For a moment, she's rather powerful. She inclines her head to one side, as she's seen Allie doing when she wants something.

"No problem, Rebecca," the nurse replies, with a broad smile which fails to reach her discordant eyes. "We'll simply add another day onto your treatment. You'll be staying with us a little longer, won't you?" She writes the notes and dismisses Rebecca, walking away.

Rebecca curses, reflecting to herself she just can't win. Still, this means spending hours with Allie. They've paired up at mealtimes and she's good company – like those boarding schools Enid Blyton writes about. She'd read about the characters in Mallory Towers; with their tuck boxes and lacrosse racquets. Allie suggests to Rebecca they spend their day exploring.

"Rrather!" she replies. Her voice is becoming more refined and slightly higher in pitch.

The pair sneak around the restricted areas in the hospital; hiding in ante-rooms and storage cupboards full of cleaning materials, if they hear any staff approaching. They happen upon the operating theatre. They are aware, of course, of the people who'd had the brain operations. Those patients don't talk much and are vacant a good deal of the time. When returning to the day room a few days after the operation, looking like animals at the vet, with their shaven heads and those frightful indentations either side. It was commonplace to avoid these patients, as though one might be infected by their severe madness if one got too close.

The deserted operating theatre is pristine; scrubbed white tiles and jars of instruments in sterilising fluid, which smell like rotten vinegar. The floor fascinates Rebecca - tiled in patterns, muddy brown diamonds, or squares, she's not sure…with black and white triangles round an inner square. The effect is of stars, stretching from one side of the room to the other. She can't avoid stepping on the cracks. Allie closes the door and begins to open cupboards and drawers.

"Watch old Wylie Coyote doesn't catch us!"

"Who?" Rebecca replies, giggling.

"Dr McKissock. He's the visiting neurosurgeon. Haven't you seen him yet?"

"I don't think so…what's he like?"

"He's got half moon glasses and peers at you over the top. A pointy nose, bit like Pinocchio! He smokes big fat cigars with thick fingers. A set jaw, you know the type?"

"Not really…"

"He's an O.B.E. mind you. Very well respected in the field – he used to treat all the brain injured soldiers during the war. Travels all round the biggest hospitals, like Maudsley and St Thomas' in London. He even does post-mortems – on the ones that don't survive. "

"I'll be sure to keep out of his way." Rebecca sees a drawer with a tiny silver key. She turns and opens, stepping back, eyes wide. "I say, Allie, look here...what the hell's this?"

Allie peers over her shoulder to what looks like different coloured fur, attached to a card. There are dates and initials under each clump. When she pokes, she realizes this is not fur, but hair. She pulls a sheet out and stares – noting the drawer is full to the brim. Rebecca takes it from her and stares at it.

"Put it back! Let's get out of here!" Allie says, panicking. They are human scalps.

Chapter Twenty-Five:

Four months into her treatment, Rebecca's established in a safe, tedious routine. She's enjoying the company of her two closest friends in St Andrews, Allie and now a thin woman, Belle, who eats like a horse, but stays inexplicably thin. Rebecca imagines her as one of those big Japanese fighters with their bellies hanging out – what are they? Satsuma wrestlers. She whispers this to Allie, as they walk into the dining hall. Allie laughs.

"Sumo, Rebecca – you are so funny. She's eating more than her fair share of laxatives, her. She keeps spares in her handbag."

"What's that got to do anything?" Rebecca asks.

"In one end and straight out the other!"

"But how does she get hold of them?"

"Her brother's an eminent surgeon darling – they're not going to question her too much. He's orfern here. Everyone knows, even the nurses. They turn a blind eye." This remind Rebecca of her mother-in-law's glass eye, with a twinge of guilt. Rebecca won't request the surgeon's name. She's learning the rules of etiquette.

"My god. Is she nesh?"

"I beg your pardon?"

"Nesh – you know, a bit…feeble?"

"Is that a local word? How quaint!"

"I…I don't think…"

"Charming! Nesh…just so. I shall take it up! Belle is indeed, nesh, yes - I should say so."

Rebecca is embarrassed by her faux pas. She feels a little patronized by Allie – and resents her a little. Scanning the room to check for new patients, her eyes meet with a man she's not seen before. He stares straight at her; slowly smiling and nodding a greeting. Rebecca returns his smile with a surge of excitement. The distant thrill of attraction returns; quickly followed by hot, reddening cheeks. She sashays to the table.

As Allie and Belle chat, Rebecca glances over to him. He's sitting with Jack, laughing and joking like old friends, waving his claret in a jovial way. He raises his glass towards her. She smiles and looks down at the roast dinner swimming in congealed gravy on her plate. Dinners taste extremely bland here – not enough salt. The vegetables are boiled to death, some even crushed – the flaccid calibrace, sprout skins burst open and flaking, stinking out the dining hall …she doesn't fancy eating now, appetite's dissipated.

"I'm going to the ladies," she says abruptly, interrupting Allie and Belle. They seem surprised, but Belle shovels the contents of Rebecca's plate onto hers.

Rebecca flees from the room, wondering who he is and what he's doing in here...what Arthur would say. She's disorientated since this treatment started. Her memories often become cloudy – particularly in the short-term. It's sometimes disconcerting and often a relief; not to be constantly reprimanding yourself or remembering what you needed to do next.

She drifts, soft-footed, to the lounge, searching for Allie. After several minutes, she remembers Allie's still at dinner. Dear Allie, only a short-time friend, but close. Allie's father's a professor. She's certainly the sort of person to be around; a good egg. When they get out of here, Allie's taking her to Glyndebourne – she's promised. What did she say earlier? Orfern instead of often. She practices the word – she'll have to find a way to work that into a conversation. She'll wait for her. Allie knows everyone in society and will tell her all about the new man.

Rebecca retrieves a magazine from the coffee table and sits in an armchair. My Home; she reads, from a bright yellow cover and a photograph of an impeccable housewife. Clearly glamorous; in her house everything is perfect. She bets her husband's got his tea on the table every night and her children are immaculate. She's probably got servants. Housework's rather depressing; hard work. All those hints and tips inside, on making a swagged pelmet and tails, ornate curtains for prestigious homes. That's how ladies spend their time. She'll make those, if she's well again. People pay a shilling for these magazines to learn to do things properly. Rebecca decides to subscribe when she gets out.

Belle walks in. "Not hungry tonight, Rebecca?"

"No. Don't you find the food rather bland?"

"No. I've eaten worse."

"Where's Allie?"

"On the way. How's Arthur getting along with the house?"

"He's finished now, Belle. I thought I told you. He's working up here now, remember? Until I'm discharged. Then we're moving in there together." She's irritable, suspecting Belle is stirring the pot.

"Perhaps you did – you must forgive my mind! I blame the meds. You're lucky – I wish a man loving me as he loves you. Your Arthur's jolly handsome, isn't he?"

"Yes, he is."

"Remind me, how long have you been married?"

"Two years. By the way, Belle, I meant to ask you something..." Rebecca leans in towards Belle, conspiratorial. "You've a wonderful appetite, haven't you?"

Belle flinches – Rebecca has noticed a little twitch under her right eye.

"What d'you mean?"

"Well, I'm only saying. You have such a trim figure and I was wondering what your secret is?"

"Secret?"

"I enjoy my food and you seem to love yours, don't you rather?"

"What're you getting at?"

"I'm in awe of you, Belle. You eat far more than I do and yet you're so...slim?"

Belle begins to fidget. This'll do, for now. She's stopped mentioning Arthur and Rebecca doesn't want to be reminded of him at the moment. She leans, satisfied, back in her chair, crossing her legs and inclining them to the left, like the lady in the magazine; as Allie approaches. Sitting down, Allie picks up a magazine and winks at Rebecca.

"I'm going on up now, I'm rather tired," said Belle. Her hand is shaking.

"So early?" Rebecca says, victorious. Sanctimonious little bitch. Belle's no experience of real life pressures. She's not married with children. She can't judge. Spoiled. No-one outside expects her to do anything.

"Yes, I'm sorry. I'll catch you at breakfast?"

"Of course. Sleep tight Belle." Allie replies.

"Goodnight Belle," Rebecca says, smiling.

Belle scurries from the room and Rebecca noticed her little calves. Arthur wouldn't fancy those legs and flat chest – or her boyish bob. Whatever had she seen in her? Troughing food like a pig and pooing, revolting. Imagine having to constantly excuse yourself for the toilet, with a husband. No, Belle's not the type of friend she wants. Allie, on the other hand...but she'd have to broach the topic gently; not give herself away. You weren't sure who could be trusted not to blab. She needs to navigate two worlds, one in here, and one outside. In each, the rules are different. Perhaps the ideal was to leave a foot in both – if either place became overwhelming, one might retreat to the other for a while.

"Allie," Rebecca starts.

"Yeees?" Allie replies, with the air of a soothsayer.

"I need to talk to you."

"I expect you do."

"Who is he?"

"Whom?"

"You saw him Allie, at dinner. Didn't you see him *watching*?"

"D'you mean Edward?"

"Edward?"

"Oh, I'm sorry – of course you wouldn't know him. He took a shine to you, though."

"You're teasing."

"I am. The man, Rebecca, is Captain Edward Napier."

"Captain?"

"Oh yes. Or rather, ex-Captain."

"Why ex?"

"Retired from service now, of course."

"Is he married?"

"What makes you ask?"

"Allie, stop playing games. Curiosity."

"Killed the cat, Rebecca."

"Bugger the cat, Allie. Spill the beans."

"He is married. The wife is flighty. Caused a dreadful scandal."

"Oh?"

"She had a love affair. With one of my family's friends. Can't say who, obviously. She became pregnant with his child, not Edward's. Edward was an utter gentleman over the whole debacle; taken the boy as his own – dotes over him. I suppose he drinks to cope, bless him.

"I don't understand. Why would he take on someone else's child?"

"Rebecca, you are so green! Don't you realise this sort of thing happens?"

"Allie, the poor man. He must be a saint. Why on earth did he forgive her?"

"What else was he to do? They live in the Channel Islands, Rebecca; such a small world. His whole family hail from there. The scandal, you understand, would be intolerable."

"Isn't he rather lovely?"

"Have a care, Rebecca. He's troubled."

"Allie, we're all in here because we're troubled."

"You like him, don't you?"

"I don't understand what you mean."

"I'm not an idiot, Rebecca. It's obvious."

"Really?"

"Yes. Take my advice - you be careful."

Chapter Twenty-Six:

Rebecca's lost her appetite and having missed lunch, she sits in the lounge for half an hour or so. She watches a waiter walking towards her with a piece of paper in his hand. "For you," he says, and walks away. She tears open the envelope. In beautifully curved letters, she reads:

"I know you are on a hunger strike, you'll be hungry by dinner time! May I take you out to dinner?" the signature says: "Your Psychiatrist".

Rebecca glances around. No-one's looking. She tucks the note into her handbag and goes straight up to her room, where she reads and re-reads, debating whether going out for dinner constitutes adultery. This life is so boring. Maybe she can excuse some excitement – as long as it doesn't go too far.

An hour later, Matron calls into Rebecca's private room.

"Mrs Denby," she says, hesitating. "I wish you would let Captain Napier take you out to dine tonight."

"I don't think I'd better, Matron. I don't think it's appropriate."

"I'm sure dinner's perfectly harmless. You must keep up your strength for these treatments and you aren't eating properly. Perhaps company will help?"

"No, I don't think I can. But you might thank the Captain for me, for his kindness."

"I will. Do reconsider, though. At least make sure you eat tonight!"

"I'll come for dinner with Allie and Belle."

"Right you are."

Edward is not in the dining hall that night, to her chagrin. She wonders if he's taken someone else out. The next time she sees him is in the corridor, the next day.

"Good morning Rebecca!" he says "Can we go for a walk?"

Rebecca is rather taken aback. "When?"

"Shall I meet you after luncheon? Or are you still on a hunger strike?"

"I orfern skip lunch. I suppose a walk would be pleasant."

"I'll meet you in front of Wantage House then, in the garden?"

"About half past twelve."

Rebecca attends a craft group for two hours this morning. Her plans were to swim for an hour between 11.00am and 12.00pm – Mario, the instructor, chastised her about non-attendance yesterday. He'd heated the pool. She decides against swimming, not wanting to have to do her make-up and hair all over again. The group construct wicker baskets and fill them with foil covered chocolate eggs for the Easter chapel service. She can't concentrate on the work and her hands shakes. She only thinks about the walk.

Edward stands, outside the magnificent sand-dust pillars of Wantage House, wearing a panama hat. Their introduction is formal, him, tipping the hat and her, extending a gloved hand to shake his, which, instead, he raises to his lips. He smiles, offering his arm. She listens to his story and ascertains he must be rich, which only serves to add to his charm. They share their reasons for being in St Andrews; Edward describing the marital problems that resulted in his heavy drinking and Rebecca her fears and the compulsions she uses to allay them. They are so at ease in one another's company by the end of two hours; that dining as a foursome this evening with Jack and Allie seems agreeable and inevitable.

They begin sitting together for all their meals. Belle is quickly dropped. Rebecca notices Edward takes a glass or two of wine with every meal and presumes his drinking is under control now. Rebecca takes tiny mouthfuls of food and is careful to chew her food very slowly with her mouth closed, dabbing her mouth daintily with the corner of the linen napkin, as she has seen Allie do. She has learned the tip of subtly licking the top of her wine glass before she sips, in order not to smear it with her lipstick.

The men's sleeping accommodation is on a different side of the hospital. The rules are strict – no visitors of the opposite sex in either quarter. One morning, Allie collects the ladies' post and finds a letter in the pile, addressed to "Captain, the Honourable Edward Napier." She shows Rebecca, who is pleased to have his title proven, but wants to keep the secret to herself. Allie needn't broadcast their business, particularly since she doesn't really understand what "the Honourable" part means, until Allie explains it. A courtesy title, afforded to the second son of an Earl, Baron, or Viscount. Rebecca feigns indifference, but is enthralled. Allie has been giving her lessons in applying her make-up, from plucking her eyebrows and sculpting them into a high arch with a pencil, to applying the lipstick four times, blotting with soft tissue in between.

Edward and Rebecca become closer over the months. His chauffeur takes them for rides in his Bentley around the grounds, while they sit in the back together, clutching hands. They take picnics on the lawn and meet for croquet. The relationship is never consummated, but an understanding is reached, the boundaries of which are cuddles, kisses and company. At the weekly dance; they are always together – Edward is accomplished at ballroom.

118

He reads Milton to her – gazes in her glassy blue eyes – "Thou with fresh hopes, the lover's heart dost fill!"

By the time Rebecca has only one month left of her treatment, Edward becomes amorous and begins to persuade Rebecca to take the relationship further. They walk past the croquet lawns, holding hands, when he turns to her.

"I must speak with you, Rebecca."

"Edward, you may say anything you wish, to me."

"I've never experienced so much happiness, in my whole life."

"Neither have I."

"Must we end things?"

"I leave next month, so I'm afraid so."

"How soon hath Time, the subtle thief of youth…?"

"…stolen on his wing my three and twentieth year!" she finishes, smiling. "How I shall miss Milton!" The name never fails to remind her of the sterilizing fluid that undoubtedly awaits her return.

"You need not miss Milton, Rebecca. You could have it every day!"

She is quite certain that she will…but she says nothing.

"I lived the good life, Rebecca. Had all the parties and even women I wanted. I've never fallen in love with any of them. Until now."

"Do you mean it?"

"I do. I want to settle down with a sensible, loving woman, Rebecca. You."

"Edward, I can't possibly. I feel the same as you, but I'm married, with a baby."

"We could tell Arthur together. I'll be right by your side."

"But what about Robert, my darling son?"

"I'll be frank with you, Rebecca. I adore my boy as if he were my own…only you know that isn't."

"You're such a good man. Life must be terrible for you."

"It was. I must also consider the question of his inheritance. There could be no question of his being… usurped in any way."

"Usurped?"

"I couldn't make him share, you understand. So far as he is concerned I am his real father and I could not introduce a…a step-child. You, of course, will be well provided for in the event of my…passing on. You trust my word."

"What are you saying?"

"I think you understand, Rebecca. I'll take you away from all this and give you a beautiful life. One filled with all the precious things you deserve. Your boy is well-loved and taken care of, is he not?"

"Of course, but I couldn't possibly leave him." She thinks him cruel, to suggest it. He took on another man's child before- so why not hers? Perhaps he is rather selfish. She looks at his mouth, which, for the first time, looks a little weak.

"Give my proposition some thought. Don't be too hasty. Your son's managed without you, hasn't he? He might adjust better to a clean break – perhaps consider his best interests, too."

Rebecca is silent. No more laundry days, cleaning, sweeping and scrubbing. She could give Edward a child of his own. With servants and nannies to help, life would be easy. Dad would forgive her, she was sure. She'll have to make the decision quickly.

"I need time, Edward."

"Time is running out, Rebecca. I'll leave you now. Say you'll join me for dinner?"

"Yes."

They part at the entrance to the women's quarters. Rebecca goes to her room to reflect. The situation is ridiculous, of course and beginning to get out of hand. The best thing to do is let him down gently, just before she leaves. Don't crush his hopes and spoil the last few weeks. She doesn't love Edward enough to give up Arthur and Robert. The thought of them fills her with remorse. She needs to try much harder when she gets home – Arthur must never find out that she considered leaving him. He's no fool and he probably realises there's a spark between her and Edward. She tried to hide it, but Edward was too friendly to Arthur on his visits, almost mocking. She feels well in Edward's company; which is certainly not to be confused with love.

Rumours abound at the hospital concerning the affair between the Captain and Mrs Denby. The other residents begin to point and snigger. All the staff seem to encourage the relationship; almost as though coerced. Edward charmed them all, she supposes. Perhaps they believe he's the best thing for her. With only two weeks left of her treatment, the days begin to pass with urgency. They walk in the evenings, stopping to kiss sometimes and continuing to talk about being together forever. Rebecca imagines herself with the title "Lady", enjoying the image and knowing she need only say yes. These Mills & Boon recollections feel more wholesome than the hand job she gave him in his Bentley.

One afternoon, Charlie Lindsay arrives to see Rebecca. He's alone and she takes care to introduce him to Edward, before they walk around the bowling green, father and daughter.

"He seems fond of you, my girlie," he says, winking.

"Who?"

"Who, indeed? You like him, don't you?"

"Dad – you must promise to keep a secret, if I tell you,"

"You'd better tell me."

"Edward wants me to elope with him."

"And shall you?"

"Aren't you angry?"

"Did you imagine I didn't know? I take a close interest in all your doings, Rebecca. I am kept informed."

"What should I do?"

"Do you love him?"

"Yes, I think so,"

"Perhaps you should go with him. You'd enjoy a better life than the other one can give you. I always thought you sold yourself short."

"What about Robert?"

"Only you can answer. I'll leave the decision to you."

When given the choice; she didn't want it.

A few days before she's due to go home, Edward becomes frantic, promising to get her free of her illness. Finally, he presses two airline tickets in her hand.

"Marry me, Rebecca. Say you will."

"I am so sorry Edward, I can't possibly!" She bursts into tears and runs away from him to her room. He discharges himself and leaves St Andrews later that day. She never sees him again.

At the end of the six month treatment, Rebecca is "topped up" with three more ECT treatments, this time with anaesthetic and muscle relaxants. She feels better than she's ever felt, keen to move into her new house, with baby Robert and Arthur. Arthur returns to his job in Cheltenham. Rebecca leaves St Andrews with various prescriptions, intended to maintain her stability. Calmdownzapine, MAOIrestinpeace, Tritofitinzapine, Wakeupzamol, Nofitsazil, Complyrazine, Noreprievezenol, Shhhoprim. She will be in and out of asylums for the rest of her life, but none as grand as St Andrew's. No further charitable funding was offered.

Chapter Twenty-Seven:

This is a good life at Morelands. They named their house after the Youth Club where they met. Rebecca's had a lucky escape from The Honourable Captain Edward Napier. She hadn't been forced to face him again, which she couldn't bear. Now she seems to have everything she wanted. The lovely house that Arthur had built, with a twenty-two foot kitchen, sporting a top-loading washing machine, three bedrooms, a lounge, bathroom, toilet and games room and a private drive. Her home is, she reflects, quite posh.

For the next two years, she enjoys feeling stable and well. Robert is nearly four, a fine lad, who the family adore. Rebecca pets him frequently, fussing over his hair and his clothing. She believes her parents love him the best, probably because they'd had him almost full-time for the six months of her stay in St Andrew's. Just as Rebecca had suspected all along, her sister Doris and Mark had returned to America about five months after their new baby, Paul, was born. He was unusually quiet, never cried. The poor little mite contracted meningitis on the boat back to the states, misdiagnosed as teething. He died. American law dictated they had to leave his little body in New York, where the death was registered - hundreds of miles from their new home. This reminded Rebecca how precious children are. Poor Doris. Rebecca hadn't seen her since, although her parents had visited once, already. How her mother managed the trip, with her nerves and all, Rebecca couldn't imagine. Rebecca is determined to hold her family together. Despite being bored, she completes the housework with a good grace. Each day, she straightens the house before cleaning. She starts in one corner of the room, picking up the toys and clothes – piling them up as she goes. She finds it difficult to be disciplined enough not to skip between rooms, but the magazines are filled with useful hints and tips.

She feather-dusts the lampshades and tops of shelves, shaking out the sofa and chair cushions and brushing the dust from the upholstery. Next, the furniture is dusted with a soft cloth and beeswax. Start high and end low! That's the way. Toilets and bathrooms are scrubbed with powdery Vim and rinsed out. She pushes along the carpet sweeper for the rugs, but nothing works better than a good old-fashioned beating in the sunshine. The floors are mopped with only a little water. Strong camphorous mothballs hang in closets between the clothing and on sunny days, Rebecca spreads all the blankets from the beds on the washing line to air them. Clothes are patched and repaired by hand and Rebecca keeps a sewing basket for repairs, which she completes in the evenings while listening to the wireless. On Thursdays, she takes Robert with her to the shops for all the groceries and she even lets him help her with the baking on Saturdays. He's quite a natural.

In the meantime, Arthur pursues his interest in boats and boat-building. He purchases second- hand books from Woolworths on the subject, at sixpence apiece. Fascinated by the latest racing boats, he teams up with two friends, Dennis Draper, a surveyor and architect, and Jack Smith, who's a local sign writer. Dennis draws up the plans for the project. At this time, the Co-Operative shop is being demolished and members of the public can purchase various discarded items at the site. Arthur buys a beautiful mahogany counter, twenty feet long and two and a half feet wide. Between them, the friends reckon they could make sub-frames, for three boats – one for each of them – bargain.

Three boats are constructed and completed over many months, in their spare time. Jack Smith's son becomes his mechanic, buying outboard motors and Bristol Marina donates engines. Arthur, Dennis and Jack sign a lease to rent a water space in the Cotswolds and found a motor boat racing Club. Jack Smith goes on to become one of the world's greatest powerboat drivers, competing in the USA, Thailand, South Africa and Russia and becomes Commodore of the Cotswold Club at one time. His career spans three decades, winning championships in Formula Three, Formula Grand Prix and Formula One. Aged 59, he competes in the Formula One Grand Prix in Singapore. His boat crashes and he's badly injured. The rescue boat breaks down, before it reaches him and he drowns.

Arthur continues his hobby at the Racing Club, until ordinary patrons become overwhelmed with rich, hedonistic townie-types, who spoil the experience for him, with their competitive nature. A few years later, a regular club member needs a co-pilot and takes a volunteer visitor from Birmingham out with him – who's desperate for the thrill. No-one checks whether he's anchored in the boat correctly. Rebecca and Arthur watch the craft reach speeds of 30-40mph, and the bouncing throws him into the water. The next boat's propeller goes straight through his stomach. Although he's rushed to Cirencester hospital, he doesn't survive. One of the nurses confides to Rebecca that they knew he wouldn't make it on arrival – his injuries were too severe. Rebecca takes two extra Thathurtzapam, when she can't sleep that night.

Arthur remains lifelong friends with Dennis Draper, but they never go to the club again.

Chapter Twenty-Eight:

One night after tea, Arthur looks serious.

"Now Rebecca, I want to talk to you about something," he says.

"Run along to the garden, Robert darling. Mummy needs to speak with Daddy."

Robert toddles outside in his shorts and began to play hopscotch on the path, scrawling the squares in with a jagged limestone.

"How are you feeling?" Arthur asks.

"I'm very well. Why?"

"I was wondering...whether you felt well enough, you know."

"For what?"

"The thing is, I was an only child. I wouldn't want that for Robert...and he's four now."

"D'you mean you'd like another baby?"

"I would. But only if you're well enough."

The thought crossed her mind several times over the last few months. How lovely Arthur feels that way. "Yes, I believe I am."

"Great! Let's get started then, no time like the present!" he grabs her breast and laughs. She slaps his hand away.

"Arthur! Not while Robert's awake, for heaven's sake. He'll see. Later?"

"It's a date."

She washes up, smiling.

Several months pass. Try as they might, Rebecca doesn't conceive. Even after a few drinks to relax them, Arthur taking her out to special places and for romantic dinners, nothing happens. Rebecca resigns herself to doing without another baby. She's not as upset about it as she thought she might be and Arthur seems happy enough, so long as she is. They get on with their lives. At the weekends, Arthur loves going fishing early on a Sunday morning, around 5.00am, coming home in time for his big Sunday roast, then retiring to the sofa for a kip. Later in the evening, they might go out with friends.

It's early spring on the River Severn; long a rich source of food for poor and gentry alike, abundant in elvers, lampreys and wild salmon. Arthur and his friend Dennis arrange to go elvering, one night. Rebecca asks if she can come, suggesting Charlie and Faith look after Robert. The night air is biting damp. He's told her to dress warm and not worry how she looks, but she doesn't much like slacks. Her Mother says ladies don't wear them. She's put them on over her stockings and is glad of them. She's assigned the task of sorting elvers with bare hands. They're in a shallow elver tray, in a wooden frame with a nylon mesh. Rebecca plunges her fingertips into the slime as they wriggle through, picking out the leaves and sticklebacks that cut if you grab them wrong, even the odd flatty. She keeps the tray near the campfire, sitting on the tump, next to Arthur's father's initials, carved into the willow tree. You need to keep them fresh and alive, but not too hot.

The three return home, happy, hungry and glad. Rebecca washes two pints of elvers in a sieve, shaking as much water as she can out, drying them in a clean tea towel; puts some bacon in the pan, to get the fat fizzing salt-smoke. When the bacon's lightly browned, she pours the elvers in, scrambles an egg in them and each of them has big mug of sweet tea. They're fishy and chewy and crispy, melt in the mouth. After they wash up, Dennis and Rebecca start on the brandy. He leans over the table.

"Worked at Boot's, didn't you Beck?"

"Oh yes, Dennis."

"You'll like this. So, I've popped into Boots now, 'cos I've got a sweet little number lined up for Saturday night and I want some Jonnies in case I gets lucky. How many d'you want, he says to me, I've got a three, six or nine pack? I'd best have the nine, I says to him, winking. She's hot to trot. Well, 'e laughs and bags them up for me. I picks this girl up, Lily her name is, but when I gets there she's got me lined up for supper with the parents instead of what I 'as in mind. Well, we sits down and I says, d'you all mind if I say Grace and she leans over to me and whispers I didn't know you was religious and I says to 'er, I didn't know your old man was a chemist!"

Rebecca laughs, holding her hand to her mouth in case she's unseemly. Dennis, encouraged, carries on in an Irish accent:

"Well, there's a whole bunch of nuns lined up at the gates of Heaven and before they're admitted, they've to speak to St Peter for admittance. St Peter says to the Sister Agnes, now, have you ever touched a penis? And she says well to be honest, I once touched one with the end of my finger. Well, he says, touch your finger in that holy water, say three Hail Mary's and g'wan your way through. He turns to Sister Mary and says Sister Mary, now, 'tis the same question for you. Well, she says I once did get carried away and I rubbed one up and down a bit. Well, he says, dip your whole hand in the holy water, say six Hail Mary's and g'wan your way through. He turns to Sister Conceptia and says, now, 'tis the same question for you. But suddenly there's a jostling and a fightin' up the line. It's Sister Ruth and she's pushing her way to the front. All in good time, says St Peter. What's your hurry, Sister? And Sister Ruth says well, if I've to gargle that stuff, I'd prefer it's before Sister Mary Thomas sticks her arse in it!"

They carry on like this until the early hours of the morning. After bidding goodnight to Dennis, who staggers off down the road with his share of the elvers, they go to bed, giggling and romping about before making love quickly and falling asleep.

Rebecca misses her period next month. And the next. She's already sure, but visits the doctor and waits for it to be confirmed. When she tells him, Arthur hits the air with his fist and shouts, YES! When they tell Robert he's to have a baby brother or sister; he asks for another biscuit. Nanny Denby and Rebecca start knitting again.

After suffering terribly with morning sickness, Rebecca is at a routine ante-natal appointment. Dr Lewis inquires how things are.

"I do wish I could stop being sick Doctor," she replies. "I wasn't this bad with Robert."

"Well, how severe is it?"

"Every morning...I'm generally better after lunch. It's more feeling sick than actually being sick. I wonder if it's the tablets."

"I wouldn't have thought so. Well, I can prescribe you something very new, if you like, to help with the nausea."

"Do you have pills for everything nowadays?"

"Not quite! I am having fantastic results with some mums though, seems to sort them out within a couple of days. It's called thalidomide."

"Do you know, Doctor Lewis, I think I'll try and manage without. I'm already rattling!"

"Just as you like. But come back and see me if you change your mind."

"Thank you."

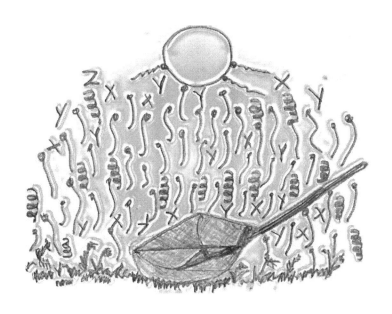

Chapter Twenty-Nine:

If God has the answers; then perhaps they can be found in the Church. There are two churches within a short walking distance from Rebecca's home. The Catholic one is grander; with mauve stained glass windows and gilded statues. The gargoyles, through which rainwater tumbles in an arc; are a little disconcerting; but inside, she is fascinated with the Virgin statue of Mary and child. Here, mothers appear to be held in more reverence. The door is never locked. Rebecca has taken to sitting in here, right at the back, for a quiet hour when she can. The prayer mats are of thick red velvet. The white leather prayer books lie sideways with gilt edges and bookmarks. She has noticed people going into confession. She has seen the priest leave and return, candles being lit and people fiddling with crucifixes on beads. They all appear to have some safety in their rituals – as she does. The priest seems not to have noticed her for the last two weeks; but today, he approaches her.

"Good day to you. Have you everything you need or can I be of any assistance to you?

"How kind of you to ask. I hope you have not minded my coming."

"Not at all, all God's children are welcome."

"I'm not a Catholic, you see."

"Yet here you find yourself. Would you like to ask me anything?"

"What made you become a priest?"

He laughs. "What an excellent question. May I sit?"

She moves up the pew.

"When I was a just an altar boy, I saw a terrible happening. A lady came to see the priest, I believe she was Italian. She had not long buried her poor dear husband; and was left with a young son. I didn't understand what had happened; but only that a month later; she sat and watched as they dug up his coffin and took it away. The hole was filled in again and the tombstone laid flat on the ground. It was carted off later. I asked why and the priest told me that he had been sinful during his life with another woman. His wife would not bring herself to share his grave and her grief at his passing, so she moved his body away."

"The poor woman. How did she find out?

"She saw the other woman putting flowers down. Never confronted her; but began to ask the right questions of the right people. For twenty years he had led a double life."

"What did you think about it?"

"I thought her belief in Almighty God incredible. In difficult times; many question their faith in a higher power. She did not. She never missed a mass or confessional. I wanted to feel that faith so strongly myself – but it was still some years before it came to me."

"Do you remember the moment?"

"Yes. It was at a weekend retreat, in Prinknash Abbey. We'd been fasting. Some were said to have visions during these times; but I'm afraid mine was rather less dramatic. The monks were mainly silent; but when they sang…I can only say the sound filled the room. More than that; it filled my heart with a sense of belonging…as though I was joined by a thread to mankind. I felt so content – rather than elated. That's when I knew I believed in more than I could see."

"I'm not sure I've ever felt…content."

"But perhaps it is possible. God will come to those who search."

Rebecca feels comforted and begins to visit more regularly. She invites Father Stephens to call on her and Arthur. Over some weeks; Father Stephens, becomes a frequent visitor at the house. Arthur doesn't hold with all that "holy stuff", but he quite likes him. Mild-mannered and a good listener, Rebecca finds his presence comforting, he seems so convinced that God holds all the answers, if only she'll listen. She tells him the bad thoughts have returned and how sick she feels, worrying about this baby and whether she'll be ill again afterwards, like last time. He suggests she might enjoy complete a term of tutelage to convert to Catholicism and she agrees.

When she attends, her tutoring is not to be with him, as she had envisaged. Instead, it's with a dour Irish nun, Sister Mary, whose eyes suggest she can read everything in Rebecca's head and disapproves of the contents. The sessions take place in the gardens of a large house in Denmark Road, a quiet, wide and tree-lined road half a mile from Gloucester's city centre. Rebecca quickly tires of Sister Mary's austere manner and talk of repentance, fire and brimstone through thin lips and how everyone's a sinner – particularly Rebecca. "Every baby is born with a stain on its back" she says. Rebecca thinks her words ridiculous, her last baby was rather beautiful and she hopes the next one will be, too. Arthur's sure she's carrying a girl, he thinks that's how it happens, the silly man. She wonders how any innocent baby can be stained, or blamed, for anything.

She has listened to a description of purgatory for half an hour, when she notices a nun in the gardens, toiling over a white rose bush with secateurs. She wears no make-up and you can't even see her hair, but her blue eyes are curtained with doll-like lashes. Her face has an almost ethereal serenity. Rebecca feels she must interrupt.

"Who is that? Isn't she beautiful?"

"Beauty is in the eye of the beholder, Rebecca. Pride is a sin and Sister Constance is married to the Lord. We have no need of the painted faces that *others* hold so dear."

"Well, I only meant she looks as though she has no cares in the world."

"She cares alright. As all should care, about doing the Lord's will."

"How do we know what the Lord's will is?"

"Ours is not to question, Rebecca. All shall be revealed in the Lord's great plan."

"What's his plan for me?"

"Perhaps for you to care less about your own appearance. In any case I think we should continue next week. You should read the papers I gave you concerning confirmation, in time for our next session."

"I will."

"We'll finish there for today then. God be with you, Rebecca," she says, crossing herself and glaring at Rebecca.

"And with you, sister."

Rebecca completes the term as she'd promised, but never goes through with her confirmation. Father Stephens seems to understand. When Rebecca next speaks to him of her fears, he suggests she might like to visit a convent in Minehead, for a rest. This would be a week's "retreat" where she could relax and live a simple life, with the other nuns. She jumps at the chance and Arthur takes the day off work to drive her there, with her little suitcase in hand. He kisses her long and hard as he drops her off.

"Don't be getting any ideas about converting, Mrs Denby. You'd miss the cock, I reckon."

"Arthur, for heaven's sake, I can hardly convert to being a nun. In my condition!"

"Well, you just remember, it's all in the word. NONE."

She laughs and gets out of the car, looking up at the building. It's smothered in the greasy red leaves of a Virginia creeper. The wooden front door, battened with blue-gray iron nails, is shut firm. Her heels sink in the gravel, becoming covered in yellow powdering dust as she approaches and rings the bell.

The nuns are friendly enough, yet detached. After explaining all the rules about mealtimes, prayer and activities, one of them leads Rebecca to a box bedroom, with nothing on the wall but a crucifix. She places her suitcase on the floor and unpacks her clothes, hanging them into a tiny mahogany wardrobe. She opens the bible. The pages are worn and smudged from hundreds of barren fingertips. She lies down on the hard single bed. The silence hits her. No children's noise, no snoring and no cars. This ought to feel peaceful, but she just feels lonely. She tosses and turns – missing

Arthur's comforting arm around her. She wonders how they live like this and determines to find out. Someone will tell her the attraction. Hours later, itchy and hot, she tosses off the thin blanket and prises open the tiny window. Even the grounds are still.

For the next few days, she watches and complies. They don't speak much, these nuns. They're pleasant enough, smiling and continuing with their tasks. Rebecca wanders about, lost and lonely. They prefer quiet time, praying, gardening and cooking – such a simple life...but boring. The nicest is Sister Katy, who affords Rebecca some attention, in the evening. She's answered Rebecca's questions with quotations from the bible and now takes up her praying stool.

"Where are you going now, Sister Katy?"

"I'm going to mass, Rebecca."

"Can I come with you?"

"Of course."

"Is this your own praying stool or do they provide it?"

"We don't own anything Rebecca – but this is mine while I am here. This one is rather worn, as you can see."

"May I see?"

Sister Katy hands her the praying stool for inspection.

"It's threadbare, but I could repair this for you. I'd be happy to, if you let me. It'll give me something useful to occupy my time."

"What a lovely idea, Rebecca. Are you sure it won't be too much trouble?"

"Not at all. Would it be alright for me to start now and then take the stool home if I don't complete the work in time? I promise I'll make sure it's sent back to you when I finish." There's no real need to take it home, but Rebecca hopes this will prolong the friendship and the contact.

"I'll ask for permission, Rebecca. Thank you for your gracious offer."

"I'll start tomorrow!"

"Very well."

Rebecca is enthralled at having a project and the trust placed in her. She tolerates the prayers, thanking God for the opportunity to do a useful and pious chore.

The next morning, she leaves the convent to find the sewing shop in Minehead. It's good to focus on a project – she must overcome the anxiety to do this for her new friend. After asking a local person, she's directed to a haberdashery. *Thodays* opens out to a larger space than first appearance from the outside. Rebecca notes the lack of staff in attendance. There are plenty of eye-catching items. She touches the bright-coloured fabrics, fingering raw silk, muslin and taffeta, pulling rolls and holding them up to the mirror, draping them round her. She searches through offcuts and selects several. As she fingers the buttons on card, diamante, plain and square shaped, some brass like military - her mind drifts back to her childhood – Mother's sewing box and the button tin, where she ran her fingers through the different shapes and sizes; sieving them through each hand into the tin from up high. It makes her sad to think how simple life was then...how much safer she felt. She takes six different strips in one hand and then moves to the long counters to flip through the pattern catalogues, searching the latest fashion designs from Butterick and Vogue. After an hour's mooching, she finds tapestry canvas, rough, hair-shirt like, crisscrossed. Doing penance, almost – this is fitting for reviving a nun's praying stool. She selects brightly coloured wools, surely Sister Katy needs this to be cheerful - she isn't allowed to be. Rebecca's not going to make something plain, as a sign, a payback, and recognition of how she appreciates the nun's kindness.

These are the items she'll purchase. Rebecca can't justify buying the others she's collected, but she wants them so much. She'll pay for the right ones, and take the bad. The diamante buttons and the patterns, some braiding and ribbons. Glancing round to check no-one's watching, she pops these into her handbag, taking out her purse and clicking the bag shut. Her heart thumps as she approaches the counter, waiting for someone to stop her and wondering what she'll say if confronted. Act confused, "why, I'm awfully sorry, I wanted to buy these things too – I couldn't carry them all." And when the police arrive, saying "This is ridiculous, you can see this is an honest mistake and here's the money to pay?" and if this doesn't wash, finally, "I'm afraid I am mentally ill...if you contact Father Stephens at St Augustine's and my doctor, they'll vouch for my character...."

No-one challenges her. She pays for the items and leaves the shop, panicking and thrilled. Rebecca quickens her step back to the convent, clutching the crinkling paper bag with her purchased accoutrements and grasping her handbag containing the illegitimate ones. She'd better go home soon, before anyone finds out.

First thing the next day, Rebecca makes her excuses, due to morning sickness, and telephones Arthur to collect her, taking the praying stool with her and the stolen items in her suitcase. No-one knows, or suspects. Arthur's pleased to see her and loads her case into the boot, lighting them both a cigarette and whistling all the way home.

In guilty excitement she makes love with her husband that night – she's missed Arthur and when he leaves for work next morning, realises she ought to get ready for Robert's return. She sits alone in the bedroom and opens up the suitcase, hesitating before removing the top layer of clothes. The loose spoils lie underneath, accusing. She's a bad woman, worst still, hiding this in a convent. A sinner. What on earth will Arthur say, if he finds out? She's nothing better than a common thief. She deserves to be punished, taken through the courts and thrown into jail. After two hours of staring at the swag and churning her plight around her mind, the porridge thoughts clear to the course of necessary action. Rebecca telephones the police.

"I've stolen some things from a shop."

"Who's calling please?"

"My name is Rebecca Rose Denby."

"Where   are   you   now?"

She gives her address. Within fifteen minutes, two police officers, one male, one female, knock at the door. Rebecca answers.

"Mrs Rebecca Rose Denby?" the male officer asks. He looks embarrassed.

"Yes."

"I'm PC Giles and this is PC Preece."

"Priest?"

"Preece! Did you telephone to confess to theft from a shop?" the female officer asks, masculine and brusque.

"Ms Denby, I think we'd better come in, please. I'm sure you don't want to discuss this on your doorstep." PC Giles's tone is appeasing. Rebecca stands aside.

"Yes, do, please. I did phone you. I...I don't know why I did it."

"What did you steal? I think you'd better show us. Right away." PC Preece shows no sympathy.

"I'll show you – this way." She leads them upstairs to her bedroom, finely dusted with the ornaments, the tiebacks, the floral curtains and the lavender bags, the bed with its periwinkled pink bedspread, upon which lies an open suitcase and threads, buttons, braid, ribbons are displayed in neat rows. "These are the things."

"Where did you steal them from?"

"From Thodays, in Minehead."

"You'll be punished for this."

"But I didn't mean to steal, I don't know what came over me. I'll return it all, of course!"

"Theft from a shop is a serious offence. You'll need to come with us to the station while we conduct further enquiries. Do you have any idea how much money shops lose because of people like you?"

"I can't...I have a little boy, he's due back today!"

"Who has him at the moment?"

"My mother in law. Please, I can't possibly go to prison! Who'll take care of him?"

"You should have thought about that before you stole things."

PC Giles looks on, calmly. "Are you married?" he asks.

"Yes, my husband Arthur is out at work."

"Did you tell him about this?"

"No, Arthur will be devastated."

"Now, now, Mrs Denby. I'm sure he won't be as angry as you think. Can you give us the telephone number of his works, and I'll arrange for him to come home and explain all this, eh?"

PC Giles's a good man. What a horrible person, the other one. She's so cold, Rebecca wouldn't call her a woman. How can she hope to understand, when she's cruel, hateful.

"Yes, yes...I'll just find the number."

PC Preece looks incredulous, but says nothing.

After an hour's uncomfortable wait, where Rebecca offers them tea; Arthur arrives. She wonders what on earth he will say. She's left downstairs with *her*.

Arthur takes the male officer upstairs, and she can't hear the conversation. She hears the telephone rise and fall by the ping, wondering if Arthur is ringing the Doctor. Only PC Preece, the malevolent force in the kitchen, glares at Rebecca like a judge passing sentence. After half an hour, they return.

"Mrs Denby, Arthur's explained about your illness. We spoke to Doctor Lewis and we're going to telephone Father Stephens now, to see if we can't straighten this out."

"Thank you. I'm so very sorry, you see, I don't understand why it happened!"

Rebecca begins to cry with relief. She makes everyone a second cup of tea, though PC Preece doesn't even sip it, the bitch. Father Stephens arrives on his bicycle, mopping a handkerchief to his lined forehead. She concentrates on the hairs in his ears, which

135

look like spiders trying to escape. His lilting Irish tones could put the devil himself to sleep.

"I'm sure, officers, Rebecca was simply confused," he says. "She wanted to mend the praying stool, you understand, and the Lord knows she's suffered with her troubles. As a woman with child, I'm sure you'll appreciate her difficulties, one might only contact her doctor to find out about her medications, and I hoped the time away would help her,"

"Well, Father, what do you propose we do about the stolen items?"

"Officer, I'm certain I can telephone Thodays and explain the situation. I'll take full responsibility to return the merchandise to them and they'll surely understand."

"I think that might be the best course of action. We'll need to fill out a report."

"To be sure, Officer and thank you kindly for your understanding. These are good people and are seeking guidance for their problems. I'm certain the owners of the shop will be glad for the return of the items when I explain."

"You'll inform us of the outcome, Father?"

"Indeed I will." As Father Stephens sees them to the door, he looks from the sympathetic face of the PC Giles to PC Preece, kindly – though she will not melt.

"The Lord moves in mysterious ways....and perhaps Mrs Denby's confession is a window into her soul."

"Hmm... Well, good day to you Father," she replies.

"God be with you, officer," he replies. He closes the door behind them and breaths out.

He returns all the items to the shop in person. No charges are pressed. Sister Katy forgives Rebecca and keeps in touch with her, by letter, offering hope and salvation in the face of repentance. Rebecca makes a beautiful job of the praying stool, hand embroidered flowers and leaves in bright threads. The following weekend, Rebecca is admitted to Coney Hill mental asylum with depression.

Chapter Thirty:

Coney Hill mental asylum was originally known as the Barnwood Mill Estate. Set in 243 acres of beautiful grounds, the driveway is lined with pine trees at one side and on the other, several well-established horse chestnuts and four lime trees, under whose shade the patients can sit, in the summer. The hospital farm has a herd of over a hundred Ayrshire cattle and supplies fruit and vegetables for the kitchens. Several architects had competed for the contract to build the asylum in 1879, which was won by Messrs John Giles & Giles of London, who had already built eleven other asylums throughout Britain. All were under strict instructions to ensure minimal fire risk at the premises.

Arthur drives Rebecca up the private road to the front gates. The clock tower stands above the arched entrance, over which is a concrete tablet, inscribed: "ANNO DOMINI 1883 – BEAR YE ONE ANOTHER'S BURDENS". She stares at the sign and repeats the words to herself several times. She will learn this is a biblical quotation from Galatians. The red brick walls are interspersed with blue engineering bricks in lines of two, with diamond shaped patterns pictured over the windows. The windows at the top of the tower are arched.

Rebecca's latest psychiatrist is female, well-meaning and pleasant, but the stupid woman prescribes barbiturates. These leave Rebecca with the constant sensation of being unpleasantly drunk. Like the time just before she was sick all over her dress and Arthur had to strip her off. She doesn't rate the psychiatrist much – no job for a woman. Over the next six months, Rebecca spends most of her time in here, but sometimes goes home for the weekend. Everyone seems to be managing without her.

The revolving door in and out of Coney Hill makes both these lives, half-lived. Rebecca is never committed to one or the other. Each carries its own set of rules; so juxtaposed that neither make any sense. Inside Coney Hill, she learns helplessness and passivity. She need only control her behaviour to a superior degree than the low-class loonies. Otherwise, anything goes – the more bizarre the better. This elevates one's status to one of high visibility, ensuring a consistent flow of attention from staff and patients alike. At home, Rebecca is expected to take sole responsibility for the cleaning, cooking and childcare.

Coney Hill is also a good place to come, if you'd rather avoid something. She's been going home for weekends for the last few weeks and is considered recovered, for the moment. Her Brother Clive's wedding takes place tomorrow. Rebecca doesn't like his fiancée, Megan. She believes Megan to be consumed with jealousy of her – sure that Megan is responsible for Clive rarely visiting her. Clive disapproves of the amount of medication

Rebecca takes, and can't see anything wrong with his youngest sister. He's such a handsome, well-dressed man and a policeman too. Rebecca is proud of him and often boasts about him to the other patients. Instead of going home, she's relapsed tonight, asking the Superintendent to notify her brother she's unable to attend his wedding tomorrow and requesting he visit her after the ceremony. She wouldn't want to appear in all the photographs in a maternity dress.

On Saturday morning, Rebecca puts on her dressing gown and best voice, as she approaches the ward attendant, her toilet bag in hand.

"Might I please go for a bath now?"

Mr Holliday sighs, putting down the pen. "Are you next in the queue, Rebecca?"

"Oh yes."

"Very well. Go and start running it."

"Thank you."

Rebecca cleans out the tub with a cloth from home and a small amount of her own Vim. She can't bring herself to get in until she's cleaned it to her standards – one never knew who else had lain in there and what diseases they might have. Satisfied, she rinses round several times and begins to fill the bath, adding the lavender bath foam. She lays out all her things along the side, toothbrush and pink tooth powder, shampoo, conditioner and moisturising cream. Realising she's forgotten something; she turns off the taps and goes back to the ward.

"I've just left my towel. I'll be going in now,"

"Alright Rebecca," Mr Holliday replies.

She returns to find fat Theresa entering the bathroom. Anger rises in her, at this violation.

"What d'you think you're doing?" she demands.

"I'm going for a bath. What's it to you, Lady Snooty?"

"That's my bath. Move aside please."

"Make me."

"I said move. Or you'll regret it." Their eyes lock. Theresa isn't quite as sure of herself as she says again: "Make me."

Rebecca slaps her hand hard, across Theresa's bloated cheek. The loud slap leaves a red mark and is drowned out by the resultant shrieking from Theresa, who runs away shouting at the top of her voice: "Rebecca's slapped me, she's just slapped me. Assault and battery! She's mental! Take her away! Put her on the shock list!"

Rebecca closes the door behind her. She is prepared for the lack of a lock on the door. She carries a plastic door wedge in her toilet bag, which she slides in under the gap, then leisurely removes her dressing gown and nightie. Mr Holliday knocks on the door.

"Yes?" she calls, imperiously.

"What happened Rebecca? Theresa says you slapped her."

"I certainly did not. She caused a confrontation trying to get into my bath and I asked her to leave. She's hysterical."

"I see. Well, we're taking her for sedation now and perhaps you can talk about this at group, this afternoon."

"If you think it'll help Theresa, by all means. She seems overwrought today. I may be busy with my visitors later though."

"Visitors?"

"Oh yes. My brother's getting married today and they'll be bringing me some wedding cake tonight. They could be here afternoon or evening visiting."

"I see. I'll leave you to your bath."

Rebecca smiles as she lies back in the steam. Those from good stock are far more plausible. She hopes Clive comes alone, but will ensure she's fully made-up with her hair immaculate, in case he brings Megan. She leaves the bathroom half an hour later to complete the process, which takes a full three hours. Her hair is set, as is her expression of bravery, as though she is vulnerable, yet stoic. She practices in the mirror and makes her way down to the day room where she waits, sipping a polystyrene cup of tea from the trolley. Afternoon visiting hours come and go. No-one arrives for her. There's a long queue for the payphone, so she asks if she can use telephone in reception. They refuse permission. They seem to know something she doesn't, as is often the case. At six o-clock she repeats the whole process. They placate Rebecca by explaining the difficulties in getting away from your wedding day. When this won't work, they eventually offer her another Pentothal. Resigned, she takes the pill and goes up to bed, hating Megan and envying the day she's had with *her* brother. She doesn't deserve him, of course – why, she's nothing more than a skivvy, from mining stock in the valleys. With her immaculate house and fresh flowers once a week, luring Clive away from his family. Trying to take over Rebecca's Mother too - always there with chocolates and creeping. Mother's too naive, of course, the silly thing. Even Dad seems to like Megan; but she knows how to get round men. She's the one who stopped Clive coming to visit tonight.

Chapter Thirty-One:

They're all crackers, of course. Take Rosemary, who looks far too big for her body and looms up in Rebecca's face in the day room with a wide, skewiff grin which emphasises quite a thick moustache. Why on earth hasn't someone encouraged her to pluck the hair out? So many of them seemed to make themselves look peculiar, as well as exhibiting bizarre behaviour.

"WHAT'S YOUR NAME?" Rosemary shouts. Rebecca starts, almost dropping her magazine.

"Rebecca," she replies.

"UGH!" exclaims Rosemary, grimacing and poking out a furred tongue. A nurse scuttles across the room and takes her by the arm.

"Don't mind Rosemary, Rebecca – she says that to everyone. Don't be rude, Rosemary."

"WHAT DID YOU HAVE FOR LUNCH?" Rosemary shouts at Rebecca again.

"The soup,"

"BORING! HAVE YOU GOT A BABY IN THERE?" She pokes Rebecca's bump.

"I am expecting, yes."

"HAVE YOU BEEN DOING SEX THEN?"

"Well, really..." Rebecca can see she isn't all there, but there's no excuse for ill manners.

The nurse leads Rosemary away with a firm grip on her arm. Turning to the drooling lady in the smock beside her, Rebecca says, "how rude!" Slack-lips looks around to see if anyone's listening and whispers to Rebecca, with no small degree of importance: "she's *authentic*. Nurse Chadwick told me. It's a learning distability."

Rebecca has no doubt the woman's genuine, but still.

After supper, Rebecca's getting anxious about her vulnerability in sleep. She imagines constructing an elaborate system of tying tins around the bed, to warn her of the proximity of another patient. Theresa will be back some time. It's always disconcerting if you wake in the dark, to find someone's returned. As the night shift takes over, the male attendant does the ward rounds.

"How is poor Theresa?" she asks, with an empathic expression.

"She's had her ECT and she'll be up later. Much calmer now. Try to rest."

"I will, thank you."

She's dirty, mind, fat Theresa. Foul inside and out. Every morning, she visits Rebecca after she's shitted in her knickers. The stench wafts with her, those big white pants in her hand – apple-catchers, Arthur calls them.

Theresa opens them up and shoves them close to Rebecca's face. Rebecca asks her many times to stop, but each time the attendants take her away. This is all an act, of course and a way of dirtying up those restraining her.

When Theresa is brought back in a wheelchair, her expression is vacant – the dilated pupils stare beyond. She gives no sense she's recovered from the shock yet, and seems placid enough. They put her to bed and she turns her back and begins to snore. Rebecca sleeps.

Next morning, Rebecca jolts awake to Theresa's screech:

"FIRE!"

She's no time to adjust to what is happening. Theresa's shit hits her full in the face – the stench is overpowering and it begins to slide down onto her nightclothes and the bed. Roaring like an animal, Rebecca struggles to her feet and punches Theresa with a left hook which sends her reeling over her bed, where she bangs her head on the radiator and lies prostrate, screeching with eerie laughter. The alarm bells began to clang and before long, both Rebecca and Theresa are surrounded by attendants – being dragged from the ward, as the other patients begin cheering, caterwauling and applauding in glee, as though they are watching a football match.

After cleaning Rebecca (roughly, she feels) they take her away to isolation. Theresa is taken for a Turkish. This treatment takes place in huge metal boxes, where only your head sticks out. Steam is pumped in until you're unbearably hot. They give you sips of water through a straw, as you sweat profusely and finally you're plunged into ice cold water.

The day passes slowly. Rebecca stares at the treetops through the high-barred window and wonders how long she'll wait. She rubs at her belly and notes with pleasure a limb sticking out and moving around. The tedium can only be relieved by dropping off to sleep, but she's buzzing with adrenaline at what she's let loose. Arthur will be visiting this evening and he'll stick up for her. If they don't understand, she'll jolly well go home. As a voluntary patient – they'd better remember she can leave any time she pleases. How dare they lock her in isolation for defending herself? When she meets the Superintendent she'll have some choice words for him.

Her left knuckles throb with the pain in her fist and she flexes them, smiling slightly. Grandfather would be proud of that one – his days in the ring were legendary. Outside, even more so, she'd heard the family lore and was shown his brass knuckledusters once. Filled with self-righteous indignation, Rebecca begins to count the minutes and hours in her head until at 5.00pm, the door opens.

"You'll need to come with us now, Rebecca," the attendant says.

"Good. Is it visiting time?"

"In an hour. First the Superintendent wants to see you."

"I want to see him, too."

"Your husband's here early."

"Oh?"

"Yes. The Superintendent telephoned him to request he attends the meeting."

"Good."

She stands and follows him down the long corridor to the service lift. The attendant is silent and the tension began to mount between floors, as Rebecca begins to rehearse her speech. She intends to lodge a formal complaint about why the staff had not anticipated Theresa's behaviour and her own conditions in isolation, with nothing to do or even read, for a whole day. He'll get a piece of her mind.

Dr Mendleson is a young man to be a Superintendent, at 32. He'd taken over the appointment last year, in the spring of 1956, and had already made many changes. Thanks to him, the wards were organised on an open door principle. He believes people thrive on trust. Consequently, he'd ordered the removal of the railings between the ward gardens, formerly known as the "airing courts." He courted controversy with the introduction of a mixed ward as an experiment. Under his charge, the numbers of patients being released increased and he cleared the entertainment hall of its beds, (a practice commonly used in asylums at times of over-crowding, of which he disapproved) instructing the Secretary to hold dances, concerts and even show films. Each night of the week offered a different activity. He intends to make his mark on the place and in the world of psychiatry. His ethos is to reward patients on the basis of their behaviour; a therapeutic atmosphere being conducive to recovery.

Superintendent Mendleson considers Rebecca's violence towards a fellow patient, who is more disturbed than her, a debacle. He's already told the husband, who listened with a grim expression, as though he was about to say something. As the attendant opens the door, Superintendent Mendleson motions for Rebecca to join them. He doesn't stand. She's pleased Arthur's early and kisses him on the cheek. He pats her hand and pulls the chair out for her. Superintendent Mendleson offers her a cigarette, which she accepts, before he leans across the table to light it for her. He sits back and lights his own, blowing the smoke towards her.

"We need to discuss what happened with Theresa today, Rebecca."

"Yes Dr Mendleson, I quite agree. I want to talk about several issues..."

"You'll have a chance to put your case in a moment. First, I must tell you from my point of view, I will not see my hospital turned into a boxing ring. Your behaviour is unacceptable. Particularly in your condition."

Rebecca is outraged. "Do you have any idea what that...woman did to me?"

"Theresa is very poorly, Rebecca. You've been a regular patient here for some time now and I would expect you to recognise that."

"She should be on a different ward, with her own kind. She's absolutely revolting."

"Her behaviour, Rebecca, may be distasteful but it is just that...behaviour. You don't know her case history as I do. I suggest you restrain yourself, from any further embarrassment. You're not a psychiatrist."

"Dr Mendleson, she's been thrusting her *faeces* in my face almost every day this week. I made numerous complaints, yet nothing has been done."

"You are a voluntary patient here, Rebecca, are you not?"

"I don't see what..."

"You submit yourself voluntarily for treatment at this facility with other patients. Some of them are not voluntary and Theresa is one of those. I might ask you to consider your position. You do not have a God-given right to special treatment and must learn to better tolerate those more unfortunate than yourself, if you are to remain."

"I beg your pardon?"

"I mean, Rebecca, if you wish to continue treatment here, you need to control yourself. Otherwise I shall be forced to consider your position."

"What are you saying?"

"If there is another occurrence of violent behaviour on your part, I will discharge you from my hospital and it will then be a police matter. Your illness is one where I believe you have the capacity to control your behaviour in the main, but suffer with anxiety and depression. You don't hit people when you're at home, do you?"

"Of course not." Rebecca is momentarily subdued, by the thought of being kicked out. Arthur is clenching his fists and his face is bright red, as he stands up. He leans across the table and points his finger at the doctor. Rebecca has never seen Arthur like this – how exciting, what will he do?

"I've had a gutsful of this. I'm taking Rebecca home now – she missed out last weekend. If she needs to come back at any time, AT ANY TIME, d'you hear me? She'll be back. YOU best remember that this is OUR hospital, not YOURS. I pay my taxes and you don't own it," Arthur shouts.

Superintendent Mendleson is taken aback.

"Mr Denby, I urge you to encourage your wife to control herself. Violence begets violence."

"Tell you what, Dr Mendleson. You sort old shitty-pants out and leave my wife to me."

He gets up and holds out his arm for Rebecca. She slips her arm through, her eyes shining with new-found admiration for Arthur. As they walk down the corridor to the entrance, the receptionist stops them.

"One moment, where are you going with this patient?" She looks concerned, yet slightly afraid.

"Rebecca Rose Denby is my wife. Check your records. She's come here voluntarily and she's leaving the same way."

The receptionist replies: "Would you wait one moment please, while I just check with Superintendent Mendleson?" she dials, frantic and continues a whispered conversation.

"Would you like Mrs Denby's clothes brought down, so she can change?" she asks, replacing the receiver.

"I'll collect them tomorrow. Good evening to you."

"Goodnight, Mr Denby."

The door swishes shut behind them and Rebecca emerges, almost skipping in her slippers, to the other real world.

Chapter Thirty-Two:

Coney Hill's getting more like a hotel every time she comes. Last year, the American psychiatrists were shown round by a proud Superintendent Mendleson, with their lovely accents, just like the Yanks during the war. They were so glamorous, compared to the Brits. Rebecca thinks of Doris enviously – no wonder the tramp loves America, spoilt for choice. But poor Mark...she'd have had him, given the chance. She wishes she was well enough to travel to America...maybe one day. Pentothal makes you believe you can do anything. She'll need a passport, mind. Later this afternoon, Rebecca has booked an appointment for the beauty parlour. She's going to have a French manicure – well, that's something to look forward to, especially as the dance is tonight.

Pity the men are atrocious dancers – not trained like Mr Brown or her father. Never seem to focus. Those were the days...not so much after she was a mother. Maybe Dr Mendleson will ask her to dance. She laughs at the thought – he's more respectful since Arthur's given him the rocket. He reckons she'll be well enough by Monday, to go home for an extended period – with regular reviews of course, but attending at the day centre after. Even Theresa shitty pants is behaving better, now she's developed a crush on Dr Mendleson. Silly bitch; simpering when he does his rounds.

The evening is cold and the ward rather draughty, as Rebecca dresses in her mauve maternity frock and clips on the pearl earrings. Theresa is attempting to launch herself into a scarlet tent and seems to be having trouble with the buttons.

"Rebecca," she hisses.

"Yes, Theresa?"

"Could you do up the top two? I can't reach!"

"What d'you say?"

"Please."

"Come here then." Rebecca strains the material enough to slip the covered buttons through the holes, avoiding any skin contact. Theresa is almost bursting out of the dress. Why would anyone let themselves get like that? "There," she says.

"How do I look?"

"Let's just say I don't think Marilyn Munroe will be losing any sleep!"

"Thank you," Theresa replies and beams. As Rebecca drapes the coney fur stole around her shoulders, she smiles at Theresa's stupidity and taps her heels down the corridor.

The entertainment hall is gay, decorated with the streamers and balloons. The five piece band plays a variety of jazz and after dinner, the dancing commences. There are many shufflers, of course, but most people are smiling and even those sitting down with vacant expressions will sometimes tap a foot or strum a rhythm on the tablecloths with one hand. To an outsider, the scene would likely be comical and Rebecca is pleased to consider herself one of them, now. The patients aren't allowed much alcohol, but a pleasant fruit punch is served in plastic cups, lumps of apple, cucumber and hard pear floating. It'll probably take at least a pint to have any effect. The men drink cloudy ale or cider – rationed at two pints each.

Theresa sits on the edge of the stage with her fruit punch, poking stubby fingers in to fish out the fruit pieces, chain-smoking and gazing dreamily at Dr Mendleson. He sits at the staff table wearing a paper hat. Theresa monitors his every move and gesture, glaring at any nurse brave enough to behave in a coquettish manner with him. The nurses seem oblivious of her presence. Rebecca supposes the patients are more like pets to many of them, than people. To be dealt with when they were naughty; patted or ignored when they behaved well. She determines to break with tradition and boldly approaches the table.

"Excuse me, Dr Mendleson?" she says.

"Yes Rebecca? Are you enjoying yourself?"

"I might enjoy myself a little more if you would join me for a dance?"

Dr Mendleson's eyebrows rise. "I'm not very good, I'm afraid..." he mutters, calculating how he can refuse without causing offence.

"Nonsense! I shan't mind. Come along, I can teach you!" she extends her hand.

He glances round at his secretary, who shrugs.

"Why not?" he says, smiling bravely and rising to his feet.

Dr Mendleson is rather good, breaking into a gentle waltz. He holds her at a respectful distance to allow for her bump. Rebecca senses her steps are a little rusty, but begins to enjoy herself. She's not danced in such a long time. She glances over his shoulder at Theresa, who is glowering at them both. Perhaps Rebecca is the only one to notice Theresa burning her own palm with the cigarette end and shudders at the spectacle. Utterly mad, but this might be enough for tonight. As the dance ends, she excuses herself and retreats to the far corner of the room. Her ribs are aching and she's conscious of the baby now. Theresa has disappeared. Rebecca is uneasy.

Eventually, the guests begin to drift away, as the band plays the national anthem. Only the staff and Rebecca remain for the whole thing and the kitchen ladies clear the tables, folding the tablecloths into the middle and gathering up all the dropped plastic cups.

Theresa's last into bed. She doesn't bother asking Rebecca to help her undo the scarlet dress. Instead, she pulls at it hard and the top three buttons ping to the floor. Muttering what sound like swear words under her breath in a monotone, she undresses and gets into her nightie, climbing into her bed. She turns her back on Rebecca to face the wall, she settles down and is quiet. Rebecca lies awake, waiting for Theresa's snores that never come.

In half an hour; all the alarms bells begin wailing.

"Keep calm, everyone!" shouts the male night attendant, distinctly flustered. He leaves the ward, keys jangling; only to return again in seconds.

"Alright, everybody, we're having a fire drill. You need to leave everything except your slippers and dressing gowns, put them on, please and form a line here – it's cold outside."

Maud Priday, ordinarily an unobtrusive mousey-hair thin woman, begins pulling at her hair and screeching, then singing:

"FIRE, FIRE, FIRE, Fire in the valleys fire down below, it's fetch a bucket of water boys, there's fire down below!"

The twenty patients on Rebecca's ward begin a cacophony of wailing, complaining and shouting – one begins driving her imaginary fire engine and making the NEENAW sound of a siren. It takes all the attendant's wits to get them down the stairs and out of the building, which is not assisted by his fumbling with the keys at every door. By the time the hospital is evacuated, the noise from the gardens outweighs the approaching fire engine. The only quiet two are Rebecca, who is frightened and Theresa, who walks a circle, in a shuffling motion, with her head down and won't look at anyone.

The fire engine arrives and when the firemen started unravelling the huge hoses, the patients cheer and jump about. The staff attempt to them back from trying to touch the firemen and generally obstructing them. Pinhead Sid, an inordinately tall patient with a tiny head and protruding ears, is so animated by the furore that he dances, with his knees held high. Rebecca stares at them, shocked in her realisation they're loonies, wondering how on earth she has ended up in this freak show. She can't be one of them. But the evidence shows otherwise. Theresa is silent, biting her nails down to the quick, the cigarette burns on her palm a deep, angry burgundy.

It takes four hours to put the fire out. The patients are crammed into other buildings and wards, including the chapel. Rebecca and Theresa find themselves shivering between the pews under blankets, with square prayer cushions for pillows. Rebecca closes her eyes and prays hard for this to be over.

The entertainments hall and adjoining staff restaurant are destroyed. They say the situation was exacerbated because of a lack of windows and the fire was burning away quietly inside for quite a time. The cause of the blaze is never discovered.

Rebecca goes home on Monday. She resolves to do her best never to return – she must think of the baby now.

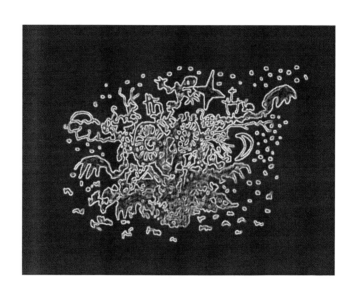

Chapter Thirty-Three:

Rebecca, eight months into her pregnancy, packs up the Victoria Sponge she's made in a tin and sets off on foot, to visit her parents. By the end of the road, the bad thoughts come back with a vengeance. The panic attack manifests with hyperventilation, palpitations, sweating and nausea. She speeds up her steps, her legs wobbling as she checks over her shoulder, convinced she's being followed. She reaches the corner where the large laurel bush overflows onto the path. Perhaps someone's hiding in it, waiting to ambush her. She stops and stares into its dark depth for a moment – as the waxy leaves move before her eyes, she turns and scurries back to her house, bolting the door behind her and sinking into a chair.

She'd wanted to hear all about their trip to America. Dad popped round after they returned last week, but he refused to gossip. Charlie and Faith Lindsay travelled from Southampton to New York on the Queen Elizabeth. Mother suffered terribly with seasickness for most of the journey both ways – but the return trip had been over exceptionally rough seas. Dad joked about being alone at mealtimes and showed what great sea legs he had, lifting up his trouser leg to show Rebecca the hair above his spats and laughing. The photographs being developed at Boots would be back by now, one of them at the Captain's table. An avid diarist, Charlie Lindsay wrote his sightseeing journal every day. He'd visited Boot Hill and various graves and landmarks, keeping a full account of his trip. He'd hinted that Doris was homesick and was having financial difficulties, but he'd "done what he could." Chucked more money at her, probably. Doris was so...materialistic. Faith was ambivalent about the visit. Rebecca resigns herself to wait for the details. She can't bring herself to leave the house today.

Over the next few weeks Rebecca's mood deteriorates and she hardly leaves the house. She believes she's losing her mind again, but can't afford to fall apart before the baby arrives. She won't give birth in Coney Hill, of this she is determined. She can't bear the thought of fat Teresa getting hold of her child. Her skin erupts in angry boils. A particularly painful one, throbs, high on her leg. One night she decides to pop it. She creeps down in the middle of the night, fetches a sewing needle, burns the end under a match to sterilize and begins puncturing the boil and squeezing out the contents.

Arthur pads down to the living room to enquire what on earth she's doing. Nothing surprises him anymore, so, weary, he makes her a cup of tea. She extracts quarter of a pint of pus, after which she's trembling and sweating. Four hours later, at 6.00am on 10 January 1959, she has the first contraction. She's already booked into hospital in Cheltenham for the birth, so Rebecca is assured that all the arrangements are in place and is uncharacteristically calm.

Arthur's arranged to go into Cheltenham to buy some electrical appliances for a woman he'd promised to assist. He knows Rebecca's in labour, but he never worries about her ability to cope. He says he won't be out long, but he also needs to pay calls in Gloucester this morning. True to his word, he returns home at lunchtime and after a cup of tea, asks if she'd like to come with him. The pains are manageable, so she and Robert accompany him in the car.

"I don't want to be too far from home, Arthur. Just in case."

"Don't you trouble; I promise I'll get you back in time."

"Alright."

"We'll drop in to your Mum and Dad's, shall we?"

"Don't tell her the baby's coming. You know how she gets."

"As you like."

When they arrive at the Lindsay's, Arthur goes straight through to the lounge and starts chatting with Rebecca's father. Rebecca's irritated to find her sister-in-law Megan in her mother's kitchen, sipping tea and eating a flapjack. Megan's getting her feet under the table – she's always here lately and making Mother laugh. Mother likes her so much. Rebecca is rather self-conscious about her bulk, but dismisses the thought. She was slim again soon after Robert – this time's sure to be the same.

Megan looks her up and down. "Hello Rebecca. You look ready to pop! I bet you can't wait."

"Hello Megan. Been here long?"

"Only an hour or so. Lots to catch up on with *Mum*."

Rebecca bristles, resenting Megan's use of the term. "Oh?"

"I must be getting along now. I'll leave Mum to fill you in. Toodleoo." Megan looks at Faith as though they share a conspiracy and leaves the house, banging the door behind her.

"What did she mean?" Rebecca turns to her Mother.

"We've had rather sad news. I'm afraid Doris and Mark have separated," Faith replies.

"What?"

"She telephoned to tell me. They're getting a divorce, apparently."

"Mark's left her?"

"Of course not. Doris left him and she's taken Greg with her. Didn't go into many details because it was long-distance – in fact we got cut off before she could answer my questions."

"That was inconvenient. How on earth is she going to manage?"

"She's been offered a job as a telephonist, it seems. And Dad gave her a little something to help out, while we were there. She won't have gone through all that already. A neighbour is going to take care of Greg during the day. I don't know all the arrangements yet. I'd be grateful if you kept it within the family please, Rebecca. You know how people *talk*."

"Yes, I shouldn't have thought you'd want this news getting out."

"Would you like some tea? I should imagine Arthur would like one. I expect he's been hard at work again?"

"He's had to pop to Cheltenham this morning."

Faith begins attending to Robert, who has plundered the cupboard where they keep his toys and is running a dinky car up and down his grandmother's shins. After half an hour's trivia about the neighbours, at the kitchen table, Rebecca begins to feel more uncomfortable and summons Arthur to take her home. He enters the kitchen with her father, who winks at her and kisses her cheek.

"Miss Rebecca, I've suggested Arthur takes the Zephyr, because of the four-wheel drive...it'll get you there safely on those icy roads if need be."

"Get her where?" her Mother says, sharp.

"Rebecca's booked into hospital tomorrow Faithy. Makes sense for Arthur to hold onto it for a day or two, baby's due any day now. I'll use his in the meantime."

"Are you sure, Charlie? Arthur's is smaller than you're used to...and you promised to take Cecily and Giles to church with us on Sunday." Faith makes no attempt to conceal her distaste, at the thought of borrowing Arthur's inferior car.

"We'll manage fine Faithy. I'll just run you through the controls, Arthur. Come along Robert, you must be a big boy now and help Granddad tuck Mummy into the car."

"Goodbye dear," Faith says, as Rebecca kissed her cold cheek. "Let us know, won't you?"

Arthur and Rebecca, holding Robert's hands, walk to the kerbside. Robert tries to make them swing him, but Arthur stops him. Charlie opens the door for Rebecca, taking the tartan rug from the boot and tucking her knees in.

"You'll telephone us?" he asks Arthur.

"Of course," Arthur replies.

As the car pulls away, Robert waves to his grandfather, kneeling on the back seat until he's out of sight. Halfway on the road home, large soft white feathers begin to fall. Robert is enthralled to see his first snowfall. They struggle to settle him down for his tea, with promises that he can build a snowman tomorrow, if the snow settles and entreaties to go to bed, like a good boy. He's only just settled down when at quarter to eight, Rebecca waters break and Arthur telephones her parents to collect Robert. Arthur begins driving Rebecca to Cheltenham slowly, although there is little traffic and the snow falls persistent and steady. The white blanket dampens sound.

By the time they reach the hospital, the contractions are strong, with only a minute or so between. Arthur's about to leave, when Rebecca realises:

"My handbag, Arthur. My tablets! In the car!"

She can't be anywhere without the tablets.

The staff fetch a wheelchair for Rebecca, send Arthur away and immediately began preparing her for the delivery room. After an agonising internal examination by a thick set midwife, Rebecca's pubic hair is shaved off and she's given an enema. Within five minutes, she rushes to the toilet and empties her bowels. Waves of stomach pain follow on top of the contractions. She's unable to stem the flow of faeces. When it finally stops, she's wheeled straight to the delivery room.

Rebecca can hear a great deal of rushing around. She's left alone for an hour while the staff attend an emergency case. A young girl's baby has died, the poor thing – Rebecca can hear her sobbing. A fat middle-aged midwife gives Rebecca a bell, with strict instructions to ring, if they're needed quickly. Rebecca feels the baby moving down and the urge to push, so she rings the bell. The fat midwife glares at her, as she washes her hands.

"Mrs Denby, you're not ready yet - it's far too soon. Stop making such a fuss!"

"Nurse, I am telling you, my baby's coming right now, I can feel it."

"And I am telling you, Mrs Denby that you have hours to go yet. Now just lie down, please."

"Nurse, it's coming – please, please check."

"Have it your way. Lie back, feet together, knees apart!"

Rebecca's right.

The birth's over in minutes. Rebecca's son is born at 9.30pm, less than two hours after arriving at the hospital. He weighs in at 7lbs 8oz and is the image of Arthur – a beautiful bonny baby. Rebecca decides he will be named Charles, after her Dad. This time, she doesn't attempt breast-feeding. She's been advised not to, because of the tablets. Charles is cleaned, weighed measured and seems very quiet, as they swaddle him and take him away to the nursery ward.

At eleven o'clock, Arthur rings the hospital from the social club where he's been out with his parents, to check on Rebecca's progress. He expresses surprise when told he has another son. He'll visit the next morning, when they'll tell him his son is jaundiced and not to worry his wife with it, Charlie's having treatment, so she can't see him just now.

Rebecca can't understand why the midwives aren't bringing Charlie back to her for his feed. All the other mothers have their babies brought to them for their bottle, every four hours, like clockwork. She keeps asking and they keep making excuses, telling her to wait. Rebecca keeps crying and asking if something's wrong with her baby, until they sedate her. It's five days before she sees him, with the explanation that he's been jaundiced and they needed to treat him without her becoming hysterical. Seven days pass before she's allowed to take him home.

#

Charlie's such an easy baby – drinking his bottles with vigour and thriving. Within two months, he's sleeping through the night. Robert isn't interested in him.

"He doesn't do much, does he?" he asks.

"You'll be able to play with him when he's a bit older," Rebecca laughs.

"He stinks."

"Robert, what a thing to say!"

#

When baby Charlie reaches six months old, he wins Gloucester's bonniest baby contest after a friend of Rebecca's sends his picture to the local paper; The Citizen. Nanny Denby declares she's nearly beside herself.

Chapter Thirty-Four:

The drugs seem to stabilise things for a while; until they fiddle with them. Rebecca has more support from her parents and Arthur's now, who often have both their grandchildren round, sleeping overnight. When she stays for a spell in Coney Hill, Rebecca's sons even go and stay with Megan and Clive, which Rebecca isn't keen on, but she can't very well dictate to Arthur about what he does with the children when she's in hospital – the man's head of the household, after all. Megan seems a little too perfect. Her house is always immaculate and she has fresh flowers delivered every week from a local florist. Everything in her life is well organised. Life's not fair.

The doctors change Rebecca's medication, experimenting with various combinations. Rebecca begins to find herself intermittently excitable and impulsive on occasions. She dresses in a flamboyant way, full make-up, high heeled shoes and matching handbags and gloves – even a hat, just to fetch groceries. One Friday when the boys are with their grandparents, she decides to go to town. She walks the five minutes to the bus stop on the main road, crossing to avoid the laurel bush on the corner. After checking the timetable, she realises she's missed the hourly bus by five minutes and perches on the narrow seat in the shelter to wait for the next one, instead of returning home. A variety of traffic passes, and men honk their horns; some wolf-whistle, or make lewd comments to Rebecca. Secretly, she enjoys this and smiles back, waving at two workmen, approaching in a white van. They slow to a standstill outside the bus shelter. The passenger winds down his window.

"Where you going, love?" he asks.

"Only into town. I missed the last bus."

"We're going your way. Can we give you a lift?"

"Are you sure you've got room?"

"We'll always make room for a beauty like you love. Hop in and we'll drop you off."

"You don't mind?"

"Not at all. Here, give me your arm and I'll help you up." He opens the door to the cab and jumps onto the pavement.

"Thank you," she replies. As she climbs into the van, he gives her bottom a squeeze. She turns and frowns, climbing into the centre seat. This frightens her a little, but she doesn't say anything. He jumps in beside, shuffling Rebecca into the middle, between him and the driver, who eyes her lasciviously and revs up the engine, pulling away from the kerb with a screech. He reaches the roundabout and careers round it without pulling into the right lane. Rebecca is dizzy.

"Where d'you live, darling?" he says, grinning.

"In Leckhampton – just back there."

"What's your name?"

"Rebecca."

"Pleased to meet you Rebecca. This here is Dan, driver Dan, we call him, and I'm Phil."

"Nice to meet you."

"No boyfriend today then? Where is he, at work?"

"I'm married."

"Well that is a crying shame, ain't it Dan?" he looks over her head to his colleague.

"A great shame, Phil," Dan replied. "We was going to ask you up to Cranham with us!"

"Cranham? But that's the opposite way from town. I thought you were going to town?" she replies, becoming anxious.

"Your old man ever taken you up Cranham, Rebecca?"

"We've been for a walk there, yes."

"D'you know that little layby?"

"No?"

"That's a little place where sweethearts can go, for a bit of a kiss and cuddle."

"No, I don't know it."

"Fancy coming up Cranham with me and Phil, for a bit of a kiss and cuddle? If you was my wife I wouldn't let you out alone!"

"Oh no, thank you. I must get to town. I've the shopping to do."

"Now that's not very friendly, is it? After we're offering to give you a lift to town and everything."

"Please, you won't take me up there, will you?"

"Aw, go on Rebecca – you know you want to, all dressed up lovely with only the groceries for company!"

"Would you stop the van please? I want to get out."

Dan, the driver, starts laughing.

"Now don't you worry, Rebecca, we're only playing with you. No need for all that. We'll take you into town straight away, if that's what you want."

"Yes, please. Thank you."

"My pleasure. Where shall we drop you?"

"By Boots would be lovely."

Her heart beats fast and her palms begin to sweat. Thankfully, they're heading into town, but she begins to realise the danger she might've been in. She mustn't get into cars with strangers again. She decides against telling Arthur. They drop her off, Phil kissing her hand with a mock bow and watching her trotting away quickly on her high heels, shaking his head and smiling before he jumps back into the van and they drive off. She's ashamed, as though she's invited this. She's obviously a bad person, deep down, for these things to happen to her.

#

Rebecca and Arthur start going out again to social occasions, the old-time music hall at the theatre, the cinema and sometimes even to dances – mainly with Rebecca's parents. Arthur would never dance, he couldn't or wouldn't, she doesn't know which. She partners other people and her father encourages her to drink brandy and Champagne with him while Arthur and her Mother's backs are turned. Arthur has stopped drinking altogether now. Sometimes he carries his wife up to bed, helping her to undress; she gets so drunk. She wonders if he ever feels resentful. She knows other people think she's a pretty woman, because they often tell her so, but somehow she doesn't quite trust their words. Her marriage is strained now. Arthur seems to stop her enjoying herself and starts being possessive, ordering her around and taking her home early – even refusing to take her out altogether. Finally, Arthur stops Rebecca going out without him. They row; but he's adamant, warning her of the dangers of her behaviour with her mental illness, she might get into any amount of trouble. He says he's only protecting her from herself – she's naive, too trusting, she doesn't realise what other people are like. They'll take liberties.

This is an up and down kind of year.

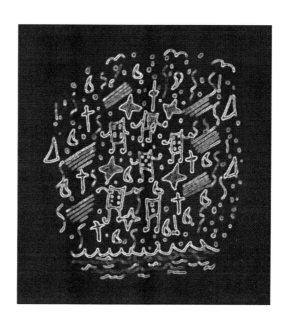

Chapter Thirty-Five:

1960 arrives and Arthur's craving independence, tired of making money for other people and having to ask for time off. He's a qualified electrical engineer with ambitions to become the boss and start his own business. They don't have much cash to get him started. They call Arthur's new business E.M.U. (Electric Motor Unit) and initially he's doing well in securing contracts. He's a good reputation for being reliable and trustworthy and the jobs flow in steadily. Many companies will sub-contract to him, pleased not to fund someone full-time. He undertakes various house wiring contracts and quarry work, factory for metal form, assisting with the workshop for Scallons; where his father-in-law works and also washing plant at Cerney. The wholesalers give him a month's credit, which keeps him going, until he can get his clients to stump up.

By 1961, Arthur's taken on several big contracts and is hoping the buggers'll pay up promptly. He struggles with chasing people for money - finds this a bit uncomfortable and embarrassing. The late payers make life stressful. Then the letter arrives from the wholesalers. Seems one of their staff has been embezzling funds, so they've no choice but to call in all monies due, by the end of the month. Since Arthur's business is running on a shoestring, he goes back to visit his clients owing money, in person. Quite a few are not at home, so he writes letters, by hand. He receives a distressing letter from a client owing one of the largest amounts, who says he's gone bankrupt and is in severe anguish, threatening to commit suicide if Arthur pushes him any further for the money. Both Rebecca and Arthur feel the weight of responsibility, given their own experiences of depression, so they decide not to push the matter.

They can't afford to write off such a large sum. The letters and demands become increasingly threatening. Arthur hides most of them from Rebecca, until the summons is served early one morning, after breakfast. He plonks down at the kitchen table.

"What's wrong, Arthur?" Rebecca asks, unnerved at his pallor.

"The jig is up, I'm afraid, love," he mutters, rubbing his forehead and looking at her.

"Who was the man?"

"He was from the County Court. The wholesalers filed for bankruptcy. They're making me bankrupt Rebecca. I'll be in the papers. We're finished."

"Oh Lord…couldn't you go to Dad? You know he'd help!"

"Too late. I can't expect him to pay out this amount. There's nothing else for it, Rebecca. We've got to sell the house."

"But where are we going to live?"

161

"I can't answer that, yet. I'll sort something out. We've always got Mum and Dad's, at Sandbanks. Only until we work things out. The boys can bunk in with us."

"I can't go back there, Arthur. Not with the boys. Let me speak to Dad."

"I've let you all down. He'll have a field day about this one."

"Dad's not like that…he'll understand. Don't forget he helped Clive, you know with Megan overspending, her debts to the florist. We'll pay him back, over time."

"Christ, Rebecca, you don't understand. I'm not crawling to him for money, not now, not ever. We'll sell the house and the furniture and clear what we can. We'll start again."

"At least let me speak to him to see if he suggests somewhere to live. Arthur, we've the boys to think of. I won't go back to Sandbanks, and that's flat."

"Ask him then. Don't dictate to me what you won't do – we might not have any choice. I presume you don't propose to leave me over this?"

"How could you even suggest breaking up? We've made vows, for better or worse, for richer or poorer. I mean to stick by those. You stuck by me, didn't you, in sickness and in health?"

"You're a good girl. Perhaps I don't deserve you."

"I'll go and talk to him now. You'll be alright with the boys?"

"Fine. You go." He lights a cigarette and walks out to the back garden, where Robert and Charlie are swinging on the washing line. He doesn't tell them off, but stands, smoking and watching.

Rebecca puts on her hat and coat and runs all the way.

#

Arthur is made bankrupt. Morelands is sold. Rebecca supports Arthur and tries to help, although she keens over her limitations. He's devastated – as they are shunned by neighbours and friends alike. Bankruptcy indicates that someone isn't trustworthy – they're considered irresponsible and feckless. Rebecca is acutely aware of the talk about her. One of her friends suggests she should leave Arthur, but at this time she appears to come into her own. This isn't her fault. He's made a mistake for once and she's determined to stand by him.

The bankruptcy is ignored by Arthur's parents; they never discuss the situation and pretend nothing's happened. They don't offer to help out financially, but often knit or purchase clothes for their grandsons.

Charlie Lindsay purchases two caravans for Rebecca, Arthur and their two sons Robert and Charlie and sites them in Blossom Orchard. One caravan is for sleeping; the other for living, with a lounge and kitchen. Within weeks, Arthur gains new employment for a specialist dry cleaning company,

Alphonse Reyer, initially as a Van Driver and then goes on to maintaining the boiler systems. Now, he's driving long distance and the money's reasonable, so he's able to keep the family, as well as paying his father in law some modest rental. The boys adapt and behave well, on the whole, and Rebecca quite likes caravans. They live here for two years, saving hard from Arthur's new job. She takes the tablets and stays out of hospital, coping well with Arthur's absence on long road trips in the safety of being close to her parents. In 1963, Charlie suggests they buy a place next door to one another. Arthur will not be able to borrow money for a mortgage until the three years of the bankruptcy is discharged – Charlie will provide the deposits. They look at a pair of cottages in rural Bussage, near Stroud. A hilltop location, peaceful. The sale is almost complete when Faith speaks to a local in the grocery shop, who tells her they were cut off in the snow last winter. She refuses to move. Charlie decides to buy a large house that will accommodate them all at Stroud Road in Gloucester. He buys Rebecca a rent book and she contributes each week. Her parents are always at hand to help with the children – the housework is shared. Rebecca loves this spacious house and feels safe.

In 1964, Arthur is appointed Under-Manager at Alphonse Reyer. Arthur wants to escape his in-laws – he finds a property he thinks they can afford to buy at Ashbridge Road, in Gloucester. He takes an unenthusiastic Rebecca to look.

"I hate it," she says.

He spends forty eight hours persuading her to ask her father for the deposit. She gives in. Charlie provides the deposit; on the condition the house is put in his daughter's name – he won't have her lose another one. They move in. Rebecca spirals down again and begins to have more courses of ECT treatments. They're not so painful now, as they give her an anaesthetic and muscle relaxants before starting. On one occasion where she begins to come round, she listens to the urgent voices of the doctors and nurses.

"Thank God, she's coming round," one says, as Rebecca opens her eyes. She never gets to the bottom of this incident, but often wonders whether they'd overdosed her and shocked her too much. Maybe they experimented with people, like guinea pigs, varying those dosages. Coming round is always disturbing for the first few hours, not remembering your name or what day it is. All this moving house is very unsettling. Rebecca wishes they could settle somewhere so she can be safe. Charlie sells the large house and moves to the same road.

As for Arthur, he does as he pleases, most of the time. He's working long hours again. When he's supposed to be at home, he'll take himself off fishing. He'll mess up the house with boat or engine parts – he's constantly collecting things to fix for other people, or messing about with another invention. Trying to get meals around all this and take care of the boys is hard – they fight a lot, these days. Robert likes to tease Charlie, who can be volatile. Last week, they were digging in the garden with their toy spades. Robert, as the eldest, had the superior metal spade and Charlie was struggling away with his plastic one. Rebecca hadn't heard any preamble, until Robert came in screaming his head off, blood pouring down his face from a big gash on his forehead. Charlie had taken his older brother's metal spade off him and dug it into Robert's head. Such an angry boy, at times.

Still, soon there'll be another baby to love. Rebecca hasn't told anyone yet, though she's about three months pregnant and is hoping for a girl this time – one she can dress up and pet. Before long, they'll be advising her against the pregnancy and telling her off. The baby wasn't planned, of course, but neither was it unwelcome. Best to keep quiet as long as possible or they might try and take some of the pills away and she can't manage that. She cancels having any more ECT treatments though, they'd be sure to kill the baby and she pretends she's managing alright. By the time she's five months pregnant and it's too late for them to suggest weaning off the drugs, she visits the doctor and tells him.

He remonstrates with her about the damage already done and books her in for an x-ray a few weeks later. The baby's dead inside you, they tell her. She'll need to be induced to push it out. Having gone through the pain of labour with no result, they don't let Rebecca see the baby, just whisk away the body and give her an injection, which sedates her, for hours. When they can't stop her crying, they give her a referral letter. Back to Coney Hill. She stays a fortnight and returns home, empty. Six months later, she miscarries again at two months. Can't even carry a baby safely any more. God is very angry with her. This is her punishment. Eighteen more months of the double life ensue, between asylums and home.

Chapter Thirty-Six:

Young Charlie Denby watches the clock behind the geography teacher's back. He has little interest in precipitation and hopes it will not happen next week. He packs no clothes in his head; but his fishing rod; feather quill floats and weights and the tin of maggots Grampy has supplied. Earlier on he has played a good trick with them, asking his friends for a crisp at play time and when the pack was offered; he took one crisp and dropped several maggots into the bottom. When his friends came to fold the packet and tip out the last crumbs into their mouths, he watched their shock as they chewed on the wriggling bodies and spat, swearing and running after him. Charlie's a fast runner, even when he's laughing.

When the bell rings; he runs all the way home. Outside, his father is packing up the camper van from the side door. He's whistling. His mother is in the kitchen among an array of Tupperware. In a quality street tin squats a simnel cake and she has arranged marzipan balls in a perfect circle around the edge. She takes a tablet from her apron pocket and downs it with the dregs of her tea. Charlie knows this is not a good sign; so he offers to help her by carrying out the packages to the van. She seems distracted and slams the lid onto the cake tin.

"You'd better get changed," she says "and wash your face. I'm not taking you out looking like a navvy." He runs up the stairs and rubs a flannel round his face, before scrambling into the clothes laid out on his bed. As he grabs his fishing rod; he notices the dirty school clothes he left on the floor. He can give her no excuses this time; so he bundles them up and puts them in the laundry basket on the landing, taking care to tuck the leg of his shorts in so the lid shuts neatly. Robert arrives from school and takes his time getting ready – he knows it winds Charlie up. His mother makes up the flask of hot tea. The last thing to be packed is the wicker basket lined with gingham, salt and pepper pot and plates held in by crisscrossed leather straps. His father takes it from her. He follows Robert outside and up the steps and waits in the van, tapping his toe. Finally his father comes out, pushing his mother gently in front. She will go back to check the cooker is off two more times before he can lock the door. His father opens the front door for her, settles her into her seat and slides the side door shut on Robert and Charlie. They are off.

Robert pinches his leg and twists the flesh, but Charlie knows better than to cry out. His father lights two cigarettes and hands one to Rebecca. It is a relatively short trip at twenty five miles; but still Robert will ask, as he always does, to stop for a pee halfway. Charlie watches his mother. Her eyes flit this way and that; and she grasps the door handle until her knuckles turn white. As they pull into the layby; Robert jumps out.

"Do you want the toilet, Charlie?" she asks.

"No thank you."

"I think you'd better try. We're only halfway."

"Okay, okay." He jumps out and runs into a gap in the bushes. He wills himself to go; and a slow trickle begins, just as Robert creeps up on him from the side. Robert aims the direction of his flow onto Charlie's shoes, then shakes and tucks himself back in, laughing.

"Fuck off Robert! You dirty bastard!"

"Now then, Charlie, I'm not the one who's pissed on my shoes. You want to aim better, you're a big boy now!" He glances full at Charlie's penis. "Although, maybe not,"

Charlie does up his trousers and chases Robert, bending down and piling into Robert's stomach with his head.

"Ah, ah Mum, look, Charlie's gone funny again!"

Charlie glares at his brother and walks away. He can't afford a scene. He's the only one who cares about all this. The gravel lakes at Ashton Keynes brim with perch, roach and bream. Charlie has maggots and worms for bait. Just as soon as the tent's up, he plans to leave them all and set up his rod, eat his bag of barley sugar and start hauling them out. As they pull into the campsite; he can see his mother's eyes darting around to see who else is there. The smell of fried onions rises from someone's camp stove. His father picks a good spot, very close to the lakeside. The dark water ripples invitingly. In the middle is the brambly island; just like Swallows and Amazons. He will swim out to it and look for eggs. There will be a whole week in paradise. He helps his father take out the canvas; thread the poles through and starts knocking in the tent pegs with a mallet. Charlie is allowed to light the gas stove so they can boil the kettle. The smell of gas and sulphur from the matches brings up all the joy of camping for him. She hasn't stepped out of the van yet, so he makes her a cup of tea and knocks on the window, smiling. She stares at him and shakes her head; so he walks round to the driver's door and offers it to her.

"Shut the door!" she says. He closes it again and sets the tin mug down on the grass. Leave her alone. Give her some time to adjust. Robert's run off with another lad and has commandeered his pushbike, riding round with no hands.

"Can I go fishing now Dad?" he says.

"Let me just sort your Mother out," his father replies.

He watches his father try her door, but she holds fast to the handle. He goes to the driver's side. As he opens it, he hears her.

"I don't think I can do it, Arthur."

"Now then, you'll be absolutely fine. You just sit in here for a while and drink your tea. Look, Charlie's made you a lovely cup here."

"No, no. I shan't be able to do it. You'll have to take me back."

"Now we've only just arrived. Have you had your tablet?"

"It won't make any difference."

"Well just take another one. It doesn't matter for today. I'll get your bed set up in the back and you don't have to do anything. I'll see to the picnic."

Charlie's stomach begins to hurt as though he needs the toilet. He must try and help. He peers around his father's legs.

"Mum, I'm just going to set up my rod and catch you a really big bream. Alright? The biggest one ever."

"Don't let him keep on at me, Arthur. I just can't stay. It's too much. I'm not well."

"Charlie, run along now sunshine. I'll deal with this. You go and set up your rod. Don't go too far away so you can hear me if I call you."

He runs to the edge of the lake and watches from behind a tree. Their voices raise. She's crying now and rocking back and forwards in the seat. He hates her so much. She's going to spoil everything again and he tried so hard. He pummels the bark with the sides of his fists and sinks to his knees on the grass, banging the back of his head against the tree. Fucking selfish bitch. She's done it on purpose. Let them get all the way here and set up. Warm tears of rage streak down his cheeks and he kicks the fishing rod, still in the bag. His father slams the driver's door and begins to pack everything away, finally shouting:

"Robert! Charlie! Back here now, please!"

He decides on one last try. Crying, he takes her hand.

"Please, Mum, please stay. You'll be safe. I'll take care of you!"

She looks at him; unmoved. He sees it is pointless. "I hate you!" he shouts. At this, she looks afraid – her eyes gazing above his head to her husband's.

He cuffs his son round the head, not hard. "That's enough. You'll not speak to your mother like that. She's ill. Now get in the van. We'll do it another time."

Even Robert is quiet on the way home. Charlie kicks the underside of her seat all the way. She doesn't stop him. She never says a word when she discovers he has tipped the maggots into the cake tin.

Chapter Thirty-Seven:

By 1967, Rebecca's physical health at age 33 is good and she's considered fit and healthy, by her doctors. Despite this, her mental illness is still a matter of grave concern to them. After all their interventions, including limited attempts at psychotherapy, insulin coma treatment, by now some 40 ECT treatments; barbiturates, anti-depressants, lithium carbonate and numerous other tablets, her overall feelings of anxiety and panic attacks, depression and obsessions are with her, more often than not. Even her stays as an inpatient at Coney Hill do little to relieve her symptoms, in the longer term. Rebecca is, by now, agoraphobic and refuses to go anywhere without Arthur – in fact she finds leaving the house at all, a complete chore, most of the time. She's a compliant patient, seeming to try everything they suggest with enthusiasm, but nothing works for her. They still don't consider her a hopeless case, but she doesn't seem to fit the profile of many other patients, with a supportive familial background. Rebecca hasn't neglected her children in the manner they've witnessed in some cases. Rebecca's something of a treatment-resistant mystery, which is becoming frustrating to solve.

After a consultation between several senior staff, they decide a longer-term referral to the York Clinic at Guy's Hospital in London for a period of nine months might work. Here, they can try all the latest therapies. Her family can visit if they wish and she may return home for one weekend a month (health permitting). Rebecca is enthusiastic at the prospect. These London experts might be able to cure her. They begin with intensive psychoanalysis, including hypnosis and questioning under Sodium Amytal. They suggest several times to her, perhaps she has suffered childhood sexual abuse and has repressed her memories. Rebecca remains adamant she hasn't. Nothing of the kind is revealed by the various therapies, one of which is a notorious "truth" drug, used for interrogation in less salubrious facilities.

Dr Stafford Clarke is Rebecca's consultant at Guy's Hospital, overseeing most of her treatments. He's a flamboyant character, appearing on television several times, which caused some controversy within the hospital establishment. Towards the end of her stay, he attends a group meeting and indicates to Rebecca the consultants feel they have exhausted all possible options – she remains: "treatment refractory". One of the psychiatrists contributes, in rather a frustrated tone, "We've nothing else for you. You'll just have to have a leucotomy." Rebecca is aware this is a kind of brain operation and panics – she remembers seeing patients in St Andrews and at Coney Hill, wandering round like vegetables. They dribble and soil themselves. The consultants are quick to reassure her.

"Those were old fashioned full frontal operations. These days, we've developed stereotaxic equipment to hold the head in place – like a frame. We give you a proper anaesthetic and you won't know anything about it. This is a ground-breaking, modified operation, a bimedial leucotomy. We remove the smallest bits of brain which cause all the anxiety and depression. Recovery times are good. We estimate around half of our patients experience a much better life afterwards."

"Isn't it terribly dangerous?"

"All surgery is risky, of course. But we have excellent rehabilitation facilities here and you'll recuperate with us for at least six weeks. Afterwards, you can return home and lead a normal life. Now doesn't that sound good?"

"It would be wonderful. But...I don't know – I'd have to discuss this with my husband."

"In any case, you'll have to be interviewed, by a panel of specialists. We won't offer you the operation without a proper assessment. If you pass, we'll discharge you for a few weeks to discuss the matter with your family. No need to make any hasty decisions. I'll put your name forward for the board, shall I?"

"If you think that's the best thing, Doctor."

"Good. I'll see you presently, Rebecca."

A week later, Dr Niall, who is in charge of Rebecca's ward, warns her she'll be asked some rather personal questions, to assess if she's suitable for the operation. She shouldn't take offence, he says – they're asking for very good reasons. Simply answer them truthfully. The Board, consisting of eight doctors, sit imperiously behind two long, covered tables, with jugs of water and glasses, clipboards and pens. They indicate she should take a seat in the middle of the room, about five feet away from the desk. Several begin asking questions; as the others make notes and observe her reactions.

"When did you first become ill, Rebecca?"

"I was twenty one. But the fears started earlier."

"Can you estimate your age?"

"I was fifteen, I think."

"But you managed for some years?"

"Yes, until just after I had Robert. He's my eldest son."

"I see from your notes you were originally diagnosed with schizophrenia?"

"Yes. But then they decided it wasn't schizophrenia. I had obsessions, deep depression and anxiety. Now I've got agoraphobia too."

"Schizophrenia was ruled out. You don't hear voices then, or imagine you're someone else?"

"No, I have bad thoughts."

"You're married, aren't you?"

"Yes."

"Get along well, do you?"

"We love each other very much. All couples have a few ups and downs, of course, but we still love each other very much."

"What about sex?"

"I beg your pardon?"

"Do you have regular sex with your husband?"

"I don't see that that's any of your business."

"Do you have a problem with sex, then?"

"Of course not."

"Have it regularly, do you?"

"As regularly as anyone expects to."

"How often d'you suppose that is?"

"That rather depends. What has this got to do with my illness?"

"D'you like sex, Rebecca?"

"I don't want to answer you."

"D'you think you like it more than other women do?"

"I've no idea. Why don't you ask them?"

"Have you got a problem with discussing sex, Rebecca?"

"I have a problem discussing it with strangers."

"What sort of sex d'you like, Rebecca? A bit of the missionary, or something more exotic?"

"How dare you ask me that?" she shouts.

At this, the doctors glance at one another. One smirks and nods.

"You can go now, Rebecca. We'll let you know the outcome tomorrow."

She stands and walks away, in as dignified a manner as she can manage, with her head held high. They sounded like perverts, what disgusting questions they asked. Wait until she told Arthur. He wouldn't be happy.

The following day, Dr Niall visits her on his rounds. When she complains about the questioning, he laughs and pats her arm.

"I did warn you, Rebecca. You mustn't take everything so personally. They have to ask, you see. Some people become a little, well, promiscuous after the operation – but generally only if they had a tendency towards immorality beforehand. It releases your inhibitions, you see. So if you had been a bit of a lush, why, you might even become a prostitute."

"Well, I found it highly offensive. I hope none of them would be doing the operation, if I agree to it."

"They're just here for assessment. Anyway, would you like to hear how you performed?"

"Yes."

"Well, they concluded that you passed their tests with flying colours. You're an ideal candidate for the operation and they are prepared to offer it to you in a fortnight's time. Your husband's picking you up this evening, isn't he?"

"Yes. I don't know about this surgery, Dr Niall. It seems…drastic."

"Of course. I'll ask Dr Svante to speak with your husband. Arthur isn't it?"

"Yes."

"Well, he will explain everything to Arthur in technical terms about the operation, before we bring him up to the ward to collect you. Then you can both go home for a rest and talk things over."

"Dr Niall, level with me please."

"Of course, Rebecca. What would you like to ask?"

"This operation is rather dangerous, isn't it?"

"It's certainly risky. There is a fifty-fifty chance of a good recovery. Patients might die, perhaps those not as young and healthy as you, but all surgery is risky; general anaesthetics have been known to kill people. The thing is, you've had plenty of anaesthetics, haven't you? And never reacted badly."

"Yes, for the ECT."

"There have been a relatively few cases where people have ended up in a vegetative state – but really that was more to do with the old operations. Technology has advanced so far; we can really be far more accurate these days and the amount of tissue removed is much smaller than it was. A few other unfortunate cases were that someone ended up needing to use a wheelchair, but again, they were considerably older than you."

"And on the other hand, if it worked – I could be a proper wife and mother? That's all I've ever really wanted. I don't want to be like this anymore."

"If this is successful, you could lead a pretty normal life. More than you've experienced, anyway. You've been ill for many years now, Rebecca. But we'll leave it up to you. There's plenty to consider, I appreciate that."

Rebecca's left alone and begins wondering however in the world she has come to this. She takes two Valium and waits until she's numb, then wanders down to the day room. Every sound seems muffled. On reaching the payphone, she rolls and lines up the coins on the top of the box and dials Arthur in a mechanic trance. As he answers, the pips start and the coins sliding down the eternal chute rattles like the Liberty Bell slot machine. The gamble is on. When he answers, she can only say his name before she burst into tears. He can't believe his wife's news and doesn't say much. She knows only a fool or a martyr would undertake this mission. She's no fool.

Chapter Thirty-Eight:

Rebecca doesn't say too much to her family, but Arthur briefs them that she is considering undergoing brain surgery. They are appalled, according to Arthur, who won't elaborate on their comments – this is to be entirely her decision and he will support her. She stops eating and can't sleep properly. She keeps weighing up the words and adding to them; she risks ending up blind, paralysed in a wheelchair, or a zombie. This would be worse than dying. If she goes ahead with the operation, she could be the perfect wife and mother, which is all she's ever craved for – being able to settle with her lot with good grace and fortitude, not always craving for some elusive other life.

After several days in distress, Arthur rings Rebecca's doctor and tells him the terrible state she's in – the dilemma is making her ill and she needs help, for her crying and panics. The GP visits her at home and eventually administers an injection, which sedates her for twelve hours, although Arthur notices she's still restless and murmuring in her sleep, tossing and turning. The GP prescribes a stronger tranquilizer for when she comes round, in the day. Arthur is sickened by the thought of the operation, but is curious whether surgery might work for her. They've tried everything else. This mental illness business is far beyond his understanding – he can't understand how things have escalated this far. He knows Rebecca's highly strung and gets herself very low from time to time, but they manage alright, on the whole. This is so drastic; like a step too far – but what can he say? This has to be her decision, he's damned sure it won't be his, he doesn't want the responsibility. He's happy with the way she is and doesn't mind looking after her, although she's bloody difficult at times. It's so frustrating; their life is pleasurable, on balance. She just needs to pull herself together and stop worrying so much. Course, her mother hasn't helped Rebecca, she's a worrywart and her Dad spoiled her to compensate. The last thing Arthur needs is an invalid for a wife, or to be a widower with two boys at his age.

He supposes he has no choice but to trust those psychiatrists – they're the experts. A modified leucotomy, they'd said. Not like the old ones – should get her right as rain if the operation's successful.

It would be a relief if he could leave her alone sometimes, without her getting in a state. This last year, she's taken to coming to work with him; sitting in the car all day and waiting for him to finish. Which can't be good for her.

#

At the beginning of June 1967; the sun pours through the kitchen window. Arthur asks Rebecca if she's up to a walk in the countryside for the afternoon, at Wainlodes, a local beauty spot by the River Severn. To his surprise, she agrees. They've walked for half an hour or so, when she stops.

"I'll have the operation."

"You will? You've thought it through – just remember what they said. If it goes wrong, you could die. Or you could be handicapped. You have considered it properly?"

"I've decided."

"Alright. If that's what you want, we'll tell them."

She's adamant and never changes her mind again. The following day, Arthur phones the Maudsley to speak to the consultant.

"Rebecca's decided to go ahead with this operation."

"Very good. She's an ideal candidate. Is there anything you need to ask?"

"Do you really think there's no alternative?"

"I must be honest with you, Mr. Denby – your wife has proved resistant to all the other treatments. She responded to ECT for a time, but you've seen the relapses."

"I've seen some other people who've had it, in the asylum mind – they didn't look all there, to me."

"Mr. Denby; some of the older operations were very primitive. This was really in the experimental stages back then. Now, the operation I'm offering Rebecca is a bimedial leucotomy operation. We take far less away, we have a frame to target precisely the right areas and a good success rate."

"I see. You're the professionals."

"Indeed. I wouldn't be offering this if it wasn't the last resort. I don't see Rebecca improving any other way now. She's still a young woman."

"Alright. If you can book her in then, I'll let her know."

"We'll send a letter."

The hardest and most terrible task Rebecca experiences is saying goodbye to her sons, knowing this may be the last time she sees them. Robert is now thirteen and Charlie, eight. They don't understand why she's going for brain surgery – she seems pretty normal to them, although they've been told the basics. They rely on Mrs P, the housekeeper, whenever their mother's in hospital, or their Grandparents, Uncle and Aunt. Mrs P's rather like one of the family now. Rebecca visits her mother and father the night before the operation, knowing it might be the last time she ever sees them. Her father is very gruff, but hugs her a long while before she leaves. She feels him smell her hair before he squeezes her. As she is about to go out of the door, her mother says, in a forlorn tone:

"You know you don't *have* to have this operation, don't you?"

Rebecca rounds on her mother.

"What d'you mean? There's no other choice now!"

"I'm just saying. You could still change your mind!"

"This is just like you! You've said nothing at all and I'm about to go in! How could you try and make it any worse than it is? I haven't taken this decision lightly!"

"We'll be on our way now," Arthur says, firmly, ushering Rebecca out of the door. "Goodnight, Faith."

Rebecca cries all the way home. She never said goodbye to her mother.

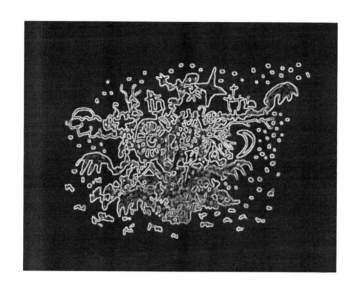

Chapter Thirty-Nine:

Both Arthur and Rebecca try to keep optimistic the operation will do the trick. Eventually they get on the road to London. They don't speak much on the way. Arthur can't stay long at Maudsley Hospital, because of his work commitments – he's already used up all his leave, taking days off when Rebecca couldn't cope. He kisses her goodbye and returns to the car, lighting a cigarette before he sets off.

Arthur visits her the following evening. He's horrified at her appearance; as the bandages have been removed. What's left of her hair is matted in blood. The colour drains from his face when he sees her – yet he's puzzling to understand what change there will be, because she seems to have come through as herself. She recognises him, at least.

Two hours after he leaves, Rebecca becomes aware of a metallic taste in her mouth, as though she is sucking a dirty sixpence. It's called an Aura. A minute later, her body becomes stiff and her arms and legs begin to twitch. Five more minutes pass, before the Nurse comes to check her blood pressure and finds her drooling, twitching and soaked through with urine. She calls for help and five auxiliaries are required to hold her down and insert the wooden paddle between her teeth. She is turned over and the diazepam is administered rectally. It is a tonic-clonic seizure, also described as a grand mal. This symptomatic epilepsy is caused by damage to the neurotransmitters, those delicate, sensitive structures, chemical and electrical impulses that facilitate consciousness. This is an unfortunate (though not unknown) consequence in at least 12% of leucotomy cases. She will require a prescription of diazepam for life. About half of all patients with epilepsy originating from the limbic structures develop depression, anxiety and psychosis. Rebecca joins this half.

Chapter Forty:

The day after the operation, Rebecca is transferred back to the York Clinic. When she arrives, she's shown to a private room. Her medication is now dispensed every two hours; she no longer has control of her tablets. On the bed, she's shocked to find a list of daily tasks, with her name on it, she is expected to complete, starting from the third day after her operation, until her discharge from hospital. The routine is relentless. All patients must rise at 7.00 to get washed and dressed. At 7.30 they are expected to serve tea to the whole ward. By 8.00am they must lay the breakfast up in the dining room and clear at 9.00am. After breakfast, Rebecca has to put the crockery away and dust the room as though she's doing a spring clean and then proceed straight to Occupational Therapy. The first tasks are physical, as she re-learns all her forgotten vocabulary and how to co-ordinate her movements enough to walk in a steady fashion. The therapists suggest various tasks available to Rebecca, such as basket weaving, crafting lampshades; rug making or knitting. She selects knitting. Perhaps she can finish Charlie's black cardigan. He'll be pleased. In moss stitch, perhaps. When she picks up the needles and yarn; she can't recollect how to knit. Staring at the rows for a few minutes, Rebecca wonders what to do next. She can't even figure out whether she ought to tell someone. One of the occupational therapists notices and comes over to assist, sitting alongside Rebecca for half an hour and demonstrating. After three or four runs, the technique begins to sink in. The cardigan will not be completed for many weeks.

Sister enters the communal sitting room and calls out: "Does anybody smoke in here?" and several patients, including Rebecca, call "Yes!" One or two, who can't speak, put up their hands.

"Get on with it, then!" the Sister says, and tosses down a kidney dish in the middle of the floor, which lands with a clang like a spittoon.

The hospital regime is strict, but productive. One afternoon, Rebecca bakes some Victoria sponges. In the evening, patients are never allowed to hang around in their bedrooms or sit in the lounge, relaxing. Every minute is filled with tasks. Even their social life is organised into playing board games. Sometimes they're permitted to cook a barbeque on top of the roof, on condition they prepare all the food themselves, or it doesn't happen. They take sausages, bacon and onions and whatever other items they can muster up, including baking their own bread, for their feast. Rebecca begins craving food, imagining different dishes, consuming more than ever before. The food at Guy's is wonderful in general, since the hospital employ an Italian chef. The headaches become less frequent. Her stitches are removed and the hair begins to grow over the bald patch; downy at first. Gradually, Rebecca begins to recover. Until they explain the "duties". The exposure tasks, they call them, are set by the consultant, Mr Macintyre.

Mr Macintyre has two Sisters on duty. One is an attractive Irish male and the other a very pretty sister, who is strict, yet fair. Mr Macintyre smiles at Rebecca.

"Now, I shall need you to do something for me today, Rebecca."

"Of course, Doctor. What is it?" she asks. She's eager to please.

"You are to walk to the nearest railway station and purchase a train ticket for me. Straight there and straight back. Alright?"

"Oh, no Mr Macintyre. I can't possibly do that. I don't go out alone. I'm agoraphobic."

"Come now, what's there to be frightened of?"

"I can't. You don't understand. I don't leave home without Arthur, you see."

"You're not at home now. You want to get well, don't you?"

"Of course I do. But this is London, too, I couldn't even find my way round."

"I'll give you directions. Here they are, look – already written out for you." He hands her a folded piece of paper.

"I'm not going. I'm sorry."

"Come along, Rebecca. No more excuses. You must learn to stand on your own two feet now. That's why you're here."

"But what if something happens to me?"

"Nothing's going to happen to you. Now, which is your favourite drink in the world?"

"Champagne and Brandy."

"I meant a soft drink; we don't recommend alcohol after surgery!"

"Coffee made with all milk."

"Right – well, this is your reward. When you get back, which won't take you any longer than half an hour, I'll arrange a hot milky coffee here waiting for you. How about it?"

"You can keep it! I'm not going."

"Come along now Rebecca, you're not refusing me, are you? Do this for me please?"

"I'll try."

"Atta girl! You'll be just dandy, I know you will. See you in half an hour. I'll get Sister to tell the canteen the time you'll be needing that coffee. Here's the money; this should be plenty." Mr Macintyre presses the coins in her palm, closes her fingers round and patting with a friendly laugh. Rebecca stands up and walks down the stairs to the hospital reception, her heart thumping and her forehead sweating.

She takes three attempts to walk to the bottom of the steps outside the front door and stay there. Her hands are trembling. The anxiety overwhelms her, the same as before, she's no better and this is hopeless. How can he be so cruel as to make her do this? Next time she'll refuse, but she's not the sort of person to renege on her word. The streets are loud and busy with traffic, smoking double-decker buses; their red colour like a danger warning signal. Bicycles, rook-black cabs, to say nothing of the pedestrians; they are all dodging one another so fast. No-one even looks at her; they're all so intent on getting to their destination. Her heels tap on the uneven paving slabs and she begins to scurry along. Best to get this over with, quickly. Stockwell, Stockwell, Stockwell – she repeats the name of the underground station in her mind. The directions are so straightforward; this is simply one long road. But she'll have to cross over, at some point – how on earth can she do that with all this traffic? She can't find a space. The noise and fumes begin to make her panic.

She spots the pedestrian crossing, although the signal changes from walk to stop in seconds – she'll have to run across the road. At least the crowds mean other people are slower than her and she isn't be the last one over, perhaps to be clipped by a car or a bus. The Underground sign is blue, red and white and in her haste to reach the entrance, she catches her heel on a paving slab, stumbles and almost falls. Rebecca walks into the station and spots someone in a uniform behind a glass counter. She joins the queue, shifting from foot to foot and feeling she needs to urinate – she'd better cross her legs. The line disperses before she can compose herself and she approaches the counter, her fingers trembling. She opens her palm and drops all five coins onto the floor.

"I'm sorry, so sorry," she stammers.

"That's alright love," the ticket seller smiles and looks her in the eyes. She bends down and begins to gather up the change, as someone tuts behind her. No-one helps. When she stands up again, she needs to refer to her piece of paper for the instructions on the destination. She can't remember.

"From the hospital darlin?" the ticket seller says.

"Yes, yes. I need to buy a ticket for someone else."

"Alright. I understand. Why don't you pass your paper through to me sweetheart? You take your time and they can wait their turn. Everyone's in too much of a hurry these days, in my opinion."

He understands, then. She can't be the first he's seen. It's obviously a trick Mr Macintyre likes to play. She wonders if everyone else knows she's a mental patient, too. He didn't really need a ticket. Now she understands. She passes the paper under the hatch with the coins and the ticket seller reads it.

"Here you are my lovely. Here's your change. Don't you worry and you go straight back. You'll be alright."

"Thank you so much. I'm sorry to keep everyone waiting."

"Never you mind anyone else. Always a pleasure serving a beauty such as yourself."

"Thank you. Goodbye."

"Tata darling. Good luck to you!"

The walk back is a bit easier, but she keeps a brisk pace. As promised, the hot milky coffee is waiting for her. So is Mr Macintyre.

"Here she is! You made it fine, Rebecca! What did I tell you?" he says, smiling broadly.

"I'll never do that again as long as I live!" she cries.

He laughs at her.

Over the next six weeks, other duties follow. One of these is to travel alone, further into London. Rebecca attends the changing of the guard and almost misses the bus back for lunch. She's terrified that she might have to hail a taxi with not enough money to pay for it, but another one pulls up within five minutes. The exhaustion she experiences from the anxiety is so much that all she wants to do when she gets back, is lie down. She approaches the Sister.

"Please, Sister, mightn't I just lie down on my bed for half an hour? I found the trip far too much, this morning?"

"Absolutely not, Rebecca. Now, pull yourself together and get down to the day room – this afternoon you'll be baking for the consultants. Let's forget this silliness."

Rebecca wants to cry, but does as she's told. They are cruel, here. After six weeks, the doctors decide she's well enough to return home, with a paper bag full of prescribed medication.

Chapter Forty-One:

Water pistols are so funny, when you think about it. Rebecca can't stop laughing at the boys, even though this only encourages them and by now, she's soaked through to the skin. Last week, the buggers had been to the cattle market and Robert came home with six ducks. She'd had to send him back to return five, she didn't mind him keeping one. As if Charlie and his bloody pet rat Templeton and Mrs Rat weren't enough – why ever he'd got a mating pair she never understood. Before long he'd bred thirty or forty. She wasn't afraid of them, they were quite sweet really, but there were far too many. In the end Arthur got rid of them for her, Charlie wouldn't listen to a word she said.

Her moments of happiness are never wholehearted – they're always spoiled later on. While the boys were at school, Arthur popped home and took her quickly at lunchtime and she'd had, for the first time, a huge thrill and satisfaction from it. She'd heard rumours about women achieving an orgasm, but never believed them – not that she didn't enjoy sex, she'd enjoyed herself, but she always felt slightly unfulfilled. Now she'd experienced this once, she couldn't wait until the next time.

"That bloody operation was good for something, wasn't it?" Arthur had said, zipping up his fly.

\#

Rebecca is beginning to notice other men looking at her and enjoy the attention. Almost a year has passed – she doesn't see much difference in herself, apart from a tendency to blurt words out – things she'd rather censor. This is causing some arguments, particularly with Mother, but also several of their friends. They'd lost touch with one couple after turning up at their house to surprise them...the husband answered the door and asked them to wait on the doorstep, which was unusual. Rebecca heard the woman in the background say "I'm not having that bloody loony in my house!" She burst into tears and ran back to the car. Arthur got in and drove away in a fury, but wouldn't talk any more.

At least Arthur still loves her. Never mind there's not much room for her thoughts and feelings to be heard, no-one cares to listen – they're all too busy. They'd given her another ten sessions of ECT recently – reckoned she'd respond even better to the shocks after the operation. Thank God for the tablets, much as she's like a bloody drug addict and can't do without them, sometimes they numb everything. A shame though, unlike having a drink, where the effects wear off in the morning. Then these other tablets, Mayos, they call them for short, the long name was Monoamine something, are prescribed, alongside a huge diet sheet. Stuff she can't eat; Marmite, salami, broad beans – there's a long list, but the one she misses most is cheese. Never to eat Cheddar again, or she'll die – these foods cause a dangerous increase in blood pressure. She probably wouldn't have thought about cheese, but now she obsesses about it, particularly when she's cooking Welsh rarebit for the children and the salt-smell lingers.

The strangest thing is those psychiatrists at Maudsley. Perhaps because when she's under pressure, she can act. People often said she ought to think about a career on the stage. Course, Mother was a professional dancer, one of those who do the French high-kicking and showing their stocking tops, The Folie Bergerac or something. Her mind drifts to a theme tune, a detective show set in Jersey, where Captain Napier lives; or is it Guernsey…what if she'd gone with him, perhaps she'd never have need the operation…where was she…How could Mother perform on stage – with her panics and all? Nothing makes sense in this cruel world, not any more. Anyway, where was she, those psychiatrists wrote her a personal letter. They think her operation was so successful; she's been invited to come and give a little talk, on stage to the student doctors. She'll be an honorary speaker and they'll pay her, £100.00 for every session and arrange her transport, a luxury hotel for the night and everything. What an outing – but she isn't going to stay overnight.

What fun, sitting on the stage while they all look at her and ask her questions. They're ever so polite. She does exactly what they've coached her to at rehearsals, tells the audience she's so much better and how the surgery saved her life. One asks if she's happy and she assures him she is. She wonders about his question for days afterwards, whether her answer was true or if happiness matters. No one's ever asked her before. But she wasn't being paid to say bad things and let down the psychiatrists and neurosurgeons, with their lovely manners and good hearts. The audience believed her. That was the main thing. Mr Macintyre and two surgical colleagues took her to The Orangery at Kensington Palace Gardens for afternoon tea when the question and answer finished. She tucked into cucumber, smoked salmon and egg and cress sandwiches with the crusts cut off, little fancies, currant scones and strawberry jam, clotted cream and tea in porcelain cups, hand painted with daisies.

She's back home now. Here's Arthur, with his tools and parts. But he's got all thrifty with everything else. Not far from their house is a slaughter-yard – run by a man called Garth. Garth is ever so friendly and manages well, really, what with his epilepsy and all. A perk of his job is getting "internal meats" – they're perfectly fine to eat, Arthur says, but most people don't tend to want them and the trouble is they're waterlogged, from washing. "Inner skirts", he calls them. Garth's given his good friend Arthur a big old bag of these, to bring home for tea. He needs to dry them out, he says, and he sticks them in Rebecca's new spin-drier. The blood and burned plastic stench is choking when he breaks the spin-drier – then he takes it all apart and cleans flesh off all the bearings on the kitchen table. It's chaos in the house at times. To top this off, her period's late.

#

When she tells Arthur, he's delighted. Rebecca can't bear to lose another baby, so she books an appointment and goes to see the GP.

"Rebecca, I really don't think this is a good idea," he begins, looking stern.

"It's a bit late for that, Doctor, wouldn't you say?" she replies.

"Not necessarily. Your menses are only twelve weeks overdue, according to your dates? We'll be able to book a termination in your circumstances. Time is of the essence."

"A what?"

"Terminating the pregnancy...you must understand it's not safe for this to proceed. You've already had two miscarriages."

"Arthur and I want this baby, Doctor. I'm telling you now, so I won't miscarry again."

"You don't understand, Rebecca. The drugs you're on mean that any fetus will either die in your womb, or be born terribly deformed. It'll be mentally and physically handicapped and won't survive."

"Then I'll stop taking them."

"You can't simply stop taking them Rebecca. You're epileptic. A seizure can kill you."

"I don't care. How dare you suggest abortion? That's what you mean. That's wrong."

"You must consider the baby first, Rebecca. Your needs are secondary. Will you bring a child into this world to suffer? Think about it again and consult with Arthur. Two doctors sign the form to certify your mental health will be damaged by continuing with the pregnancy. The procedure can be done discreetly. No one need find out. While we're at it, we could sterilise you and prevent this happening again. You should have been more...responsible, Rebecca. You didn't cope well with the other children, did you?"

"There's nothing wrong with my boys. I couldn't cope because your lot turned me into a bloody drug addict. I won't change my mind, Doctor, so you'd better get used to it."

"Rebecca, I shall consider having you committed if you are set on this course of action. You've always been a voluntary patient. Won't you agree to reconsider?"

"Are you threatening me?"

"Don't be histrionic. Go home and tell Arthur what I said. I'm going to book you both an appointment first thing in the morning to discuss this further. He must be made aware of the implications."

"Do as you like. He'll say the same."

"Calm yourself, Rebecca. No need for all this. Can you make 9.00am?"

"We'll both be here. I'm warning you Doctor, I'll run away if need be – but I am having this baby and you are not going to stop me."

"Don't get excitable; think of your nerves. Got your Valium here?"

"Obviously. I can't go out without them, can I? Thanks to all of you!"

"I suggest you take one and get a good night's sleep. We'll talk this over tomorrow."

"Fine. Goodbye."

"Goodbye, Rebecca."

Rebecca and Arthur tell Robert and Charlie there'll be a new baby in the family. Robert's thrilled. Charlie says: "I think you're absolutely disgusting, at your age!" They are taken aback, but laugh.

The pressure continues on the couple, appointment after appointment. They don't budge. Arthur is willing to deal with the consequences – even if their baby is born deformed and handicapped. After some weeks, the doctors relent and persuade Rebecca to come into Coney Hill, to be weaned off the more dangerous drugs. First the seizures come, where she foams at the mouth and convulses. They strap her down with a wooden paddle between her teeth, to stop her biting her own tongue. Then the hallucinations begin, colourful and terrifying. A disfigured girl appears, covered in postulating boils, red and angry, with a hump back and claws instead of hands, shakes Rebecca's body, screaming at her. She can't speak aloud and tell them, though she tries. She's sedated for the last four of the nine months, paralysed by drugs and fear. Sister Bredon watches over her and makes notes.

Time and again, the doctors return to Rebecca and Arthur, certain there's something wrong with the baby. They want to inject the fetus to do further tests and she becomes terrified about a conspiracy to abort without her knowledge, fighting with every instinct left, to protect her unborn child – she refuses permission for the injection. Still a voluntary patient, she discharges herself from the hospital and returns home – against the advice and the odds. Once back, she begins to settle down. Rebecca continues with the Valium – nothing else. She wishes they understood her – thank God for Arthur. She might be a junkie, but she won't become a murderer for anybody.

Stella Faith Denby is born on 17 September 1968. The Denby family celebrate their daughter and Charlie Lindsay opens champagne to celebrate.

Rebecca sips it, ecstatic with the thrill of the familiar bubbles and real high. No-one can find anything wrong with Stella. She's perfect.

Chapter Forty-Two:

Rebecca's finding it hard to *bond*, as they say now, with baby Stella. It's hard being stuck to someone else where you're never alone but a person hangs on or off you, needing things you haven't even got for yourself. Stella is like a perfect china doll – smooth white skin and soft hair. Thank goodness for Arthur taking over the bottle-feeding; he worships his daughter. Rebecca's afraid – she watches Stella for any signs of a problem. The consultants at the hospital said she might look fine – but she probably won't be, we'll have to keep an eye on the situation. They refer to Stella as a situation. Arthur is washing her, changing her, chatting and cooing over her. He wasn't this way with the boys. Thank goodness, really – Rebecca loves Stella, dressing her up in outfits; but love seems different now, inexplicably blunted.

Life at home is tedious, in comparison to Coney Hill. She finds she's always got something to deal with. Changes are afoot at Arthur's firm. Alphonse Reyer's factory is being rebuilt and he's offered a job at Wembley Laundry in London; or a position in their specialist dry cleaning division for furs, leathers and suede in Leicester. Due to Rebecca's ongoing medical problems, and after much thought, he declines both offers. He's unemployed for a time and focuses on bringing up his baby daughter. He'll remember this as one of the happiest times of his life.

Six months later, Rebecca's falling into despair again. A locum GP visits their house and takes Arthur to one side.

"You ought to get her into Coney Hill, now Arthur. For a rest. She's obviously not coping."

"D'you think that's for the best?" Arthur asks.

"I do. Arthur, I'll level with you. This is an absolutely ideal opportunity. Rebecca's been obsessed with Stella from the minute she was born. Hasn't brought her for the proper post-natal checks we routinely do. We're all worried she won't let us check the baby over, for any signs."

"Signs?"

"The things we warned you about. If you persuade Rebecca to get into Coney Hill this time, you can bring Stella in for the tests."

"What tests?"

"For abnormalities."

"I reckon you'd better leave now, Doctor."

"I beg your pardon?"

"I suggest you go, before I say something I regret."

"I don't understand you, Arthur. Now look, you'll appreciate we want to do everything to help, and the sooner we diagnose any problems, the better chance your daughter will have in the world."

"You've spent years buggering up my wife. She was a beautiful woman and now she's a bloody invalid. I'll deal with her, I've dealt with everything else. You've all tried to make us kill our baby, and we've stopped you. If you think I'm going to let you fuck up my daughter, think again. Get out of my house and stay away from us. You're bloody meddling, I've had a gutsful of all of you. Piss off – now, or I won't be responsible for my actions!"

Arthur stands, and opens the front door. The doctor shuts up and leaves, shaking his head. Arthur goes up to his daughter's bedroom and stares at her, sleeping peacefully. Anticipating his wife's drug-induced stupor in bed, he resolves to let her go for a rest in Coney Hill again. He checks on Rebecca, whose mouth is lolling open on the lace-edged pillow and a little dribble of spittle trails into a damp pool, dampening her hair, bless her. He pops a finger under her chin and gently levers up, until her mouth closes. Rebecca begins to breathe through her nose and snore, softly. Going back downstairs, he makes a cup of tea; which goes cold as he sits on the sofa enraged, with his head in his hands and allows himself to feel overwhelmed, for the first time. Only the silent walls absorb his sobs.

Fuck them all. He won't let this happen again. Not for his little girl. He gets himself together and slides in beside his sleeping wife, placing his arm over her and cupping her breast, as always.

Chapter Forty-Three:

They won't be able to manage without Arthur's earnings any longer. Their savings are nearly wiped out. Arthur begins looking for another job and spots one, in the local paper, as the Manager of a newsagent in Innsworth, near the RAF camp. They sell toys, sweets, cards, books and other small hardware items. The owner calls Arthur for an interview and offers him the job with a flat above the shop, which he accepts. Rebecca tries to carry on, but now begins to imagine herself in a big dark hole, with no hope. She stops caring how she looks; can't work and wanders around like a zombie, most of the time. She realises the doctors don't want to her suffering, but they can only do so much – she's beginning to lose faith in them. Rebecca overhears people whispering, "She's mad". She starts believing them. She's often left embarrassed, after her verbal outbursts, she finds herself blurting out every fleeting thought in her head; however daft – and often she recognises how ridiculous some of them are, too late. She watches people's facial movements with detached interest. She doesn't interpret their responses in the way her family seem to. Instead, she learns emotions by rote - hurt, anger, and guilt. When her words cause these expressions, she apologises - but they are disconnected from her.

Rebecca and Arthur rent out the Ashbridge Road house, without taking up references, to the postman and his wife and their enormous Great Dane, which is sized more like a small horse. Between them, they wreck the place, causing more stress.

Grampy Denby falls ill with cancer. People avoid him as he loses weight and wastes away, confined to the upstairs bedroom at Sandbanks – except young Charlie, who visits him often and sits with his grandfather, but he won't share what they talk about. Charlie is the only one who still cuddles him. Rebecca, sits with him for hours, holding his hand. Sometimes she reads to him, from Daphne Du Maurier. People whisper that he is *riddled*. After he dies, he visits Charlie in his dreams and Charlie is always pleased to see him. His own young life is a mixture between the misery of fighting Robert off tormenting him and fighting at school. He's getting better at fighting all the time. From the dirty early years of Robert bursting in on him in the bath; turning out the light and telling him to open his mouth and then urinating in it – Robert has progressed to further degradation of his younger brother. He is left in charge of Charlie one afternoon while their parents go to the flicks. They've scarcely been out the door five minutes before he has held Charlie down, stripped him naked and hog-tied him with rope on the lounge floor, laughing. This time; Charlie's cries are heard by Arthur, who's forgotten his fags. Having taken in this disturbing scene, he shouts: "what are you doing, you queer bastard?" and knocks Robert about the head. As

Robert snivels and runs upstairs; Arthur releases his youngest son and goes back out to join his wife, with his cigarettes, shaking his head.

Rebecca can't stand to live in the flat any longer – feeling claustrophobic, as well as agoraphobic, but neither can she bear to go back to the other house, now she's seen the damage. She doesn't regard this as home, after the invasion by those dirty people. She's always hated that house – never wanted to live there anyway. So they give the postman, the wife and the Great Dane two month's notice and sell up.

Chapter Forty-Four:

In July 1971, the family moves again, to Trenton Road, Gloucester. Arthur starts his own dry cleaning company. Rebecca is able to help in this business, he's the boss. They clean, do repairs on clothing, dying things to different shades on request and hold contracts with the prison, police and fire service. She watches his hairy arms, fixing, mending, and doing. Everyone loves Arthur. Members of the public bring odd items in, for Rebecca to advertise in the shop window and sell on. From the commission on these, she manages to save £300.00 and they purchase a cruiser, intended for pleasure boating. They moor the boat at the junction of the canal, but the owner soon points out this is illegal and needs to be moved to a legal berth, which Arthur purchases. He lashes an engine onto the boat and Rebecca, along with her Mother, accompany him to travel down the canal to Gloucester docks. Both of the women are very anxious, since neither can swim. They book the lock to traverse onto the River Severn and forget about the safety of the matter, in order to moor the boat by Westgate Bridge. On dry land, Arthur rebuilds and redecorates the boat. Rebecca begins a sideline business, selling Avon products to river-goers, including gypsies in the area. When the rain falls for six weeks; they return to find the boat filled with water, but thankfully still afloat. After a couple of years, they sell it to Sailor Bill, a chap from Tuffley.

Over the next two years; Robert progresses from his former torture of Charlie to inviting a group of his friends round, for what he calls an *exhibition wank* where they masturbate in front of his younger brother, who is encouraged to come in and watch. Finally Robert; having spent the evening out drinking with his friends; returns to their shared bedroom giggling and drunk. Charlie is initially asleep when he becomes aware of his brother's presence in his bed. His brother overpowers him with his weight and attempts to insert his erect penis into Charlie's anus, laughing all the while. This time Charlie will fight him off successfully, shouting "fuck off you gay bastard" and Robert will treat the incident as a big joke; he hadn't intended to go through with anything and the evening's events; when raised in later life by Charlie – will be referred to between them mysteriously as "Worthington E" episode – the beer Robert had been drinking before his incestuous attempt on his brother was made. Their parents never knew.

#

Meanwhile in America, Rebecca's sister Doris causes quite a scandal by having several love affairs in her workplaces. She announces she's become engaged to a well-to-do insurance broker, called Jasper. Her family don't attend the wedding, but she brings her husband over to England to meet them. Jasper is portly and bespectacled, though well mannered and besotted by Doris. It hardly seems a love match on Doris's part, but perhaps his attractions are fiduciary. Now, Doris appears to be living the high life and has been accepted into the congregation of Jasper's church. He's a Jehovah's Witness. Doris's not what Rebecca considers the church-going type. She's changing into someone pious, but still outgoing – that's how she seems after such a long absence. Rebecca's Mother, Doris and her sister-in-law Megan have formed a clique, from which Rebecca feels subtly excluded. For the fortnight Doris stays, she only visits Rebecca once. Rebecca is discomfited about visiting her parent's house during this time, as though she's surplus to requirements, not *one of them.*

Robert adores his little sister and spends many afternoons taking Stella out in her pushchair and showing her off. Charlie isn't the slightest bit interested – except in teasing Stella on occasion and pinching her sweets. The children are growing self-sufficient. Rebecca doesn't get much trouble off Robert – though the boy's in a dreamland. Wants to be a chef, of all things. Well, he's far too clever; no-one ever appreciates cooks. Service isn't a proper trade. Robert's a wonderful cook, she's always taught both her boys – not for them finding out the hard way, like she did. But that's not a proper job for man. He'll never make any money and no-one will respect him. Despite his mother's reservations; Robert pursues his dream of becoming a chef and leaves home to move into digs in the hotel where he works.

Charlie is, well, disrespectful and needs to be taught a lesson. Headstrong. Grampy Lindsay adores him, of course, even when Charlie'd found his shotgun and taken the heads off all his prize roses. What did Dad say? "He's a proper boy, that one." Charlie and his bloody carrying on, bringing his friends round. One of them, Derek, has a violent black father and they aren't the sort of family she feels he ought to be associated with...South African, or something and she tells Charlie so, one night – get that bloody nigger out of my house! Although he's pale-skinned; she knows his background. Charlie had looked at her contemptuously, when she shouted at Derek and turned to him, saying, "Ignore her Der. She's *mental*."

Mental, is she? Not mental enough to let that boy rule the roost. Arthur's got to discipline him. He's never been smacked and nor was she, but she was a good girl and Charlie goes too far sometimes. His attitude's worse, now he's taken up boxing at India House. Fast with fists of iron, the coach says. She went to watch him in the ring and is proud of his lithe fitness; dancing around with a dangerous look in his eye – fighting men are a legacy from her side. He needs reigning in, before he gets too big for his boots. Charlie's kept on and on at her to get him a Staffordshire Bull Terrier and they've had their names down at the animal shelter for months before one has come in. It's been kept in a shed and used for fighting. One side of it's face is like leather from bites and scratches and it's cropped ears and whip-like tail make it a fierce looking creature. The red eyes don't help. She's not at all sure about it; particularly since they say it'll need to be sedated for the first night. But have it he will; and Arthur let him. Charlie and the dog have been inseparable since. He's called him Mutley.

He doesn't treat that dog nicely – coaching him to fight too. Charlie's so proud to be first one of his peers with a Staffordshire bull terrier. Mutley waits for him to finish school and walks home with him off the lead. But Charlie's an irresponsible little sod. Rebecca's sure he hasn't fed Mutley today. She's fixating on this issue all afternoon and when Charlie comes home in the evening, she starts.

"Did you fed Mutley today?"

"Course I did."

"I don't think so, Charlie. Don't lie to me. I know you."

"Mum, I've fed him. I'll feed him again later."

"Charlie, if you don't feed that dog right away, I'm telling your father."

"You do that."

Charlie marches upstairs; Mutley at his heels. No doubt the little sod will be out again and still won't feed him. He's snoozing on his bed like a layabout. She paces the room, watching the clock and waiting for Arthur. He's later than usual – two hours late. As soon as he walks in, she starts again.

"You've got to speak to him, Arthur."

"What's your trouble?"

"He's not fed Mutley. I've told him, and he's lied to me,"

"Can I just get through the door?"

"What time d'you call this anyway, where were you?"

"Rebecca, I've been to the wholesalers to get new stock. I told you."

"No you didn't."

"I did, you probably don't remember."

"I can't be expected to deal with all this, while you're out gallivanting. I'm ill. I've had an operation!"

"Don't I know it?"

"What did you say?"

"Someone's got to earn some money to keep this family going!"

"Dad always said I could do better than you. He was right!"

"Your Dad always had too much to say,"

"You leave my Dad out of this!"

"Gladly."

"You're a failure, aren't you? You're jealous of him, because you're not the provider he is!"

"Who knows what I might have been, if it wasn't for you?"

"Don't you blame this on me. I'm ill. What's your excuse?"

"I think you'd best shut up, woman, before I say something I regret."

"All I've asked you to do is speak to him about the dog. I mean it, Arthur. Now!"

Arthur doesn't reply. He picks up a cup from the draining board and launches it into the sink, where it smashes. Rebecca shuts up and turns away, starting to cry. He storms up the stairs to Charlie's room, finding his son fast asleep on top of the bedspread and Mutley curled up on his feet. Arthur, overwhelmed with rage at the scene, approaches his boy's head. Mutley's cropped ears prick up and he stands, wagging his whip-like, half-bald tail. As Arthur brings his fist down on his son's nose. Mutley begins to growl and bark at Arthur. Charlie starts up, jumping to his feet.

She hears them shouting, from the kitchen. It's exciting.

Feed that bloody dog!

Then a thud, and then a bump bump bump bump down the stairs. Barking, growling

Arth - you ever touch me again, I'll kill you."

Silence. She takes two Valium and sits at the table, watching the dresser as her son, crying, is storming past her with Mutley at his heels, not looking at her but muttering *fucking mental bitch* and slamming the back door – he hasn't fed Mutley, but that's not the point. Rebecca hears Arthur go upstairs, run the tap in the bathroom and slam their bedroom door.

Chapter Forty-Five:

In late 1973, Charlie & Faith Lindsay take a flight to America, to visit Doris and Jasper. Before they leave, Charlie Lindsay is worried about his health. He won't elaborate, but entrusts Arthur with money to cover his funeral arrangements. Arthur is instructed to make sure his body is returned to the UK, should he die in America. Arthur's taken aback; but promises to take care of his wishes in the event. He tells no-one. During the second week in America, Charlie suffers a massive heart attack. He's rushed to the hospital in time to be saved. Although he survives for a further two weeks, he dies after a second attack in the hospital, leaving Faith, his anxious widow, with the task of making the arrangements and travelling home alone. Doris's husband Jasper telephones Arthur long-distance.

"My condolences Arthur. Sure is a bad situation,"

"I think he saw it coming, Jasper. He's left me with instructions."

"He has? Jeez. What were they?"

"His body's to be returned for burial here."

"Well now Arthur, I'm not one to go against a dyin' man's wishes, but ya know, I can't advise it – between you and me Grace sure is cut up. If you'll take my advice, we'll deal with it this end. I know it's awkward – but has he left you funds? You'll be able to wire them?"

"Jasper, I gave him my word I'd carry out those wishes. The money's here. I'll contact the airline myself. If you have any expenses you just let me know and I'll cover them. You can send the receipts."

"Now Arthur, I don't think you understand. Now see sense. That poor woman's real shocked. I just think if we can bury him here, it'll be a whole lot simpler all round. It's gonna cost a whole lot."

"I'm not discussing it any more Jasper. Put Faith on please." He hears a tut and Faith being handed the phone.

"Arthur?" her voice is shaky.

"He's left me money and instructions Faith, in case this happened. We'll bury him at home. I know it's hard, but you don't want to leave him over there, do you?"

"Oh Arthur, do you think it's for the best? Jasper's sure he's better left here."

"Listen to me Faith, this is what he wanted. I promised him. And his family are here and this is where he's from. He needs to come home so they can say goodbye to him."

"Alright Arthur, just as you say."

Charlie Denby was 75 years old. No-one is available to accompany Faith home and so she sits in first class, being comforted an air hostess for

197

the entire journey. When they reach England, HM Customs & Excise search her husband's coffin and his body for drugs.

#

Rebecca is grief-stricken and the world seems even more unsafe. No one loves her like her father. She keeps trying to telephone him in America, not believing he can be dead. Arthur removes the phone and locks it in the cupboard, to stop her. Faith becomes anxious and needful. Frightened to return to the marital home, she stays with Rebecca and Arthur for a few months. During the first three weeks she's plenty to do, making all the funeral arrangements. As they attend the funeral, Rebecca holds her mother's arm and tries to comfort her. Rebecca can't cry, or believe any of this is real – she blames her drugs. He's bound to come home eventually, this must be a mistake. He's not in there. Her father cannot be in the coffin, which is being lowered into the ground. Faith is throwing a handful of soil in when she sinks to her knees as if to throw herself on top of the coffin. She is held up by her eldest son, Clive.

As the family, friends and work colleagues congregate outside the chapel, Rebecca makes her way to the cloakrooms. Two of the cubicles are already occupied. Walking on tiptoes, she closes the door and sits on the toilet lid, on the far left. Opening her handbag, she takes out two Valium and swallows them. The other toilets flush in tandem and she hears the occupants leave their cubicles and begin washing their hands, whispering. She strains to hear them. One of the voices is familiar.

"Did you see her then? Her face?"

"I know, nothing at all, was there?"

"She doesn't care about anyone but herself. Selfish, I told Clive. That's her real problem. Selfish and spoiled. Fancy not even crying at your own father's funeral."

"He was a lovely man. Poor Faith; having to deal with that mental cow, all on her own now. I hear she's stayed with her ever since she got back."

"I'm working on that. Come on!"

The outer door slams, as her sister-in-law and one of her friends, leave. Rebecca clenches her fists and bangs them on either side of her ears until the Valium takes effect. Hateful, hateful, hateful Megan.

#

Faith decides she will never return to her home and arranges the sale. Charlie has left no money or pension, although the house, at least, is paid for. She's enough money from the house sale to purchase a luxury flat, but can't settle there either and buys herself a bungalow in Tuffley. She subsequently develops a heart problem, meaning she won't be able to live alone, without care.

Clive and Megan suggest she might sell the bungalow and they could pool their resources to buy a bigger place together. In return, Megan undertakes to look after Faith, until her death. On several occasions, Faith discusses the proposition with Rebecca and asks for her blessing. This will mean no inheritance for Doris or Rebecca. Rebecca knows she's not in a position to take care of her mother and asks whether the move will make her happy. Faith assures her this is her wish. So Rebecca gives her blessings.

Rebecca's sister Doris visits England again, after her father's death. On the first occasion, Rebecca and Doris are alone in their mother's kitchen.

"Is life wonderful in America, Doris?" Rebecca asks.

"God, yes, Rebecca. Each state's like a different country. I could never live back here again. The people love Brits, the food's great and service is amazing. There's no comparison. And as for the men...well!" she nudges Rebecca, laughing.

"You're so naughty, Doris! D'you know, I think I might be well enough to come and visit you, if I came back with you. I'm so much better now."

"You haven't got a passport though, have you Rebecca? Let's wait and see. How's Mum been?"

"Frail, since Dad passed away. She won't be left alone."

Doris says, "She only misses Dad because there's no one to chauffeur her out and about now!"

Rebecca laughs. "You're probably right!"

"No one to make a fuss of her!"

"No. But Doris...d'you think I might be able to come back with you on the plane, for a visit? America sounds so wonderful."

"Rebecca, try to understand. I don't think it would be a good idea, really. You're not awfully well, are you, let's face it?"

"I'm better now. Please?"

"I don't think so. I simply couldn't be responsible for you, if you became ill. It's not like here - you have to pay for all your healthcare. Try to understand, dear. You're better off here, where you're safe."

"I see."

"Make the best of things. Come on, we'd better go and join Mum."

Rebecca suppresses the urge to cry, as another short-lived fantasy joins the scrapheap. Later, Rebecca's mother confronts her. Doris reported the conversation, attributing the comment about her only missing her father because there was no-one to ferry her around, to Rebecca. Rebecca denies this fervently. This prompts the start of a coolness between her and her mother.

Six months later, Doris visits again. She doesn't come to see Rebecca. Rebecca believes she's come to ask their mother for money, but is never told. She shouldn't need any more money, now she's married Jasper. Rebecca never sees her sister again.

Chapter Forty-Six:

Charlie's either out at school or socialising with his friends. He still gets into many fights – sometimes both he and Mutley are arrested for petty crimes and the dog can be heard howling from the cells when his parents arrive to collect him from the police station. The crimes are petty, mainly; setting fire to a farmer's hedge and badger baiting; but Rebecca could do without all this aggravation.

Even little Stella is independent - she dictates what she will and won't wear. The outfits she chooses are outrageous, often mis-matched. Arthur indulges her and Rebecca tries to influence her; but they're more like companions than mother and daughter. When Stella starts school, she's particular about her food. If she doesn't like the school dinner, she'll refuse to eat anything. Rebecca ends up making her packed lunches each day.

Rebecca still invites Mother round for dinner twice a week; always cooking her favourites of roast pork, or lamb. They wash up together and settle down for an afternoon nap. This goes on for several months. One Sunday after they wake up; Rebecca recounts an anecdote about her father in Bournemouth, saying how much she misses him. Faith stares at her.

"Of course, he always did show off," she says, rather sharply.

"What d'you mean?" Rebecca asks, taken aback.

"All mouth. You don't know what he was really like."

"Please...don't talk about Dad like that, Mother."

"The things I went through with him. He's left me destitute, with all his capers and spending."

"But he bought you the house,"

"What good is a house to me with no husband and no money? He never put something aside for a rainy day. I always presumed he had. Now I'm just a guest in someone else's house."

"I thought you were happy with Megan and Clive?"

"I am. They're kind to me. I'm saying he wasn't all he was cracked up to be."

"Mother, please, I don't want to hear this about my Dad. I loved him."

"Well, you always were two of a kind."

"What d'you mean?"

"The apple didn't fall far from *that* particular tree."

"I'd like you to go now, please Mother."

"I beg your pardon?"

"Please, leave. We'll meet next week. I can't bear to listen anymore."

"Fine. Truth hurts, doesn't it? I'll be off then; I know where I'm not welcome."

Faith storms out. She fails to turn up for her meal the following week, or the next. Rebecca writes to her mother and petitions her brother Clive. Faith declines to contact her.

#

In 1978, Rebecca and her family move once more, to Oxford Street, in the heart of Gloucester city centre, next to the iron railings on the corner, situated in a vibrant, ethnically diverse neighbourhood with thriving brothels, fish and chips shops run by Greeks and mechanics run by Italians. A vegetarian restaurant opens; with no insight to their carnivorous community and fails, within ten months. The Hindu community fair better with the curry house. The smells and sounds of the fishy-fat and spices permeates bedroom windows into the early hours. After *The Welsh Harp* public house kicks out, later than closing time after a lock-in, Charlie listens in his bedroom to the familiar sounds of the motorbike's two-stroke engine ringa dinga dinga ding and waits for the barking chain-saw of the Harleys that will follow dug dug dug dug. This pub is frequented by the Gloucester Scorpions Hell's Angels, who take over the rear bar as their territory. Further down is the less salubrious England's Glory, with crossed matches on the swinging sign; named after the popular matches made in the Moreland's factory in Bristol Road, where their parents and grandparents faces rotted away with phossy jaw, glowed in the dark like the luminous Jesus's on mahogany crosses which saw them out of this life.

Belching, hiccupping drunks in ill-fitting pinstriped suits, wobbling one-footed lecturing with finger pointed at those who swerve by them, pissing in doorways and over their shoes, straggling hair and unkempt beards like nests homing only fag ash, spittle and crumbs.

In daytime, where children play in back streets and alleyways running behind Wanton Lawn Lunatic Asylum behind the Royal Hospital, picking up still lit fag butts and drawing and coughing and stepping in dog shit no-one clears up. The railway line cuts over the top of them all; diesel stinking shoostacoo with people and coal and goods across the charcoal-coloured bridge, stained spray-paint white with the delinquent adolescent autographs and monographs of the non-invested, seventies molested, children's home neglected in their nylon stay-pressed flares and ribbed polo necks (donated).

The three storey house is little more than a shell, requiring complete refurbishment. The residents use the meagre back of each terrace to plunder and exploit the daylight and space of their neighbours in their hunger for anonymity, exclusivity and autonomy. Rebecca and Arthur continue the dry-cleaning business as an agency from home. They're losing money rapidly; so Arthur also works for a newsagent as a relief morning manager, putting up paper rounds and running the shop. He takes on picking up the local paper from Cheltenham and delivering it to all the shops en-route to Gloucester.

The following year, eight years after Grampy Denby, Nanny Denby lies dying in bed. It began in her lungs and spread rapidly. Rebecca visits regularly and talks with her. The shared female intimacies might appear strange to the outside world, but seemed quite natural to Shelagh & Rebecca. Having helped Nanny change from her clothes to a fresh nightie, Rebecca wonders why she's never worn a brassiere. Instead, Nanny Denby places two folded handkerchiefs over the top of her breasts and attaches them to her vest with safety pins.

"That'll see me through the week!" Nanny Denby chuckles one day, as Rebecca finishes polishing the glass eye for her. Nanny Denby replaces this in her eye socket.

"Well now, Rebecca,"

"Yes, Nanny?"

"Just imagine you had lots of money. What would be your heart's desire?"

"I need to consider. Maybe a house in the country!"

"No dear, how tedious! You'd be bored stupid. Something else."

"Perhaps I'd employ a butler and a maid, to wait on me hand and foot and I would never do the housework!"

"Not staff, either dear. Come on now, think hard."

"Money no object?"

"Money no object. But this must be something for you."

"Arthur promised me a mink coat, years ago. I never got one."

"An excellent choice. Perhaps one day, then."

"In my dreams."

Nanny Denby holds her birthday party the following Saturday. Perhaps she already knows this will be her last. Others treat the evening as a farewell party. She dies the following Tuesday. They do say, those Macmillan nurses, the dying brighten up for one last dance, before they pass away.

#

Shelagh's funeral is so well-attended, people queue outside the church in the rain, jostling together under black umbrellas. The last of them to press her warm hand in Arthur's, is his Aunt Edith, of whom he's very fond – she's shared a certain closeness with Shelagh all her life. After the wake; Aunt Edith's husband George asks, in a quiet voice, if he might have a word with Arthur.

"Not today, obviously, but we need to talk with you sometime soon, Arthur. We've something to tell you."

"Alright," Arthur replies. He's puzzled. "Why don't you come to tea with us on Saturday?"

"Thank you. I'm sorry for your loss, Arthur. Shelagh was a special lady. Edith loved her very much."

The following Saturday, Edith and George visit. Rebecca serves cucumber sandwiches with the crusts cut off, a pot of tea and a selection of cakes, while they reminisce about Shelagh and her organisations – her women's institute and community activities. She was a marvel, despite being somewhat disadvantaged by losing one eye, in childhood and tall, too, for a woman, six feet at her peak, although the cancer made her seem shrunken in stature. Several hours pass before George can speak with Arthur alone. Arthur, bored with the chit-chat, invites George to come and look at his latest project in the garage. Amid the plywood and three in one, cogs, wires and engine parts, Arthur fiddles with a carburetor. Eventually George speaks:

"I need to show you this, Arthur. I can't fathom how else to tell you, but you need to know. Shelagh gave Edith this in an envelope at the birthday party, with instructions not to open it until she died." He takes a folded piece of faded green paper from his inside breast pocket, shaking. Arthur wipes his hand on an oily rag and opens the brittle folds carefully. At first glance, he thinks this is his mother's birth certificate – her maiden name is the first thing he notes. He is mistaken – she's listed as "mother". He scans the page to the word "father" next to which is *unknown*. The name of the child is "Edith Mustoe". He realises the woman sitting in his kitchen is not his Aunt, after all.

"So Edith…is my sister?" he ponders, leaning against the vice. The cold metal handle digs in his back.

"Yes Arthur. Edith is worried about how you'll take the news. Her childhood was miserable – her mother was a lovely woman, but her adoptive father was a cruel man. Edith suffered at his hands, Arthur."

"Poor Edith."

"A real bastard, between you and me, Arthur. He often took the belt to Edith and when she finally went out to work, he used to take all her wages off her. 'Course, they sacked him as a schoolteacher. I don't know why…but I've got my views." George narrows his eyes and taps his nose with his forefinger, pausing to watch Arthur's reaction. "This must be a shock for you, I'm sorry."

"D'you know…I overheard talk when I was a little boy – mysterious talk of a baby – I didn't really understand. So my Mum had Edith before she met Dad?"

"Yes."

"I wonder if Dad knew"

"Who can say, Arth. I think he probably did. But he adored your mother."

"Poor Mum, keeping her secret all these years. I'll speak to Edith,"

"Thank you Arthur. I love her, you know, and she's cut up about how you'll react. Edith is lost now, you see, her adoptive parents are already dead and now her real mother too – she didn't want you hurt, but you're her only family alive in the world. She wants to be close to you."

"She needn't worry. This isn't her fault."

Arthur walks back into the kitchen, handing the birth certificate to Rebecca. Edith looks at him, her eyes filling with tears. George sits next to her and pats her arm.

"Well, Edith," Arthur says.

"Arthur…I couldn't think what to do for the best," Edith replies.

"I'll tell you what I reckon. If I'm to have a sister in the world, I couldn't choose a nicer one."

At this, Edith begins to sob. Arthur walks around and put his arm around her.

"Come on now. Don't upset yourself. What a rum thing then! Fancy them keeping this quiet all these years! I'll say this for them, they were stoic liars."

Rebecca doesn't understand. "What's going on, Arthur?" she asks, puzzling over the birth certificate, which makes no sense.

"Rebecca, I've only just realised. Mum had Edith, before she married Dad. Edith is my sister."

"Good God! I don't understand…why didn't Shelagh tell you?"

"Rebecca, you don't realise how life was, in those days. You couldn't have a child out of wedlock. Women were locked up in asylums and their babies got taken away for adoption."

They talk long into the evening. Poor Edith never believed she belonged to her adoptive parents. Her adoptive mother, in fact her Aunt, (Eddie Mustoe's sister) had long-hoped for a child of her own, but they were never blessed. Eddie was friendly with the Head Gardener at a stately home in Cheltenham, with servant's quarters well away from the main house. Ashamed of his daughter's condition; when Shelagh was three months pregnant, he drove her over, late at night and deposited her with the Head Gardener and his wife. They kept her indoors for the last six months of her confinement, until two weeks before the baby was due. Eddie borrowed a car, picked her up at midnight and brought her back to the family home, Sandbanks. Edith was born in the middle bedroom, where the neighbours wouldn't hear the noise. Shelagh could keep her for six weeks. She was told to say goodbye to her daughter. Eddie drove Edith to his sister's house in the early hours – wrapped in a knitted blanket on top of cushions in a drawer taken from a chest of drawers, on the back seat.

A week later, Eddie accompanied his daughter Shelagh and grand-daughter Edith, alongside his sister and brother-in-law to the Register Office to register the birth and sign the adoption papers. Shelagh returned to the family home, alone and empty in hand and body. Edith never found out who her real father was. Arthur found a faded photograph of a soldier from the First World War amongst his Mother's possessions and he wondered. There was no name on it.

When the will has gone through probate; Shelagh leaves all £9,000 of her estate to Rebecca and Arthur – the most money they've ever had. She leaves nothing to her daughter Edith. At this time; a family home can be bought outright for £4,000.00.   Rebecca visits Cavendish House in Cheltenham and buys herself a white mink coat, costing £1,200.00. Two days later, she's dissatisfied with her purchase and returns to the shop. There, in a locked cabinet, is a full length light brown mink coat – the most expensive one in the shop, costing £4,500.00. Rebecca buys it.

The dry cleaning agency eventually peters out completely; in line with the development and mass-production of static polymers and artificial fabrics. Charlie leaves home. Two years later, the mink coat is sold to repay debts.   In 1981, they sell the house before they lose it. With the inheritance and the house sale; there is just enough money to downsize even further in a house just off Moors Street. Arthur takes Rebecca to look at it; and inside, all the walls in every room are painted luminous yellow. Seems the vendor had a job painting the lines on the roads. She wants another house in Stroud Road; but he tells her this is where they're buying, because they can buy it outright. She is not given the choice. When asked where she lives; Rebecca will reframe this as Moors St Augustine's - because it sounds better. Rebecca, Arthur and Stella move into the house in the poor area. There will be no more house moves.

Chapter Forty-Seven:

Robert lands himself a prime job as Head Chef at Coney Hill asylum. It's well paid – the canteen is merry with banter, which Robert encourages - provided he is the Banterer-in-Chief. Part of their role is to feed the nurse orderlies and Robert enjoys taking the piss out of them. He's a bit perturbed about their locking the patients up, in the afternoons and getting drunk, but not enough to complain, or hand in his notice. Drunken disorderly's, he calls them. These people are all dirty. He washes his own hands all the time and showers twice when he comes home, to wash the smell of the place off him. Some of them shouldn't be in an asylum; he senses this, least of all his mother. Particularly the businessmen – he watches them come in with a nervous breakdown and leave with something worse. Madness is contagious; as is hanging around with the mentals. Half the psychiatrists and staff seem weirder than the patients. One Sunday afternoon, Winston, a placid second generation Jamaican, eases his wide backside into a chair, in the staff dining room and begins to tuck into his meal. Robert approaches his table, twirling and snapping a tea towel in the air.

"Eh Winston, me bwai, what d'yam tink of de chow?"

"Messa D! Rispeck! Yadam food feet for a king!"

"You ever thought about joining Egon Ronay, then, Winston? Sampling the food in all the restaurants and giving it your low-down?"

"Yar funny bwai, Messa D. Hee hee hee. Egon Roaanay...You make me laugh Messa D. Winston can be King o' de dumplin!"

"Winston, you want to be a restaurant critic. I've never seen you turn a meal down. Say Whaaaaat? C'mon brother, das goooood chicken!"

Winston keeps right on chewing, slowly. He tinks he knows something real funny that might shut this honky up. Bombaclat.

"Robert, my man. Keep on going wi ya dam faistey! Ya food good for a white bwai!"

Robert laughs, as he nudges one of his audience; an apprentice from the local tech. He slaps his thigh and raises his knee. "YO SHORE ENJOY YOUR FOOD, MY MAN! WAY BETTER DAN DEM BANANAS ON THAT BOAT!" And he whoops, like Michael Jackson. The apprentice scratches at a big yellow zit on his badly-shaven neck, laughing his thicko laugh, conspiratorial.

Winston watches, his grin showing large white teeth. "Mmm...ya ganna be real famous, Messa D, my man. Lip out ya irie name two time?"

"SPEAK English boy?"

"Yo surname. Lass name."

"Denby, Winston. Denby – hear it and weep. One day my name'll be up in lights and you can say, that man shore cooked for me. Me, Winston

Wilkins. Robert Denby, that world-famous chef, he done prepared my dinner when he started. You want an autograph, Winston?"

"Yes Sir, I'll take your autograph, Mr Famous Robert Denby with dem Meechalin stars an ya name im plenty. Denby, you say? Mmm, clever bwai, me tink ya Madda on ward 2."

Robert pales momentarily, but recovers quickly. His left eye twitches. No-one notices except Winston.

"What you talkin about, Willis? Don't get you, Winston, you shore you ain't been taking some of them drugs you been dishin out? You sure you ain't been on the ganja, Winston? Your secret's safe with me Winston, but we wouldn't want those inspectors finding out what goes on on the ward at night, hey?"

"Messa Denby, ya fool with Winstan, but Winstan av de las laugh." Winston sucks saliva through his teeth and shakes his head, chuckling. "Tschhhhh Rasclat. Foolish bwai. Hee hee hee."

Robert secures another job, within a month – head chef at an Italian restaurant in town.

Chapter Forty-Eight:

Robert begins a relationship with a lady called Ruth. This is an up and down sort of affair – Ruth is already engaged to someone else. He is now the youngest ever Head chef at a local hospital. Ruth attended public school and her parents, The Giles's, are millionaires. After a spell at secretarial college, Ruth breaks off her engagement and takes a low-paid job to be with Robert, who quickly proposes to her and she accepts. The Giles family don't approve and refuse to attend the engagement party. When Rebecca learns of this, she's upset and telephones Ruth, asking if she believes Robert is good enough for her. Ruth assures Rebecca that her parents have no problem with Robert, but are angry with Ruth. At the party, Robert hands a hand-crafted box of chocolates to Ruth, which also contains the engagement ring. Rebecca has never seen him so enamoured with a woman and is delighted for the couple. They're bound to be compatible, of course, being both Gemini's. Eventually, Ruth's parents come round to the idea. Rebecca purchases a special bone china cup and saucer in order to serve tea to Mrs Giles, should she ever deign to visit.

Nonetheless, attending the wedding causes Rebecca tremendous anxiety. How can they live up to the upper classes? She needs a beautiful hat. They must hire a Rolls Royce for the day, to fit in with the other guests. She suggests this to Arthur.

"We'll take the Rolls Canardly," he jokes.

"What are you talking about?" Rebecca snaps.

"It rolls down the hill and can 'ardly get up the other side!"

"Don't be ridiculous Arthur."

"I'm not hiring a Rolls Royce, Rebecca, and that's final."

"What about a Mercedes-Benz?"

"We might just manage that. Leave it with me."

"And a chauffeur."

"I'll put a bloody hat on and drive – you can sit in the back like Lady Muck, if you must."

Pacified for the moment, Rebecca telephones Ruth for advice on her outfit, in order not to embarrass her new daughter-in-law.

"I don't care what you come in, as long as you're there!" Ruth replies. Rebecca still spends a great deal of time and money on her outfit. Her dress is brightly coloured and laden with chiffon over the top in two layers, teamed with a black hat laced with hundreds of long, tiny feathers. For her daughter Stella, who's now 11, Rebecca buys a suit with a matching hat. Stella refuses to wear it and instead wears a skirt with a tank top and a straw hat. She will not be persuaded otherwise and Rebecca gives in – the child is so headstrong. The wedding day arrives and Rebecca spends four hours getting ready; as all her routines are repeated multiple times. She takes double her usual dosage of tranquilisers and slips the packet into her handbag. She passes their little van in the street, Rebecca sticks two fingers up, walking past to the waiting Mercedes. "Not tonight, Josephine!" she says. Arthur has even arranged a chauffeur.

Faith, Rebecca's mother, also attends the wedding with Rebecca's brother Clive and his wife, Megan. They sit at a table far away from Rebecca. Although Faith acknowledges Rebecca by saying hello, she remains very cool and distant and avoids getting into any protracted conversation with her. Every few hours, Rebecca slips to the ladies and tops up her medication. As the reception continues around her, she floats away to staring into space on many occasions, damning her need for the tablets and how they spoil everything; flattening the happiest of occasions to indifference. Arthur and Rebecca leave the evening party early. She sleeps solidly, for fourteen hours.

Chapter Forty-Nine:

Arthur begins work as an electrician in the maintenance department of Gloucester Royal Hospital. The early eighties bring new government policies into practice, with the notion of "care in the community" pushed. Later that decade, Horton Road and Coney Hill are sold off piecemeal, for sprawling match-box housing. Two estates called Abbeydale and Abbeymead satisfy a growing market for modern red-brick, thin-walled houses. They are quickly filled by young professionals and families. With it, Thatcherism promotes a culture of every man for himself, capitalism and greed. Those with diagnoses of mental illness are herded out and encouraged to attend day centres, or live in sheltered housing. It is felt that their problematic behaviour can be well-controlled by tablets, anti-psychotics, neuroleptics and the like.

Rebecca is probably one of the first to attend day centres, to help get her out of the house and address her obsessions and depression. The first she attends is at Denmark Road in Gloucester. There are a few nice women - Rebecca feels she can identify with them. They all smoke and have a lot in common, discussing their various issues and how to cope with them. The centre even has a sewing group. A matron is in attendance and a lady called Dot, who heads the social scene. Dot arranges dancing on Fridays, which they all enjoy, and a session of bingo. All the patients are given tasks to complete, which might be washing clothes, washing up, making drinks, tidying the kitchen and cooking home produce. The consultants meet at the centre every Friday at four o-clock. Rebecca's job is to boil a piece of ham early in the morning, cool it and slice it in the afternoon and make sandwiches for "the big boys". She dutifully cuts them into triangles and arranges them, with a parsley garnish.

In order to try and introduce some normality into Rebecca's life, the psychiatrists recommend she be offered a placement at the Central Sterile Supplies Department, a unit annexed to Gloucester Royal Hospital. Rebecca is paid a small wage. The instruments and dressings for surgical operations require specialist sterilization and packaging, ready for issue. A meal is also provided, as is transport between home and work. Rebecca begins to feel useful and productive again. Two years later, they announce this unit is to close and transfer to the rear of a mental health unit within the hospital. Meals are provided in the hospital catering section. By this time, she has progressed to a "top table operative" and begins to train new members to the team. Unfortunately, the unit then shuts down completely – making all the workers redundant.

Financial cutbacks to the day centres mean the activities are curtailed. The NHS takes over funding some of them for a time, constructing a canteen and an activity building in the grounds. Both enterprises fail and are closed down. Various new schemes are started, with each patient being offered a counsellor, but finally the NHS convert all the rooms to offices. The patients are ousted. Rebecca is directed to another day unit, run on the same lines as the previous one. After a few months this too closes down, with no alternative provision. Other venues in Gloucestershire are offered, but Rebecca's agoraphobia and fear of travelling longer distances makes attendance impossible.

Later, a new day centre called "Salvus Sanctuary" opens in Warford Road and Rebecca begins to attend. This is intended to help with mental health problems and employs a manager, a day officer and a doctor who tries to get patients back on track, should they become overwhelmed by anxiety or depression. Rebecca finds her agoraphobia worsening and eventually realises she can't walk unaccompanied any more. Arthur needs to take her and collect her, but finally she becomes too frightened to leave home. She's saddened, because she likes the sewing group and was learning quilting – she's already sewn two full sized quilts and a few smaller ones for prams and pushchairs.

The centre also holds fetes, which she's always enjoyed. All the items made by the patients are sold, their woodwork, pottery, painting, home-made preserves, pickles, hard-boiled eggs, scones, plants and bric-a-brac. The patients serve soft drinks, tea and coffee and at the end a raffle is held, to raise funds. The money goes into the "amenity" fund, which is used for day trips for them, to exhibitions or stately homes.

In 1986; Rebecca is asked to take part in a televised report for Go West News, publicising the work of the Salvus Sanctuary Day Centre. Eager to please, she agrees.

In the Go West Newsroom; the fresh face of the presenter is framed by his Christopher Biggins over-sized spectacles. He wears a tweed jacket, bland as his expression of caring, serious stance, required for such a delicate topic as this. He clutches his pen as he reads the autocue:

"One in five people will suffer from mental illness at some time in their lives...some will be treated in mental hospitals, but with many now closing down, a new type of day care is evolving and with it, new methods for helping *the mentally ill*. In a special report now, Len Sneddon looks at a centre which is helping to shape the care of *the mentally ill* for the future."

Cut/cue to a street scene and then Rebecca, in her white dress, copied from Dynasty by Debenhams, flecked with bold-patterned black and a fake handkerchief sewn onto the breast. Curled, short cut auburn hair, styled like Princess Diana. Her blue eyes sparkle in a benign fashion, head tilted in compliance.

"If you've got a picture in your mind about going to hell - if anyone's got a picture in their mind about going to hell, it's like that. It's uncontrollable feelings of panic and fear." The brush with Catholicism stayed with Rebecca.

Could Hell really be worse? She can't imagine this existence between terror and hopelessness as a life worth leading. She doesn't have much imagination anymore; so she acts. Rebecca speaks with poise and delicacy, very well spoken, hardly any trace of an accent. The camera cuts to her wedding rings, clasped ladylike together on her lap, her legs, tucked to the side as she sits in the darkened blue room, on the cosy-carpeted floor.

They cut to another patient – male this time, this is Vernon Compton. Vernon's pupils are dilated. He speaks slowly, with a broad Gloucestershire accent; his eyes downcast, the pale and thinning hair framing the face of someone rather beaten.

"Well I was in a roit old state, I been upturning the table when I gets depressed and I grabs the kitchen knife and I asks moi mother to stab me, I does, you know like when iss reely bad. Thing is I can come ere and there's others like me. There's a lot of stigmata you know, with mental illness..."

Here is the reassuring male voice of Len Sneddon once more, to narrate the viewer through the scene:

"Rebecca Denby has suffered from severe depression for thirty six years. To try and cure her, she's had a lobotomy. That's an operation on the brain, and has had more than forty sessions of electroconvulsive therapy, where electricity is passed through the head. That's as well as a lifetime on drugs. She says the centre was her last hope."

Smiling brightly now, Rebecca continues: "They have a different approach to...mental health. We're helped to run the unit as far as possible, which gives us motivation. We have *sane* things that we do – our groups, and they ask us. They don't just push you to one side, they actually follow it up."

"What d'you think you'd have done, without the day centre?"

"I don't think I'd be here. That's a dreadful thing to say, but um, here they just worked on me for a whole week. They never stopped and I saw the light through and I carried on. So whenever I feel depressed, I get in touch with the centre!"

"Are you saying they saved your life?" It is important Len Sneddon makes the point about the *value* of these facilities, for the viewers.

She pauses for one moment: "I would say yes, on that. Yes."

Cut to some beautiful artwork being painted by *the mentally ill*, Munch-like anguished faces and features daubed in garish red and orange contained in a whirling rook black sea of torment. Then - two rows of patients with their arms outstretched towards one another, clasped at the hands, as though re-creating a square dance of old. Instead, one patient stands at the end and dives, headlong, onto the limbs of her peers, exhaling with a long groan. OOOOOOOOOOOH!

213

Cut to the beautiful people, the social workers, and therapists/carers. Young, male, virile – denim casual shirts opened up at the neck. Floppy 80's hair, thick and abundant. They look like Richard Gere and Brian Ferry, who talk about drama therapy in their plummy voices, yah, obvs and how integration and confidence-building is the answer.

Cut to a refined lady in her fifties, who talks, too, of her panic attacks. She gives every appearance of a coherent mother. Like Rebecca, she is the regal female ambassador for the day-centre. They are the publicity scunts – saved from certain death by Richard Gere and Brian Ferry.

Cut to the last scene of the group, where they swiftly remove the lens from the shaking man with his tardive dyskinesia; Parkinsonian-like symptoms, from years of neuroleptics. He's not such good television as Brian Ferry-carer, who now strokes and then passes round the imaginary cat to *the mentally ill* and encourages them to do the same. They play along. They want to make sure the centre gets enough funds to carry on. Where will they go, if it shuts?

This is therapy.

Several weeks later, drama-therapist Richard Gere is admitted to the emergency department of Gloucester Royal Hospital with a wound to the back of his head, which requires six stitches. An hour earlier, green-fingered Vernon assists the Head Gardener with the bedding plants in the border surrounding the day centre. Richard Gere stops by, to check on his progress and compliments him, suggesting that if Vernon's interested – he'll bring him in a book on gardening, from home. Vernon's really pleased. As Richard walks away, Vernon begins to fret, that Richard Gere will forget his promise. He can't seem to think of the right words to shout, so he launches the trowel at the back of his head instead, to get his attention. As it strikes, Richard Gere is felled to the ground, rolling and holding his bleeding head with both hands.

"What the fuck did you do that for Vernon?" shouts the Head Gardener, wiping his hands and running towards Richard Gere. Vernon runs with him.

"Sorry, sorry" he says. "You won't forget my gardening book though, will you?"

"Get back inside and ask them to phone an ambulance, Vernon, oh my God!"

Richard Gere does not return to the day centre, but takes up work teaching Drama at a local primary school and running Amateur Dramatics Societies, in the local community. Five years pass, before he decides to go for some counselling sessions for the nightmares. Fifteen years later, he takes his own life with a concoction of anti-depressants, making sure he won't be found. His wife finds him, after her night-shift in the nursing home.

Chapter Fifty:

Rebecca spirals in and out of depression with the occasional passionate outburst. By the time her teenage daughter Stella starts dating Andy, she realises she's missed the boat in terms of being able to control her. Sometimes Rebecca's rows with Arthur are violent and passionate and Stella seems to take this all in her stride. Apart from one occasion where she hears her mother screaming. She comes out of her bedroom to find her father dragging her mother upstairs by the hair. She takes in the scene, then shouts:

"Leave her alone!"

Artthur stares at his daughter for a moment, confused. Then he lets go of Rebecca and continues up to the bedroom, closing the door behind him. Rebecca gets up and hanging on to the stair rail, staggers to the kitchen. Stella follows, watching through the balustrade. Rebecca doesn't see her. Rebecca takes a carving knife from the kitchen drawer and rolling up her right sleeve, slowly carves five lines into her right forearm, holding it over the sink. Stella puts her hands over her mouth, so as not to cry out. Her mother watches the wounds bleed for a moment or two and then wraps her arm in a bandage, combs her hair and continues with her housework.

When Stella returns from school the next day, she will learn that her mother has visited a solicitor and shown him her wounds, saying that Arthur has inflicted them and she wants a divorce. Her father visits the solicitor and explains her mental problems, so that the matter is dropped.

Soon enough, Stella even joins in becoming Rebecca's carer and boss. In protest, Rebecca behaves angrily when Stella's young man comes around to call. He's a lovely looking chap, but he looks rather cheeky – the sort who might mess Stella about. Rebecca knows his mother from Coney Hill – her name is April. She's a brilliant artist; but her mental troubles mean she's been in and out of there for years. She's even painted Rebecca's portrait.

Stella and Andy sit cuddled up on the sofa, in front of the television. Rebecca; who has remained in her dressing gown all day; glares at the plant pot on the nest of tables, the sagging geranium leaves of burgundy and green seem limp and useless. This has been annoying her, each time she glances at it, today. She walks across the room and picks it up, brushing past the couple's legs. Opening the window, Rebecca launches the pot outside onto the pavement. It lands with a thudding crash and soil spreads out on the paving slab.

"Mum! What on earth are you doing?" Stella remonstrates.

"I don't want him in here, Stella. Get out Andy!"

Andy stands up, looking a bit worried.

"Sit down, Andy, and ignore her. She's having one of her turns!" says Stella, equally bossy.

"I think I'd better go. I'll ring you tomorrow," Andy walks out, closing the door behind him. Rebecca races to the letterbox and shouts through after him.

"Don't come back, either. You're not seeing Stella any more. I FORBID IT!" She rattles the letterbox and walks away.

Andy strides back, opens the letterbox and shouts: "I'll see her whenever I want, you nutty cow. You'd better get over it. D'you hear me?" and he walks away.

Rebecca wonders what on earth had got into her, later on – but the matter is never discussed any further. Stella and Andy continue to see one another, despite Rebecca's protestations and occasional changes of mind, where she considers Andy a charming man. When they become engaged; Stella visits her grandmother Faith several times, persuading her to attend the wedding. Faith agrees, but tells Stella not to hold out any hope of a reunion with Rebecca. Over six years, Rebecca has sent cards to her mother, filling her in on the news and asking her to get in touch – she never has. Perhaps she'd ask Megan's son to have a word with her Mother and see if he couldn't persuade her to get back in touch. Rebecca can't recollect any reason why Mother stays away – this is so cruel and hurtful. Perhaps Megan's responsible; whispering poison in her ear. But Clive should have stuck up for her. He always was weak when it came to his wife.

Faith attends Stella's wedding in 1988 as promised; but once again she is distant with Rebecca, who is terribly hurt. Rebecca finds herself in a variety of roles on this day, babysitter and entertainer of her grandchildren, waitress to the older relatives, who are content to allow her to run round serving them. Keeping busy distracts her, but this is tiring and at times she feels disorientated and dizzy. She's making the fourth serving of teas and coffees on a large tray when the front doorbell rings. Arthur rushes off to answer and begins chatting quietly with a woman on the doorstep. Rebecca pokes her head around the door. A brassy looking piece from Arthur's work – she's been after him for months, to no avail. She isn't even particularly pretty and he's a silly sod for encouraging her. Perhaps she ought to kick up a fuss, she's cheeky, coming round on their daughter's wedding day – she certainly wasn't invited. But Arthur's already showed her in and sloped off to the kitchen with her.

After serving everyone and making small talk, Rebecca wonders where Arthur's got to. She takes the empty tray out to the kitchen. As she opens the door, they don't even hear her. Arthur and the woman are kissing with their mouths open, their arms all round one another's bodies, in a clinch. Rebecca stares for a moment – the medication doesn't allow things to register quickly these days. Arthur looks up, pushing the woman away and turning, but doesn't say anything, just puts the kettle on. Rebecca closes the door and walks upstairs to her bedroom drawer, taking two more Fuckthazopam, which are so hard to swallow without water, they clag and stick at the back of her throat, dry and acidic as they dissolve slowly. She does not confront Arthur, but remonstrates with him about it on several occasions. His response is always, "You don't want to take any notice. Stop making such a fuss. She's nothing to me, it was only a little kiss on a wedding day. These things happen." Somehow, Rebecca is aware the rest of the day is tainted, but can't recollect why or how.

She supposed these things did happen, with hindsight. The friend of Arthur's who used to visit all the time when he was working on the lorries. She'd had a kiss with him, hadn't she? Or perhaps she'd imagined it. He was married too – had levelled with her. Said he was in love with her and they could have a bit on the side, no harm to anyone. He'd never leave his wife for her, mind, she ought to know. What about the occasion the postman invited her back to his house? She'd been in the pub with him and thought she jolly well would go. They left together giggling, and were almost back, when Arthur appeared on the other side of the road, crossing over with the look on his face. He'd pushed her, hadn't he? Told her to get herself off home. She ran away, just as he'd commanded. She flushes at the humiliating recollection of his bending her over his knee and spanking her bottom when he got home. The beast.

What about Edward Napier at St Andrew's, too? They weren't lovers though; never saw it right the way through. He wasn't faithful to his wife, was he? But she'd had an affair first, hadn't she; you couldn't blame the poor man. Just imagine if she'd gone off with him – she could have been having the high life in a posh house by now. Pointless dwelling on it.

Chapter Fifty-One:

A year later, Stella suddenly seems to need her mother, in the last stages of her pregnancy. Rebecca stays with her throughout a difficult labour and is the first to hold the baby, Cathy. Rebecca comes to love Cathy with a freedom and passion she's never experienced with her own children. She's always offering to look after her, even almost full-time, when Stella returns to work. The lovely bathing with the soft sponge in the kitchen sink and then all these new-fangled baby bouncers and walkers – these times bring Rebecca and Arthur joy. Arthur hopes this might pull Rebecca out of her depression and for nine months or so, this does, until he begins working longer hours. Rebecca begins to obsess about something happening to Cathy and becomes frightened she might become too ill; she mightn't be able to look after her.

Rebecca believes her safety lies in her house –but her problems don't stop there. Her fear escalates to such a degree; she refuses to be left alone at all. She pressurises Arthur to stay at home with her, in case she has a panic attack. She returns to Coney Hill for a lengthy stay of three months and more changes in medication. After her discharge she is referred back to "Salvus Sanctuary" as a day patient. Jackie Bambridge, a psychiatric nurse, writes up Rebecca's review notes:

"Rebecca has just returned to the centre after a long spell in Coney Hill Hospital. She was on "Severn" ward from 4th February to 24th May, under supervision whilst her medication was reduced and changed. She has long been on Paustellen, but has been prescribed a relatively new drug, Moclobemide. Rebecca maintains she feels no better for the change of drugs but has been advised she will have to wait up to four months before she notices any benefits. Rebecca suffered severe withdrawal symptoms whilst coming off the Paustellen. This has resulted in her feeling a complete failure with the return of suicidal feelings. Her husband has taken the next two weeks off work to be with her. During this time she will only be attending the centre on a Wednesday morning to do the sewing group, on the understanding that she can ring on the other days if she feels in need of support. Mr Denby has been in touch with the National Schizophrenic Association. He is hoping they may provide him with financial help to provide care for Rebecca as at present her state of anxiety makes it impossible for her to remain home by herself. Although all her energies have been devoted to her family in the past, she presently feels too exhausted to undertake too much and can no longer babysit for her grand-daughter. This state of affairs upsets her greatly and as she derives great support from the centres, she will probably increase her days of attendance when she feels more in control of her anxiety panic attacks. She claims she feels more in control when attending the centre and it is hoped by eventually increasing her days,

Rebecca will feel better able to cope at home. Rebecca has always had great insight and determination to overcome her problems. She has been a caring wife and mother and is now at a very low ebb. Our aims and objectives are to offer Rebecca regular counselling as required and to encourage Rebecca to attend the centre on more days so that her problems can be addressed and her self-esteem raised."

Chapter Fifty-One:

When Rebecca's brother Clive dies in April 1990, Rebecca and Arthur attend his funeral and are avoided by the rest of the family. A reporter for the Citizen comes round to list everyone's names. Rebecca spells out their names and tells him their relationship, the sister and brother-in-law of the deceased. Two days later, they scour the paper for the report. They are not mentioned as relations, but are grouped in with the also-rans in attendance, simply as Mr & Mrs Denby. Rebecca cries for the whole day and Arthur throws the newspaper into the fire, disgusted.

Chapter Fifty-Two:

Rebecca often attracts the disenfranchised, the outcast and the eccentric in society - sometimes she meets them at a therapy group or day centre, neighbours and people randomly encountered and befriended in a supermarket. Many of these characters appear to integrate within their communities, with little talk of sectioning or drug treatment. She's an empathic listener and Arthur is a mender and fixer of all things, consequently as a couple their company, time and attention is much in demand. They have an open-door policy, where visitors – colourful or otherwise, are welcomed, fed, watered and comforted, with as much care as the stray animals their three children brought home over the years.

The children have forged lives of their own – all with a hard-driven work ethic and married young. Charlie's on his second marriage and has taken on two step-sons, as well as his son from the first marriage. Robert and his wife have two children. Robert and Charlie own their own businesses and her daughter Stella first trained as a hairdresser; then a nursing auxiliary and now works in a mental health care setting; with vulnerable and sometimes dangerous patients, released from prison. Stella manages them with a half-bossy, caring and common sense approach and they appear to respond well to her, for her part, the peculiarities of their behaviour never trouble her. Stella is fervently committed to the medical model of mental illness – if these people would simply take their medication, all would be well.

It was to Rebecca that Lorena, perhaps the first post-operative transsexual prostitute in Gloucester, confided about her sex-change operation and one day took an unwilling Rebecca upstairs to show her the results of the surgery. Arthur asked how this looked, Rebecca said "actually, it was all very tidy." When he later recounted the story, he would say "of course they took his John Thomas and tucked it all up inside, that's how they do things, you know..." Lorena drank too much in local pubs and become engaged in bawdy conversations with rough men, which once resulted in them throwing her into the canal. She survived; frozen through and humiliated, yet defiant.

The upper-class chain-smoking Fiona became a frequent visitor at the Denby's. She put them in mind of an actress Francis de la Tour, who played the whimsical spinster "Miss Jones" in a popular sitcom called "Rising Damp". Her plummy voice and mannerisms were similar; her neck and head movements that inclined whilst listening, as a canary might. Unlike Miss Jones, Fiona was not sleight in stature, but was a heavily-built woman who sat with legs akimbo in front of the fire. One day Fiona stood up to retrieve her lighter from the mantelpiece and veered forwards into it, banging her head and oblivious to the guffaws of Rebecca's visiting son Charlie.

A homeless war veteran Jack, who couldn't bear to sleep anywhere indoors, once housed himself in their garden shed for several months. He was often arrested for petty crimes committed in the local area, as a likely candidate. Arthur always defended him and provided the necessary alibi, knowing full well Jack was harmless and asleep on the mattress he had given him.

Club-foot Joe, a hunchback with one huge built up parody of a platform shoe and dodgy hips, often called for Arthur's assistance in constructing a variety of contraptions in his garage. Theirs is a busy life, if not always happy. The majority of Rebecca's encounters with others are lived through a surreal looking-glass, where she often feels disconnected from what others appear to be experiencing – but they interest her. The cycle of drug-treatment, variations of which sometimes cause painful and distressing side-effects, weight gain and joint pain alongside periodic bouts of hopelessness are interspersed with spontaneous levelling. With few high points; the best Rebecca can hope for is stability - when this comes, she finds life tedious.

Rebecca and Arthur become more insular and dependent on one another for everything, carving out an independence from the rest of the world aside from family and relying less upon the psychiatric profession – becoming jaded about what they'd promised to fix and couldn't. They focus more on their physical complaints, which for Rebecca are debilitating as she becomes frail with arthritis – resorting to using a wheelchair on occasions. They develop a language of their own and role-play various characters encountered in their lives together, imitating a mixture of those accents and attitudes.

Rebecca is given a hysterectomy and Arthur develops prostate problems. He's offered an operation where they say they will *scrape it all out to stop it turning to cancer* and he goes along with it. Both are vexed when their sex life ends in their seventies after his botched operation. He can maintain an erection, but his ejaculation is so dry, the burning sensation all the way up spoils everything. He stops approaching her for any kind of sex and pushes Rebecca away if she approaches him. He sees no point in sex if he can't climax. She resents him, but sometimes they still sit together on the sofa and hold hands. They still sleep in the same bed, cuddled up, frustrated – but neither really wants things any other way. Together, they are safe.

#

The latest psychiatrist, Dr Peso, is a sweet chap. They both like this little man with a kindly expression. He's passionate, bless his heart, that's what you get with the continentals – they know (never having been abroad) – foreigners can't help themselves with their natural tendency for being over-emotional. His warmth is probably down to the Spanish climate he's been raised in. Dr Peso sits in the session, having read Rebecca's medical notes from cover to cover. When he looks Rebecca in the eyes and asks how she is, he genuinely cares. His English is excellent, had to admire him, not like some of those paki doctors – can't understand what they're on about half the time.

"Meeses Denby, you 'ave been through so much! It makes me ssad...for you to have been treated thees way."

"Well Doctor Peso, my life hasn't been easy. But I've done my best, you know."

"May I call you Rrebecca– I feel it ees important for us to know one another well. I read these notes, you see, and I feel I understand, as though I know you already, before you come here today."

"Of course you may."

"Rrebecca, what do you feel about all these tablets that you take?"

"Would you like me to speak frankly, Dr Peso?"

"Of course."

"I feel they have turned me into a drug addict. I can't do without them anymore, you see. I can't leave the house without them."

"I see thees. I feel, so sad for you. Do you want for me to help you to try to stop them, fairy slowly?"

"No. I can't manage without them...I see that now. It's hopeless. You won't take them off me, will you?"

Dr Peso's brown eyes fill with tears which he wipes away with the handkerchief from his breast pocket. "Rrreebecca, what hass happened to you is terrible. At your age, for me to take thees tablets away would be too cruel. I do not think you should have had them all and been on them for so long. But I see you cannot manage without them."

"I really can't, now. Perhaps twenty years ago – I might have had a chance. I wish you'd come along then, I might have been strong enough. But I'm old now, Dr Peso. You see how it is."

"I see how thees ees better than you know. I tell you something, Rrreebecca. But you must promees thees ees between us."

He lowers his voice, conspiratorial. Rebecca listens intently. This is strange, quite exciting – he seems not to be in charge of her. She is the listener. She wonders why he's so upset. Her instincts are not to be trusted – she knows, deep down.

"I too have the depression, you see Rrreebecca. You are not alone. And I take the anti-depressants for thees, for many years now. I do not think I would manage so well without them. It is a terrible illness. Peeple they don understand it ees not your fault – you cannot help that you feel thees way."

"Dr Peso, I am glad that you told me. You mustn't worry. I'll be alright, you see, I have Arthur to look after me and so long as they don't take them away, we manage most of the time."

225

"It would be cruel to take you off thees things at your age – I know thees. We'll carry on then Rrreebecca – and I don wan you to worry, I put thees into your notes and you weel come to see me, once a month and we talk about eet. Eef you have a problem in between, you telephone me and then we weel have an appointment."

"I will, Dr Peso. Thank you."

"Now, you don' worry and you carry on."

#

Dr Peso leaves, within the year. They wonder what happened to him. His replacement is an Oxbridge psychiatrist, who dismisses all personal contact aside in favour of discussions concerning her "symptomology" and "treatment refractory" depression.

Chapter Fifty-Three:

Rebecca watches her son Charlie grow thinner and tenser. The two year tax enquiry has taken a toll on his tired marriage. All he seems to do is work. He tells her he is lonely and she worries about him for months – even offering him some of her anti-anxiolytic medication; but he won't take it. In early 2008; he announces that his second twenty year marriage is over. His wife asks him to leave and he moves out. Both of his stepsons and his eldest son continue working with him in the business; but his youngest son of fourteen is devastated. By October; he tells Rebecca he is in love with Poppy, a counsellor and divorcee with three children he met at a dance class. In November he brings Poppy to meet his parents. Rebecca is intrigued and loses no time in telling Poppy her troubles.

In a matter of months of visits and talking, the pair form a friendship.

"Perhaps I should write a book about my life!" Rebecca announces, rolling her eyes.

"I think you should," Poppy replies.

"D'you think anyone would be interested?"

"I would be. I could help you, if you want."

"Would you really? But how would we go about it?"

"I suppose you could write it and I could type it up. Or you could record it?"

"Record it?"

"Yes. I've got a digital voice recorder I could lend you. It's ever so simple. I could play it back and type it up."

"I don't think I could manage that."

Arthur, gets up to rummage in his desk drawer. He returns with an ancient Dictaphone, dusty but working, with a two inch tape inside.

"This is just the job," he says. "I'll teach you to use it."

It takes two years to finish. They discuss the title – which begins as "One Flew Out of the Cuckoo's Nest" (at Poppy's behest – after her favourite film); but ends as "Bear Ye One Another's Burdens" after the inscription from Galatians; which sits on the clock tower of Coney Hill Asylum. The work is painstaking for Poppy, who must stop, start, rewind and erase each tape, returning the transcripts to Rebecca to check the content. She undertakes background research; interviews all Rebecca's children and writes up the results. She takes the manuscript to a local printer for binding into four hard covered books with a selection of photographs. Poppy buys gold lettering from a local artwork dealership and tweezers them on by hand to each cover and spine. All this is done in secret and she presents the finished article to Rebecca.

For one day Rebecca is elated; re-reading her foreword. She will not read the whole book – but next she flicks to the section relating to her eldest son Robert's interview. Her fury at his words cannot be placated by Arthur. She rings Poppy.

"It's all lies. I can't believe he said those things about me! How dare he? I shall never speak to him again as long as I live! And for you to write it up – I can't believe you did it."

"Rebecca, just a moment. What's upset you so much?"

"How could he believe I was jealous of his life? I've never wanted anything but the best for my children!"

"But surely you understand this is about his perspective? It may not be accurate in your eyes; but interviewing people is to find out how they feel?"

"None of it is true!"

"I can assure you I made nothing up. I interviewed him and I wrote down what he said. Maybe you should speak to him about what he shared – so you can understand?"

"I'll be having this out with him, don't you worry!"

"I'm so sorry you don't like it. You can destroy it, if you want. It's your property."

Arthur takes the phone from her. His voice is calm, yet reproachful.

"This is a bad business and she's very upset. Robert shouldn't have said those things to you."

"Perhaps not. I'm so sorry the chapter troubled her this way. But it is her book and if she wants it taken out, we can take it out."

"I think that would be best. I'll get her settled. We'll see you on Thursday?"

"Of course."

Poppy is perturbed. When an unsuspecting Robert arrives to visit his mother two days later, he encounters a verbal backlash of epic proportions from his mother. He denies everything and snatches the book from her, scanning the pages she is quoting.

"I never said that. It's ridiculous. And SHE'S NO AUTHOR!"

After they make their peace; Rebecca still suspects him. The matter will be periodically brought up and dropped with Poppy over the next eighteen months, until Poppy tires of her attempts to elicit a bearable untruth about the matter. Each time Poppy visits, she is regaled with tales of Stella and her amazing work in mental health and what a wonderful daughter she is. Each time Stella visits, she is regaled with tales of Poppy's wonderful relationship with Rebecca and how she is just like a daughter. Stella is trying very hard not to become irritable about this. Rebecca notices and steps up the praise for Poppy.

Poppy and Charlie's wedding invitations are posted in mid-July 2010. The ceremony is to be a small affair at a local church with a reception at home. Immediate family are invited, but the invitations do not extend to the children of friends and siblings. Tension quickly arises between Stella and Poppy on this issue. Poppy will not change her mind and Stella refuses to attend the wedding without her children. Poppy accepts her decision sadly – but the relationship becomes strained. Rebecca is diagnosed with hyperparathyroidism and will require a surgical operation on her throat. This takes place a week later and she makes a full recovery. Ten days prior to the wedding; Arthur wakes up in distress. He has no recollection of who and where he is. He can speak and walk; but something is awry. Stella is called, followed by an ambulance; and Arthur is admitted to hospital; having suffered a small stroke.

Rebecca spends the first night alone in the marital bed with Stella and her daughters staying in the spare room. She doesn't ask after Arthur. This situation quickly deteriorates; Stella is unable to attend her job and Rebecca refuses to be left alone. They begin to quarrel.

"Now look Mum, Andy and I have offered you this many times. We can sell our house; you and Dad can sell yours and I'll give up my job and look after you. You can move in with us. It's just not practical; you living like this anymore."

"Well I'd love to live with you Stella, but you know your father won't hear of it!"

"But he's not well enough to look after you. I've got to work – you are both ringing me to leave my job and come out every time there's a problem! I'm going to get in trouble!"

"Can't I come and live with you? I'd like that."

"It would need to be both of you. We'll need to buy a bigger place – you know ours isn't big enough and you couldn't get up those stairs. Just think about it again, it would be so much more practical for everyone. What's Dad's problem anyway?"

"He doesn't really trust Andy."

"What's Andy ever done to him?"

"Your father's worried that we'd all lose our home if Andy couldn't pay the mortgage. You know after that bankruptcy he couldn't bear to lose his house again Stella."

"We're not going to lose our home! We both work!"

"But what if you over-stretch yourselves? We'd have to go into a care home – oh I couldn't bear that, we'd be parted!"

"You wouldn't have to go anywhere. Just talk to him again. Look, we can take care of you much better this way. I can't keep leaving my work to come and stay here, I've got my children and my dogs to think of, too!"

"Well you have to persuade him. I'd love to live with you."

The crisis team are called the following evening and Charlie also visits his mother and sister to try and negotiate a course of action. The initial suggestion is for Rebecca to be taken into Wotton Lawn Hospital until Arthur is out of hospital; but the crisis team say there are no beds available and the next option is a mental health unit outside the county. After Charlie applies pressure to the crisis team; a bed at Wotton Lawn is found; by which time Rebecca has changed her mind and wants to stay at home. She is offered the usual choice; agree or be sectioned. She agrees.

The likelihood of either of Charlie's parents attending his wedding decreases to nothing during the next fortnight. Arthur develops a severe stomach bug in the hospital, which leaves him very weak. He is given an operation where a stent is inserted into the jugular vein to prevent further clots. His memory and faculties return and he makes a good recovery. His wife is situated for the first night about three hundred yards away in Wotton Lawn where she telephones Poppy and requests a visit. Charlie can't visit as he has a large wedding to cater - Poppy's parents are away and the children are now at home for the summer holidays. She drives the children into Cheltenham to stay with her best friend Maria for four hours, so she can visit Charlie's mother and then father; stopping to collect two individual bouquets for each from the local florist.

Poppy drives to Wotton Lawn. She is intrigued to be entering the place she has written about. This is a modern building with a good deal of security; one must report at reception and sign in and the door is automatically locked behind her. She follows the nurse up two flights of stairs down dark corridors. The linoleum on the floor is navy blue and the walls are sky blue; which somehow gives an aura of gloom. She passes an area with two snooker tables and a table tennis arrangement – all of which are deserted. Rebecca is fetched from her room into a day room with easy chairs, while Poppy waits. The place seems deserted. Rebecca looks very well; although still in her nightclothes at lunchtime.

"Hello my Poppy!" she says

"Hello darling! These are for you."

"For me? They are beautiful, thank you."

"Do you have a vase?"

"I don't think so."

"Shall I ask?"

"Yes, please."

"Would you like some tea? Come through to the kitchen with me."

"I would, thank you. How are you feeling?"

"Not so bad, better today. Stella wants me to go and live with her."

"And shall you?"

"I don't want to. She's very bossy."

Rebecca makes tea in a communal kitchen. There is another patient in the room with bandages round both wrists. Poppy smiles at her. The smile isn't returned; but the woman says "hello" and shuffles her feet through the open door to the lounge; spilling her tea as she moves – the dirty pink dressing gown cord trailing on the floor behind.

"Attempted suicide…" Rebecca whispers, matter of fact.

"Oh…dear,"

"They don't talk much, the others. Disturbed. I've made one nice friend though,"

"Good. Did they say how long you must stay in here?"

"They're moving me tomorrow. To Charlton Lane."

"What, to the dementia ward?"

"Yes. I'm not ill enough to be in here."

"Nor there either! What a shame. How long since you had a ciggy?"

"Too long, I'm dying for one. I have asked, but they don't take me."

"I'll ask. I could do with one."

Poppy searches for the ward security and asks. She is told they will come and accompany them both in half an hour – they're short staffed. Poppy asks whether she is qualified enough to take her - but apparently Health & Safety rules say not. Rebecca shows Poppy her room. This is sparsely furnished and small; with barely enough room for the single bed. There are Yale locks on the outside. After returning to the lounge; they are joined by a woman whose lank fringe barely covers two black eyes. This one is more talkative and shares how many times she has stayed here. So many; she's lost count. A further hour passes before Poppy asks once more whether they can go outside for a cigarette. They may not.

The door to the day room bursts open and Stella strides across the room, followed by her two daughters. This makes Poppy jump. Stella stands between the two chairs where Poppy and her mother sit and ignoring Poppy; kisses her mother on the cheek. She begins to speak loudly as though addressing a child.

"Now Mum; I've arranged to come and see you and I shall be there at the start of Dad's visiting time in twenty minutes. I've spoken to Robert and want to make it very clear that I don't want ANYONE ELSE visiting him and upsetting him by telling him you're in here. He's not to be worried. Robert agrees with me."

Poppy stands and kisses Rebecca on the cheek. "I'm going to go now Rebecca. Look after yourself." Rebecca looks shocked and begins to try and answer her daughter; as Poppy leaves, shaken and upset. In the car park; she telephones Charlie; explains the scene and asks whether he still wants her to take the flowers over to Arthur. He advises her to do so and then leave before his sister arrives.

Arthur is looking frail and is half-asleep. Poppy leaves the flowers with him and kisses his cheek. "I'll visit again soon," she whispers and he nods his thanks.

Charlie rings the hospital to enquire after his father. He is told they have been given instructions by Stella not to give any other family member information on his condition. Rebecca is moved to Charlton Lane in Cheltenham; on a ward with elderly patients who have senile dementia. Despite the encouragement of the staff to Rebecca and offers from her son Robert to drive her there and back, Rebecca will not attend the wedding. She expects a visit from Poppy and Charlie after the ceremony and is very disgruntled when they don't attend. Robert attends without his wife at the church and leaves before the reception. It rains softly all day.

When Charlie and Poppy return from their honeymoon, he contacts Stella to enquire after his parents. She behaves in a cool manner. She has everything in hand. Arthur is out of hospital and there is to be a meeting with the psychiatrists to discuss Rebecca's care plan, prior to her release. Charlie suggests that he also attend – and Stella agrees that he may, provided he comes alone. Armed with a variety of his own questions about whether the whole family ought to be offered advice and therapy in order to better care for his mother; he arrives at the meeting. A general practitioner and psychiatrist sit behind a desk; his father, mother and sister are already seated. The female care home manager smiles at him in welcome, for which he is grateful; since he already senses hostility. He kisses both parents on the cheek and is greeted warmly. Stella won't meet his eye.

"Hello Stella," he says. She ignores him.

"HELLO STELLA," louder this time. She flinches. "Hello Charlie."

The discussion begins. The professionals discuss medication. To a perturbed silence; Charlie asks about diagnosis and counselling. The psychiatrist and general practitioner listen with patient disengagement.

"Don't you think we would all benefit from family therapy?"

"I don't need therapy, even if you do!" Stella responds.

"You might need counselling, Charlie, but that doesn't mean the rest of us do!" Arthur says. Rebecca remains silent; her eyes gleaming.

The meeting is swiftly concluded with further prescriptions and paperwork; and Rebecca is released. After the meeting, a crestfallen Charlie walks to the front door. The manageress of the care home takes his arm.

"Don't you worry about it, Charlie. I know you did your best. People won't always listen."

"Thank you,"

"You live your life happy. You and your wife have a good thing going,"

"I will."

"Take care."

Perhaps once a year or so, Rebecca experiences what the family describe as an "episode" where the new-fangled "crisis" team are called out – first with patter; then with threats. If she won't agree to come in for treatment; they'll "section" her. This is always sufficient for compliance and then after a brief period with the youngsters, the self-harmers (cutting is fashionable these days) or the anorexics and bulimics, with their bigger doses of the newer drugs that don't appear to be working either and single-bedded cell-bedrooms. She'll be assessed as not ill enough to be with them. One might enter voluntarily, submitting to the psychiatrist knowing best, but then he becomes omnipotent; he will decide if and when she leaves and what treatment can be forced on her. Some relish the power above even the law of the land. One or two enjoy the ultimate submission – they can recall Rebecca at any time her husband (as her designated carer) decides he cannot manage her behaviour.

For a week after, she'll be interred in the same dementia care unit with the elderly people who wander about crying, fighting, lonely with no visitors or bombed beyond all recognition, rocking in their armchairs and waving their arms when the Coronation Street theme tune begins – latching on to a semblance of familiarity where nothing is familiar or comfortable any more. Arthur returns home lonely. He sleeps solidly for two nights and then becomes despondent about how to fill his days outside visiting times. She is his reason for existing. He asks to have her back now.

Rebecca assumes the role of compliant patient (to begin with) and then dictates to the nurses about when her medication is due, complains about the other residents, the food and why on earth they can't simply leave her alone. After a week or so, all parties become bored and frustrated – Rebecca won't fit in because she doesn't have dementia – a care plan is hastily drawn up and passed between departments until filed. The staff are relieved to fulfil their duty of targets and discharge her to husband's care as usual.

A letter arrives from Rebecca's GP asking whether she will give her consent to see a trainee psychologist. She's keen to assist anyone in training and hopes this process will be ongoing. Poppy says psychologists are different to psychiatrists and might have other ideas. She arrives for the first session. The psychologist is in her twenties and as Arthur is asked to wait outside; Rebecca takes an instant dislike to her.

"Would you like to tell me how you're feeling?"

"I'm feeling quite angry about what's been done to me, since you ask."

"What do you feel has been done to you?"

"All the drugs. They made no difference at all and turned me into a junkie. And that operation was dreadful. It didn't work, did it?"

"Operation?"

"I'm talking about my leucotomy – as well you know."

"I'm sorry, I've not been made aware of this operation. When was this?"

"1967. You don't know?"

"The information might be in historical notes. Could you tell me about it?"

"Why am I surprised? None of you know what you're doing. NOT ONE! I'd like to see you sitting in this chair and being me for a day. I'd swap places with you any time. Utterly useless, the lot of you!"

"Now Rebecca; I'll have to ask you to stop using abusive and threatening behaviour; or I'll have to recommend treatment as an in-patient. I'm sure neither of us want that, do we?"

"Don't you think I'm entitled to be angry?"

"Anger is an ordinary emotion, Rebecca. But we need to find ways in which to express it safely and manage it. What do you think would help you?"

"Can you fetch my husband in now please? I've had enough for today. I want to go home."

"Certainly. I'll see you at the same time next week and we can talk about your operation then, if you like."

The trainee psychologist presumes this is part Rebecca's "illness" and hopes she will be able to calm herself – if she exhibits more symptoms, a period of "respite" might be required. She sees the patient fortnightly for the token six sessions that will enable her to complete the abnormal psychology module and discharges her; congratulating Rebecca on her progress. Rebecca is often sent away – sometimes a few home visits through the care squad will be organised to provide a bit of light relief. Company is the thing – she loves conversation, but all too quickly the minimum-waged leave within weeks, due to lack of funding. Rebecca doesn't tend to like those silly young women they send – they're always patronising – prurient interest, yet not really caring - ambitious types looking to forge themselves a name in the profession, but the young men are rather charming. Jolly and affectionate too; up for a laugh and joke. Might even give her a hug – well women need that don't they – she might be old, but she isn't dead yet. The family begin to refer to the regimen as "don't care in the community."

Chapter Fifty-Four:

Now Rebecca is Poppy's mother-in-law. Rebecca and Arthur visit Poppy and Charlie or go out with them; to summer village fetes, jumble sales, or car boot sales; the temporary joy of which seems to over-ride Rebecca's agoraphobia – particularly if it ends in tea and cake. Rebecca treats Poppy's children as her grandchildren; indulging them with sweets, comic books and colouring pencils. She even lets them play on her stairlift, laughing as they squeal and giggle going up and down at a snail's pace hum at the touch of a button; while Arthur tutts and worries about the mechanics of it all. Fun is all well and good - unless they break it.

Poppy and Charlie visit Rebecca and Arthur every Thursday evening after the children are in bed. They observe the scene in the two roads as they drive in. Inner city Moors Street is filled with newsagents and hairdressers and takeaways, mosques, music and book shops, four pubs and a theatre. It is a diverse, cluttered and multi-cultural area. They pass the barber's that puts them in mind of the 80's tv series "Desmond's". The black proprietors work late into the evening; and always appear to be having a real good time with their clientele. Further down, the street darkens and overflowing wheeled bins cluster in the corner, white house numbers daubed on them in ownership. Women in full hijabs and white trainers, haul green and white carrier bags from Asda, through the alleyway to their homes, accompanied by children with flawless skin, deep brown innocent eyes and topknots or veils; stepping off the pavement to avoid the haggard white sunken-cheeked piss-soaked drunk, or the man on the council-supplied mobility scooter, mowing down the pavement with his obese arse straddled horizontally beyond the seat; or the pock-marked acne of the impossibly-heeled pasty white blonde that pulls her stricken roots into the harsh ballet-bun atop her wide head – eyebrows tattooed on in a Barbie-barbaric grimace. She can't afford the 6-month re-do; so now, they are grey-blue, as is she.

Charlie squeezes the car through the narrow back streets; parked up on both sides; where they glance at the banner declaring "The only God is Allah!" eventually pulling up to Rebecca and Arthur's corner house. It's raining soft and sadly – the rain where you could do your crying anonymously; and Charlie flips the door handle; which activates the doorbell in their lounge. Poppy waits. Arthur greets them at the door with a broad grin. He sticks his head out the door to check what is happening in the street and salutes a neighbour wearing overalls, spilling oil from his half-fixed motorbike on the pavement. "Howdo!"

Poppy kisses Arthur on the right cheek. He holds her arm as she wipes her feet.

"How are you?" she says.

"Struggling on, you know how it is!" he replies with a laugh and a wink.

"I do."

He stands aside as she enters the hallway. Father and son shake hands and squeeze arms. To the right hand side is a glass door, a window to Arthur's garage; where ingenious projects are always underway; some complete; some not. His latest is building a vardo; a traditional gypsy caravan; that he hopes to bring to Poppy and Charlie's house and park in the field one summer's day and he and Rebecca will stay the night. One spring and summer has already passed; and they all secretly doubt it will happen in reality; but they all hope so. The project was halted this spring; because a blackbird nested next to the glass door; and could not be disturbed. They were saddened when it deserted the nest. Outside is a small courtyard; with raised flowerbeds and knee high ornaments of Laurel and Hardy and fountains and bird tables and a little set of steep wooden steps to an upstairs raised balcony; which is surrounded by lush plants. Rebecca can't get up there anymore.

There is a little downstairs toilet; with a raised disabled seat; where Arthur displays his oil paintings of boats; he feels unskilled; but he enjoyed his painting, back in the day. Poppy follows him into the kitchen; which is blinding with the fluorescent overhead light. There is a sliding glass door to the lounge; where they spend most of their time. There is a two-bar electric fire in the grate; with a stuffed bee alongside. On the mantelpiece above are two ornaments; one of which Poppy has been told reminds Arthur of her. It is an elegant lady from the 1950's with bobbed hair. Poppy bought the other one (though she loathes ornaments) for Rebecca last year; entitled "friendship"; it portrays two women, one behind the other, apparently offering support. All of these "willow" ornaments are faceless, open to interpretation.

A lone goldfish swims in futile circles in a tank on a shelf. There used to be a budgie in a cage above Rebecca's chair; but he died two years ago. Poppy never heard him sing. An oak dresser sits to the left of the room, on which family photographs; fine china and ornaments are arranged. The room is painted magnolia and is divided into two sections; the part where they all sit; Rebecca on the right leather chair, next to a cream chair, under the cushion of which old newspapers are stored.

Poppy and Charlie sit on the two-seater settee in the middle; and Arthur sits on a leather chair next to the television; with his arsenal of remote controls. The television is large, and has a second screen, so they can have two different programmes on at once if they wish. Underneath the television is their female Japanese spaniel dog "Tottie", and her basket. Tottie is spoiled and petted and has only the finest food, hand cooked, each day. The dog quite likes Poppy, who detests dogs. Tottie smells rancid – suffers from cataracts and a permanently uncomfortable; snotty nose which she snorts and licks clean. Sometimes Tottie sits in "Poppy's place" on the sofa when she arrives; and is removed accordingly. The last time Poppy visited with her girls, who are obsessed with Tottie; Tottie began what Arthur calls "a performance" with her toy dog. The adults studiously tried to ignore Tottie as she "dry humped" the toy dog, enthusiastically. Poppy wanted to laugh – particularly when her daughters asked what Tottie was doing. Playing with her toy.

The back section of the room is open; but is divided with sumptuous cream curtains in the winter. There are expensive cream leather sofas and beautiful cushions; tapestries that Rebecca has completed over the years. Arthur's computer table is hidden away here; but otherwise no one ever sits in that end. The only time Poppy has seen it used is when she takes her children over; who unceremoniously and disrespectfully throw the cushions around and dive on the sofas. Poppy is embarrassed by this; but Rebecca is amused by it and allows it. The ceilings are high in both rooms. There are ashtrays; strategically placed for Rebecca and Poppy in their conspiratorial habit; of which their husbands disapprove. Having controlled their own indulgences; which were always a secondary need; control is their replacement addiction. It is more powerful.

Poppy can instinctively read Rebecca's mood when she enters. If her face is slightly puffy, or she is recumbent in the chair; it's a bad sign. If she is upright and has re-applied her lipstick; it's a good sign. The television is on loud; but soon after they arrive; it is turned down; but left on; providing a continual distraction, on which anyone can focus if ever conversation dries up. They carry out the usual rituals; Poppy puts her coat down carelessly and Rebecca worries about the quality and it being crushed; and eventually they settle by leaving it on the back of the settee. Rebecca fetches Poppy her first gin and tonic; (after which she will encourage Poppy to help herself) in a delicate stemmed glass, where the measure is huge. Poppy lights two cigarettes and passes one to Rebecca. Rebecca persuades Arthur to have a cup of tea; which he doesn't want; and she offers food, cakes, or scones, and although Poppy's full up, she takes one, so as not to offend. They buy special gluten free cakes for Charlie; who is also full up, but eats and shares with Arthur, who quite likes them They have many conversations; where they all talk across one another periodically; eager for their opportunity to interrupt.

Arthur or Charlie might interject to take a potshot with his rifle at a rat feeding from the birdtable through the window. They always miss. Eventually, Rebecca may steer the conversation to more serious matters, concerning her present lack of wellbeing or the past; which sometimes deteriorates over the evening. She is tired; but doesn't want her guests to go home yet. Poppy will listen and empathise; Charlie will try to change the subject and Arthur will often cut through all this with a humorous, common sense response which tends to break the atmosphere. Poppy and Charlie pick up the cues; making it alright and safe to leave and return again next week. At the door, Poppy will turn to Arthur and say "don't forget the ashbox!" – it's their thing. Tonight, they've strayed onto politics; prompted by subtitles of the news on the muted television. Chancellor George Osborne has announced the highest post-war cuts in public spending.

"I've never seen anything get better when those private companies get hold of it!" Arthur begins.

"You're so right!" Poppy jumps in. "Look at the NHS – farming out the cooking and cleaning –it's crap. And more expensive!"

"We go to that many hospital appointments – and none of these departments seem to talk to one another anymore."

"You're right, they don't. It should have got better with all that technology – but again they've wasted all this money on I.T. systems. And what about those Private Finance Initiatives? I can't even believe that was down to Labour. They only did it to keep the figures off the books. It's bloody shameful. That's what's bankrupting the NHS."

"D'you know what Margaret Thatcher said when she was asked what her greatest achievement was?" Charlie says.

"What's that?" Arthur replies.

"New Labour!" He waits for this to sink in. It doesn't.

"She's a marvellous woman," Rebecca interjects. She purses her lips.

"She's an embarrassment to women!" Poppy says, incredulous.

"No. I won't have a word said against her."

"Best not speak to me about her then. Can't stand her."

"You don't know what it was like! All those people holding the country to ransom!"

"What, fighting for their rights, d'you mean?"

"Those unions just destroyed this country!"

"I think you'll find it's greed that destroyed the country. Now we have no unions; no-one has any rights at work, at all. Scargill predicted it. He was proved right."

"Don't you think they're just jealous?"

"Who's jealous?"

"You know, those socialism people. Jealous of people with money."

"What? I've got money now and I still feel the same way. I didn't earn it."

"Jealous. Yes. Now, I think I want some cake. Would you like some cake?"

"Sorry?" she is reminded of Marie Antoinette – let them all eat cake.

"I've got some lovely carrot cake. You've not eaten anything tonight!"

"No…really - no thank you."

"Arthur. Arthur!! I'd like some cake now!"

"What's your trouble?"

"I want some cake Arthur, please." She turns back to Poppy. "I'm a conservative."

"Yes, I know you are."

"Robert's a conservative, too."

"I know Robert is. I remember when he was going to stand as a local candidate."

By this time, Charlie has his coat on. "C'mon Mrs D, time we were off!"

Rebecca realises they are leaving; as Poppy puts her coat on. "Course, Robert doesn't think much of you. I expect you know that."

"Pardon?" Poppy is taken aback and wonders if she misheard her.

"Robert – he doesn't think much of you." Rebecca's eyes glitter as she smiles.

"Oh well, I don't think much of him, either. Still, there we are." Irritated now, Poppy does her best not to show it; and kisses Rebecca goodbye.

In the car; Charlie says: "You bit, there."

"Well, I'm a human being too."

"She's a cantankerous old bitch."

"She doesn't even know why she's a conservative. Never mind. Let's go home."

Chapter Fifty-Five:

Poppy enrols on a Masters Degree in Counselling Psychotherapy. She'd love to attend university; but there's nothing local – so it needs to be a distance learning course. Her preparatory work over the next six months focusses on the theory of diagnosing and treating "mental illness" - because she has come to believe the process is pseudo-science and wants to prove it. Having successfully passed the modules relating to research methodology and design; she encounters the "life history" method. Although she feels reticent about bringing up the subject of "the book" again – she decides to ask Rebecca the question.

"Rebecca, I have something to ask you…"

"You can ask me anything, Poppy. You know that!"

"This course – you know I have to submit a research project?"

"Is that for the desertion?"

"That's right – the final dissertation."

"Dissertation. Yes, you have talked about it."

"All the work I've been doing is about challenging the mental health system."

"I hope they listen to you. They wouldn't listen to me!"

"I want to make them. I'd like to do an analysis of how you've had all these treatments, yet none of them really worked for you."

"I see. Now let me think." She peels open the cellophane on the cigarette packet, rips off the silver foil and takes two out. She hands both to Poppy, who lights one and hands it back, then the other. After drawing and exhaling, Rebecca says: "Arthur! ARTHUR!"

"Whas your trouble woman?"

"Listen to what Poppy has to say."

Poppy repeats the last sentence.

"I hope it's not going to be like that book. That caused a lot of trouble, you know," Arthur says.

"Those things Robert said about me were terrible. But of course he says he never said them."

"I know you were upset; and I'm sorry for that. But what I really want to write about is your experiences of the treatments and how you came to be given them."

"I think that would be very good. If you think it would help. If I could just stop this happening to someone else – it would be worth it."

"So do I. We could at least try. You could read everything I write before I submit the work – and you could take out anything you weren't comfortable with sharing."

"You should do it. I don't want anyone reading those things Robert said. They were lies."

"Understood. I'll take his interview out completely. It will just be about you. But you don't have to decide tonight, anyway. Talk it over with Arthur and think about it. I won't be offended if you don't want to do it."

"I know you won't. I can speak my mind to you."

"Thank you....Ah that's brilliant...Good. I'll have to run it by my tutor Joy, anyway. They'll have to agree. Then I'll have to put in a research proposal – so it'd be some months away."

"Very good," Arthur says, changing channels and scratching Tottie's head.

Chapter Fifty-Six:

It is January and sunny outside, but a sharp minus four. Charlie's offered to drive Poppy to the university; an hour and a half away. He isn't happy about her going; he has a bad instinct about it. So does Poppy - but feels she must brave it out. She selects her outfit with care; just the right balance between the slick black Jaeger she wears to her "real" job and the hippy and beads brigade, rainbow warrior uniform of a counsellor. Arthur advised her to "dress warmly" and she's glad she did – it's freezing out. Extinguishing her cigarette and taking an extra strong mint; she kisses Charlie and leaves the car.

"Good luck love," he says.

The main university building is overwhelming; the grandiose entrance in pale scrubbed sandstone is surrounded by ancient elm trees and guarded by a tall black security guard; who talks into his radio. Poppy tries to inhale the delicious academia; and reminds herself - in theory she's a student here; not attending her own trial. The meeting is not in the main building, but in a Cotswold stone cottage alongside. After checking the digital recorder in her handbag; she realises the light won't come on. But she checked the batteries this morning and put fresh ones in. It is no use, the thing is dead. She will have no witness. She tries it twice more; feeling nervous – but there is no response. She must accept it, so she does.

She rings the doorbell; spot on time. The place seems deserted. She shivers and waits; at least five minutes, before she rings again. Still no answer. A tabby cat with white socks and his tail held high trots up, his little furry balls sashaying like buttocks on a catwalk; wrapping himself round her legs and purring. Poppy bends to stroke him and he bounced his striped cheek into her clammy palm.

The guard at the gated entrance to the main building; watches her. She smiles – she hopes, reassuringly. In a minute; he strolls over and enquires if he can help? She checks with him whether she is in the right place and he confirms she is – then walks back to his post. Poppy checks the appointment letter again; starting to feel anxious. It's not unknown for her to be scatty when it comes to practicalities. No, it's the right time and date. She rings again, longer this time - she's getting very cold now. She wonders if keeping her waiting is a power trip; then dismisses this as paranoia. Finally she hears someone descending creaky stairs; heavy-footed. The door is flung open, and Dr Walter Crock looks her up and down appraisingly. He looks taken aback. Poppy recognises him from his university photograph. Silly hair. Charlie had looked at the photograph on the university website. What a prat; why's he got that hairstyle and why is he wearing a leather jacket. Who's he trying to be? She'd laughed. Don't be like that; he's probably "down" with the stooodents.

His plentiful gray hair is brushed up high.

"Dr Crock?" she says, extended her hand. He takes it for a second. "I'm Poppy Denby."

"You're the lady with the maternity leave!" he says, in a loaded tone. She wonders what he's talking about and pauses before replying.

"No, I don't think so, my maternity leave was 5 years ago. Maybe another student?"

"No," he says. "We had to change our policy on accredited prior learning because of you."

She recognises his reproach. "Oh... yes," she falters.

She follows him up the stairs to his office. It's white walls are very bright as the sun pours through the sash windows. Two desks are untidy and littered with paperwork. There are foreign postcards on the notice board. She thinks as he is obviously well-travelled – she hopes he's broad-minded, too. He motions for her to sit in the opposing chair at a round table; where "his n hers" chairs are safely removed from hers. She realises she has been categorised as "the lady with the maternity leave" - a non-conformist; which rarely bodes well.

As they waited for the now-late Fatima; Dr Crock makes conversation.

"So. You're a full-time counsellor are you? Where do you practice?"

"Oh...no. I do some private practice; but I work part-time too."

"Doing what?"

"I'm Administration Manager. Of a horse riding trust."

"I see...Tell me, does your trust offer courses?"

"No...we have lessons. But we're thinking of becoming an accreditation body...in the future."

"Interesting. You might want to consider something I'm developing."

"Oh?"

"We're going to be offering accreditation programmes to small businesses."

"Right." Poppy feels confused, but feigns polite interest.

"I'll write my mobile down on my business card." He takes a pen from his shirt pocket and scribes on a card, handing it to her. "Here. So when you're ready to start looking at accreditation – give me a ring,"

"Thanks...I'll pass it on." Poppy slips the card into her purse.

She sees Fatima through the balustrade, lumbering up the stairs; sweating and puffing. She glares at Poppy as she takes off her coat, hanging on the back of the chair next to Walter's.

"Hello," she says, looking at Walter. Poppy stands and extends her hand. Fatima touches it briefly. Her hand is hot.

"Hello, I'm Poppy, nice to meet you!"

"Hmmm."

Fatima wears a blue fleece track suit; which cut into three spare tyres. She sits down, heavily, exhaling. So begins a barrage that will last two hours.

"Shall we begin?" Walter says, taking up pen and paper and nodding to Fatima.

"There are just *so* many ethical issues around this project," she begins, curling her fingertips on the desk into a spider.

"Oh?"

"Yes. I don't understand why you're doing this….I mean, who is it for? What on earth do you want to write about this for? They don't do even lobotomies any more!"

Poppy is very taken aback. Doesn't she know? But she's a senior lecturer in the field…she recovers herself to answer calmly.

"Well, in fact I thought that too; but they are actually still going on in two centres in the UK, one in Ninewells Surgery by Dr Samuel Eljamel and also in the University College in Wales...these are just the ones I know of ,so far."

Fatima waves a hand in dismissal.

"In any case; you appear to be trying to compress someone else's life story."

"I must admit, I have struggled to keep within the word count, but…" (she had intended to say she hadn't realised that the transcripts she was analysing need not form part of the word count, but rather an appendix)

"This is really not suitable for a small scale project. You might not believe you are coercing or persuading your mother-in-law into doing this project. She's vulnerable; and you might be taking advantage of her. And what about the researcher bias? How can you possibly be objective?"

"Ah. This type of research really isn't intended to be objective. Researcher bias is addressed using reflexivity and transparency. I can assure you I haven't persuaded or coerced my mother-in-law to take part. In fact originally, she asked me to write her life story – two years ago. The project is about examining the mental health treatments she received; in relation to the life problems she was experiencing."

"But she might be doing it to please you, she might not be able to say no to you."

"That's a fair point. But she's been able to say no to me on other matters, so I don't think that's the case."

"There are just so many ethical issues involved here. You are just failing to hear our concerns."

"I honestly have listened to your concerns; but I genuinely believe I can address them. I did actually prepare a 5000 word essay to cover all the points you raised. I have this here, if you would like to read it?" Poppy takes the essay from her handbag.

It is now Walter's turn to take charge. "The ethics board certainly wouldn't be prepared to read 5000 words. They might possibly read a 300 word executive summary."

"I'm not sure I could address the issues sufficiently in just 300 words...but I could try, I suppose."

"You know; you really seem to be writing at PHD level...I don't know. I have to tell you; I wouldn't recommend you put this to the ethics board. I'm a member of that board; and they'll ask my opinion. They'll also take Fatima's opinion into account. She won't support it. And the one with the most clout will be the opinion of the external examiner. And they certainly won't support it."

"Still...I think I would like to try...."

"Well, listen....I know how these ethics boards work. It could tie your project up for months as it gets referred back and forth. I mean, if you had been able to come to me and say, Walter, here are 10 or so published papers where academics have researched and written about their family members; I might be willing to support it at the board, but..."

"I think I can do that."

Walter raises his eyebrows and shoots a worried glance at Fatima.

"Well, even so. I just think you should postpone this. I'm not saying abandon it. If you just get through this Masters, and you told me you wanted to do it for PHD, I might even draft in a supervisor from elsewhere, if necessary. At PHD, you can do all sorts of things, why I even once had....."

He goes on to cite some unrelated projects and Poppy's mind wanders.

"Joy has asked to give up being your supervisor, as she feels compromised. So you need to be aware of that," Fatima smiles, just with her mouth. At this, tears threaten to overwhelm Poppy. Not Joy...Joy who said it was original; and worthwhile and a great idea. Joy who had promised to support her through the ethics board. Joy who had phoned to wish her luck at the meeting.

"Oh my god, really? I had no idea....I'm sorry if she felt compromised, I thought she was in support of the project."

"Errr, yes..." Walter shifts in discomfort. "We do need to make you aware of that, of course. Joy believed you would change your mind and consider other projects and when you went back on it, she felt compromised and specifically requested you be found another supervisor."

"Oh...poor Joy...I hope she is okay...I had no idea she felt like that..."

Fatima adopts a lower tone. "We also had concerns about your ability to *manage* the disappointment of a *rejection* from the ethics committee and whether you could cope with it. You seem, well, rather *passionate* about it. Maybe a bit *too* passionate!"

Poppy wonders whether it is possible to be too passionate about women's brains being chopped out to make them conform in the world.

"I think I could manage...I just wanted the chance..."

Walter wants to wrap the meeting up. "So. The situation will be; even if you select another project; that Fatima and I will take over your supervision jointly. I'm not trained in counselling psychotherapy and I don't really know anything about it; so I will oversee, shall we say, the *process* side of it and Fiona will oversee the counselling element. You'd have to agree to this if you want to continue with the university."

"Oh, I see. I'll have to give this some thought."

"Well, shall we move on to talk about alternative projects then?" says Fatima.

"Right...."

"Perhaps recruiting participants via online questionnaire would be good. There shouldn't be any ethical issues with that. You'll have to think of a suitable topic."

"One thing I discussed with Joy, was the use of focus groups; discussing their views on psychiatric diagnosis and treatment. I think I could do that relatively easily; I had investigated the possibility as an alternative and had some candidates in agreement....."

"Oh no, I don't think that would be appropriate at all. Focus groups can be used in some circumstances; but not for this. Who were these *people?*"

"Well, I had a variety; a psychology teacher, a doctor, former counselling colleagues and some of their contacts....supervisors and so on,"

"No; I think recruiting participants needs to be much more objective."

"Objective. Right...."

"Well, perhaps you need to go and give it some thought," Walter says, twiddling his pen round in his fingers. "Come back to us when you're ready with a decision on your new project and we'll consider it. You'll have to draft a new research brief, obviously."

"Even though I've passed that module?"

"Yes, well you won't have to pay for it again. We'll waive the fees. It's still a pass. Otherwise you can take your existing credits and exit the university with a Postgraduate Diploma. You've enough points."

"Exit? You mean leave?"

"Yes. Or you can propose another project. And you'll need to confirm in writing that you would like to accept our offer of supervision."

"I see."

"Well, I think that's it for now. We'll wait to hear from you." He stands, holding out his hand to indicate the meeting has concluded. Poppy shakes it briefly. Fatima does not offer hers.

"Okay, well, goodbye then."

"Goodbye. You can find your own way out?"

"Yes, it's just downstairs."

Poppy walks softly down the stairs. Her head is aching and her legs tremble slightly. She grips the bannister to steady herself and watches her step. She contains herself until she reaches the car, in case they are watching from the upstairs window. Charlie looked at her and can tell, immediately.

"Please, just get me out of here. I'll tell you on the way."

He shakes his head and starts the engine, pulling away quickly.

"D'you get the recording?"

"No. It was dead."

"Oh God – and you checked it this morning, didn't you?"

"Yeah. Bastard thing. Must be fate!"

Poppy, reeling, recounts a few choice snippets to begin with. Charlie, infuriated, spends the first hour of the journey ranting about the unfairness of it all and their stupidity. She isn't even heartened by this and just gazes out of the window as they fly past the trees and fields.

"You must fight it Poppy."

"I will; I'll just have to reflect on this and regroup first. Perhaps it's not meant to be. I need to think about it."

She realises there are other lives and voices in this family affected by Rebecca and they all need to be heard. And when she has listened to them all for enough years, she is also affected by Rebecca. Perhaps one day Poppy needs to be heard, too.

Chapter Fifty-Seven:

"You know my greatest wish, Poppy?" Rebecca says.

"What's that?"

"For you and Stella to be friends again. You're so *alike*."

"I don't think we are. I don't think you'll be getting your wish this time, sorry,"

"Well I shall pray for it."

"Fine. Did I tell you my tutor rang to apologise about that meeting, by the way?"

"Did she?"

"Yeah. And she never said she didn't want to be my supervisor – they lied about it."

"They don't want to hear it, do they Poppy?" Rebecca asks.

"It doesn't seem that way, does it? Maybe we'll make them hear it. I'll take it somewhere else if I have to. Another university."

"Would you really do that?"

"Yes."

"I've printed out the consent form again; by the way – just in case we should be asked for it. It's exactly the same as the last one; but if you're happy, I'll read it all to you both and leave it with you to sign. I just want an up to date one. Don't want to give them any ammunition."

"Fine."

"No rush – take as long as you need."

Poppy reads it all through – explaining the jargon, right to withdraw at any time, anonymity. She leaves the form with them. Early on the Sunday morning, Arthur telephones Poppy.

"We've got a problem this end,"

"You do? What's up?"

"It's this form. Rebecca's watched a documentary about neurosurgery for children with brain tumours. She thinks if she signs the consent form, then those children won't get their operations. She doesn't want to sign it and I think it's best if we just leave it,"

"Okay, if you think that's for the best. I'm so sorry she's upset – but do tell her for me it's not a problem."

"I knew you'd say that. I told her you would. We'll leave it then, if you don't mind,"

"I don't mind. Tell her I'll see her Thursday as usual,"

"Look forward to it, I'm sorry about this. But you know, we can't really agree about that operation. It was good for some things."

"Don't worry about it." She knows what it was good for in his eyes. Sex.

Poppy replaces the receiver and returns to the bedroom in a daze. Charlie looks up.

"What was all that about?"

"It's over. She won't sign the consent form,"

"What? Why the hell not?"

"She's watched a documentary or something and it's frightened her. But it wouldn't be ethical for me to push it – if that's how she feels I have to respect it." She puts her head in her hands and lies down, facing the wall.

"No way. Not after all that work! This is what she's like Poppy, I warned you. She plays games,"

"She won this one."

"Does she realize what this means? All those years of wasted work?"

"I don't know."

"I'm not having it. I'll ring up and explain."

"Don't do that. Just leave it. I need to think what I'm going to do next."

Poppy swims at the local pool. She swims half a mile, plunging into the blue depths, thrashing hard with a back stroke until the frustration is worn out physically. She does this every day for a week. Her ears fill with water that muffles everything. The sunlight pours through the full length windows. She notices the shades of green in the Poplar trees waving outside, people in the park walking their dogs. She prays, too – please God, tell me what to do. On the seventh day; the answer arrives. Let it go. She is tired of fighting the world and considers how life will feel if she isn't threatened any more by the decisions of others. It is a relief to be free.

Two days later; Poppy is given a promotion to full time Operations Manager at work and doubles her salary. She is returning from picking the children up from school when her mobile rings. Stella. They have not spoken since the incident at Wotton Lawn. She hesitates before answering.

"Hello?"

"Poppy? It's Stella,"

"Hello. What can I do for you?"

"It's about our Mum,"

"Okay…"

"I've just had a massive row with her,"

"Oh dear. Well, join the club."

"I'm sick to death of it. Every time I go round there she's criticizing me. You know when we had that…trouble?"

"Yes, I do."

"Well, I think she's been playing us off against each other. She just kept telling me how wonderful you were every time I went down there and I got sick of it."

"Did she?"

"And she wouldn't stop going on about that book again – the things Robert said."

"Well, that was over a long time ago. I told her to destroy it. In fact, even my degree is over now. It's all over, now. She won't sign the consent form - so I can't put my dissertation in at uni – even if they do agree to let me submit,"

"Really? But why not? You've done so much work!"

"She's watched some crap on the telly about children's brain tumours and decided that's the same as a lobotomy. I don't know. I've almost given up with it, really."

"That's awful. Look, I never wanted us to fall out, but this is what she does. Don't you ever wonder why she lost touch with all her family?"

"I did wonder – but then I never heard their side and it's too late now. Her mum and dad are dead, her brother's dead, and I heard that Megan's in an old people's home with Alzheimer's – so she won't remember. We don't know where her sister is, or even if she's still alive."

"I know. D'you think we could get together, to talk?"

"I guess so."

"Trouble is, she's got a personality disorder."

"I don't really believe in those."

"We learn all about them at work."

"Mmmm. Trouble is, no-one can be sure, can they? It's easier to believe she's ill than just being spiteful."

There will never be an apology from Stella. She explains this by her belief that apologies are meaningless words – she worked with the information she had at the time; albeit wrong. Poppy will have to live with this explanation. The truce begins. It will be nurtured into an friendship and then an alliance.

Charlie rings his mother and father and explains the meaning of Rebecca's decision. By this time, Rebecca is feeling better and realizes the implications. She was having a bad day, she said. She signs the form, Arthur counter-signs it and she asks Poppy to see it through – as far as she can get.

Poppy's research proposal is declined by the ethics board. Poppy takes her case to the Office of the Independent Adjudicator for Higher Education. It is upheld. The compensation pays a third of her fees towards a creative writing course at a different university. She gives up counselling completely and will never take another client. She passes a masters in one year with distinction. Rebecca and Arthur attend Poppy's graduation ceremony. A picture of Poppy in a cap and gown, holding a scroll still sits on top Rebecca's dresser.

Chapter Fifty-Eight:

Stella and her husband have booked their holiday to Tenerife and are due to leave in three days. Robert and his wife are away, too – in the Bahamas. Arthur got shingles two weeks ago – he's coped quite well but Rebecca doesn't tolerate him being poorly much. He's told everyone to stay away while he's contagious – so she's had very few visitors either. She's become more demanding as he recovers.

"I want you to kill me. Just get your gun and shoot me!" Rebecca says.

She's been saying this to Arthur for two days now – waking him up in the middle of the night. He's tired out. It's so distressing that she can't snap out of this. He's rung Stella and she can't come away from work again; she's already been round three times to try and calm her mother down. She's advised him to ring the crisis team. He tries some humour:

"I can't shoot you. I might miss."

"I'll take an overdose then!"

"What if it didn't work? You'd be in a right old state. Now put all this talk of death aside – you know it doesn't do any good. Shall I get you some of that carrot cake?"

"I need help! Get me to the psychiatrist! I need to see him now!"

"Well, I'm here for you. I don't know why you always have to reserve this for the weekends. You know the only ones available are the crisis team."

"Ring them then!"

"If you want me to ring them, I will. But all they'll do is take you back in. You shouldn't have come out the last time, really. Not when they were trying to get you better."

"I need to talk to someone!"

"Just as you like."

Within three hours the team have arrived. She begins to shout at them.

"You're all bloody charlatans! You're trying to kill me!"

He notices the plastic bag beside her armchair. It appeared yesterday – he presumed her knitting was in there; but now he's wondering. As he reaches over her to take it, she glares at him.

"Leave that alone!"

He pulls it from her firmly and takes it upstairs. Inside are boxes of valium. He counts up the blister packs. There are over a thousand tablets in here she has been stashing. He realises he cannot know how many she has been topping up with and when. He takes them downstairs and hands them over the crisis team.

"That's my property!"

They explain to her she cannot keep them. Some are out of date. It will take a great deal of persuasion before she will agree to accompany them back to Charlton Lane. Once in; she cries when he visits.

"I will never forgive you!"

"Then I'm leaving. I'll be back tomorrow."

"I want a divorce. Get me a solicitor."

"I'll see you tomorrow. Try not to upset yourself."

He leaves. The nurse enters.

"How are you now, Rebecca?"

"I am ready to leave."

They continue in this vein for three days

"That isn't really a good idea. We've only just changed your medication and it's going to take a while to get into your system and start helping you."

"I'm a voluntary patient. I can leave whenever I want,"

"Rebecca, you must understand we are trying to treat you. You're ill."

"I know my rights. I want to see a solicitor. How dare you try and make me stay here against my will?"

"Rebecca, I'm afraid if your behaviour continues; we're going to have to section you under the mental health act. Do you know what that means?"

"You're threatening me! I shall telephone my husband to collect me."

"I'm sorry, but it's not possible for you to leave just now. You're really not well enough. Do you remember asking us to come out because you weren't coping at home? And Arthur's had shingles. He's in quite a lot of pain and isn't really well enough to look after you at the moment. You both need a break – can you see that?"

"I'm not listening to any more of this. You'll get me a solicitor and I'll sue the lot of you!"

"You're putting us in an impossible situation. So we're going to apply for a temporary section; just for seventy two hours until you've had a chance to calm down. It's for your own safety."

Somehow, Arthur persuades them to discharge Rebecca the following day.

Chapter Fifty-Nine:

Poppy continues recording Rebecca's fragmented memories and researching all the treatments Rebecca endured. The photographs came out this week, from Arthur's collecting box. Rebecca's mood swings tonight, between helplessness and anger. Poppy tries to listen to Rebecca, but Arthur and Charlie keep interrupting her. Eventually, Rebecca rallies in spite, lashing out at everyone and saying she wishes they could feel what she feels for a day – then they' d know. Poppy wonders how she could wish this on anyone. Within minutes, Rebecca begins to weep. Poppy feels helpless and can only hold her hand as she watches her disintegrate, wondering how her own mood capsizes and begins to slip underwater alongside Rebecca's. But Poppy knows she can walk away where Rebecca can't.

Rebecca telephones Poppy first thing, one summer morning. She's back in Charlton Lane.

"Hello *my* Poppy, it's Rebecca." Her voice sounds frail.

"Hello darling, how are you?

"Well, I'm not so good."

"Oh dear...I'm sorry to hear that..."

"Yes. I expect Arthur's told you. I have fluid on my lungs now; just like Charlie with his Chronic Obstructive Lungs. I'm getting breathless. And I have an enlarged heart. I really am ill, you know."

"Yes, he did tell me....that must be so uncomfortable for you. How are you feeling with your nerves; is that any better?"

"Quite a bit better, yes. They've moved me into a different room today"

"Have they?"

"Yes. Stella wants me to move in with her."

"And shall you?"

"I would, but Arthur, won't hear of it."

"Oh dear."

"How are the girls? And James? I know what motherhood is like, you don't get a moment to yourself."

"They're well, thanks – I took them swimming, trying to work as well – other than that, not much to report!"

"Anyway....I know you Poppy, and I'm sure you were waiting for an official invitation from me before visiting; just in case I wasn't up to it?"

"Well...."

"I knew, you see. I *know* you. We understand each other, don't we?"

"I like to think we do. I'm sorry I haven't managed to make it so far. The kids have been off on summer holidays; and my friend's daughter staying

255

round for two nights. And Charlie's got loads of work on. I don't know when I can; but I'll try to make it in the next few days."

"It would be lovely to see you...How's Charlie?"

"He's fine, thank you....I'd like to see you too.."

"Okay. Well, I won't keep you, I know how it is, with young children."

"OK darling, see you soon. Keep safe."

"Goodbye, *my* Poppy."

The day is sweltering and close. Even in the early evening the temperature reaches twenty eight degrees. Poppy leaves the three girls with Charlie, to put to bed. She feels light-headed; driving to Cheltenham. The car windows are wound down; and she experiences an uncharacteristic anxiety about finding her way. Aware that only one hour of visiting time will remain by the time she arrives; she takes a convoluted route; past many of the areas where she used to live. She settles as she reaches Leckhampton; taking time to admire the cleanliness and the tall oak trees lining the road.

Poppy pulls up in the car park in the brand new purpose-built hospital block. Someone wolf-whistles as she locks the car. She looks around; but can see nothing through the one-way windows. Arthur calls out; we're in here! Poppy laughs. "Thank you," she mouths. Poppy rings the doorbell and waits for a nurse to answer. The building is secured; patients with dementia are prone to wandering out. The walls are painted pale blue. Inside is hot and stuffy; although the back doors to a small walled garden are open. One elderly resident conducts a silent, solitary waltz. The action reminds Poppy of the Mancini character in One Flew Over The Cuckoo's Nest. A male and female patient turn on one another; their turkey necks waggling.

Male: They'll kick you out of here, you horrible old bag!

Female: They'll kick YOU out! She scowls at him and hits him, on the arm.

Small male Nurse: Come on now, Patrick.

Stella greets Poppy at the door, leading her through the lounge to Rebecca's room.

"She's playing up, Poppy," Stella says, rolling her eyes.

"Oh dear."

Stella nudges Poppy. "Look!" She points to a shirtless man, outside. He runs his hands up and down a metallic water feature; consisting of four or five stainless steel pipes of varying height. He splashes himself with the droplets, which cling like jewels to his silvering chest hair.

"This is why I LOVE mental health!" Stella giggles.

"I don't know how you do it." The splashing man does not appear disturbed. Poppy supposes his behavior makes sense in this heat, but she absorbs the despair here like a sponge. People's relatives, real people, who are lost in their sense of who, and where, they are. Some clutch at her hand, asking when their daughter, husband or father is coming. Others ask her for directions to the Superintendent. Too many sit in chairs, their rocking and weeping -ignored. When they get a flash of recollection; they become enraged over trivia; with the strangers surrounding them. Poppy can't understand why Rebecca's here and how this can be better than being in her own home. If only she could try a little harder to consider her family's feelings.

Rebecca greets her warmly. Poppy hands over the Thornton's chocolates she's kept in the freezer; so they didn't melt. Rebecca opens them straight away; offering them around. Kisses are exchanged, arms are squeezed.

"You look beautiful, Poppy. What a lovely dress!"

"Thank you...second hand shop Rebecca, maybe a bit OTT tonight, but it's too hot."

"You have such an eye for the bargains. I don't like this room much. I don't know if I shall sleep here tonight."

"Don't you? What don't you like?"

"It feels like a prison."

"Well; you've got your own key."

"It feels like a prison."

"It's stuffy and close, I know. It seems to be everywhere, tonight."

Rebecca gets up and down, first to the toilet, next to the wardrobe; unpacks her clothes and hangs them up – smoothing the shoulder pads; picking off fluff. Offering the chocolates around again; eating one or two. The nurse enters. Suddenly; Rebecca sits down.

"Hello my darling; how are you doing?" the nurse says.

"Oh, oh....not too good."

"Oh dear; what's wrong?"

"I don't like this room. I shan't sleep here, tonight."

"Oh, don't you? Why's that, my love?"

"It feels like a prison."

"Oh dear! But you're not locked in here; you can leave this room any time. The key is there for your use; and we all have a key; if yours got lost."

"Mmmm. But I don't like it."

By way of a demonstration regarding the door key; Arthur gets up to demonstrate how to lock and unlock the door. He manages to get the key stuck in the lock and it cannot be removed.....at which point a different nurse "2" is called to assist. She can't budge the key either. Stella begins to laugh.

"Look Dad, you've broken it, you're in trouble now!"

Arthur says something grumbly under his breath in response. Rebecca is disinterested.

2nd nurse: (briskly) "Not to worry! We'll have to get maintenance to see to it later. You can still open and shut it."

The first nurse extends her arm to Rebecca.

"Well, come with me a minute, my love."

"Me?"

"Yes, not very far."

Stella throws a poignant glance at Poppy. Arthur rolls his eyes. She acknowledges them both; with a half shrug, half smile. The nurse leads Rebecca out. They re-enter, two minutes later.

"Yes, that seems much better."

Poppy and Stella saw the other identical room on the way in, next door to this one.

"Well, I'll need to call the cleaning team; because it hasn't been used for a while - but if you prefer it, we'll move you in there later. We'll just shift your bed to start with; you don't want to bother with all your wardrobe dear; we can do that for you tomorrow."

"Thank you." Rebecca seems satisfied.

Poppy's phone buzzes. She picks it up. Stella. Poppy wonders why Stella is sending her a text message, when she's sitting beside her. It reads: "She's going for a BAFTA". Rebecca is immersed elsewhere. Poppy is shocked, yet wants to laugh - but she feels bitchy, conspiratorial. She resists the urge to respond; but she looks at Stella and nods acknowledgement.

The nurse is sweet; caring; seems of a competent age. She pats Rebecca on the arm; and says; "well, I don't mind doing that for you, because I love you."

Rebecca's facial expression turns malevolent for a moment. Poppy watches and wonders if Rebecca *senses* she is being patronized and lied to. Rebecca is contemptuous of this woman. Her tone is querulous and she leans close to the nurse's face.

"*What* did you say?"

The Nurse's temple twitches. Poppy hears the slight quavering of her first few words as she puts on a silly tone, as though she was only joking.

"I said I'll do it for ya cos I luvs ya!" The nurse reddens with embarrassment. Rebecca sees she is in control. She switches to affable old lady and sits back in her chair.

"Oh, go on with you! *You* love *me? Mee? Ahhh*...Thank you!"

She clutches the nurse's sweating hand, which is squeezing her arm.

"How rude of me, I haven't introduced you! Have you met my daughter-in-law, Poppy? She's a *counsellor*."

"Is she? Yes I've met Poppy, I didn't know you were a counsellor."

"I *was* a counsellor. Nice to meet you."

"And my daughter, of course, you know?"

258

"Yes, hello Stella! Keeping well?""

"I'm fine thank you!"

"Well, if you're all settled here for now, Rebecca, I'm going to sort out that room for you."

"Yes, yes, you go dear. And thank you!"

"You're welcome. 'Bye all!"

Poppy leaves first. As soon as she's out of earshot, Rebecca turns to Stella.

"I thought Poppy looked rather tarty tonight."

"Don't be nasty, she looked lovely! It's a summer's day, what did you expect her to wear?"

"Hmm. I'm just saying. I don't think it's appropriate."

"I thought she looked pretty tasty!" Arthur said.

"You would."

"Anyway Mum, we're off now."

The visitors return to their houses, Arthur his empty one, Stella and Poppy their homes, filled with husbands and children. Later, Rebecca joins the other residents, in front of the television in the day room. She listens empathically to Squadron Leader (ret'd) Jones – one of the care workers stole his receiver and so his orders for the next mission are delayed.

"Without the bloody receiver, it's hopeless, Mrs D."

"Rebecca, call me Rebecca. It's abominable, Captain. You must see the Superintendent first thing and put in a complaint."

"Who are you talking to? I'm the Squadron Leader, not Captain. There's no writing paper in the room! I'm sure they're lying to me. There's a conspiracy afoot."

"I know quite what you mean. They've stolen my glasses, too. And my medication is overdue – I've told them several times."

"They must think we're stupid."

"It's a good job we know the truth."

"What's that you say?"

"I said, it's a good job we know the truth."

"You'll have to speak up, Nurse. I'm hard of hearing, you see."

Chapter Sixty:

In 2013, Rebecca catches pneumonia. Poppy and Charlie go to Gloucester Royal to visit her. She's getting hungry. The hot ward stinks of school dinners and musty bodies. She's on floor 9 of the tower block, high above the city where the dirty window view is of rain-laden clouds at sunset. A pink gingham nursing auxiliary arrives with a clipboard and glares at Poppy until she relinquishes her chair, next to Rebecca's bed. She needs to take more notes – seems to have some trouble writing them. Behind her, a grey-haired-page-bobbed lady has slid halfway down in her chair, clutching a plastic spoon like manna. Another patient, slim, long-legged, bruised feet upon the floor, slams down her hands as they continued to ignore her buzzer. The noise agitates her. Her bed is strewn with bags. She gives up four minutes later, her chin slumping onto her chest and her eyes glazed. The urine drips slowly on the floor.

Poppy leaves the ward to request another blanket for Rebecca, whose feet are cold. The nursing station is busier than the ward – they'll try to find one. A young Australian doctor is doing the rounds. Poppy smiles as he waits for her to open the door, glancing at the anti-bac hand wash alongside the warnings of MRSA and wonders if she should use this again. As she pushes the door to the ward, the Aussie doctor frowns and says:

"You guys should really use that stuff."

"Sorry," Poppy nods and obeys. By now, she's been here two hours and washed her hands four times. Arthur says Rebecca told him to take all her money and just piss off, this afternoon. Right after she threatened to jump out of the window. *She doesn't mean it,* he said. *Anyway I doubt she'd get up on that window sill!* Rebecca tells Poppy how the staff are mistreating her; she hasn't had a cup of tea since eight o-clock this morning. Arthur says he's seen her drink three.

"My medication's due!" She says, when Poppy returns. "Look at her ignoring me. My feet are so cold Poppy,"

"They're just finding a blanket. D'you want me to fetch her?"

"No, I'll get her. Nurse!" she calls out, quietly. The nurse doesn't hear.

"Have you pressed your buzzer?" Poppy asks.

"No," Rebecca replies and reaches for the button for the radio, which lights up. Arthur wrestles with the cable underneath the tight sheets, to find the buzzer. Buzz buzz buzz. The nurse comes over.

"What can I do for you?"

"My medication's due."

"When the doctor's done his rounds – he won't be long now. You're having a CT scan soon, aren't you?"

"Yes. I must have my medication."

The nurse turns to Arthur, Charlie and Poppy. "D'you want to go down with her for the scan?"

"Yes." Arthur replies.

"D'you know where it is?"

"Course, I worked here for twenty years, you know. Until I retired!"

"Did you dear?"

"I'm so hungry," Rebecca interjects. "Can I have something to eat now?"

The nurse checks her charts. "That should be alright."

"Shall I get you a sandwich from the canteen?" Poppy asks. Arthur slips her a tenner.

"Anything but cheese Poppy. D'you know the way?"

"I'll find it."

Poppy gets lost, but Arthur meets her in the shop and buys her a box of orange matchmakers, which she devours by Rebecca's bed, as Rebecca tucks into a ham sandwich. On the way down to the CT scan, the porters struggle to squeeze Rebecca and her bed, Arthur, Poppy and Charlie into the lift. Arthur's last in, and the doors open and close on his backside. Poppy giggles. "Two rashers off the back!" he says, and moves further in. The CT scan reveals there are metal plates from the leucotomy, still in her brain. Seems they weren't aware from her records – apparently an MRI scan could have killed her if the magnets moved the plates. They discharge her the next morning with antibiotics. Just another bladder infection.

#

Historically, Rebecca had 48 ECT treatments. Vast swathes of her childhood memory were lost, each time. Now and again some percolate back; unreliable now – disconnected from the feelings which once accompanied them. Sometimes the professionals accused her of repressing childhood sexual abuse. Rebecca is adamant that never happened – says she'd have told them about it right at the start, if it had. "You don't forget the traumas," she says. "You forget the good things."

Her mouth looks a little different tonight. She has new teeth. They don't fit properly and protrude – it is difficult not to laugh when she looks like Esther Rantzen. This evening, Rebecca remembers a bit more - her father used to cough and spew up foam and his body would shake, because he'd got shell-shock and had been mustard-gassed, having survived four years at Ypres and the Somme. Rebecca would scream in fear as a little girl, yet her brother and sister would laugh and run away, her brother jumping out of his bedroom window to escape. She recollects Father was a red-cap; a military policeman.

"You've got that wrong, he wasn't a red cap," Arthur says.

"That's what I was always told. Why must you do this, Arthur? He's always doing this to me, spoiling things,"

She remembers too, that her mother was a dancer in a chorus line on a stage, before she had *her trouble*. Course, Faith's own father was a cruel man who once beat a cat with a poker. One day he'd tried to take a poker to Rebecca's son Robert, and she fought him off.

Poppy says: "it's no wonder your mother was anxious, is it?" but no one is listening.

Rebecca says "Arthur's mother once said to me: *he should have left you and he'd have had a better life!*"

Arthur laughs. "Well, Rebecca, she was just thinking about her son's wellbeing!"

Rebecca scowls at him. "I remember how hurt I was that she said it and staying away from her, refusing to go into the house, but your Dad, *your Dad*, came out to talk to me in the car, he was a lovely man!" Arthur changes the subject. Rebecca turns back to Poppy.

"There are two things I think I want to say, about the reasons for my problems. The rest of the world looks on and thinks poor Arthur, he has had no life, because of me. And they're right! I wonder if I was spoilt. I want somebody to tell me the truth."

"Well, if you were spoilt, that's not really your fault."

Rebecca fixes Poppy with the canny, piercing blue eyes, nodding slowly. "I see what you mean."

"You've been brought up in a family where your own mother is incredibly anxious. What sort of message is that giving to a child? The world is going to seem pretty unsafe, isn't it, if your own mother's terrified? And where there are bombs going off and there's a war on?"

"Yes."

"It's not about blaming people – just understanding. She's still cutting up your dinners when you're 14! Most people probably didn't do that, did they?"

Arthur interrupts again.

"Well, I had this out with her mother once. I just said, if you poke that dinner about any more it won't be worth eating!" Hohoho, the men laugh.

Charlie looks at her mysteriously and says "The answers are all within you."

Poppy ignores his interruption. The men have started another conversation and Rebecca is distracted for a moment. Then Poppy presses, "but you said there were two reasons for your troubles. What was the other, Rebecca?"

"I don't remember," she replies. There is a short pause. She clenches her fists. "I want to hurt myself."

"You seem really angry, Rebecca?"

"I am, Poppy."

"I know."

"I didn't feel like going to Asda yesterday."

"No?"

Arthur steps in. "Well, 'course we ran out of food. Stella went for us, before she went to work,"

"She's a good girl," Rebecca says.

"Yes," Poppy murmurs.

"She wants us to move in with her."

"And shall you?"

"Oh no. She's just so bossy."

"She gets things done though, eh?"

"Stella thinks we should get someone in to do shopping for us. But I said no. Otherwise the world is closing in on me Poppy, getting smaller. I do need to get out, I know that."

"I know," Poppy replies. She glances at the clock surreptitiously; knowing soon she must leave Rebecca, to pick up her children from school.

Poppy finds it difficult to leave Rebecca behind every week and thinks about her a great deal in between visits – trying to find some hopeful or explanatory news, an answer to help. So she keeps reading more academic papers the next day. Papadatou-Pastou et al; (2008) found in almost two million left handed people, the odds of a man being left-handed were 1:23 times more likely than a woman. Perhaps Rebecca is a very special case. Had she been born male, she might have the opportunity to become a prime minister, an entrepreneur, a chess champion or an architect, or have an increased chance of being creative. She might not be taking that lumpy frog-chalk casserole of 11,000 psychotropic drugs each year, swilling round the bland, unforbidden food – no cheese, Grommit. No marmite. No brandy and champagne. An occasional gin and tonic mind, (small because of my meds) with Poppy. *Doctor* said that would be alright.

Poppy can never be sure how much physical damage has been done to Rebecca's brain. Of one thing; Poppy feels certain – she'd have had a better chance of recovering and managing her distressing feelings, with no treatment at all. Poppy realises she doesn't know best, after all. She doesn't *know* anything, really. Poppy needs to believe Rebecca is still in there somewhere.

Life, unlike fiction, is filled with rather unsatisfactory endings...so Poppy looks forward to next week's visit.

Chapter Sixty-One:

Poppy's period arrives Thursday morning. The finale of a week's irritation at any noise which seems amplified and jars in her head like cymbals clashing. Blood pours down her legs and onto the floor tiles as she runs up the corridor to the bathroom. She scrambles to clean herself and the floor up before her daughters wake up. No good frightening them about these things. Her periods have been heavier these last two years and more painful – her legs ache, as well as her stomach. Now she takes painkillers. Life must carry on, since neo-feminism dictates the denial of female bodily functions. One must carry on with all one's tasks as normal; whatever one's body may do to betray a private disgust. "Bodyform" advertises women during their period, dancing through meadows in white shorts; which belies the arsy chocolate scoffing of the silent majority. Poppy still feels dirty and sweaty after the shower.

She sits in the passenger seat of the car, as her best friend Maria chats amiably, asking for directions; despite assuring Poppy she knew the way beforehand. Poppy loathes being late. She used to hate her clients turning up late – felt like they didn't care enough. Poppy and Maria are on the way to Newport to meet the Treasurer and the external auditor of the trust where they both work. Poppy doesn't believe she really needs to go and resents how she'll need to contain the mood and the bleeding which is already threatening to defy the supersize tampon and pad – maybe she's got fibroids or polycystic ovaries or the big C. Perhaps she should stop being a hypochondriac, this is probably the menopause threatening. They pass through the Forest of Dean; where there's no telephone signal to look up the directions. The trees overhang the road in dark threatening places which seem isolated; but she would give anything to stop the car and walk among them alone, wallow for a while in their stoic solitude that endured – people crashed, died and were murdered in these woods and the trees are indifferent in silent longevity – alive in the summer, withering in death in glorious technicolour in autumn, dry and dead in the winter, reborn with their buds in the spring. Not like people.

Poppy hopes it won't be too awkward to pop to the loo on arrival...hopes she doesn't smell...prays no-one will know from her glare and the hard tone that replaces her ordinarily-calm-in-a-crises one. At least she can share it all with Rebecca tonight. They understand each other. As they emerge from the forest, Maria says to ring her husband for directions. Poppy expects him to take the piss about them getting lost, but he doesn't, the bastard. They are twenty minutes off-track, and take a minor detour. Poppy watches the clock, her jaw set.

They arrive at the perfect three-bedroomed executive box of the young professional graduates, newlyweds, where the children are yet to come and where the sweet, hyperactive young Treasurer greets them with hugs, coffee and bacon sandwiches. Poppy excuses herself to the toilet, which is difficult to flush. The competent Germaine Greer of an external auditor arrives. She's impressive alright, no-nonsense. The meeting progresses with mumblings of Gift Aid and government gateways and aren't the revenue in a mess because of all those redundancies and isn't it a shame they don't cause all these problems for the big corporations. Five hours and three toilet breaks later, they leave. Maria drives too fast down the cul-de-sac and the car mounts the kerb nearest Poppy with a bang. Maria laughs it off; of course as they were prone to do in these crises, back from their days in police cadets at 15; all twenty seven years ago - when their lives stretched ahead of them safely. Now Poppy stays jittery for the rest of the journey. Her vigilance makes Maria so nervous; she keeps making silly mistakes.

The evening progresses like a predictable river - until Poppy constructs a dam to try and divert the current, but instead it began to overflow in all the wrong places. Her stream of consciousness travels this way with their weekly routine:

She gets home and baths the children, reads them a story, sets them up a DVD, puts her make up back on, kisses them goodnight and bangs on James's bedroom door to remind him to babysit and check on them. Charlie's already running the car engine. She locks the back door and gets in the car. He fails to put on his seatbelt as usual and the beep beep beep sounds. Put your seatbelt on. Sorry love. Can you stop driving so fast round the corners? Sorry love. You know, if you didn't drive up other people's arses you wouldn't have to jam the brakes on. Poppy, I'm only doing 50. But you have no room to stop. I'm perfectly safe. Into Tesco, the bright lights glare, the trolleys crash and crowds of slow movers block the aisles. She buys flowers for Rebecca and Charlie buys Haslet (not faggots this time) for Arthur. Shall I get her a custard doughnut? She likes those. No, best not to encourage her. Seems all the traffic lights are red. Past Gino Fatico the Italian mechanics shop. The lower high street with neon takeaways, Rooster Chicken, Pizza to go, Kebabs, Afro-Caribbean cuisine, curry houses and gaming emporiums, Salvation Army shops and evangelical red brick churches. Past the park and four storey homes split into dingy flats with bedspreads covering the grey windows and into Moors Street. People with disabilities, limps, wheelchairs, breathing apparatus. A place for sugaring the hair from your body. They imagine what's going on in their lives: What's going on there then Poppy? I don't know, maybe troubled childhood, loveless marriage. He will joke that the man who walks with legs akimbo has been shafted with a huge dildo by his wife. Dark damp bedsitters with dim lights and dinner for one in front of the television.

Aren't we lucky to live where we do? Yes, we must never take it for granted. Why are you going the wrong way around the mini-roundabout Charlie? Because I can. Gaylord. Bitch. I adore you mind. I adore you too. He hits the kerb when he parks badly. Oh Austin! She says and laughs. He parks in the disabled bay outside his parent's house next to the fucked up motorbike with oil making purple green swirls underneath. They try the door handle. There's fumbling as Arthur arrives to open it. She kisses his cheek as he holds her arm. How are you? She says, Oh struggling, you know how it is! He replies as always. I do, she says. You won't forget the ash-box tonight, will you? I won't.

"She's been a bit difficult the last few days," he whispers.

"Oh dear."

"I didn't cancel your coming, cos she perks up when you're here,"

"That's nice of you to say. Thank you."

The fluorescent light in the kitchen buzzes. He slides open the door through to the lounge and Rebecca smiles broadly – her eyes are glassy tonight. Although her skin is wrinkle-free and her cheeks soft; Poppy can tell she's over-medicated. She looks puffy and swollen. Poppy and Charlie take the usual places on the two seater sofa in the middle of the room, with Rebecca in her chair with the ejector seat on the right and Arthur next to all his remote controls and gadgets on the left. One bar is on the electric fire and the air is thick with cigarette smoke. Rebecca's ashtray is full. The television dominates the room with Coronation Street and the volume right up. Charlie flips through the Betterware catalogue, pointing out object d'art to Poppy.

"I'll get you a drink, Poppy. Arthur, will you make Charlie a cup of tea please?"

"What's your trouble woman?"

"Will you make Charlie's tea?"

"Right."

Rebecca struggles to stand – almost getting stuck halfway and groaning from the pain in her legs, but once up she moves quite well. Poppy gratefully sinks the first gin from her special glass. The green bottle is already placed on the worktop and the individual tonic waters are in the fridge. Rebecca always pours the first, as hostess. Rebecca is itching to share something, *justify* something. Poppy already knows what; Stella rang up crying last night. It'll have to be dealt with decisively, if raised, so Poppy buys herself some time in talking about trivia; takes two more gins – larger each time as she listens. She won't swerve the subject, tonight; but she could cry with exhaustion.

"I told her, Poppy. I said, Stella, I don't want you doing my hair anymore; you're not a good hairdresser. Well, she said to me, that's fine. She took it very well. Then I asked her to recommend a good hairdresser. Between you and I; I've been quite spiteful to Arthur, but you know I just can't help it and Lord knows why he puts up with me, but it's my illness, you see."

"Hmmm. That was a bit...tactless, wasn't it?" Poppy says it quick.

Rebecca looks aghast. "What d'you mean by that?"

"Well, she's your daughter. Don't you think that might have been a bit...hurtful?"

"Oh. I hadn't really thought about that. D'you really think so?" She looks thoughtful.

"I do. You know, if you don't want her to do your hair any more, that's fine – you can always find another hairdresser...but did you really need to ask her to recommend someone else? How must that have felt to her?"

"You're right, Poppy. What should I do?"

"Wow...I don't know. What d'you think you should do?" Poppy's voice is hard toned.

"I don't know. D'you think I was wrong?"

"Yeah, I do. Why don't you ring her and apologise? We all fuck up sometimes and say hurtful things. You just have to say sorry and learn from it."

"Perhaps she won't speak to me."

"You'll just have to try again then, won't you? You can do without losing touch with another family member."

"I'll try. Arthur! Bring me the phone!"

Arthur brings the phone. Rebecca struggles with the buttons while dialling.

"Hello darling," Rebecca says. "You know I love you." She smiles.

She listens for a while. Poppy hears Stella's tone rising but can't hear her words. Rebecca continues: "But you know, I don't like how you cut my hair and I pay you, so I'm entitled to say. I was just speaking the truth, about how I felt."

Poppy shakes her head. Rebecca hands the phone to her and Stella offloads her point of view. Poppy goes out to the kitchen and assures Stella that her mother is trying to apologise and may be doing so in a clumsy fashion...perhaps she could sleep on it? Stella agrees, with the proviso that her mother doesn't ring her any more tonight and leaves her alone for a bit. Poppy placates, hangs up and helps herself to a large gin-half-tonic, before returning to the lounge – wondering if anyone gives a fuck about how her day isn't.

The Denby husbands are discomfited. Their wives appear tense. These tensions are best averted or postponed, in their experience. Passion's all very well and good – but when they get out of hand – hysterical – there are occasions where you've got to put your foot down. They glance at one another and attempt to interject in the conversation, but their wives are having none of it.

"Well, you see what I'm dealing with, Poppy! Stella won't listen!" She holds her hands in supplication, as though she is dealing with an errant child.

"Did you listen to her? You don't really want it to go on, do you?"

"I don't. But she just won't see reason."

"Trouble is, you phoned her to apologise, but it wasn't really an apology, was it, because you then starting justifying what you'd said?"

"I don't know what you mean."

"Okay, well, if you're sorry for what you said – then you don't start telling someone that what you said was fair?"

"I don't like the way she cuts my hair. I'm just speaking the truth."

"That's fine – if you don't like her hairdressing, find another hairdresser. What you don't do, is ask her to recommend a good one. It's insulting."

"You're right. I've been ever so nasty to Arthur, too. Sometimes I just can't help myself."

"Is that right? Couldn't you just stop?"

"What d'you mean?"

"Look, if you're saying spiteful things to people – you do know you are, because you've just told me you are...why don't you just, stop doing it?"

"Stop? But I can't."

"Yes, you can. Just stop saying spiteful things. That's your daughter and your husband. You're hurting them."

"I don't want to talk about it anymore."

"I bet you don't."

Arthur and Charlie have gone quiet and are exchanging knowing, warning glances. Poppy senses them and is irritated – why don't they tell her straight? Arthur makes a *Poppy's had too much to drink and out the door* gesture. Charlie takes the hint and stands up.

"I think we'd better go now..." he says.

Poppy rounds on him. "I don't," she says.

"Yes, I think I'd like you to go now!" says Rebecca, closing her eyes and turning her head to the wall, away from Poppy. She thinks Poppy has been very cruel tonight. Arthur will stop her in a minute and she can tell him all about it when they go.

"I'm going nowhere."

Charlie tries again, "I really think we should go now."

Arthur stands up and tries a soothing tone. "Perhaps it's for the best," and looks at Poppy sympathetically.

"Stop fucking saving her. Fuck off out of here, the pair of you. I mean it – leave this to me. Stop fucking rescuing her – it's what you always do. She needs to face up to it." Poppy stands up and looks from her father-law's eyes to her husband's; her own glassy with exhausted rage and gin.

Both standing now, Arthur and Charlie look at one another, in consternation. Charlie looks into his wife's eyes and realises she means it. Part of him wants her to do it, too – so he takes his father by the arm and indicates they should go to the kitchen. They slide the door across behind them. Poppy sits on the edge of sofa. She hears Charlie quietly say to his father: "Just trust her. She knows what she'd doing."

Rebecca keeps her eyes shut and her face to the wall.

"I want you to go," she whispers. Poppy feels an overwhelming urge to slap her.

"I don't care what you want. I'm not going anywhere."

"Please....JUST GO!"

"No. If you really want me to leave here, I will. You can jolly well look me in the eye and say so."

There is a pause. Rebecca opens her eyes and looks at Poppy. Poppy sees what she has always been afraid to see in this woman and in herself – that perhaps, after all, she is selfish and trivial, cruel and fake. But most of all – she sees that she, Poppy, has won. Rebecca is not satisfied; as she sometimes seems after managing to make other people lose their temper. No, she is afraid. This is a Pyrrhic victory and Poppy is a bit deflated and a bit guilty, too. And the rush of compassion comes – the more familiar one.

"Thank you. Now then, if you're telling me you want me to leave, I'll go. And d'you know what, unless you say you don't want me to, I'll be back here next Thursday and every Thursday until I can't any more. I do love you, but you just need to stop. It's not fair, what you're doing. You just keep hurting people."

"I know. I'm tired."

"That's fine, I know you are. We'll go, tonight. D'you want me to come back next week?"

"I always want you to come back. I love you."

"I love you too. Come here," Poppy leans over the poor old lady, and hugs her close. Rebecca hugs her back.

"I don't want us to fall out," Rebecca says.

"I don't either. But you know what, falling out's okay, so long as you make up. No bad endings, here, eh? No falling out for years. Say what you feel and say sorry if you're wrong."

"Alright Poppy. Fair enough."

"Are we alright then? Don't you be saying something different when I leave, will you? If you need to say it, say it now. Don't piss me about."

"We're alright."

"Right. I love you. Give me a kiss, please. We'll see you next week."

"I love you too...goodnight Poppy."

Although neither of their husbands understand their exclusion - sometimes there is a need for victims, bullies and rescuers to switch roles for a bit. To scratch at the veneer of sanity.

-The End-

Epilogue:
"Guinea Pigs"
An ethnographic case study on Neurosurgery for Mental Disorder:
By Poppy Denby
Abstract

"Leucotomy" is the preferred term for "lobotomy" in the United Kingdom. Psychosurgery has been rebranded in the last decade as Neurosurgery for Mental Disorder (NSMD). There were at least twenty different modifications of this procedure. The basis of them all was to surgically ablate (destroy) healthy brain tissue, in the hope of relieving feelings of anxiety, depression or obsessive compulsive behaviour. NSMD procedures were always controversial, even among professional psychiatrists and neurosurgeons.

Many countries outlawed the procedure. In 1996, the Norwegian Health Department offered compensation to anyone who had received a lobotomy in the past, equivalent to £10,000.00 each. 2005 patients had a lobotomy in Norway, but only 500 were still alive. The Ministry said: "the decision follows the government's recognition of the long term side effects of this operation, which include intellectual impairment, disinhibition, epilepsy, apathy, incontinence and obesity....lobotomy is no longer considered an acceptable treatment in Norway." Goldbeck-Wood (1996:1).

Breggin (2002) testified that "his criticism of psychosurgery had stopped most of the projects in the United States and helped to establish the standard that psychosurgery is experimental and unacceptable as a routine clinical procedure...two Harvard professors who are noted advocates of psychosurgery testified on behalf of the neurosurgeon...their failure to sway the jury was a serious blow to the aspirations of the few remaining psychosurgeons in the United States." The patient in question was awarded $7.5m – the jury were unanimous in their decision.

The United Kingdom is the only country in Western Europe where NSMD is still available. It is still practiced (albeit in small numbers) for so-called "intractable" mental illness – by the North Bristol NHS Trust and the National Hospital for Neurology & Neurosurgery in London. 14 operations were carried out between 1991 and 1995. Goldbeck-Wood (1996:1). In England, the Care Quality Commission has a duty under section 5 of the Mental Health Act (1983) to appoint a panel of assessors – who approve (or decline) all ablative NSMD operations taking place within England. Referrals have more than tripled between 2009 and 2014 – although approvals have remained steady - at an average of two per annum.

I would like to make my researcher bias transparent from the outset – I have come to disbelieve many conventional notions of "mental illness" which have no scientifically-demonstrable basis. Blind faith in science is no less naïve than it's nemesis -organised religions. I concur with Sacks (1985): *"we are far too concerned with defectology and far too little with narratology, the neglected and needed science of the concrete."* Long may the mind elude "sciences" and continue to inspire us with its ingenuity – to find reason and purpose beyond what we think – at least today – we can measure. We would do well to remember that the definition of a "scientific fact" is one which, with new learning; may yet be disproven.

In this paper, I utilise an ethnographic case study, reflexivity and feminist-critical literature review to address the question: Is it time to call for an end to ablative Neurosurgery for Mental Disorder?

Introduction:

I met my case study participant in 2008, when she was 75 years old, in a personal capacity, as the mother of my partner. I was a counselling psychotherapist, specialising in Cognitive Behavioural Therapy. Over the next year; we became friends. She recounted stories about her life, which were harrowing.

Some months later (at her behest), we embarked upon a two year journey of co-writing her biography, including 56 years within the British mental health service, as she was treated for depression, anxiety and obsessive compulsions. In 1967, she received a bimedial leucotomy operation, which was considered by the psychiatrists in charge of her care to be the last resort. I gave up counselling practice; in order to focus on this person and completed a Post-Graduate Diploma in Counselling Psychotherapy, followed by an MA in Critical & Creative Writing; in order to re-construct my participant's whole biography. My participant chose her own pseudonym: Rebecca.

Despite putting in a formal request for access to her medical records under the United Kingdom Freedom of Information Act, we never received these and Rebecca was never given any explanation as to why. Therefore, some elements of this research have been limited to a balance of probability. During the course of my research, I conducted a critical literature review on neurosurgery for mental disorder; which forms the basis of this case study.

The work has been conducted in full collaboration with Rebecca and her husband/carer Arthur; who have both given signed consent to participate. I may be considered as a participant observer within this process. The data was collected from oral history taking in person and personal observation over a five-year period as a weekly visitor and friend. In addition, I received dictation from Rebecca onto tapes in my absence, which I later transcribed. I have also had access to both my participant and her husband's historical written notes.

Data and discussion:

I believe Rebecca's bimedial leucotomy operation was performed by Dr Peter Shurr in June 1967. Fenton (1999) quotes Schurr as having carried out the "bimedial leucotomy" for 20 years in England. The British Journal of Psychiatry published a report in 1968 citing Schurr as the surgeon at The Guys-Maudsley Neurosurgical Unit, London, which coincides with where and when Rebecca's operation took place. This was verified by the Patient Action Liaison Service (PALS) at the Maudsley Hospital in 2010. Schurr and two colleagues (Felix Post & W. Linford Rees) published a paper entitled "An Evaluation of Bimedial Leucotomy", in 1968, studying 64 patients undergoing the procedure between 1953 and 1958. Many serious potential side-effects were well-known by the authors before Rebecca's operation.

The explanation of the limited success rate was: "it would have been astonishing if any procedure could have rendered completely symptom-free patients with long-standing psychiatric illnesses of a kind which had been little influenced by previous therapeutic efforts." Post et al; (1968:1226).

Key phrases appeared somewhat at odds with a statement later in the paper, particularly "little influenced" and "responded up to a point". Post *et al*; (1968:1228) stated: "We were not dealing with a chronic mental hospital population, but with patients admitted voluntarily or informally, who in most instances had good family relationships, and who in spite of severe symptoms responded up to a point to psychiatric nursing and occupational therapy".

Rebecca spent the preceding nine months being treated without success at Maudsley; when she reported being told: "we've tried everything else; you'll just have to have a leucotomy." Rebecca was sent home for a fortnight to consult with her family on the implications of a decision to proceed. She and her husband were forewarned the risks of the operation were she could be left "blind, paralysed or a vegetable", but the chances of a successful recovery were "50/50". This was an ambitious estimate. Post et al; (1968: 1234) wrote: "In summarising undesirable leucotomy effects, it has to be conceded that...undesirable effects occurred in just under two thirds of cases... in slightly under one third these were not negligible". This appeared closer to 67% failure rate. "Certainly, only two patients below the age of 40, and none under 30 improved after leucotomy in a really satisfactory fashion". Shurr (1968:1238) Since Rebecca was 33; a statistically poorer outcome might have been predicted.

Rebecca's husband left the final decision to her. Over the next fortnight, she became increasingly anxious and required sedation on several occasions. She made the decision to proceed.

Post *et al*; (1968:1242) wrote: "In our view, there exists no royal road along which the therapeutic value of leucotomy or of any of its derivatives can be proved or disproved once and for all". If the therapeutic value can't be proven; the ethics of this procedure are questionable. I perceived a juxtaposition: a person's "brain" was considered sufficiently dysfunctional to require dangerous and irreversible surgery and conversely, (particularly if diagnosed with "hysteria" or "inadequate personality"), the person was considered competent to consent.

Persaud *et al*; (2003:195) raised concerns about the validity of informed consent "in a population seeking a last resort for intractable and severe psychiatric disorder". As Gostin (1980:153) stated: "This presents the paradoxical situation where practitioners purport to limit their interventions solely to cases of grave disablement but maintain, at the same time, that the patient is capable of sufficient understanding and competence to provide legally effective consent."

A patient diagnosed with "depression" who had experienced suicidal ideation might feel ambivalent towards their future wellbeing. If experiencing guilt, shame or low self-esteem; the decision to submit oneself to such a procedure could be self-harming. Despite concluding that there was still a role for neurosurgery for mental disorder, Fenton (1999:265) made the point: "one needs to check that consent is not a consequence of the patient's psychopathology, for example, a desire for punishment in a severely depressed patient with feelings of guilt or unworthiness." Fenton did not indicate how this could be checked.

Post *et al*; (1968:1243) acknowledged in their results that: "during the extended observation period (i.e. beyond the first three post-operative years) the natural course of illness is seen to have taken over once again". If mental illness has a natural course capable of withstanding or repairing dysfunctional brain tissue; (white matter); we might conclude that the white matter was not the cause. If it was the cause; but the brain was capable of repairing itself sufficiently for the illness to "take over" again; then surgery would be ineffectual. The clinical efficacy of this procedure is questionable.

Luria (1973:64) spent 40 years as a neuropsychologist; entirely devoted to the psychological study of patients with local brain lesions. He acknowledged that insufficient material had been collected on lesions in the medial zones; since lesions confined to these zones were rarely identified in clinical settings. Luria suggested that patients with relatively minor lesions of the medial zones: "exhibited no defects of their higher mental processes, frequently complained of a defect of memory...their increased inhibition by irrelevant, interfering stimuli, so that even the slightest distraction inhibits existing traces". No definition was given of "relatively minor", but in comparison with other procedures; bimedial leucotomy was less invasive.

There was insufficient evidence to suggest that Rebecca was easily distracted. Despite a room filled with people; several conversations occurring simultaneously and a television on; Rebecca could filter out all these distractions and remain completely focused on her own thoughts. When Rebecca was engaged in one-to-one conversation; she selected parts of that conversation which contributed to maintaining her own views and discounted (or gave limited value to) alternatives. If she could be easily distracted; it might be reasonably straightforward to effect some (albeit temporary) shift from her catastrophic thought processes.

Conversely, Rebecca interrupts when a point comes to mind; as she fears losing her "thread" if she doesn't say it immediately. Her family have adapted to this, so there are no negative consequences or expectations in terms of "norms" or "manners". Still, Rebecca continues (without exception) to apologise in advance: "Excuse me for butting in; but I must say this now; or I'll lose it." It could be argued that this behaviour results from a rational knowledge of what is required, rather than association with negative emotions. For example Damasio (2006:49) cites the case of "Elliot", whose records of social knowledge could be retrieved under experimental conditions. Damasio also points out that "real life has a way of forcing you into choices."

From a cognitive behavioural therapy perspective, I initially believed Rebecca's behaviour was based on her thoughts being connected with an emotion. In order to experience sufficient motivation to apologise; Rebecca must be able to connect a negative emotion or consequence (reward versus punishment) to being judged or perceived by others as "rude". If she did not experience emotions; this would be irrelevant. She would not "care" whether she was perceived as "rude". I rationalised that she must consider what she has to contribute as relevant or important; which implies some measure of self-esteem. There was motivation to contribute to a discussion. Aside from a perceived positive emotional experience, I could not identify another explanation for this behaviour. Rebecca's level of conscious choice to be "distracted" remains a mystery. She sometimes chooses to be distracted by an outing or a visit from friends – and at other times decides to stay home feeling miserable. Other internal physical factors may influence this; such as recurrent bladder infections; changes in medication and arthritic pain.

Luria (1973:29) cautioned against mechanistic theories of "narrow localisation" of brain areas; suggesting instead that these could not be isolated from complex systems activity in the brain. 'Naturally all mental processes, such as perception and memorising...cannot be regarded as isolated or even indivisible 'faculties' which can be presumed to be the direct 'function' of limited cell groups or to be 'localised' in particular areas of the brain." Luria believed that "premature schemes" narrowly working on the theory of localisation would prove baseless in the future. He proposed instead that in furthering knowledge of the brain, there must be reconciliation and gradual progression utilising "morphology, physiology, psychology and clinical medicine". This appeared to be a holistic approach. Damasio (2006:144) points out that "current body representations do not occur within a rigid cortical map as decades of human brain diagrams have insidiously suggested."

Neurosurgery for mental disorder continues to rely upon the localization principles Luria considered lacking in evidence, as early as 1973: "fundamental forms of conscious activity must be approached as complex functional systems; consequently the basic approach to their localisation in the cerebral cortex must be radically altered." Luria (1973:30). Similarly Damasio (2006: 250,251) also cautions against explaining the mind "solely in terms of brain events, leaving by the wayside the rest of the organism and the surrounding physical and social environment."

Some modern literature suggests that localization in the relationship between neurochemical correlates remains theoretical. NICE (2006:22): "Treatment with either medication or CBT is associated with a reversal of the functional neuroimaging findings to the pattern found in control individuals." Schwartz et al; (1998) *cited in* NICE (2006). "The neurochemical correlates of these differences are not known..." If these correlates remain unknown; presumably neurosurgical ablation of brain tissue remains experimental and potentially inaccurate.

Eljamel (2008:1) is one of the few remaining neurosurgeons in the UK still performing neurosurgery for mental disorder at Ninewells Hospital in Dundee. He acknowledged the inaccuracy of the procedure: "the exact location of the target is not clear...Over the past 10 years, I have used the surgical techniques presented here with little variation. Nevertheless the size and location of the resultant lesions varied from patient to patient on long-term postoperative MR image analysis." Trimble (2007:467) observes that the same alterations in behaviour can emerge from lesions at different sites in the brain and "lesions at apparently the same sites in different individuals may lead to different behavioural manifestations."

This experimental surgery is carried out on those now legally considered as "vulnerable" groups in the United Kingdom. Fenton (1999:263) also points out that there is no consensus on the optimum target site for lesions in NSMD. "The lack of a precise neural model of how NSMD works remains a valid concern".

Rebecca continues to experience "terrible anxiety" (another emotion); but behavioural interventions, e.g. graded exposure, boundaries (conducted post-operatively) had short term benefit. These could have been attempted without surgery. Had surgery proved successful; one might reasonably expect an immediate marked alleviation of anxiety/panic, obsessions or compulsions, or depression symptoms, since the healthy brain tissue destroyed was purported to be the cause. Rebecca's post-operative experience of anxiety was as acute as pre-operative – but strong boundaries steering her towards behavioural experimentation were more successful. "There still remains the possibility that the progress of patients beyond the immediate post-operative period had been strongly influenced by the later treatments received." Post et al; (1968:1243). This is borne out by an observation of neurosurgery in the United Kingdom, by Breggin, (1972:374):

"Their lobotomised patients are thus given extensive often long-term services probably made available to very few if any other patients in Great Britain, certainly not to patients suffering from "anxiety syndromes" and yet they never once mention the possibility that whatever useful effects they achieve may be due entirely to these massive efforts mobilising psychiatry, social work, welfare, rehabilitation and psychological services. Typically, they have no control groups who are given these services without lobotomies!"

Gostin (1980:151) makes a similar point: "One cannot discount the fact that in many of these studies, there was intensive nursing and medical care before and after the surgical intervention...these may well have contributed to the patients' improvement." Gostin also points out that in some cases, clinical improvement commenced prior to the operation. This suggests surgery was not the last resort and indeed that these symptoms were not completely "intractable". The use of the words "intractable" and "treatment resistant" imply that the "symptoms" are so chronic that the patient has some kind of physiological brain impairment. Freeman et al (2000:7) suggests: "Much neuropsychological research has been defensively framed and carried out by researchers who are not independent of the neurosurgery for mental disorder programme."

Persaud *et al*; (2003:195) point out that "sham intracranial surgery...would never make it past a contemporary ethics committee". NSMD, as a treatment, appears to have acquired impunity from the robust evidence-base that is required for other types of surgery. It was, therefore, difficult to research the potential of a placebo effect. As Gostin points out: "the elaborateness of the psychosurgical procedure may provide a potentially significant placebo effect."

Bridges, (1973:858) was a psychiatrist who promoted and referred patients for psychosurgery, in the form of stereotactic tractotomies at the Brook General Hospital in London. He made the observation that if this surgery was viewed by the patient as "a last, hopeless resort, it can prove to be so for that reason alone". If the "belief" in surgery is the deciding factor about whether or not it proves effective; it cannot be considered evidence-based. It is not necessary for a patient to believe an appendectomy will cure their appendicitis for it to do so.

If surgery failed; the responsibility for this could be attributed to the patient's belief system, or the chronicity of their "disorder" rather than the procedure. This provides the psychiatrist and neurosurgeon with a great deal of power over the patient. Success may be attributed to their expertise and failure may be attributed to the patient's attitude towards psychosurgery.

I found the implications of such control over the seat of consciousness of others; rather a disturbing concept. This was not lessened when I discovered that in 2000, at the age of 70, Bridges was tried at Guildford Crown Court and pled guilty to two counts of indecent assault on a male and taking an indecent photograph of a child. He was struck off by the General Medical Council and received a suspended sentence. At the "Association for Convulsive Therapy", a group of psychiatrists, (proponents of Electro-Shock treatment in America), three of the six founders would be involved in serious scandals. Breggin (1975:234). One agreed to revoke his medical license after former patients accused him of sadistic and sexual abuse. A second used ECT to make her a "suitable housewife." When we consider that female patients for ECT outnumbered males by 3:1 in one state (California) we might begin questioning received wisdom concerning the validity of any mental health "diagnosis". Szasz (1974: xiii) states that any claims that mental illnesses are diagnosable disorders of the brain are "not based on scientific research; it is a lie, an error, or a naïve revival of the somatic premise of the long-discredited humoral theory of disease."

Bridges describes his patient's improvement as "curiously delayed" after surgery; for a period up to 2 years and suggested patients should be warned not to expect immediate alleviation of their "symptoms". In this way, he stated: "disappointment is avoided." I reflected that in the context of the provision of subsequent services; it would be difficult to identify which intervention (if any) provided symptomatic relief.

Post et al (1958: 1245) concluded: "Best results may be expected in elderly patients with uncomplicated chronic depressions". Most patients had variable diagnoses and "uncomplicated depression" was not defined. I suggest "chronic" depression is unlikely to be simple. Despite receiving the procedure, the following groups were excluded from the sample for analysis:

- 6 patients who exhibited "a schizophrenic reaction type", (undefined) as this group was "too small for evaluation".
- Four cases where data "were insufficient or had been lost". It is indeed unfortunate that medical records can be "lost"; particularly when one is collecting data for a study to support their surgical interventions.
- Two patients who died, 6 days and 3 months after operation. One might question whether the cause of death was related to the surgery; but this was not stated.

The remaining 52 patients were included: "after abstracting from the case notes various diagnostic pronouncements made by senior psychiatrists".

Clearly, diagnostic agreement was not achieved. None had received a diagnosis of "uncomplicated depression". "At different times, these patients had been labelled one or several of the following: anxiety hysteria, hysteria, anxiety neurosis, neurotic depression, or inadequate personality". Their stated "ideal" (to have a psychiatrist and psychiatric social worker interviewing both patient and relatives) was achieved at 3 year follow-up in only 10 cases; which could call into question the validity and reliability of the data. "Hysteria" (*of the womb*) and "homosexuality" have subsequently been removed from the discourse of psychiatric diagnosis. The latter still exists; but is no longer considered an illness.

Rebecca experienced side effects as a result of the operation, including epilepsy (which I will cover later) and "disinhibition". Her husband considers her "disinhibition" positive; as he believes it resulted in her post-operative ability to achieve orgasm - not experienced previously. He was considerably more enthusiastic about this than Rebecca; who stated that she had always enjoyed sex in any case. She did not consider this sufficient compensation to negate the other effects.

Baker et al; (1970:39) cite a reduction in anxiety and tension as the "most striking and beneficial effect of leucotomy". This presents one possible reason for this improvement/change. However, later in the paper they state "moral standards may be reduced following leucotomy "but these "fell within the range of socially acceptable norms". Neither moral standards nor socially acceptable norms were defined. Perhaps it is more likely that that sexual proclivity was enabled as a further known side-effect.

This theory might be evidenced by the pre-operative assessment questions, which focused on prurient sexual questioning. Rebecca found it very offensive. She reported being asked whether she liked sex and how much, by a panel of male doctors who would make the decision to refer. Since she defended herself against these questions, saying "How dare you ask me that?" the decision was made that she was suitable for operation. Having demonstrated that she found the questions offensive; perhaps the board concluded that she was less likely to be at risk of post-operative promiscuity.

(Tan et al; 1971 *cited in* Bejerot, 2003:242) discussed the social consequences of "disinhibition" in bimedial leucotomy patients. Out of 24 patients; two female patients "caused embarrassment" to their husbands by "being slovenly, over-demonstrative or swearing in public". These subjective assessments by matrimonial partners may be unrelated to the surgery and are of limited statistical significance at 8%. They might reflect paternalistic, hegemonic discourse at the time; but one male patient began "making excessive sexual demands "to his wife and 3 years later was cautioned by the police for "making improper advances to young girls". Rebecca's husband recollects (with amusement) a vicar who received the operation around the same time as her. After the operation, he began to "swear like a trooper!"

Rebecca interprets her "disinhibition" as the occasional inability to censor what she says. I felt this must be further investigated as an ethical issue for consideration during the research. This represented a further reason to facilitate, encourage and respect Rebecca's ultimate veto on content; after substantial opportunity to reflect upon what content she chose to share. There were confidences shared during our relationship; which I kept. This illustrates very effectively the limitations on ethnography in this context. I felt respect for the participant and the trust she had placed in our relationship took priority over the research.

Luria (1973: 224) suggested some patients with lesions in this brain region uttered "uncontrollable confabulations" which were explained as unknowing untruths; in other words, untruths (inaccuracies) that the patient believed to be true. Since the data was validated as a true account by her husband; this was not Rebecca's experience. She was also consistently able to maintain confidences I shared.

There have been; however; occasions where close family members were subjected to censure by Rebecca (post-operatively). Because this can happen in familial relationships on occasion; (with or without justification) it was not possible to be categorical that this was a side effect of any of Rebecca's surgery or indeed, other treatment. Thus, familial frustration abounded; in knowing how to manage their own responses when feeling hurt or insulted; and indeed manage their responses to Rebecca effectively. They were rendered impotent by an inability to differentiate with any confidence and had to manage as best they could.

Fenton (1999:268) discussed the paradox that could follow improvement after surgery. Increased independence and assertiveness often placed strain on familial relationships. Whereas a patient might have been relatively passive to care for previously; assertiveness and a desire for independence might lead to tensions between them and their care-givers. It was advised that any relapse should not be regarded as a return to "the chronicity of the pre-operative condition" and need to be "treated effectively by conventional methods". There could be a loss of role, and/or loss of control, for the care-givers.

(Bentall, 2009:134) suggests that there is firm evidence dating as far back as the late 1950's that family relationships influence the "course" of the "illness" rather than the "onset". It was surprising to note that patients discharged from hospital back to their parents or siblings, were more likely to become ill again, as were patients who had been married and returned to their spouses. The reasons for this were "high expressed emotion" on the part of the families. Such emotions were closely linked to frustration at seeing the loved-one "behave in an apparently irrational and self-defeating manner". Unfortunately, the net result of family carers' frustrations was that they could behave in a "critical, hostile, highly emotional or over-protective manner" towards the "patient". In turn, this provoked hostility from the "patient", "leading to an escalating spiral of anger and distress to both". This unfortunate vicious cycle would often lead to "the patient" needing further treatment, which often further damaged the "patients" self-esteem, maintaining the problems. Best outcomes were consequently associated with families who displayed "laid-back indifference" towards the "patient". Bentall (2009:134).

It is interesting to note that one of Rebecca's children behaved in precisely this manner over many years. It was not contrived; but more a matter of self-preservation. This family member is possibly the one who retained the utmost respect from Rebecca over the years. It would seem clear that further support for families would be preferable, to share key skills in caring for a family member suffering from "mental illness" or "mental distress"; in order to avoid maintaining the above cycles.

Did Rebecca participate in her own downfall prior to the leucotomy operation, by over-reliance on her diagnosis to abnegate herself from responsibility? I believe it is possible. Sometimes Rebecca becomes very angry with her husband. Perhaps this reflects a human need to rebel against the authority, upon which you are dependent, in order to achieve autonomy. It may be Rebecca has inadvertently swapped one male authority figure for another; a father, a husband and then a series of psychiatrists - none of whom have really encouraged her to take responsibility for her own recovery. Rebecca learned to be helpless. To date; she believes wholeheartedly that "a man should be in charge of the household and have the final say," even if they are not the financial breadwinner, are unfaithful, feckless or violent.

Given that the statistics indicate people receiving psychiatric treatment do better when they leave hospital for a different environment that their familial home – it seems clear that the families/carers need clearer guidance from health professionals about how the environment also needs to change. We could not expect a psychotropic drug to be prescribed to the patient to enable them to cope with that environment; without seeking to address the environment itself. As Damasio (2006:267) points out: "If the proposed solution to individual and social suffering bypasses the causes of individual and social conflict, it is not likely to work for very long."

Rebecca expressed to me that she wishes she had not had the operation. Her husband remains undecided. I have three feminist-biased theories as to why. First, if she has a diagnosis, no responsibility could be attached to his behaviour, as a partial cause or contributory factor for her distress – she was "mentally ill". Second, she enjoyed sex more, which he acknowledges was gratifying for him. Third – no-one could really question his actions in "dealing" with her – for her actions could always be attributed to mental illness. He has received a great deal of empathy over the years, as the stoic character who "loved her anyway" – the carer. As with the psychiatrists and neurosurgeons, being a carer was, and remains, a tremendously powerful position. It is interesting to note that he always speaks very positively about his life – he has no regrets.

Surgical ablation is a permanent destruction which may render recovery impossible. My observations over the last six years indicate that Rebecca holds extremely rigid attitudes to life. She will not, for example, discuss why she holds certain views. Rebecca appears to project her most enduring feelings of sadness, anxiety and anger onto others and in this way, she can empathise with them. Whether or not the other person is experiencing these emotions; Rebecca is certain they are. She seems incapable of advanced empathy – unable to empathise with a different viewpoint from her own. This may be the reason why all subsequent efforts at rehabilitation and psychotherapy have failed.

I imagine Rebecca would prove an exceptionally frustrating client, for a professional. This is because she remains unmoved and unaffected by any therapeutic interventions and appears to "know" categorically that they are futile. It is most unfortunate that her benign facial expression at these times could be perceived as "smug", as though she is very kindly tolerating their efforts. I suspect it provides little more than a short distraction from a "rather boring" (in her words) day-to-day life.

The leucotomy operation also left Rebecca with epilepsy. (Miller, 1948:1103) estimated this happened in 12% of cases. Such seizures, originating in the limbic structures can cause: "depression, anxiety and psychosis... depression in epilepsy may result from iatrogenic causes, both pharmacologic and surgical." (Warren, 2011:27) Fong: *cited in* Warren 2011:27) wrote: "studies have estimated that up to 50 per cent of patients with epilepsy develop psychiatric disorders, the most common being depression, anxiety and psychotic disturbances".

Trimble (2007: 51) points out that epileptic seizures arising from the parietal lobes cause a number of somatosensory symptoms. These included "a variety of visual illusions and hallucinations...and also complex hallucinations." Since this surgery; Rebecca has reported a variety of frightening and disturbing hallucinations; one of which she described as "all in colour." These occurred when her medication for epilepsy was reduced (under medical supervision) during her final pregnancy; in order to minimise pre-natal damage to the fetus.

As a known side effect of a procedure designed to alleviate these specific symptoms, this seemed counter-productive. This would limit anyone trying to help or offer treatment to Rebecca; rendering it impossible to differentiate between symptoms resulting from surgery, epilepsy, (or iatrogenic causes) versus the original "symptoms". McLeod (2008:4) suggests that ECT was offered as a treatment for schizophrenia on the basis that one could not have schizophrenia and epilepsy simultaneously. If epilepsy is induced by ECT "the schizophrenic symptoms will be forced into submission!"

Five years after Rebecca's operation, (Breggin 1972: 356) wrote: "the psychosurgeon picks out the symptom that he wants to focus upon, then destroys the brain's overall capacity to respond emotionally, in order to "cure" the symptom which he focused upon, completely neglecting that he has simply subdued the entire human being." Holden (1972) *cited in* Breggin (1972:366) added: "The frequent effect of such over operation was irreversible change in mood, emotion, temperament and all other higher mental functions..."

A fuller understanding of the area of the brain tissue destroyed (in Rebecca's case) was critical to analysing the potential effects. This proved a highly complex topic. Damasio (2006:60) wrote extensively on the effects of lesions/damage to various brain regions. He suggested that damage to white matter subjacent to medial regions of the frontal lobe "drastically reduced" emotions and feelings. Specifically, this loss of emotions and feelings caused impairment in reasoning and decision making. This suggested that deliberately subduing or altering emotions was counter-productive in terms of future progress in patients; since reasoning and decision making would be crucial for recovery.

Any possibility of "impaired reasoning/decision making" was of great concern to me in relation to the ethics of this research. Despite all previous evidence to suggest Rebecca's capacity to give informed consent must be presumed as a default; I felt it was necessary to reflect further on this particular issue; reviewing all the evidence to date. This was extremely difficult to assess as a layperson. I wrote to two authors cited in this study for professional advice, (Damasio & Bentall) but unfortunately neither responded. I also requested advice from a senior lecturer, who's MSC was in Neuroscience; but he felt unqualified to assist and advised me to consult a neurosurgery practitioner. I have not done so, on the basis that anyone practicing this type of operation must believe wholeheartedly in what they do. I did research for academic papers by neurosurgeons against neurosurgery for mental disorder, but found none. I reflected how much more difficult it might be for someone considering this surgery, to gain access to both sides of the debate.

In the midst of this ethical dilemma; Rebecca's psychiatrist wrote to her personally, requesting her consent to be a "practice subject" for a trainee psychologist. He obviously considered she had capacity for giving consent intact. Rebecca has historically been involved in many research projects; giving paid talks at the Maudsley about her operation and even publicising the work of her local day care centre on television, so much of this information was already in the "public domain".

Rebecca agreed to participate in being a "practice subject" for the trainee psychologist. Unfortunately, she was not informed that there would only be six one-hour sessions. On no level could this be considered an adequate amount of time to discuss her long-term issues. She was perturbed to note that when she began to discuss her operation; the trainee psychologist was "shocked" - having no idea Rebecca had been the subject of neurosurgery for mental disorder. Either the trainee psychologist had not read the case notes, or they had not been made available to her. In any case, this was a profoundly dissatisfactory experience of participating in research for Rebecca – but one for which her psychiatrist considered she was capable of giving informed consent.

Miller (1948: 1095) described 7 modified procedures of the original frontal lobotomy. The first was Rebecca's procedure and the second that of Howard Dully (2007):

"Bimedial lobotomy – in which the medial half of the frontothalamus radiations is sectioned".

"Transorbital lobotomy – in which the frontothalamic fibres are sectioned through a leukotome introduced supra-orbitally into the front lobes". (above eye sockets).

The major difference between these two procedures appeared to be the entry method the surgeon used. Despite experiencing life difficulties, Howard Dully (2007) continued to experience emotions. He survived and recovered sufficiently to research and co-author his autobiography entitled "My lobotomy". As Bentall, (2010:38) notes: *"In a way Dully was lucky, being surprisingly unaffected by what was done to him and able, in later life, to tell his tale. "* Perhaps Dully's capacity for recovery was assisted by his very young age (12) at the time of the surgery.

Cingulectomy is "the bilateral excision of Brodmann's area 24". Fenton (1999:263). The bimedial leucotomy appears similar to the "cingulectomy", which targets the "cingulated areas on each side", but on closer inspection of a diagram by Valenstein (1976:I-23) (shown in Appendix 1) I could see that neither Dully's transorbital lobotomy, nor the cingulectomy, were in precisely the same region as Rebecca's operation. Damasio (2006:67,217,218) noted that impairments in reasoning, decision making and emotions/feelings often occurred from damage in other sites. This would render such patients incapable of making appropriate decisions of a personal or social nature. They have discarded what their brains acquired through socialisation and education, in terms of anticipating future consequences. This results in a tendency to make spontaneous decisions; which are not always in their best interests and further, compromises the opportunity for new learning.

However; a clinician's interpretation of impaired feelings and reasoning remains subjective. Damasio mentions psychological tests that can be administered; for example the MMPI (Minnesota Multi-Phase Inventory) and the Wisconsin Card Sorting Test. These tests can only be administered by trained professionals; but remain open to interpretation and are based upon observational experiments, relating to behaviour in various scenarios. It still remains impossible to categorically assess the notion of "free will" being completely retained or discarded. Tests; for example; which do not represent real-life situations or threats (e.g. gambling) could be taken by patients with ambivalence about consequence; perhaps for interest or possibly even manipulatively; particularly in cases where the patient remained highly intelligent.

(Fenton, 1999:267) also highlights "outspokenness" and used the word "disinhibition" as having been described after surgery; but indicated the possibility that these changes could be regarded as signs of improved assertiveness and less dependence. Fenton believes that these changes were not "socially incapacitating" but rather positive "psychosocial adjustments" not related to organic defects. In this paper, Fenton cites (Kartsoussiss et al; 1991), who identified one modified leucotomy procedure (the stereotactic subcaudate tractotomy) where patients showed no deficits in frontal lobe functioning. The measure used to test this was the Wisconsin Card Sorting test - the same measure applied by Damasio (2006:42) to formulate his theory.

I experienced considerable difficulty understanding Damasio's differentiation between "emotions" and "feelings". Damasio, (2003:103) theorises that "feelings" are the bodily (physiological) sensational response to emotions. He believes he has identified the key regions involved in producing the *"emotive"* responses behind the pleasurable states. These are the right orbitofrontal cortices, the left ventral striatum and the right amygdala. Regions identified that were "strongly associated" with feelings related to pain or pleasure were the *"insula, SI and SSI"*.

The engagement of one apparently very critical region, (the insula) is reduced by two drugs; Fentanyl and Valium. Rebecca takes both of these on a regular basis. The *"SI"* is strongly implicated in the ability to experience empathy.

There were occasions where Rebecca would "go for the now"; e.g. go out for the day if she was feeling well; but equally there were occasions where although feeling well; she would predict feeling worse later that day;

and stay home accordingly. It was unfortunate that this often led to loneliness and boredom. McGilchrist (2010:407) points out that "social isolation leads to exaggerated fear responses." I observed no consistent tendency to take risks, perceived or otherwise. If anything the opposite was true; and her behaviour would err on the side of caution, as is often the case when people experience anxiety.

Unfortunately, Rebecca didn't appear to retain more than a short-term association with activities and positive emotions. For example, despite enjoying her weekly quilting group; the positive feeling quickly dissipated, resulting in a regular dilemma about whether to attend next time. Still, it was significant that she still experienced positive emotions; albeit for a limited period. I asked whether she felt better during and after attending; she thought and said: "Yes, always." However she felt about going; she acknowledged that she did indeed feel better during and after attending. This motivated her sufficiently to continue attending. She said: "I remember what you asked; and I go, because I know I'll feel better for going".

I reflected how tragic it would be if the operation had only rendered the capacity to retain positive emotions impossible. More enduring were familiar (perhaps safer) negative thoughts and feelings of hopelessness, anxiety and boredom.

Each time I felt I might be getting close to a balance of probability – another possibility would present itself. As I felt myself becoming increasingly frustrated with my lack of understanding; I took a break from the research for several months and then returned to review.

Damasio (1994:131) discusses two types of "emotion". Early (or primary) emotion appears to be pre-programmed almost from birth. Humans would appear to have an innate survival mechanism to respond automatically to certain environmental stimuli. For example (the size of what we can see – e.g. large animals), the "span" of what we can see (e.g. wing span – say, flying eagles), types of motion in others (e.g. as in reptiles), certain sounds (e.g. growling) and certain configurations of body state (e.g. hunger, temperature and physical pain/discomfort). Although "depression" is not mentioned; perhaps it may transpire that this is a primary emotion related to metabolism and hibernation – perhaps a shutdown in order to conserve energy when other basic needs are unmet.

According to Damasio's theory; these "primary" emotions are detected and processed by the amygdala. (The amygdala does not appear to be an area anywhere near Rebecca's surgical ablation.) It's important to note that the human being does not need to "code" (or recognise/categorise) the "threat" at this stage. This process alone can accomplish useful goals to survival, e.g. speedy concealment (hiding) a display of anger towards a competitor (fight) or the ability to run (flight).

Nonetheless, the physical (sensory) perception of external threat (either visual, physical, auditory or olfactory) appears to trigger the involvement of many processes (or signals) from the brain to the body and back again - first of the body state. However, the actions of the amygdala alone "are not sufficient to support the process of secondary emotions." Damasio (1994:131). So what happens next?

The anterior cingulated gyrus becomes activated. The role of the anterior cingulated gyrus appears to be one of "inhibition"; in other words inhibiting (or mediating) the driver of the next response. Allman et al; (2001:109) defines the anterior cingulated cortex as "a specialised area of neocortex devoted to the regulation of emotional and cognitive behaviour." It almost appears to be the brain area responsible for a very fast assessment (or evaluation) process. I like to think of it in layman's terms as the "count to ten" factor – although these processes may be realistically too quick to be brought into consciousness (as I perceive it). It may be the primal instinct, subsequently mediated by the anterior cingulated cortex, that some refer to as "nature versus nurture".

I wonder whether it is desirable to reduce the capacity to experience anxiety as an essential human emotion – the fight or flight mechanism seems essential to human survival. Is it possible that people could inadvertently expose themselves to high-risk situations as a result of a reduced capacity to evaluate risk? Could this result in a surgically-induced naivety? After this surgery; Rebecca certainly demonstrated behavior which could be considered naive – on several occasions. The consequence of this was that her post-evaluation of these occasions resulted in terrible guilt – which contributed to a continuation of a low mood. However, I would imagine "guilt" itself as a secondary emotion, following evaluation.

Vago et al; (2011:288) describe the anterior cingulated cortex as being "critical for self-regulation and adaptability...it is assumed to be involved in regulating somatic, visceral and autonomic responses to stressful events, emotional expression and social behaviour." Again I was most concerned to note the discourse "assumed"; not a particularly scientific word. I wondered how damaging such an area would impact on someone's consciousness. Presumably they would be unable to regulate their cognitive and physiological responses to external cues; for example danger – with the benefit of previously acquired social learning.

Vago et al; (2011:7) posits that "white matter lesions throughout the frontal-striatal-thalamic circuitry are associated with depression." Anxiety and depression are often cyclical. As Bentall (2009:10) points out: "the majority of people whose symptoms meet current criteria for major depression recover within a few months." Far from alleviating anxiety and depression; neurosurgery for mental disorder appears not only to contribute to a worsening; but reduces the ability of the patient to cognitively or physiologically mediate spontaneous recovery.

Luria (1973:198) discusses patients with frontal lobe damage: "it is only the higher forms of organisation of conscious activity that are significantly disturbed." While I have been looking at Rebecca's demonstrable range of emotions and attributing these to a contradiction of Damasio's theory – (i.e. there was no evidence to suggest she was not "feeling" emotions and therefore no reason to presume she had lost "capacity") I may be mistaken in presuming one logically followed the other .

Rebecca was indeed experiencing emotions – but perhaps what I witnessed constitute "primary" emotions (with the exception of guilt, mentioned above). Part of the anterior cingulated gyrus has been destroyed in Rebecca's surgery, but not all. McGilchrist (2010:125) describes the anterior cingulate as "a deeper lying region profoundly implicated in social motivation." I have imagined this as like being on a hamster wheel, in her case. Rather than being able to step out of that wheel, it is as though she is suspended in one circular process that serves only to maintain exactly where she is. It must be utterly mentally (and consequently physically) exhausting and at some point, I believe her brain and then body periodically shuts down, in what outsiders perceive as a "depressive" state to protect itself from the exertion of continual adrenaline production.

If "secondary" emotions are acquired through experience – unique to the individual, then the loss of these is monumentally damaging. One cannot mitigate or avoid detrimental situations, or people, and therefore learn to our benefit (as all human beings have the opportunity to) from the experience of making mistakes and acquiring new learning.

Robinson *et al;* (1998) *cited in* Manes et al; (2002:625) state that "secondary mood disturbance (both depression and mania) is well-documented following frontal cortex damage." I found it very difficult to understand how; with this knowledge; neurosurgery continues to be practiced with the aim of damaging the frontal cortex. Perhaps the answer lies later in the paper: "Human lesion research therefore remains particularly valuable as a means of assessing the role of PFC (pre-frontal cortex) in cognition and moreover, provides direct information useful for diagnosis and rehabilitation after brain damage." Manes et al; (2002:626).

"Passive avoidance" is defined by Bechara et al; (1996:221,222) as "withholding a response to avoid punishment. Because patients with pre-frontal lesions do not seem to learn from previous mistakes, and they frequently engage in behaviours that lead to negative consequences, the issue of passive avoidance learning must be considered."

Neurosurgeons currently advocating modern techniques of neurosurgery for mental disorder (NSMD) recruited 27 participants awaiting surgery to elicit user-perspectives. For inclusion of all user-perspectives, I included these views.

> "When asked to comment about scenarios involving post-operative personality change, both positive and negative, almost all patients…noted that surgery was still justified as long as the patient understood the risks beforehand. This was the case even if surgery rendered an individual paralysed, or unrecognisable to family members as a result of personality change." Lipsman et al; (2009: 380)

A crucial point was that the "patient understood the risks". I considered the likelihood that these patients realised the potential implications and effects of irreversible personality change; including the loss of their emotions, (possibly leading to impaired reasoning and decision making) or whether they could devalue their existing personality in their situation. Access to and understanding both sides of the existing controversial debate between psychiatrists, psychologists and neurosurgeons would be required to facilitate truly informed choice. Given that there was substantial professional disagreement, I found it unlikely.

I was concerned about several parts of the discourse in this paper. Twice the suggested target areas were described as "believed" to drive "maladaptive behaviours". The term "believed" implied faith rather than evidence. "Behaviours" were targeted rather than emotion/mood. Terms later in the paper included: "diseases of mood and cognition" implying organic disease (which remains theoretical). It was proposed that this research was:

> "Placing emphasis on patient autonomy, and that patient choice should be respected, even if deciding to participate in risky surgery".

"Risky surgery" is not always offered to other medical patients, when their physical survival is not dependent upon it. If we truly respected patient choice; we might also allow voluntary or assisted euthanasia – even in the case of those for whom there is no immediate physical threat – in other words, suicide. Yet we balk at those who consider their lives so painful – physically or emotionally – being allowed the autonomy to decide whether they end their own lives.

> "Regardless of their personal, political and/or religious feelings, patients generally accepted the choice of competent adults to go ahead with risky surgery".

"Competent" user perspectives (pre and post operative) were used to make the case for offering surgery. "Competent" implies adequately qualified or capable, effective, having ability. These descriptors of mental

291

illness lack congruence with past and current definitions of mental illness. The ethical discussion proposed that:

> "Every surgical intervention has the capacity to alter personality and that NSMD is only unique because the organ at issue is the seat of awareness and consciousness."

Alterations to personality may be a side effect of other surgery; but they are not the goal. If the brain is "the seat of awareness and consciousness"; then retaining the brain as intact as possible would surely be more desirable for recovery, rather than destroying parts of it, however selectively. The "competent" user perspective was returned to, (now post-operative – assuming competence existed and has remained intact) who have a *"new identity" ("disregarding the opinion of family and friends" – i.e.* those that know the patient personally). "Identity" implies sameness, individuality. It was proposed that the "new identity" is in "perfect temporal continuity with their old identity" (presuming patients recollect and are not dissociated from their old identity). "They may, in other words, not feel any different at all". Lipsman et al; (2009:380,381,382). I suggest that "feeling different" is probably the aspiration of those electing for surgery.

Conclusion:

If neurosurgery for mental disorder is an effective and sophisticated treatment, it seems incongruous that it remains a treatment of last resort. As Damasio points out: "We must remember also that we still have no way of knowing whether the long-term effects of such (psychotropic) drugs on the brain are any less destructive than a selective form of surgery might be." The largest UK Mental Health Charity MIND (2000) advised the Royal College of Psychiatrists, reporting on neurosurgery for mental disorder that in their opinion:

> "There was absolutely and emphatically no place for neurosurgery in the treatment of mental disorder".

I agree with their view. What is clear; is that there is a substantial proportion of people whose diagnosis of mental illness is not alleviated by any physical or psychological interventions currently available. It is also clear that many of the physical interventions cause physical harm and addiction. I am advocating an approach to mental health which mirrors the Hippocratic

Oath: "First, do no harm". We must consider an uncomfortable truth: whether no treatment is preferable to the wrong one.

But what about Deep Brain Stimulation (DBS) and Vagus Nerve Stimulation (DVS)? These experimental areas of neurosurgery for mental disorder are beyond the scope of this paper and are not relevant, because neither of these procedures involve a permanent destruction of brain tissue. In common with NSMD, both procedures continue to rely on unproven theories of localization.

Despite reaching the conclusion that Rebecca's capacity for decision-making may have been irrevocably damaged as a result of her leucotomy operation; I am no longer uneasy about the ethics of conducting this research. Petryna (2005:191) states that "ethics is used variably and tactically by all actors in a chain of interests involved in human-subjects research". I am aware that this statement applies equally to me. While conducting experimental surgery on "vulnerable" patients remains legal (and by default ethical); researching first-hand accounts of patient outcomes in later years cannot be unethical – it is essential. If this surgery leaves patients without "capacity" and therefore by law, "vulnerable" – this surgery should not be happening.

When wrestling with ethical questions, I have considered: should I intervene if a counselling client expresses suicidal ideation? In doing so; by reporting their words to a third party and breaching confidentiality (whether negotiated/contracted in advance or not); I abnegate both my client and myself from responsibility and forfeit it to a higher authority (the existing NHS mental health services) in which I have no faith. Do I believe that people have the right to end their own lives? Yes. Suicide is not illegal. Would I hope to offer them enough hope and perhaps respite to reconsider? Yes. Would I be responsible if they ended their own lives because of my views? No. Would I feel responsible? I probably would. I have found myself in this scenario twice and have stuck by my principles. It is luck alone that both parties remain alive and have had partial recoveries; through making changes in their environment and behaviour – in no way attributable to my interventions, but on their own authority.

Bentall (2009:xii) was pilloried by his peers at a British National Health Service conference, for daring to suggest that a variety of psychiatric "abuses" (including prefrontal leucotomy) had been possible, "because patient's objections had been systematically ignored, on the grounds that their mental illness disqualified them from offering a reasoned opinion about their treatment." It was Bentall's view that recent psychological research showed that "even severely ill patients are usually capable of reasoning about their experiences."

Goldbeck-Wood (1996:1) quoted a spokesperson for the mental health charity MIND: "We remain very unhappy with any irreversible form of treatment, particularly when it carries such serious risks. We are concerned that a failure to relieve suffering could lead to an increase in such invasive procedures."

Damasio (2006:218) believes that in relation to patients with surgically damaged brains: "the only redeeming aspect of this tragedy resides in the window it opens for science. Some insight can indeed be gained into the nature of the processes that have been lost." Freeman et al; (2007:7) wrote in their report to the Royal College of Psychiatrists: "Long-term contact with patients post-operatively needs to be encouraged to get more realistic data about adverse effects, especially the incidence of epilepsy."

The emphasis at present seems to be on continuing to experiment with neurosurgery for mental disorder (with monitoring) rather than learning from history. In the same report Freeman et al; (2007:21) writes: "inadvertent departures from operative technique could lead to useful clinical information and should be reported systematically." An interesting use of discourse that could be translated – we could learn a lot about the brain when we make mistakes; reported by neurosurgeons. There appears to be a tendency to objectify the patient as a subject for experimentation and study; rather like guinea pigs.

I believe that we should continue to learn from patients with brain injuries due to physical injury; be that accidental (e.g. a road traffic accident) or from removal of tumours. I think there is no justification for the wilful destruction of healthy brain tissue in order to alleviate "symptoms" of human distress. That it continues to be performed under the radar of publicity or public care demonstrates a wilful blindness - to address human distress in anything other than a clinical context.

This view continues to be peddled by the media and the government – in whose financial interest it remains clear to medicalise human distress. Concentrating on diagnosis of symptoms, rather than evaluating the potential causes, negates collective responsibility for the mental wellbeing of the nation; in terms of policy and environment. Recently, my local GP surgery displayed leaflets on psychological and drug treatment for those "depressed" about the recession. How long before "recession depression" appears in DSM? The British Psychological Society issued a consensus statement in 2010 to endorse the American Psychological Association (APA's) open letter to the DSM-5 taskforce:

"A major concern raised in the letter is that the proposed revisions including lowering diagnostic thresholds across a range of disorders. It is feared that this could lead to medical explanations being applied to normal experiences, and also to the unnecessary use of potentially harmful interventions."

At one university, I was upbraided by a Senior Lecturer in Counselling Psychotherapy when I submitted my research proposal, who said: "What on earth d'you want to write about that for? Lobotomy doesn't happen anymore!" If those working in mental health are not aware, it seems even less likely the public are aware. In the meantime, those people legally categorised as "vulnerable" continue to be experimented upon.

I don't profess to have the solution to this situation; but I suspect it comes from a greater examination of our expectations about "normality" and "happiness" and examining our environment - rather than treating "symptoms". As Professor Marlys Witte says: "why would we cut and burn an organ if we understood it?" The World Health Organisation recommends that reducing gender disparities in mental health involves looking beyond mental illness as a disease of the brain. Not only have gender bias and stereotyping in the treatment of female patients and the diagnosis of psychological disorders been reported since the 1970's; but women are 48% more likely than men to use any psychotropic medication. Gender acquired risks include violence, abuse, poverty and socioeconomic disadvantage; heavy workloads, the gendered division of labour and unremitting responsibility for the care of children.

I remain extremely grateful to Rebecca and her husband for participating so frankly in this research and sharing their life stories with me. It has been a genuine privilege and our friendship continues. Rebecca's aim for this research was "to stop this happening to someone else." I promised to do my best.

Postscript 2014:

In 2012; Dr Samuel Eljamel published a paper for "Surgical Neurology International". He subsequently retired from practice. The paper was entitled "Strategies for the return of behavioral (sic) surgery". It is interesting to note that the neurosurgery for mental disorder has now been reframed as "behavioural" surgery. The objective of the surgery would appear to have reverted once more from attempting to enhance patient's "feeling" better, to altering their "behaviour". One of his patients (Mary Ramsey) who received four operations for ET (Essential Tremor) married for 33 years; relates her delight at her treatment and recommendation of surgery for others. ET, unlike other mental "disorders" included in the DSM – has a physical basis. She relates her mirth at her husband's statement:

"I have not been so embarrassed by what he said to Professor Eljamel ever, he said that he had every man's fantasy, a remote control for the wife but the mute button does not work. Professor Eljamel's shoulders were going up and down the other doctor was straight faced."

The idea of a "remote control" is probably synonymous with DBS or VNS, the mechanisms of which can be controlled by other parties. One might question again - who this surgery is intended to benefit – is it carers, society, or the patient? Previous proponents of this surgery were keen to defend it; by suggesting it was not about behavioural control. There are 172 neurosurgeons in the UK; 31 of whom are women and none of them are offering, or performing neurosurgery for mental disorder or behavioural surgery. With such high quoted statistical success rates, it is difficult to ascertain the reasons for this.

Despite Dr Eljamel's disclaimer, stating "The authors of this paper have received no outside funding and have nothing to declare" – publication of the manuscript was funded by an education grant from Swedish private company : Elekta, whose goal is "to provide shareholders with a favorable return and value growth." Among Elekta's product range are the equipment for DBS and VNS, as well as stereotaxic equipment. Eljamel cites a survey of North American Functional Neurosurgeons, where 50% of responders conducting "behavioural surgery" (perhaps unfortunately shortened to the pseudonym BS) saw BS "as a growing field of business".

Dr Eljamel warns that the future of behavioural surgery is dependent on one condition: "patients must have failed adequate therapies". We can note that the responsibility for failure of therapy is, once more, assigned to the patient. McLeod (2008:6) uses similar discourse: "Surgery is used only as a last resort, where the patient has failed to respond to other forms of treatment and their disorder is very severe." Those therapies have included comprehensive psychotropic drug treatment, ECT and behavioural therapy. Dr Eljamel also estimates that despite all these previous interventions; 20-40% of OCD (obsessive compulsive disorder) sufferers "become either resistant or refractory" and in MDD (major depressive disorders) the failure rate is 20%. Pre-operative and post-operative assessment are measured using the Yale-Brown Obsessive Compulsive Scale (HDRS) and the Montgomery-Asberg Depression Rating Scale (MADRS) and the Clinical Global Impression (CGI) scale. It should be noted that all three of these are self-reporting instruments. As yet, there is no method of ascertaining how neurosurgery itself might impact on the results of such instruments. Other commentators such as Posner (2014) are more forthright in their conclusions about the effects of lobotomy and suggest that the effects produced by lesions in the frontal lobes might be understood as deficits: "a lack of self-control, indifference to one's surroundings, and an inability to reflect on one's behaviour." When questioned about whether lobotomy worked, Posner questioned the definition of an improvement. Psychiatrists tended to measure this in terms of the ability to leave an asylum; perform household tasks or return to the workplace; in other words reflecting a subjective view of value and worth. This did not extend to demonstrating "self-knowledge or insight". Without these skills; how much validity and reliability can studies based solely on self-reporting instruments have?

Dr Eljamel's results for behavioural surgery appear impressive – with 40-60% of OCD and MDD cited as "responded" and "remission" occurring in MDD of 40%. I wonder what became of the others. In 2014; Dr Eljamel himself was been suspended from the medical register by the General Medical Council and is currently under investigation. In the interim, he cannot practice in the NHS or privately.

References:

1. Allman, J.M., Hakeem, A., Erwin, J.M., Nimchinsky, & Hoi, P. (2001). "The Anterior Cingulate Cortex: The Evolution of an Interface between Emotion and Cognition." *Annual of New York Academy of Science*. (May 2001). Vol 935. Pp 107-17.

2. Bechara, A. Tranel, D., Damasio, H., & Damasio, A.R. (1996). "Failure to Respond Autonomically to Anticipated Future Outcomes Following Damage to Prefrontal Cortex." *Cerebral Cortex*. Mar/Apr 1996:6. Pp 215-225.

3. Bejerot, S. (2003) "Psychosurgery for obsessive-compulsive disorder – concerns remain". *Acta Psychiatrica*. Vol. 107. Blackwell Munsgaard. Scandanavia. Pp241-243.

4. Breggin, Peter R. (1972). The Return of Lobotomy and Psychosurgery. *The Congressional Record*. Issue February 24, 1972. P 356,366,368,374.

5. Breggin, Peter R. (2008). Practical Applications: "22 Guidelines for Counselling & Psychotherapy". *Ethical Human Psychology and Psychiatry*. Vol 10. No 1: 2008. (Online). Available from URL: www.breggin.com. Accessed on: 1.4.2012. P 43-57.

6. Breggin, Peter R. Toxic Psychiatry. Chapter 3. *Cited in* "Psychiatric Drugs: Neuroleptics". FTR. (2012). (Online) Available from URL: www.sntp.net/drugs/tranquilizers.htm. Accessed on: 18.4.12. p.9.

7. Christmas, D., Matthews, K, Eljamel, M.S. (2004). "Neurosurgery for Mental Disorder". *The British Journal of Psychiatry*. BJP 2004. Issue 185: 175-174. London: Royal College of Psychiatrists. p 174, 194.

8. Damasio, A. (2006). *"Descartes' Error"*. Vintage: Croydon. Pp. 60,61,67,75,96,217,218,250,251,255,256,267.

9. Eljamel, S. (2012) "Strategies for the return of behavioral surgery". *SNI Stereotactic, a supplement to Surgical Neurology International*. (Online). Available from URL: www.surgical neurologyint.com. Accessed on: 29 October 2014. Pp S34-S39.

10. Goldbeck-Wood, S.A. (1996). "Norway Compensates Lobotomy Victims". *British Medical Journal*. Vol 313:708 published 21 September 1996. P1.

11. Gostin, L.O. "Ethical considerations of psychosurgery: the unhappy legacy of pre-frontal lobotomy." *Journal of medical ethics*. 1980, 6. MIND (National Association for Mental Health.) pp 149-154.

12. Lipsman, N., Zener, R. & Bernstein, M (2009). "Personal Identity, Enhancement and Neurosurgery: A Qualitative Study in Applied Neuroethics". *Bioethics*. Vol 23: Number 6. Pp 375-383: Blackwell publishing: Oxford.

13. McGilchrist, I. (2010). *The Master and his Emissary: The Divided Brain and the Making of the Western World*. Yale University Press: New Haven and London. Pp125, 407.

14. Manes, F., Sahakian, B., Clark, L., Rogers, R. Antoun, N., AitClive, M., & Robbins, T. (2005). "Decision-making processes following damage to the prefrontal cortex." *Brain*. (2002). Vol 125. Pp 624-639.

15. Miller, A. (1967). "The Lobotomy Patient – A Decade Later: A Follow-up of a Research Project started in 1948." *Canada Medical Association Journal*. April 15, 1967. Vol 96. Pp 1095-1103.

16. National Clinical Practice Guideline Number 31. (2006). "Obsessive-compulsive disorder: Core interventions in the treatment obsessive-compulsive disorder and body dysmorphic disorder". The British Psychological Society & The Royal College of Psychiatrists. London, Leicester. P 22.

17. Newman, J.P., Widom, C., & Nathan, S. (1985). "Passive Avoidance in Syndromes of Disinhibition: Psychopathy and Extraversion." *Journal of Personality and Social Psychology*. 1985, Vol 48, no. 5. The Americal Psychological Association. Pp 1316-1327.

18. Persaud, R., Crossley, D., Freeman, C, (2003). "Should neurosurgery for mental disorder be allowed to die out?" *British Journal of Psychiatry*. Vol. 183. The Royal College of Psychiatrists. PTM Publishers. London. Pp 195-196.

19. Petryna, A. (2005). "Ethical Variability: Drug development and globalising clinical trials." *American Ethnologist*. Vol 32, No. 2. pp 183-197.

20. Posner, M. (2014). Blog: "Frequently Asked Questions About Lobotomy". (Online). Available from URL: http://miriamposner.com/blog/frequently-asked-questions-about-lobotomy/ Accessed on: 18.12.14. Digital Humanities Programme, UCLA.

21. Post, F., Linford-Rees W., & Shurr, Peter H (1968). An Evaluation of Bimedial Leucotomy. *British Journal of Psychiatry*. Vol. 114. The Royal College of Psychiatrists. PTM Publishers: London. Pp 1223-1246.

22. Sacks, O. (1985) *The Man Who Mistook his Wife for a Hat*. Gerald Duckworth & Co Ltd: London. p. 193

23. Schwartz et al; (1998) *cited in* NICE (2006). National Clinical Practice Guideline Number 31. (2006). "Obsessive-compulsive disorder: Core interventions in the treatment obsessive-compulsive disorder and body dysmorphic disorder". The British Psychological Society & The Royal College of Psychiatrists. London, Leicester. P 22.

24. Tan, E. Marks, M., & Marset, P. (1971). "Bimedial Leucotomy in Obsessive-Compulsive Neurosis: A Controlled Serial Enquiry." *The British Journal of Psychiatry.* Royal College of Psychiatrists. Vol. 118. Pp 155-164.

25. Trimble, M.R. (2007). *The Soul in the Brain: The Cerebral Basis of Language, Art and Belief.* John Hopkins University Press: Baltimore. P 62, 45, 51, 467.

26. Vago, D.R., Epstein, J., Catenaccio, E., & Stern, E. (2011). "Identification of Neural Targets for the Treatment of Psychiatric Disorders: The Role of Functional Neuroimaging." *Functional Imaging.* Neurosurgery Clinics of North America: Elsevier. April 2011, Vol 22, No. 2. Pp 1-18.

27. Valenstein, E.S. "The Practice of Psychosurgery: A Survey of the Literature (1971-1976). Report to the U.S. Commission for the Protection of Human Subjects in Biomedical and Behavioural Research." August 1 1976. U.S. Department of Health, Education and Welfare: DHEW Pub. No. (OS)77-0002. Pp 1-497.

Appendix 1: Valenstein (1976:)
Location of target site for Rebecca's operation marked in:

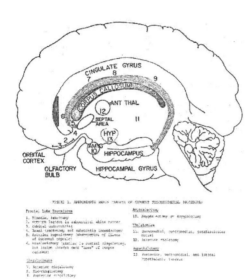

FIGURE 1. APPENDIX: BRAIN TARGETS OF CURRENT PSYCHOSURGICAL PROCEDURES

Frontal Lobe Procedures
1. Bimedial lobotomy
2. Various lesions in subcortical white matter
3. Orbital undercutting
4. Bimedial lobotomy and substantia innominata
5. Bimedial supra-orbital destruction of fibres of internal capsule
6. Tractotomy (similar to rostral cingulotomy, but lesion includes more "knee" of corpus callosum)

Cingulumotomy
7. Anterior cingulotomy
8. Mid-cingulotomy
9. Posterior cingulotomy

Amygdalotomy
10. Amygdalotomy or amygdaloidectomy

Thalamotomy
11. Dorsomedial, centromedian, parafascicular nuclei
12. Anterior thalamotomy

Hypothalotomy
13. Posterior, ventromedial, and lateral hypothalamic nuclei

1-23

301

About the author:

Jane Durston was born in 1972 in Cheltenham. *The Good Housewife's Frontal Lobotomy* is her debut novel. She lives in rural Gloucestershire with her husband and three children.